GRIN AND BEARD IT

WINSTON BROTHERS BOOK #2

PENNY REID

WWW.PENNYREID.NINJA/NEWSLETTER/

COPYRIGHT

DEDICATION

To the very capable engineers responsible for Microsoft Windows 10.
Bless your hearts.
Bless. Your. Hearts.

CHAPTER ONE

"Not all those who wander are lost."

— J.R.R. TOLKIEN, THE FELLOWSHIP OF THE RING

~Sienna~

I WAS LOST.

I was *lost* lost. My throat was tight with how lost I was. A desperate lost, half wondering if I'd crossed over into a new dimension and would never be found *lost*. I hadn't seen another car, let alone a pedestrian, in over an hour.

Perhaps I was now the last person left on the face of the earth. Perhaps everyone else had been abducted by aliens. I was so lost not even aliens could find me.

Whatever. Alternate reality, body-snatching aliens or not, I was now beyond frustrated. And when I'm extremely frustrated, I cry.

At present, I was very close to crying. I hate this about myself.

Which is why I pulled my tiny rental car off the side of the mountain road as soon as I spotted an overlook. Driving while crying is like eating while crying, or having sex while crying: weird, wet (not in a good way), and dangerous.

I tried to ignore that this overlook felt suspiciously familiar. I was fairly certain I'd pulled off at this exact spot an hour ago in a futile attempt to consult the paper map now crumpled on my passenger seat. This was the same paper map I would again have to consult, and likely with the same outcome—another two hours spent driving up and down this godforsaken mountain road.

Calming breaths were coming out as slightly hysterical huffs as I snatched the map from the passenger's seat. I shook out the map. I enjoyed the violent sound of the paper rumpling in my hands. I cleared my throat. I glared at the map. I continued glaring at the map.

I decided the map was clearly written by masochistic-doodling ancient Egyptians because everything was hieroglyphics and unreadable doodads.

I cursed the map.

"BY MOTHRA'S NIPPLES! I FUCKING HATE THIS MAP!"

Irrational anger bubbled to the surface and all I could think about was murdering the map. I would show the map who was boss.

I was boss.

Not some evil, wrong map from hell. I had no choice but to hit the map against the steering wheel several times, grunting and releasing a string of curses that would have made my sailor father proud. And maybe blush.

Then I opened my driver's side door, still grunting and raging, and slammed the map against the car, threw it on the ground, stomped on it, kicked it, and just generally assaulted it in every way I could think of. I'm a little embarrassed to admit, in my mindlessness I was also taunting the map, questioning its virility, flipping it the bird, and cursing now in Spanish as well as English.

It was the most cardio I'd done in over twelve months.

Stupid map, making me do cardio. I'll kill you!

Awareness I was no longer alone didn't occur all at once. I kind of realized a truck had driven past my map-assault-breakdance but had ignored it. If it had been twenty minutes ago I would have flagged down the truck or followed it. But I was now red-faced, snot-nosed, and sweaty. The last thing I needed were red-faced, snot-nosed, sweaty pictures of me all over the Internet . . . again.

But then the truck returned. The sound of tires crunching over gravel pulled me out of my fit of violence.

"Oh, crap."

I inhaled a large, steadying breath, leaned against my car, and closed my eyes. I needed to piece together my wherewithal as soon as possible, prepare to flash my dimples, unleash the charm.

It was at this point I almost wished I'd agreed to let my sister—who was also my extremely capable manager—accompany me. But, no. I'd wanted some time away. Some quiet and peace. The world had grown too loud, the studios too demanding, the paparazzi cameras too suffocating.

My house in LA had been broken into four times in the last month; three had been over-exuberant fans. But one of the break-ins had been a reporter. She'd gone through my stuff, digging for dirt. I had no dirt. I didn't even have sand or dust. My life was an open book.

So, no. I hadn't wanted my sister to come. And I'd left my security team in Knoxville. And now I was lost. I'd wanted a break from being Sienna Diaz. Maybe if I'd had a proper map—or any innate sense of direction—then a break might have been possible, but now . . .

Sliding my eyes to the side and glaring through the curtain my dark brown hair provided, I tried to sneak a peek at the newcomer through the truck's windshield—specifically, I wanted to determine whether I was being filmed—and that's when I spied the lights on the roof and the emblem on the hood and side of the car.

This car was official. And the man in it—now getting out of it and removing his sunglasses—was also official, wearing a uniform complete with a hat and a tool belt. A public servant.

THANK YOU, UNIVERSE.

I flipped my hair away from my face, wiped the backs of my hands across my slick cheeks and forehead, relieved I didn't need to gather my charm or wherewithal. Law enforcement didn't typically use phones to shoot amateur videos. If they did they were usually fired for misconduct.

I could leave all my figurative masks on the ground, along with Satan's torn and tattered map to hell.

As I straightened from the car and faced him I saw his steps falter. He was clearly surprised and I was pretty sure he recognized me because abrupt interest tempered his surprise. I pressed my lips together and gave him a quick smile, allowing him time for the shock to pass. But he didn't need the time; he quickly covered his surprise with a swaggery brand of attentive amusement. His left eyebrow cocked just a hint as his eyes swept over my body, and his mouth a suspicious looking line, like he was fighting a smile.

Eventually he abandoned the fight and grinned. "Evening, ma'am," he said, his accent just as sweet and thick as his voice was low. The man even tipped his hat.

And that's when I noticed Officer Grins-a-lot was adorable.

Six foot something; smiling eyes framed by thick lashes; brown beard covering a strong, angular jaw. Maybe most people wouldn't describe him as adorable. In fact, I'm pretty sure most women would call him a hot piece of ass. But after working for the last five years in Hollywood, all good-looking men were regulated to benignly adorable in my headspace.

In my early acting days, I'd dated a lot of hot guys—short hot guys, tall hot guys, muscular hot guys, thin hot guys, voluptuous hot guys—I'd tapped all manner of hot guys. But over the years I'd found the hotter the guy, the more the guy behaved like an entitled and incapable child.

Plus, I just couldn't afford to date. My career had to come first. As my sister frequently reminded me, if I wanted success, I didn't have much time for hot guys. Or any guys.

I nodded once at this hot guy's polite greeting, as a new gust of wind meant I was again forced to push my long hair away from my face. "Howdy, partner."

I cringed, because that wasn't at all charming. That was unintentionally awkward. But I really needed any help he was capable of providing, and based on his hotness, my expectations were low. I sent up a prayer that he wasn't my least favorite kind of hot guy: the hot guy asshole.

In my defense, at least I didn't follow up my earlier statement with, *"Someone has poisoned the waterhole."*

His lips compressed like he was wrestling laughter.

I braced. I never knew what or how people would react. Sometimes they'd ask me to quote one of my more famous movie lines. And that was usually fine. But right now I was lost and I was hungry and I desperately needed a shower and he was too freaking cute for me to repeat one of my most popular catchphrases—which included:

"I'll make you a sandwich if you make me a woman," and *"Fat chicks love fat dicks."*

But instead of asking me for my autograph or telling me how much he enjoyed my latest film role as Frankenstein's accident-prone, chubby younger sister, he surprised me by clearing his throat, tipping his cowboy hat back, and asking, "Ma'am, do you require assistance?"

"Yes." I reached out automatically, rushing forward and grabbing his arm. Hot guy or not, he was a life preserver in this sea of mountain road sameness. His eyes followed my movements and focused on my hand where I gripped his sleeve. I was also perfectly fine that my voice betrayed my level of desperation. "Please. Yes. I am totally lost. The GPS failed me three hours ago. I've been up and down this road a few dozen times. My phone has no reception. I have hardly any gas. I am so fucking lost. You are my hero."

At that he stood a little straighter. When he spoke his voice was calm and soothing, and he covered my hand with his, patted it; the warmth, size, roughness, and solid weight of him felt wonderfully reassuring.

I'd never been successfully reassured by a hot guy before.

It was actually really nice.

And weird.

"Where are you headed?" he asked gently.

"I'm trying to get to a place called Bandit Lake, and if you can get me there I will give you anything you want, including but not limited to a map written in hieroglyphics."

I noticed his eyes narrow when I mentioned my destination. "Bandit Lake?"

I nodded. "That's right."

"You have a place up there?"

"No, it's not my place. It belongs to a friend, Hank Weller. I'm just borrowing it for a few weeks."

"Hank? You know Hank?"

I nodded again. "Yes, officer. We went to college together."

"I'm not the law, miss. I'm a national park ranger."

I took in his uniform again. It was green and not blue. I shrugged, not caring what kind of official he was just as long as he helped me get out of this Twilight Zone episode before the banjo music started to play and the flannel-wearing bloodhounds arrived.

"Oh. Okay. Then, what should I call you? Mr. Ranger?"

He bit his lip, again fighting laughter, and squeezed my hand. "You can call me Jethro, miss. You say you're out of gas?"

"Your name is Jethro?"

"That's right."

I stared at him, feeling like his name wasn't quite right, didn't match his hot-guy status. If he were in the movie business he'd have to pick a new name. Something like Cain, or a Dean, or a Cain Dean. Four letters each, easy to remember, monosyllabic to ensure he didn't forget how to spell or pronounce them.

Because, in my experience, that kind of hot guy didn't usually know how to spell . . . or pronounce.

"How much gas did you say?" he asked again.

"The red light is flashing. I think I'm running on fumes."

"That's all right." A warm, interested smile remained behind his eyes. "I can drive you up to the lake, and we'll get this car filled up and towed."

"As in Jethro Tull?"

"Pardon me?"

"Your name? Jethro as in Jethro Tull?"

His friendly gaze traveled over my face as he grinned. Again. Wider. "As in Jethro, father-in-law of Moses in the Old Testament. Do you have any bags, miss?" He gave my hand one more reassuring squeeze then released me, moving to the driver's side door—which was still open—and plucked the keys from the ignition.

"Bags?"

"Yes. Luggage."

I snorted, saying, "Yes. Lots. But don't worry, I'm in therapy," and then chuckled at my own joke.

Meanwhile, cutie-pie Jethro straightened from the car and lifted his eyebrows at me in expectation.

"Pardon?"

Seeing he hadn't heard—or possibly hadn't understood—my attempt at humor, my chuckling tapered, and I cleared my throat.

When I'm nervous, or uncomfortable, or faced with heavy feelings, I make jokes. It's my thing. It's what I do. Some might even call it a compulsion. It's like, *Hey! Look at the funny! Focus on that, not on my pit stains or the disturbing way my nostrils are flaring* . . .

Which was how I realized Ranger Jethro was making me nervous. Which was completely bizarre because I was pretty sure I'd been inoculated against hot guys after my last boyfriend.

So. Weird.

I blamed the cardio.

Being funny is entirely dependent on timing. I'd learned early in my career to move on instead of repeating a joke, though I mourned those unheard jokes. They were the comedy equivalent of throwing seeds on rocks.

Stupid rocks.

"Sorry. Yes. Bags. In the trunk." I tossed my thumb over my shoulder and tucked my hair behind my ears, resolving to speak as little as possible.

His eyes lingered on my face, still warm and interested. We stared at each other. And then we stared some more. So I waited.

A bird chirped.

The wind rustled the trees.

And still he stared.

The way he was looking at me, all dreamy-eyed and flirty, I wondered if I had a super-fan on my hands. Or maybe he'd never met anyone famous before. Whatever it was, I needed him to get a move on, because I had to use the bathroom. I refused to pee behind the big tree at the end of the gravel patch because I'd already peed behind that tree over an hour ago, the first time I pulled onto this overlook.

I was just about to make another joke when he blinked and the moment was broken. He nodded once, bent at the waist, and popped the trunk. I turned and moved to the back of the car to retrieve my bags.

But he was right next to me, reaching into the trunk before I had it all the way open, grabbing my suitcase and overnight bag.

"Allow me," he said, shooting me another of his wide grins.

"Really, Ranger Jethro, I can carry my own bags."

"This is a full-service rescue, miss." He stood straight, placing my eighty-pound oversized suitcase on the gravel, then slung my overnight bag on his shoulder. Instead of rolling the suitcase, he lifted it by the handle and carried it to the bed of his truck.

I frowned at his retreating form. "It has wheels, Ranger."

"Don't want to ruin them. This gravel'll tear them up," he explained on a grunt.

I lifted an eyebrow at his retreating back, completely caught off guard by his thoughtful observation and helpfulness.

Narrowing my eyes in suspicion, I moved to the back seat to grab my backpack. This really was a Twilight Zone episode. A hot guy who was also capable?

Does not compute.

Unless he's gay. Yeah, he's probably gay.

In my experience, most hot guys who were both friendly and capable were gay. These were my favorite kind of hot guys. I hoped Ranger Jethro was gay.

When I straightened I saw him standing at the passenger side of his truck, watching me. He'd opened the door and was waiting, his flirty smile still in place. Now it was smaller and his eyes were just visible beneath the rim of his hat. His gaze moved up then down my body.

Yeah . . . no. Ranger Jethro isn't gay.

I faltered, my steps slowing, because I felt a little flutter of something unusual just under my ribcage, a quick intake of breath. It might have been attraction . . .

More likely, it was hunger and the fear of being murdered.

I wished my cell phone had reception. Though he was official, I'd feel a lot better about getting into a stranger's car if I had the ability to tell someone else about it. Or at least tweet the details in one hundred forty characters or less: *If I'm found dead, it was the cute park ranger named after Moses's father-in-law.*

I drew even with him and the open door to the truck. Glancing inside, I asked, "So, Moses's father-in-law was named Jethro?"

"That's right." He tilted his head to the side and took my backpack from my shoulder.

My stomach fluttered again. I swallowed to combat the sensation. "How come I didn't know this?"

His eyes followed the line of my hair past my shoulders. "You must've missed the memo when it was sent."

Taking a deep breath for bravery, I climbed into the truck. "Next thing you're going to tell me that Moses's uncle was named Darnel or Cletus."

"Nope. His uncles' names were Izhar, Hebron, and Uzziel." And with that, he placed my backpack at my feet and shut the door.

I watched him walk around the front of the truck, his steps unhurried, his hands resting on the tool belt around his narrow waist. I liked his tool belt; it made him look even more capable. Plus he had a nice walk. Not at all the sort of walk a murderer would employ.

As soon as he opened the driver's side door, he said, "But Moses's mother was also his father's aunt. Seatbelt."

I stared at his profile as he shut his door. "His mother's name was Seatbelt?"

"No." He flirty chuckled, his hazel eyes all twinkly as they moved over me, like he thought *I* was adorable. "Put on your seatbelt, miss."

I did as instructed while I sorted through his earlier statement rather than allow myself to be flustered by his capable and reassuring attention. "So, Moses's mother was also his father's aunt?"

"That's right." He nodded once, starting the ignition and checking his mirrors. "Moses's mother was named Jochebed, and her nephew, Amram, was Moses's father."

9

My mouth opened, then closed, then opened. I was finally able to manage, "So that would make his mother his great aunt?"

"And his grandfather was also his uncle, and his father was his cousin."

The ranger made a U-turn, heading in the opposite direction I'd been going, and we were off.

"Huh . . ." I thought about this fact and not necessarily my words as I mumbled, "Well, you know what they say."

"What's that?"

"If you can't keep it in your pants, keep it in the family."

His eyes bulged, and he choked on his astonishment, throwing me a shocked glance.

Poor adorable Ranger Jethro. He looked like he didn't know whether to laugh or shriek in horror. I'd shocked his delicate man-sensibilities.

He coughed out a strangled response, "I've never heard that before."

"Really? I would have thought—well, you know. Being up here, in the backwoods of Appalachia . . ."

Oh. Shit.

"Did I just say that out loud?" I groaned and shut my eyes.

"Yes. You certainly did." Now he was laughing, a robust belly laugh. It sounded nice.

"Well, I thought, you know, I thought you people, um . . ." Now my face was red again, and this time it wasn't due to my cardio-map-assault workout. But the fact he was laughing actually helped ease my mortification.

I honestly didn't care if people laughed with or at me. It was the laughter I was after, by any means necessary.

"*You people* what?" he pushed, his chuckle deep and wonderful.

Still, I was embarrassed because the words betrayed the narrow-minded direction of my thoughts. "Wow. That really came out wrong, garbled."

"Don't be so hard on yourself. You're an eloquent speaker, and it sounded very clear to me," he teased.

Did he just say eloquent?

Rather than respond, *That's an awfully big word for a hot guy*, I said, "I'm sorry. I'm so sorry. I don't know what I'm saying. Please accept my apology. I've been driving around for hours and I haven't eaten since . . . I don't know when. In fact, what is my name? Where am I? I have no idea."

"You haven't told me your name, so I can't help you there. But you're in Green Valley, Tennessee, on Moth Run Road."

Wait . . . what?

I peeked at Ranger Jethro. "You don't know my name?"

"I suppose you could always look in your wallet if you're desperate." He indicated with his chin toward my backpack, a smile still hovering on his features. "Once you figure it out, and if you're inclined to share, I'd like to know it as well."

I straightened and twisted in my seat, gaping at his profile. "You really don't know who I am?" I'm sure my tone betrayed my surprise because Ranger Jethro's smile fell away.

He stopped at a red light, switching his blinker on even though we were the only vehicle on the road. His gaze flickered over my expression, and his was unmistakably anxious.

"Should I?" he asked warily.

I blinked once, downright dumbfounded by his response.

Slowly, the wheels turned and the curtain was lifted, exposing the truth of my present situation.

The flirty smiles, the lingering gazes, the gallant rescue—Ranger Jethro fancied me.

Me.

He'd been flirting with *me*.

Not Sienna Diaz, the movie star, comedian, millionaire, Oscar winner, America's sweetheart.

By Rodan's nostrils, I couldn't remember the last time I hadn't been recognized.

Plus, judging by the way he was looking at me now, I surmised he was worried we'd met before and he'd forgotten my name. Perhaps he even thought we'd slept together and he'd forgotten that, too.

And I finally realized what kind of hot guy he was. He was the serial-dating hot guy, the most dangerous of all. Because they're smart, they're funny, they're capable, and they're typically charming.

Also, they're easy to fall for, because who doesn't want a hot, smart, funny, capable guy?

The problem is, they're not very nice. They're dangerous because they only want one thing—hot ladies. Lots of them. All the time.

And good for Ranger Jethro.

He should have his hot ladies. A year ago I would have gladly been one of his hot ladies. But just as I had no current interest in dating, I had no interest in losing my heart to a serial dater.

He swallowed thickly, looking acutely worried and bracing. And I couldn't help it, I honestly couldn't.

I threw my head back and laughed.

CHAPTER TWO

"I'm not lost for I know where I am. But however, where I am may be lost."

— A.A. MILNE, WINNIE-THE-POOH

~Jethro~

I'D LOST MY touch.

Instead of giving me her number—or even, you know, her name —this pretty lady was laughing at me. It was difficult not taking it to heart. Her loss of composure was clearly at my expense.

Except her laugh was as artless as it was contagious. So I laughed, too.

"Oh, Ranger Jethro." She wiped at her big brown eyes; tears had darkened her lashes. I stared at them. She had the longest lashes I'd ever seen. "You are so adorable. I just want to take you home and put you in my pocket."

I'd prefer her pants, but I guess I'd settle for her pocket.

For now . . .

I flexed my fingers on the steering wheel, this last thought unsettling. Five years of self-imposed celibacy had me questioning what the hell was happening. What the hell was I doing? Why now and why—apart from the obvious—her?

Also, "adorable"? I successfully fought to keep a grimace off my face.

"You have a real nice laugh," I remarked instead, because she did.

She gave me the side-eye and a flash of white teeth. My breath caught. Her smile was unreal.

And those dimples.

Wow.

She was speaking again, so I forced myself to look away from the dimples and listen. "Thank you, Ranger. I don't think anyone has ever complimented my laugh before."

I reluctantly put my eyeballs back in my head and made a left onto The Parkway, clearing my throat before remarking, "Then everyone you've met prior to me must be deaf."

It wasn't just her laugh, it was her voice. It was melodic. Plus there was something else . . . an intangible, magnetic quality. Natural and unforced.

She laughed again, not as loud this time. "I'm not usually the one laughing," she muttered. I glanced at her and saw her eyes were focused on the road beyond the windshield. "I guess I should pay attention to where we're going if I'm going to be driving around up here and not be abducted by aliens or locals. Or local aliens."

She may not have realized, but we were close to the turnoff for Bandit Lake. I debated whether or not to drive around the mountain once, keep her in the truck talking to me, because—though I'd sworn off women, stealing cars, and hurting people half a decade ago—this woman was all kinds of my type.

Long hair, dark eyes, tall, more curves than straight lines. And she had lips that could only be described as luscious. Yep. I had a physical type, and this woman checked all the boxes. This made her dangerous, a temptation.

I didn't miss that she'd yet to tell me her name. Her reluctance, given the way I was instinctively responding to her, might've been a good thing.

I cleared my throat, oddly anxious. I couldn't remember the last time anyone made me nervous. Maybe the female sheriff two towns away who'd booked me for suspected grand theft auto six years ago. She was real pretty. Strong. But she'd also carried a firearm.

Despite all the warning bells, the good, excited kind of nerves had me wracking my brain for a way to ask eyelashes and dimples for her name again without coming across as eager.

"Would you like a tour?" I drawled. "I make an excellent tour guide," I continued, purposefully layering on the charm. Man, I was rusty.

She glanced at me, her eyebrows raised in question.

"Of the mountain?" I clarified, keeping my tone easy, gesturing to the road in front of us. "I could drive you around, show you where every-thing is so you don't get lost anymore." Then I added with a wink. "Though I wouldn't mind rescuing you again."

"What? Now?" She was inspecting me like I was unhinged, appar-ently immune to the charisma I was throwing her way. Or maybe it was going over her head.

"Sure." I shrugged. "The loop isn't too big."

"Um . . ." She squirmed. "See, I would. But right now I have to pee like a hooker with a UTI. So if we could go directly to the lake house, that would be ideal," she explained, her tone conversational.

I firmed my mouth, schooling my expression so I wouldn't smile again. I didn't think she was trying to be funny. She just said funny things. Funny and charming. Likely, they wouldn't be so charming if she weren't so goddamn gorgeous.

"If there's no food at Weller's place, I have a cooler behind your seat with a sandwich." I slowed and turned on my blinker. We'd arrived at the gravel road circling the lake.

"No. No, thank you. I can't take your lunch."

"I already had lunch, that sandwich is for emergencies."

She turned in her seat, giving me her full attention. "See, now I should carry an emergency sandwich. Good job. What a great idea."

I cocked an eyebrow at her tone and set my jaw, my defensive hackles rising unexpectedly. Her voice gave me the impression she was surprised I was capable of good ideas. It was the kind of tone city people used down here when they ordered a large coffee and called it a "Venti Americano." I milled this over, plus her earlier words about backwoods Appalachia, and came to the conclusion she thought I was a hick.

Now, I admit, we have our fair share of hicks in Green Valley, Tennessee. We have hicks, hillbillies, rednecks, bumpkins, and the occasional reclusive yokel. But I was none of these things. Usually people making assumptions didn't bother me. I wasn't one to get needlessly twisted over the little things.

But coming from Miss Dimples, the unflattering assumption bothered me plenty. I didn't much like being dismissed or patronized.

"Yes, ma'am. Real genius idea. And I thought of it all by myself," I deadpanned, lowering my eyelids so I could squint at her. "And I dressed myself this morning, too." I paired my last statement with a smirk so she'd think I wasn't irritated, though I was irritated.

She hesitated for a moment, studying me, clearly not sure whether or not I was serious. I saw the wheels turn and her wince when she put two and two together. She heaved a great sigh and buried her face in her hands. "I promise I'm not usually this awful. I'm just tired and hungry and have to pee."

I chuckled, rubbing my chin as I pulled into Hank Weller's drive. "I guess I'll have to take your word for it, since you won't even tell me your name."

Real smooth. Guilt her into it. Nice. I shook my head at myself. I'd never had such trouble with a woman before, especially not when I was trying. Even nowadays they were offering their number before I'd offered my name.

"It's Sarah." She spoke from behind her fingers, so her words were a little garbled.

"Sarah? Nice to meet you, Sarah." I cut the engine.

"No, it's—" She lifted her head, her attention snagging on the building in front of us. "Where are we? Why did you stop?"

"We're here."

"We're where?"

"At Hank's place, at the lake." I tilted my chin toward the cabin. Well, it used to be a cabin. Hank's parents made some serious improvements over the years. Now it more closely resembled what my brother Cletus called "a McMansion."

Her mouth opened and closed as she sputtered incoherently for a few seconds, finally asking, "You knew how to get here based on a person's name? You know which cabin belongs to Hank? Does everybody know everybody here? How do you know Hank?"

I hesitated, her deluge of questions requiring some strategic thought, debating my options regarding how honest I should be.

She seemed astonished by my familiarity with Hank's address, not worried by it. I reckoned she wasn't used to the dynamics of a small town. Everybody knew Hank Weller. Everybody knew he went to Harvard, knew he was a troublemaker, and knew he'd been a source of disappointment to his parents.

Just like everybody knew me, Jethro Winston, my younger five brothers, my beauty queen sister, my con-artist daddy, and my librarian heart-of-gold mother. There were no secrets in Green Valley.

Now, to the issue at present, I knew Hank because he and Beau were good friends. Also, Hank, Beau, and I went fishing together. Additionally, I knew him because I'd stolen his daddy's Mercedes when I was sixteen.

But mostly, I knew Hank as a business partner. He'd bought The Pink Pony, a local strip club, some years ago. I did the carpentry and general contracting work around the place in return for being a silent partner. I'd built the bar, installed the stage, and—more recently—managed the expansion of the main building. He wanted to add a champagne room, only he'd serve his home brew instead of champagne. Hank was also a microbrewer.

Hence, I had lots of options regarding how I could answer her questions and still be truthful.

I turned to face her, bracing my hand on the back of her seat, and addressed her questions at a leisurely pace. "Now, let's see." I scratched my chin. "Yes, I knew how to get here based on Hank's name. There are a few Hanks in this town, but only one Hank with a cabin on Bandit Lake. That's because there's only about fifteen lots up here that don't belong to the government. The land can't be sold; it can only be inherited."

"Really?" She turned to face me again, angling her shoulders this time. Her temple fell to the headrest as her eyes moved over my face, clearly fascinated.

Now I felt the weight of her full attention, I had to concentrate. "To your other question, most everybody knows most everybody here, except there's a few reclusive families up in the hills who live off the grid. We're not quite sure how many or what their first names are, but we see them about town every so often, coming in for supplies or wanting to barter at the Sunday market. They're called the Hills."

"Because they live in the hills?"

"No. Because that's their last name. Hill."

Her pretty mouth formed a silent *Oh,* her eyebrows jumping a half-inch. She nodded thoughtfully, absorbing this information.

"I've known Hank for a long time, since he and my brother used to run around naked in the backyard of my momma's house."

She grinned at this, her mahogany eyes warming and dancing. "He used to do the same thing in the dorms, so I'm not terribly surprised."

That made me chuckle. "Yeah, well he's never been a fan of clothes, on himself or others."

"He runs a strip club now, right?" she asked, the friendliness and lack of judgment in her tone catching me unawares.

"That's right." I nodded slowly, assessing her with renewed interest. "The Pink Pony."

In my experience, there were three kinds of women: those that stripped at strip clubs, those that liked going to strip clubs, and those that disliked strip clubs. I understood all three perspectives and now I wondered which of the three she belonged to.

Damn if I didn't hope it was the first one.

We stared at each other for a protracted moment and I noted her gaze narrow, sharpen as she lifted a single eyebrow and grinned. "Ranger Jethro, are you wondering whether I'm a stripper?"

I was surprised by the suddenness and bluntness of the question, but recovered quickly. It was the closest she'd come to flirting with me, so I mirrored her sharp look and her grin, and shrugged. "Can't say it didn't cross my mind."

"Well, I'm not. But I have taken lessons." Her voice dropped a half octave, the curve of her mouth growing less friendly and more seductive, playful.

"Oh?" I tried to contain my own smile, adopting a mock serious expression though I couldn't quite fill my lungs with enough air. Now this was more like it. "Tell me more."

"I had to take them last year for research."

"Research?" I nodded thoughtfully, encouraging her to continue.

"That's right." Her gaze dropped to my mouth, a subtle shift that made the hairs on the back of my neck stand at attention.

My pulse quickened. Christ, she was pretty. I admit, now that she was no longer talking to me like I was a simpleton, I was having a lot of trouble focusing on the conversation. Got to love the irony.

"Really? Care to share what you learned?"

She shook her head, her long hair bouncing around her shoulders and settling on her chest along the swell of her breasts, her lips saying, "No," with an enchanting velvet cadence, making it sound like a *yes*.

I blinked.

Well, hell.

She was good at this.

Really good at this.

Like recognizes like, and what I had on my hands here was a professional charmer. This revelation was as shocking as finding moonshine in Reverend Seymour's Sunday punchbowl, because her earlier appearance of honesty and awkwardness had been downright disarming. Whereas now she had me wondering if it had been an act.

Impossibly long eyelashes lowered to half mast. An alluring smirk that hinted at devilish dimples played over her lips. Her eyes had changed from a rich mahogany to a dark Peruvian walnut . . . Excuse the clumsy comparison, but I'm a man who knows and loves my wood.

I waited to see what she'd do next, enjoying the building and thickening tension, impressed with her game. Yeah, this girl had game in spades.

At length, her smile grew and she sighed. It sounded whimsical. "This is fun."

"What's that?"

"Flirting with a national park ranger."

My eyes widened because I was both surprised and delighted by her candor. Perhaps the honesty hadn't been an act after all.

Hell . . . I *liked* this girl.

"Is that what we're doing, Miss Sarah?" I was sure to say her name in a low rumble, making it sound like a dirty word.

She gave me a teasingly reproachful look and unfastened her seatbelt. "Come now, Ranger. None of that. We're all adults here. Plus, I can't sit in this car all day with a full bladder, otherwise I'm going to pee on your upholstery. And just think of the headlines."

She gripped the handle and was moving to disembark. Remembering myself, I quickly popped open my door and jumped out, jogging around to her side just as she'd pushed her door open. I held it and reached a hand out to help her out.

Her attention darted between my offered hand and my face with a quizzical look. Shooting me a suspicious stare, she accepted help down from the cab.

Now, something odd happened just then. Odd because she'd grabbed my arm back on the mountain road and I'd felt nothing in particular. Perhaps it was merely a residual after-effect of our recent flirting, or perhaps it was the dry mountain air—or perhaps it was the five years flying solo—but an unexpected shock of warmth traveled up my arm as her palm slid against mine. Her expression didn't change. Whereas for me, the earth tilted, time slowed, and I was momentarily caught.

When I didn't release her straight away, she gazed up at me with round eyes. "What? What is it?"

I held her stare and her fingers for another beat, searching. She seemed oblivious, so I dropped her hand.

"Uh, nothing." I couldn't quite swallow. "Look for a key under the rug. Let me grab your bags." My words coming out gruff, I stepped around her and moved to the bed of the truck.

Combating the lingering and uncomfortable sense that something significant just happened, I shook my head to clear it and lifted her luggage from the truck. Just as I had all the bags lowered to the ground, my phone buzzed in my back pocket.

I glanced at the screen before accepting the call and raising it to my ear. "Hello, Cletus."

"Jethro," came his typical greeting. Cletus was number three in the family, by far the smartest, and the oddest. "You need to head over to Jeanie's right now."

"I do?" I glanced at the phone again, making note of the time and returning it to my ear; it was just past four, too early for beer and line dancing at Jeanie's place. "Why's that?"

"Claire needs rescuing."

My head cleared at the mention of Claire and habit had me mapping out the quickest route to Jeanie's. Claire McClure was my former best friend's widow. For the last five years her welfare had been my primary focus, the reason for every good decision I'd made.

"Claire never needs rescuing," I responded.

And she didn't. As much as I'd felt it my place to see to her well-being since Ben McClure's death in Afghanistan, she saw things differently. Recently—and more and more—I got the sense she was merely putting up with my meddling. I did my best to look after her, stop by her house to see if anything required attention, but that woman was tough as nails and as capable as a honey badger. More often than not, she'd give me a beer, let me hang a picture or fiddle with her gutters, then send me on my way.

"Well, she needs rescuing now."

I sighed, peering through Hank Weller's open door where the charming and mysterious Sarah had disappeared. "What's going on?"

"Come to Jeanie's," Cletus whispered ominously, then promptly hung up.

I glanced at the screen of my phone and cursed quietly. I knew Cletus wouldn't answer if I tried to call back. His custom of undersharing and treating everything as top secret was usually funny. But sometimes it was just plain irritating.

Slipping my cell into the back pocket of my uniform pants, I grabbed Sarah's bags and carried them over the gravel and stone pavers of the driveway. I mounted the steps and rolled the largest bag into the spacious entryway.

"This is a huge foyer." She spun in a slow circle, taking in the high ceilings.

She'd said the word using its French pronunciation, *foy-ay*. Cletus said it that way. The rest of us said *foy-er*, like it's spelled, because we lived in the United States and weren't pretentious nut jobs. Not that I thought Sarah was a pretentious nut job or made such a judgment about all people based on their pronunciation of that single word.

Just Cletus. He said *foy-ay* and was most definitely a pretentious nut job.

Sarah was from a big city so odd quirks could be overlooked and forgiven. I got the sense I'd be happy to overlook and forgive quite a bit of her quirks, should the situation present itself.

"Where would you like your bags, ma'am?"

Her attention settled on me, giving me a warm feeling in my chest, confused amusement playing over her features. "I'm back to being a *ma'am*? What happened to *miss*?"

Needing to do something with my hands, I hooked my thumbs on my tool belt and grinned down at her. "I'll call you whatever you'd like, Miss Sarah. But I'll need a phone number first."

What are you doing? Yeah, I wanted her number. I probably wouldn't call—because I shouldn't call—but I wanted it nonetheless.

Sarah laughed at that, and I loved the sound just as much as I had earlier. "Real smooth, Ranger. Come on inside; Hank stocked the kitchen. Do you want something to eat?"

I shook my head, irritated with Cletus for his interrupting call. "Can't. I've got to get back on the road."

Her face fell a little, and damn if that didn't make me feel good.

"Rain check?" I offered, tilting my head to the side and getting one last sweep of her. Something about her . . . made it hard to look away, or think, or talk.

She nodded, a lingering smile on her lips. "Sounds good."

I tipped my hat, forcing my feet to uproot. "Well, Miss Sarah. Pleasure to rescue you."

"Such manners," she said with a hint of sincere wonder.

I felt my grin hitch higher, unleashing my best—though out of practice—flirtatious eyes. But before I could turn, she surprised me by stepping close and stopping me with a hand on my arm. Leaning forward and lifting up on her toes, she placed a feather-light kiss on my cheek. Her breasts brushed against my chest—not on purpose, but because she had a huge rack—and my body awoke with a start. All blood flowed south. The smell of something flowery, warm, and expensive curled around me, arresting my pulse.

She didn't withdraw completely. Not right away. But rather stayed close, glanced up at me from beneath her long lashes, and whispered, "Thanks for being my hero."

I swallowed thickly, another wave of warmth unfurled in my stomach, hotter than before, exhilarating. It felt like an echo of an old addiction.

"Anytime," I managed to say, though what I wanted to do was grab her and find out what she tasted like. In fact, I was about to do just that when she backed away.

I watched her retreat, keeping my eyes locked on hers. She had me out of sorts. And by out of sorts I mean really, really wanting to put my mouth all over her body.

She gave me a wide, intoxicating grin, and I got a little lost in it until she dismissed me softly. "Goodbye, Jethro."

I clenched my jaw, affixed a tight smile to my face, and nodded once, maybe even successfully hiding the inexplicable effect she had on me. I wasn't used to this side of the equation. I was used to doing the charming, not being the one charmed.

I walked out the door. I admit, I was in a daze as I strolled back to the truck. I heard the house door click shut and I exhaled on a low whistle.

This woman . . . holy hell.

I needed a beer.

Or maybe seven.

CHAPTER THREE

"Out of all the things I have lost, I miss my mind the most."

— MARK TWAIN

~Jethro~

CLAIRE DIDN'T REQUIRE rescuing.

I did.

From my surprise birthday party.

"Happy birthday, Jethro!" was hollered at me from every direction just as the lights in Jeanie's Bar flipped on. What felt like a hundred flashes went off, scaring me half to death.

Also shouted, mostly by my brothers and some of my fishing buddies: "Happy birthday, asshole!"

My heart had nearly jumped out of my chest, so I was sure the pictures of my entrance were going to be hilarious. I had a suspicion I'd find print copies of my shocked face in odd places over the next few months. Cletus had been known to sell our more embarrassing pictures on stock photo sites. Whereas my youngest brother, Roscoe, would make them into photo calendars and gift them at Christmas.

In defense of my complete surprise, during the entire drive over and as I'd entered the bar, I'd still been preoccupied with thoughts of a certain brunette I'd helped earlier. The last thing on my mind was finding half the town grinning at me like I'd just eradicated all the rabid raccoons on the mountain.

Nothing I could do now about my scaredy-cat expression, so I decided to shrug and laugh it off.

Cletus and Claire strolled forward from the grinning crowd of at least fifty people, probably more. Her smile was huge. His smile was satisfied. He was clutching his camera.

She wrapped me in a big hug and pressed a quick kiss to my cheek, wiping away her lipstick with her thumb as she stepped back.

"Happy birthday, Jet." She used my nickname, her blue eyes happy. It was good to see her happy.

"You're in trouble." I pointed at her and shook my head. "I'll get you back for this."

"Oh, you don't know the half of it," she replied ominously.

But before I could question her further, Cletus clapped a clean hand on my shoulder. "I see we've surprised you."

I should have known Cletus was planning something when I spotted him scrubbing his fingernails earlier in the day. Cletus, along with our twin brothers, Beau and Duane, owned the Winston Brothers Auto Shop. If any of them had clean hands, then chances were they were up to no good.

"You certainly did, especially seeing as how my birthday was last month," I conceded as two of my work colleagues stepped forward to wish me a happy birthday.

Cletus waited until my friends had walked off before addressing my last comment. "Last month Naomi Winters and Carter McClure had birthdays. You know I don't like eating cake more than twice a month."

"How inconsiderate of Jethro to be born in April." Claire fought a smile and nudged my arm.

Cletus shot her a confused glare. "It's not his fault he was conceived in July, even if it makes no sense. They didn't get air conditioning in the

26

cars or the house until 1997, so you know it couldn't have been pleasant."

Billy, the second oldest of my brothers, had been hovering just outside our threesome while nursing a beer and a sour expression. Billy always wore a sour expression when I was around, but others had told me—mostly women—he was the best looking of us Winston boys. Objectively, I knew they were right.

He'd been listening to and watching our conversation, but saying nothing. At Cletus's statement he rolled his blue eyes and grumbled something under his breath.

"Have something to say, Billy?" Cletus asked, cocking an eyebrow at our brother.

Billy was dressed in a suit, as was usual, which meant he'd just come from work. Truth be told, I was surprised to see him. First of all, he worked eighty-plus-hour weeks at the mill where he was intent on climbing the corporate ladder.

And secondly, he hated my guts.

I studied him, wishing for the same things I always wished for when I looked at Billy: that I'd been a better older brother growing up, that I'd protected my momma from our daddy's abuse, that Billy hadn't taken the beatings for all of us, that I hadn't been a good-for-nothing asshole.

But currently, since none of those other wishes were likely to come true, I mostly wished I had a beer.

I turned to shake hands and exchange a greeting with Claire's father-in-law, the local fire chief, but caught the irritated glance Billy shot Cletus.

"I've got nothing to say," Billy said, a hard edge to his voice. Then his eyes flickered to Claire. He gave her a tight, uncomfortable smile, like he regretted his words. Then he asked in an infinitely softer tone, "Did you want anything to drink, Claire?"

Claire shook her head, not quite meeting his eyes. "No thanks."

He gave her a curt nod, his attention lingering on her profile for a brief moment. Then his eyes skipped to mine, and he frowned at my undemanding expression. Billy's frown became a scowl, and he abruptly walked away.

"He's so rude," Cletus said, watching our brother disappear into the crowd. "What if I wanted something to drink?"

"He's fine." Claire frowned at her hands, which had suddenly become very interesting. "He just doesn't like Jethro much, but he'll get over it eventually."

"Jethro isn't the problem," Cletus contradicted, eyeballing Claire while I accepted a hug and exchanged a few quick words with Daisy Payton, my momma's best friend. She was also the owner of Daisy's Nut House in town, the local doughnut shop and diner.

"Your momma was so proud of you, Jethro." Daisy gave me a big squeeze, then stepped back, holding my face in her hands. "Never forget how much that woman loved you."

I nodded down at her, feeling a pang of guilt as I always did when someone mentioned my mother. I hadn't been a good son, hadn't made good choices until the last three years of her life.

"Yes, ma'am. Thanks so much for coming."

"Such good manners now you're no longer stealing cars." She patted my cheek, giving me a large smile.

I gave her my very best *who me?* grin. "Well now, Mrs. Payton, I don't know what you're talking about."

"Sure you don't." She glanced heavenward and sighed. "You're too charming for your own good. I'm getting myself a drink. It's been a long week. See y'all later." She waved at Cletus and Claire before crossing to the bar.

The music finally started up and I glanced at the small stage. A few fellas were picking out the first lines to "Hey, Good Lookin'" by Hank Williams.

"That's our cue." Cletus lifted his chin toward the stage while offering his arm to Claire. "I'm on banjo duty tonight and Claire is singing. So we're leaving you to fend for yourself."

"I think I'll survive."

"Maybe . . ." A devilish glint flashed behind Cletus's eyes. "Just so you know, I invited the Tanner twins."

I froze, staring at my brother with immeasurable dismay, and croaked out, "You did what?"

I was glad I didn't have a beer because I would've spit it out in horror.

"And Suzie Samuels. And Gretchen LaRoe," Claire added, not trying to hide her amusement at my expense.

I grimaced, stepping forward, and asked through clenched teeth, "Did you invite all my old girlfriends?"

Claire threw her head back and laughed while Cletus answered, "What? I didn't know you had a girlfriend. Did you go steady with one of these fine ladies?"

I rolled my eyes. "You know what I mean."

"No, no, no." Claire giggled. "Tell us. Tell us what you mean."

I glowered at her, and she glowered back, but her uncontainable laughter ruined her glower.

Meanwhile, Cletus answered my question as though he were giving the matter serious thought. "Jethro, I merely invited some of your more colorful past exploits."

"Oh my God." I closed my eyes.

"Think of this evening as a retelling of a Christmas Carol. You are Ebenezer Scrooge, and you're being visited by the awkward escapades of years past."

"You are the worst. I'm getting you back for this. Both of you." I opened my eyes to glare at my brother and Claire, to show them I meant business.

"It takes a lot to get you this riled up, so I certainly look forward to whatever retribution you have in store." Claire patted my shoulder while Cletus ushered her toward the stage, leaving me alone in the sea of people.

Strike that, leaving me alone in a minefield of people.

I couldn't bring myself to lift my eyes and instinct told me to sprint—not walk—for the exit. The problem was, this crowd was mixed. Childhood friends, friends of my momma, my siblings, extended family, work colleagues . . .

And fuck buddies from over a half decade ago.

If it had been six years ago, any inconvenience would've made me hop on my motorcycle and leave without thinking twice. But I couldn't leave now. I wasn't that person anymore. I had to stay.

"Jethro Winston, you owe me," a shrill female voice accused from behind me.

I tensed, bracing myself. I didn't recognize the voice, but that didn't mean much. Just because I couldn't place it didn't mean I hadn't known the woman at some point. Plastering a smile on my face, I turned to face the music.

Then I sighed in relief, my hand covering my heart. "That's not funny, Ashley."

Ashley Winston, my only sister. She'd left Green Valley for college some eight years ago, mostly because living with six heathen boys drove her insane. She'd made her home in Chicago after becoming a nurse. Last August she'd returned to Green Valley to help our momma go through hospice care. During Ashley's six weeks in town, she'd fallen for my boss, Drew Runous.

She'd returned in March, partially because of Drew and—I flatter myself—partially because of us boys. This time she was staying for good.

My only sister laughed—outright laughed—at my distress, her big blue eyes dancing, then pulled me into a hug and using her real voice, said, "I really had you going."

Ashley and Billy looked like twins, although he was born number two, and she was number four in our family of seven. She used to be a local beauty queen. I might be biased as her brother, but I thought her exterior beauty had nothing on the loveliness of her heart.

Except tonight.

Tonight she was being a shrew.

I clung to her. As far as I was concerned, she was my ticket to safety. I doubted any of my past mistakes would corner me—as they'd done a number of times over the years—if I was with my sister.

"Jethro?"

"What?"

"Are you ever going to let me go?" she asked after the hug had lasted too long.

"Nope."

She squeezed me and rested her head against my shoulder, and I could feel her cheek curve with a smile. "I'll protect you. You just stay with me, big brother."

"I'm going to take you up on that," I said, releasing her from the hug but lacing our fingers together. "You're my date tonight."

She tossed her thick hair over one shoulder and grinned at me with a stunning smile. "You mean your bodyguard."

I shrugged, searching the crowd and avoiding every female gaze. "Same difference."

"What's that?"

I lifted an eyebrow in question. "What's what?"

Truth be told, I was searching for Hank Weller. Now my immediate safety was in check, my first thought was of Sarah.

Yes. I know. I'm incorrigible.

I may have sworn off women, causing hurt, and stealing cars, but this Sarah didn't strike me as *women*. Something about her had me thinking in clichés of the *she's different* variety. Maybe her dimples? Her odd, charming honesty? How easily and naturally she'd switched between endearing and seductive? I wasn't interested in falling back into old habits, treating a woman as disposable. That wasn't who I was anymore, or who I wanted to be.

But the simple truth was, less than one hour after making her acquaintance, finding out more about Sarah was a compulsion, not just curiosity.

"What's that face you're making?" Ashely poked me.

"That's my happy-birthday face."

"It looks like your, I hope I'm not about to be murdered face."

I gave her a flat smile, and she giggled at my discomfort. Spotting Hank by the end of the bar chatting with the sheriff, I kept my eyes on him as I pulled Ashley across the room. We had to stop several times to accept well wishes from the crowd.

"Where are we going?" Ashley asked when we broke through the thickest portion of the gathered group.

"I need to talk to Hank. He's got a guest staying at his place on

Bandit Lake, and I want to know who she is," I admitted, confessing my intentions to my sister. Ashley was a safe repository for my secrets. She wasn't one to leverage or blackmail, like the rest of my siblings. Or Claire.

"Okay, fine. But I want a margarita at some point, so after talking to Hank we should place our order."

"I'll buy you a trip to Mexico if you stick by my side for the night."

"You make it a trip to Costa Rica and you've got a deal."

I pulled to a stop directly in front of Hank and the sheriff, prepared to grill my friend about his guest, but stopped short when I heard what the sheriff was saying.

". . . it's not a secret anymore, seeing as how most of the movie folk are arriving this week, and they start filming the week after. So, sure, I don't mind if you tell people if they ask. I've already talked to Kip about the motel. He's known for months since that's where the crew will be staying—you know, the camera guys and the like."

Hank nodded thoughtfully until his drifting gaze caught sight of Ashley standing at my side. Then his face split with a sly grin. "Hey, Ashley. I didn't know you'd be coming tonight."

He made like he was going to hug her, so I stepped forward and intercepted the embrace. "Well, thanks for the hug, Hank. I missed you, too."

Hank Weller may have been my business partner and my younger brother Beau's best friend, but that didn't mean I wanted his paws on my sister.

He pushed me off, scowling, knowing I was interfering with his attempt to cop a feel. Really, I was doing him a favor. I was just one of her six overprotective brothers, and probably the nicest. Her man was Drew Runous. And Drew was six foot five of scary federal game warden.

"Hank. It's been a long time," Ashley drawled and offered her right hand for a benign handshake, issuing him a single eyebrow lift of distrust.

He gave her a wounded look—which impressed her not at all—and she pointed her question to the sheriff. "Evening, Sheriff. What are y'all talking about?"

Sheriff James scratched his chin, openly inspecting us. "Well I suppose there's no harm in telling, since everybody is going to know soon enough. Some Hollywood types are filming a movie out at Cades Cove and the surrounding areas, permission came down through federal channels. I imagine Drew knows all about it, has for months, I suspect."

Ashley's eyes widened with bewilderment. "He's said nothing to me about it."

"The man is good at keeping secrets," Hank said darkly.

I scowled at my business partner, then turned to Ash. "You know how Drew is, he probably forgot about it. That or he thought Hollywood people using the park wasn't important enough to mention."

My sister's smile was soft and warm and her gaze grew introspective. She was obviously thinking of Drew and his peculiar manner. "You're probably right. He'll spend an hour describing new bear cubs he spotted on the prairie, but he'd likely pay no mind to the making of a movie in his backyard."

"How fascinating," Hank deadpanned, frowning.

Although I considered Drew a good friend, I couldn't be too irritated with Hank. Half the men in Green Valley were in love with my sister. Just like half the women were in love with my brother Billy. Hank's envy was amusing as hell.

"The whole thing will be over in three months, or so they told my office. They'll be holding auditions for extras next Friday," the sheriff remarked offhandedly, as though the entire situation was perplexing, and he was trying to sort through it.

"Anybody famous in it? Anyone we would know?" Ashley asked the question most people would likely ask sooner or later.

"Not anyone I know." The sheriff shrugged. "But then I don't watch many movies these days. They're not what they used to be."

"Tom Low is in it." Hank stared past me unseeingly as he recalled several more names. "Jon Will, Ken Hess, Janice Kenner, and Sienna Diaz are all I can recall."

"Whoa." Ashley's eyes grew round and her mouth fell open. "Sienna Diaz? *And* Tom Low? Holy moly pudding pie."

Hank gave Ashley a small grin. "Holy moly pudding pie?"

"Kiss the wind and make it cry," Ash continued her odd rhyme, still too stunned to speak anything but nonsense.

"Should we know who these people are?" I asked, glancing between my sister, Sheriff James, and Hank. The sheriff was no help.

"Sienna Diaz just won an Oscar this year, first Latina to win Best Actress ever, and only the fourth to be nominated. And she won for a comedic role, which is unheard of. Her last few movies were huge hits."

"Then who is Tom Low?" I asked, none of this ringing any bells.

"He's Sienna's ex-boyfriend, and his career has kinda been suffering since they split."

I squinted at Ash. "How do you know this stuff?"

She shrugged and wrinkled her nose at me like I was the weird one. "Everybody knows this stuff, except for national park rangers who don't watch TV."

"She's right." Hank nodded. "I know this stuff."

"Well, I don't know this stuff." The sheriff shot me a commiserating glance. "Regardless, these people will be descending upon us next week. I need to go find Daisy and give her a heads-up, likely they'll be wanting some of her doughnuts and pie."

I pointed to where Daisy Payton was standing at the far end of the bar. "She's over there, said she was getting a drink."

"Thanks, son." Being a man of few words and fewer sentiments, Sheriff James gave Ashley and me a tight smile, then moved to intercept Daisy.

I watched him go and inadvertently made eye contact with a female. Hastily, I yanked my eyes to Ashley and turned us so my back was to the woman.

"Oh good grief, Jethro." Ashley's sigh was both amused and exasperated. "Haven't you figured it out by now? Cletus didn't invite any of your old lady friends to this shindig."

I glared at my sister, mouth agape. "Are you serious?"

Hank tried to hide his laughter behind his hand. "You're so gullible, Jethro. Cletus told me all about how he was going to make you think he'd invited the Tanner twins. He was just messing with you. They ain't here."

Ashley reached forward and pinched my cheek. "My big brother, scared to death of women."

"Not all women," I clarified. "Just those I've scorned."

"Have you been scorning women recently?" Hank asked, clearly finding my discomfort hilarious.

"No. I've done no scorning in the last five years."

"That you know of," Ash added with a laugh.

I frowned at my sister and my friend, irritation swelling in my chest. "Y'all make me sound like a scoundrel. I am not."

"You were." Hank shrugged. "But, you're right. You aren't anymore, not on purpose anyway."

Before I could protest his last comment, Ash said gently, "You can't help it, being as cute as you are."

"I'm not cute. I'm just friendly. Nothing wrong with being friendly."

"You're a huge flirt, is what you are," Hank said dryly before taking a sip of his beer. "You and Beau inherited the gene from your daddy. There's no competing when either of you are around."

Being told I had anything in common with my father used to fill me with pride. Now it left me hollow. I had a feeling Hank was speaking from some recent personal experience with Beau, because Beau definitely wasn't celibate.

I decided to change the subject rather than rub salt in the wound. I still wanted to know about this Sarah.

"So Hank, I came upon your houseguest on the high Moth Run overlook earlier today."

His eyes widened then narrowed. "My houseguest?"

"Yeah, Sarah."

"Sarah . . ." His tone was noncommittal.

"Said she was staying at your place on the lake, said you two went to college together."

I saw he understood who I meant, though his gaze was still cagey. "You just . . . came across her?"

"That's right. She was lost, so I drove her up the mountain to your place."

"Hmm." He took another drink of his beer, peering at me.

I wanted to ask him who the lady was, but the way he was staring made me think the more interested I sounded, the less likely he'd be to share.

"Anyway, uh, I just wanted to let you know I showed her the way to the house. I called Duane on my way over here to have her rental taken to Bandit Lake."

Infuriatingly, "Thanks," was all he said, confirming my suspicion that he wasn't inclined to expand on the subject.

This realization left me frustrated, though I covered it with an easy smile and said, "No problem." Turning to Ash, I offered her my elbow; I wasn't going to get any information out of Hank. "Do you still want that margarita, Ash?"

She slipped her fingers onto my arm and nodded. "Sure do."

With measured politeness, I led my sister away from Hank and toward the bar, greeting those we met with thanks and my very best show of affability. But my thoughts were in mild disorder. This Sarah had seemed interested, at least I'd thought so. But then, I was so rusty these days, maybe I'd been mistaken. Maybe it was just flirting. Maybe I was misreading natural charm as interest. Clearly it was time for me to get back in the game.

Regardless, if Sarah did belong to Hank then . . . well, maybe that was for the best.

CHAPTER FOUR

"I have lost friends, some by death . . . others by sheer inability to cross the street."

— VIRGINIA WOOLF

~Sienna~

COMING TO GRIPS with my inability to order Chinese takeout was a momentously horrendous moment. It would go down in infamy as one of my "First World Problems Hall of Fame" moments, along with that one time I couldn't find a nail polish color I liked at the manicurist's, and that other time the Starbucks drive-thru was unexpectedly closed.

The horror! I WOULD NEVER RECOVER.

. . . just kidding. It was fine.

Hank had packed the fridge, pantry, and spice cabinet—very nice of him—so I decided to make tacos instead. I made a mental note to have him provide me the receipt for the groceries so I could reimburse him when I made the monthly rental payment.

I was frying up the ground beef when the landline rang. I picked it up immediately, hoping it was Marta. I'd called her earlier. She hadn't picked up, likely because she hadn't recognized the phone number. I'd left a message explaining my lack of cell reception, but left out the part about me being lost. No need to freak her out unnecessarily.

"Hello?"

"Sienna?"

"Yes." I was relieved; thus, I shouted my answer. "It's so good to hear your voice."

"Oh my God, Sienna. We have been worried sick. What were you thinking, leaving the guys at the airport like that? And renting your own car? Using your own name? You could have been kidnapped."

For being the most business-minded of my siblings, Marta was dramatic. My brother Pedro, an interpretive dance performance artist and insurance actuary in New York, was the only one more dramatic than Marta.

She would've made a great actress but had eschewed any desire to do so when my first movie hit it big. As it was, she claimed she loved running my life. She was my manager, and usually I adored her for it. But increasingly over the last year, things between us had grown tense.

I kept telling her I needed a break. She kept telling me to wait until after the next movie. She'd been saying that for the last three movies.

"Marta, for heaven's sake, I'm twenty-five. It's only been five hours since I touched down in Tennessee. I do know how to drive." *I just can't read a map to save my life.* "And what do you mean 'we' have been worried sick?"

"When I couldn't reach you on your cell phone, I called Mom and Dad."

"Oh, no."

I love my mother, but she'd been one of those parents who used to make us watch *America's Most Wanted* on Sunday nights. When it went off the air, she made us watch taped re-runs on an old VCR. Without fail, at the end of each episode, she'd say, *"And that's why you never talk to strangers, because they will murder you."*

"Please don't tell me Mom called the police."

"She didn't call the police."

"Thank God."

"She called the FBI."

I moaned, closing my eyes.

"The FBI told her she needed to wait twenty-four hours before filing a report. So Mom called Jenny." Jenny being my agent.

"What? Why?" My agent was great, really great. But like any great agent, she was also an opportunist. If I were kidnapped, I'm sure she'd be both sad and thrilled. Sad for obvious reasons. Thrilled because of all the free publicity.

"I just got off the phone with Jenny." I heard Marta shuffle some papers in the background. "In fact, let me text her. She was just about to inform the studio and local police."

I sighed, my head falling to my hand. "I called you as soon as I arrived. Did you not get my message?"

"But you weren't answering your cell phone."

"My cell doesn't get reception up here."

"That's unacceptable. I need to be able to reach you. I have, like, ten scripts for you to look at. You haven't checked your email in hours. Jenny needs to know whether you're going to the London premiere for Kate's new film and who you're bringing. Travel hasn't been booked because you need to tell me the dates. You haven't given me the okay yet on the social media posts for June. *Esquire* sent over the final pictures and editorial for your approval. Creative wants your input on the campaign for—"

"Marta, stop. Just. Stop." I could feel my blood pressure rising the longer she spoke. "None of those things are critical or constitute an emergency. I told you this was going to be a writer's retreat. I told you I need a break."

She sputtered for a few moments and then finally admitted, "I didn't think you were serious."

"You didn't—"

"You're always saying you need a break, but you never actually take one."

The meat sizzled angrily, so I turned off the gas range. "I meant it the last sixty times I said it, so I'm taking one now."

"Sienna, darling." Marta hesitated, as though she were at a loss.

"Baby, listen. You know I want what's best for you. You know I love you."

"Yes. Of course." And I did. Marta was my older sister by fifteen years. She'd struggled as an actress, waiting tables, waiting for her big break. Just before I sold my first script, she'd landed a regular spot on a network TV show, and she'd given it up to manage my career.

"Then you have to believe me, now is not the time to take a break. You will lose all your momentum. You will become irrelevant. And then all the good you've done, breaking that ceiling for Latinas and women in this industry, will disappear."

I sighed, tired of this argument. In fact, I was just plain tired. I'd cranked out twelve feature film scripts in four years, all of them had been optioned. I was constantly on the press junket for whatever movie I'd just filmed, or was filming, or was about to film. Or I was speaking to crowds and supporting charities dedicated to diversity in film. I agreed with Marta, all of it was worthy of my time.

And yet, I used to love writing, acting, making people laugh, and connecting with my audience. I still liked it, but I was in danger of hating it.

"I just want a break." I hated how small my voice sounded. "I just want to sleep for a week and wear pajamas without someone taking my picture, or someone breaking into my house, or someone going through my trash."

"I know, baby. And you will. Just not yet."

I huffed a helpless laugh. "Please tell me you haven't hired someone to go through my trash."

"No. But we need people to take your picture. We need you to answer calls, respond to interview requests, post on social media. We need you to be visible and accessible. And if you're visible, you need to keep your security team close."

I nodded, hating she was right about the security team. "Okay. I'll get online somehow and send Dave my address. There's enough room here for him and the other guys."

And there went any plans I might have had of peace and quiet. I liked my security staff, but they were such guys. They never did their dishes and left stuff all over the place.

I ended the call frustrated but covering it well. I promised to call her again in the morning and returned my attention to the ground beef on the stove. It wasn't the shredded beef I preferred for my tacos, but I wasn't complaining. However, if my mother had been here, she would've been horrified.

I'd just figured out how to turn the heat on again when I heard the front door open and close, followed by a bellowing, "Sienna?"

I smiled, my spirits immediately lifting at the familiar voice. "I'm in here, Hanky-panky. But don't come in, I'm naked. And getting a gynecological exam. And having a mole removed."

"You aren't naked." His rumbly chuckle greeted my ears, and he appeared in the doorway at my right.

I glanced over at him. My good friend was leaning against the door frame, his thumbs hooked in the belt loops of his jeans. A crooked, happy grin made his typically stoic features handsome.

"Well, I *was* naked. But I got dressed really fast when I heard the front door open."

"And sent your doctors away?"

"No. I was conducting my own GYN exam with a mirror and an ice-cold speculum, and removing my own mole. I hope you don't mind if I used your steak knives for that. I'll sterilize them after if it's a problem."

He made a face and strolled to the fridge, grabbing a beer. "You're so gross."

"Yes. Yes, I am. And I can't wait to tell you all about my colonoscopy."

"Just stop." He lifted his hands to ward off my words, though he was laughing.

I'd taught Hank this ritual. It was a game I'd played with my siblings growing up, one we'd indoctrinated Hank into when he'd spent a weekend with my family during our freshman year of college. At the time, we were kinda, sorta dating.

The purpose of the game was to disgust each other. After the weekend ended, we quickly moved into friend-zone territory. It was a good lesson for me to learn about being too open—being my true, odd, gross, kooky self—too soon. I knew better now.

My willingness to share this tradition was based on his claim of being impossible to offend. Our backgrounds were as different as two people could be, but we'd bonded over disgusting boundary pushing. As a result, all romantic spark quickly fled and was replaced by poop jokes and buddy drinking. I became his wingwoman, he became my wingman, and the rest was history.

"Fine. I'll stop. But I really wanted to show you this polyp that looks like Pluto's heart-shaped crater—" He stepped behind me and closed a hand over my mouth, cutting me off, and bringing the back of my head to rest on his shoulder. I felt his body shaking with laughter.

"No polyps," he demanded.

I lifted my eyebrows. He knew what I wanted to hear.

Hank sighed, his hand slipping away and squeezing my shoulder. "You win, okay?"

"Say it," I pressed.

"Fine. Fine," he grumbled. "You disgust me."

You disgust me was the key phrase. It meant I won this round. I hadn't been keeping track, but I was pretty sure I held claim to the championship at this point.

My grin was immediate, and I did a little victory dance in front of the stove. "Spatula, spatula in my hand, who's the most repulsive in all the land?"

"Come here, doofus." Hank started to laugh again as he swatted the wooden kitchen tool away so he could pull me into a proper hug.

I wrapped my arms around his torso and sighed against his chest, relaxing into the comfort of his embrace. Hank gave good hugs; quality, full-body hugs. They reminded me of my family's hugs. I decided if this was my only chance in the house without my security team, then I might as well make the most of it.

Separating from him, I pointed the spatula at the fridge. "You stocked the fridge. Thank you. Make sure to send the receipt to my sister so we can reimburse you with the rent."

He nodded. "Yep. Already done. She transferred the money yesterday."

"Excellent." I motioned to the kitchen with a grandiose, sweeping hand movement and bellowed in an odd voice, "In that case, stay for dinner, eat my tacos, drink my wine."

He grinned. "I accept. Why didn't you call? I thought you were coming into town on Wednesday."

"I took an earlier flight, as I needed to get out of L.A. My mother was trying to set me up on another blind date." I turned back to the stove; the meat had been neglected for too long and was now hissing. "Crap. I don't know how to use a gas range. I feel like I'm burning this."

"Your momma still doing that?"

"Yes. She thinks I need a man to 'see to my needs.' Every time she says it, an angel loses its wings and I know Baby Jesus cries."

He smirked. "Your momma wants to make sure you get laid."

"I don't know where to start with her. She makes no sense, trying to set me up all the time. She raised me to believe everyone is an axe murderer."

"Is this about that Layorona lady? The one your brother told me wanders around looking for her kids?"

"It's pronounced La Llorona, and yes. She is the ghost of a woman in white, searching for her children, because she murdered them. Fear of strangers is second only to fear of La Llorona when you're a Mexican kid."

Hank's grin was pained, like a wincing grin. "Your momma is funny."

"It's not funny. It's terrifying. We all grew up knowing who she was and being told we *must listen or La Llorona will find you*. I'm still not sure if the lesson is listen to your parents or La Llorona will find you and kill you, or listen to your Mexican mother because she might go crazy and kill you. Oh sure, she'll spend eternity crying and searching for you, but she *will* kill you."

"Maybe if you'd listen to her, you'd find a good man."

I scoffed and snorted, shaking my head. "No. She just enjoys flinging random men in my direction."

"Little does she know . . ." Hank's attention caught on the meat, and he bumped me out of the way, snatching the spatula from my grip. "Here, let me do this. You go cut the tomatoes."

I relinquished control of the beef and began my search for a cutting board and knife. "How did you know I was here?"

He didn't answer straightaway. I glanced over my shoulder and stared at him for several seconds. He was stalling.

"Hank?"

"I ran into, uh, the guy who helped you get here earlier. He mentioned he'd taken you up the mountain."

"Oh! Ranger Jethro with the sexy eyes and the George Clooney jaw." I grinned at the wooden cutting board I'd just discovered, recalling how much fun it had been to flirt with the ranger. Too bad he was so adorable. In retrospect, I decided if he'd been slightly less of a hot guy I might've let him kiss me. And if he'd been a good kisser then I might've given him my number for . . . whatever.

Yes, it has been a while, and yes, he had been that tempting.

I wasn't planning on entertaining any gentleman callers while in Tennessee, but plans can change. Although, my cell was getting absolutely no reception. Even if I'd given him my number, it would've led nowhere.

"Was he flirting with you?"

"Yes. He was flirting with me." I lifted an eyebrow at Hank's sharp tone. "And he was rather good at it, actually. You don't see that kind of flirting skill out in the wild very often."

"Yeah, well, he flirts with everybody," Hank mumbled, stirring the meat with jerky movements.

I studied my friend's sullen expression for a beat, mulled over his words. "If he flirts with everybody, then why did you ask if he flirted with me?"

"Because . . ." He huffed. "Fine. He doesn't flirt with *everybody*. Well, he doesn't mean to. He's a con man is all, a charmer. People like him 'cause he's easy to like. Regardless, if you see him again, avoid him."

"He's a con man?" This made me smirk. Ranger Jethro didn't seem like the con-artist type. He didn't give off a smarmy vibe, not with his penchant for rescuing red-faced damsels in distress and not wrecking the wheels of their luggage. Though, the intensity of the look he'd given me just before leaving made me think Mr. Hot Guy Park Ranger was more than a tad dangerous beneath his cowboy hat and tool belt.

"I should say: he was a con man. But, yeah, I mean, he's turned his life around in the last few years. Used to be, if a car went missing, you knew who took it."

"Ranger Jethro used to steal cars? When did he get out of jail?" My mouth dropped open.

Hank looked uncomfortable. "They never actually *caught* him. He was arrested a few times. The charges never stuck, but everyone knew it was him."

"And people still like this guy?"

My friend rolled his eyes, looking even more uncomfortable. "Yes. He only ever stole tourists' rentals, never any locals' cars. Except one time he stole my father's Mercedes."

I winced. "He took your dad's Mercedes?"

Hank's father had been an extremely unpleasant man . . . possibly the nicest way to describe him. He was demanding and cold and, honestly, a prejudiced asshole. When he'd met me over spring break at Harvard, he'd asked me if I'd been accepted on one of those special charity case, minority scholarships—you know, *for women like me.*

When I replied that, no, I was accepted because of grades, test scores, and my parents paid for my tuition, he asked me if they were drug dealers.

So I lied, said yes, and implied I could make him disappear with a phone call rather than telling him my parents were physicians in private practice as well as militant about saving and education.

"Yes. Jethro stole it when he was fifteen or sixteen."

"I can't believe your dad didn't have him arrested."

Hank's smile was wry as he filled in the blanks. "First of all, my dad couldn't prove it. And second, Jethro returned it after three days. It was spotless. Of course it smelled like the inside of a urinal, but he returned it nevertheless."

I'm not ashamed to admit, this made me giggle. "Ha ha! That's hilarious."

My friend chuckled too, his eyes growing hazy. "It was. No amount of shampooing or detailing could remove the smell."

I gave him a minute with his memory, what I knew was likely one of the few happy ones from his childhood, before getting the gossip train back on track. "So, he stole cars and gave the proceeds to the poor? Like Robin Hood?"

"Uh, no. Nothing like that. He stole for the local biker gang, the Iron Wraiths. They had a chop shop and Jethro was the best at delivering inventory."

"Well, if he was so good, didn't see anything wrong with it, and he didn't get arrested, why'd he stop?"

"He did see that it was wrong, eventually." Hank turned down the heat and stirred the meat unnecessarily, his expression contemplative. "You know, lots of people think it was because of Drew Runous, the federal game warden in these parts. Drew was new to town a few years back and Jethro tried to steal Drew's classic BMW motorcycle. Drew caught him in the act, beat the shit out of him, but didn't turn him over to the cops. After that, Jethro got out of the Wraiths, got his GED, went to community college, worked his way up to become a wildlife ranger at the park . . ."

Whoa.

My eyes widened by increments as Hank relayed Ranger Jethro's history. What I'd considered harmless gossiping about the locals had turned into something different. I was about to suggest we change the topic when Hank continued, unprompted.

"But I think it was Ben McClure who did it."

Oh, crap. Now I was curious. "Who is Ben McClure?"

"Ben was Jethro's best friend. They grew up together, but Ben was always the straight and narrow sort. He died in Afghanistan around the same time Jethro got his shit together. Plus," Hank switched the gas off completely and rested the wooden spoon against the edge of the frying pan, "Jethro takes care of Ben's widow."

"What do you mean, *takes care of?*"

He shrugged. "You know, looks after her house, does repair work, yard work, cleans the gutters, man stuff."

I made a face. "Man stuff?"

Hank gave me a flat look. "Don't give me that. This ain't Los Angeles or Boston. This here is Green Valley, Tennessee. Men do men's work."

"Oh, like run strip clubs?" I batted my eyelashes at him.

He snorted. "No. That's just *work* work. I'm not saying men don't clean ovens around here, and I'm not saying women don't mow lawns. I'm just saying, more often than not, a man has his place and a woman has hers, everybody pulls their weight and no one minds it much. We all do our chores and help each other. So stop with the cosmopolitan, enlightened judgmental shit."

Hank was easy to tease when it came to his roots. If I wanted to get him worked up, I'd call him a yokel. I didn't think of Hank as a yokel. In fact, I wasn't even sure what a yokel was.

But his retaliatory slurs—about women and Latinas—never bothered me since I knew he didn't mean or believe them, kind of like when your big brother calls you a poopy-head. Well-meaning revenge slurs between friends were one thing, well-meaning ignorant slurs between strangers were quite another.

I held my hands up. "Fine, okay, whatever. I won't pick on your precious cultural norms, your white privilege, or your fried chicken."

"Good." He nodded once. "Then I won't pick on your telenovelas or tortillas."

"That's right, you won't." I lifted up the knife I was holding and narrowed my eyes. "Besides, listening to this Jethro guy's tale of woe is much more engrossing than a telenovela. He steals cars for a motorcycle gang, then his best friend dies in the war, he gets beaten up by a federal game warden—"

"A federal game warden who is now his boss and engaged to his sister."

"Whoa. Okay, beaten up by the warden, currently his boss, engaged to his sister, and now he's a law-abiding citizen."

"And his momma just died last year of cancer."

I sucked in a breath, my head and heart flooding with shock and sympathy for Ranger Jethro. I couldn't imagine losing my mother. She was my touchstone, my rock. "Holy crap. This guy . . ."

"And Jethro's daddy is a good-for-nothing, and he has five brothers."

"Jethro's father has five brothers?"

"No. Jethro has five brothers: Billy and Cletus, then the twins, Beau and Duane, then Roscoe. And his sister, Ashley. Jethro is the oldest."

I shook my head. "This is a telenovela, or it should be. Why is his dad a good-for-nothing?" I couldn't help myself, I now felt involved—if not invested—in this Ranger Jethro and his happily ever after.

"Let's see, I don't even know where to start. Darrell Winston, Jethro's daddy, knocked up Bethany Oliver when she was fifteen. Jethro was born when she was sixteen. Bethany came from some money and was the only daughter of—"

I waved my hand in the air, motioning him to move it along. "Give me the CliffsNotes version."

"Fine. Darrell was a bastard to his wife, cheated on her all the time, beat her up, the works. He's part of the Iron Wraiths—"

"The motorcycle guys?"

"Yep. And Darrell is in deep, tried to get his kids involved. That's how Jethro started stealing cars. Jethro was basically that bastard's shadow for the first twenty-five years of his life."

"How old is Jethro?" I tried to recall his face in detail, the wrinkles around his eyes that were becoming on outdoorsy men, but which actors and actresses avoided like B-movie roles. "He can't be more than twenty-seven."

"He is older than that. He's thirty-one. And there's another reason you should avoid the man. He's too old for you."

I snort-laughed. "That's funny, Hank. You know Tom is thirty-eight, right?" I was referring to my last sorta relationship and current co-star, Tom Low. If you asked Tom, we'd been on the road to matrimony when I'd called it off. If you asked me, we were together for one long weekend before his inability to function without constant reassurance grew oppressively irritating.

As an example, he didn't know how to do laundry. Any laundry. At all. Sometimes he threw clothes away instead of washing them, buying new outfits weekly.

"Yeah. Tom was too old for you, too."

I shrugged, not wanting to argue, but disagreeing. Tom may have been thirteen years older than me, but he was a big baby. A big, adorable, metrosexual, helpless, wee little man of a hot guy baby. He was pretty good in bed, though. Like, a solid six or seven out of ten (six or seven orgasms out of ten attempts).

Whereas Ranger Jethro, at just six years older, and based on Hank's description, very well may have been beyond my maturity level. I still liked being goofy and winning the *you disgust me* wars.

I crossed to the fridge, opening it and pulling out drawers, searching for tomatoes. "So, now Jethro looks after widows and children."

"Just widows. Just really gorgeous, redheaded widows, with pretty blue eyes and a voice like an angel." Now Hank was batting his eyelashes.

"Aha." I nodded my understanding. "Ranger Jethro is sweet on his best friend's widow?"

My stomach dropped a little with disappointment as I said the words. It was like feeling disappointed when you discover a shop doesn't have an awesome dress in your size, even though you weren't sure you wanted the awesome dress to begin with. But knowing *definitely* the awesome dress was off limits was disappointing.

I quickly pushed the feeling away. I didn't need any dresses.

"Actually, no." Hank scratched his neck and leaned back against the stove, crossing his arms. "If Jethro were sweet on Claire, then he would've made his move by now. I think he just likes taking care of her. In fact, I think he likes taking care of people."

"Then tell me something, Hanky-panky: why do you want me to stay away from reformed Ranger Jethro? He sounds fantastic. I could settle down here in Gangrene Valley. I could learn how to do woman's work. We could have all the babies. Side note, I hope they get his beard and my forearms."

Hank dipped his chin and narrowed his eyes on me, fighting a smile. "First of all, it's Green Valley, not Gangrene Valley, smart-ass."

"Honest mistake."

"And second, I don't want you to stay away from Jethro for your sake. I want you to stay away from Jethro for *his* sake."

I gaped, sputtering at my friend for several seconds before I managed, "I am insulted."

"That may be, but I'll ask you to stay away, nevertheless."

"You are an asshole yokel." I thought about throwing the tomato I was holding at him but decided against it. I'd found only one tomato, and I needed it for tacos. Tacos without tomatoes was like cake without frosting. Pointless.

"And you've always been opposed to settling down, or has that changed?"

"Absolutely not. Settling down implies settling. I have no plans to settle."

"Exactly. You're a man-eater, leaving a trail of broken hearts longer than I can list." Hank set his hands on his hips and grinned at me like he knew me . . . which he did. "You and your dimples and your sexy *everything*."

"I am not a man-eater. I don't even like giving head usually, my gag reflex is very sensitive. All that hair, I hate hair in my mouth. And it's the worst kind of hair—"

"You know what I mean, baby doll. Leave the poor guy alone. He's been through enough."

"Did you just *baby doll* me? You don't baby doll me. I *baby doll* you."

Hank ignored my outrage and grabbed the tomato from my hand, moving to the cutting board. "Jethro might have been a con artist, but he's mostly reformed."

"Keep your diaper on, baby doll," I grumbled.

"I'm serious, Sienna. He's out of bounds." Hank chopped the tomato, though he kept his eyes leveled on me as he mumbled, "Poor man ain't ever met anything like you."

CHAPTER FIVE

"The art of losing isn't hard to master;
so many things seemed filled with the intent
to be lost that their loss is no disaster."

— ELIZABETH BISHOP, THE COMPLETE POEMS

~Sienna~

BANJO MUSIC FREAKS me out.

I've always associated it with the movie *Deliverance*. It's like, I hear a banjo and my hands go to my bottom in an automatic Pavlovian response. Ring a bell and nothing happens, strum a banjo and I'm covering my poop shoot.

Also, flannel.

Also, bearded men with hound dogs and rifles.

Likely this has something to do with the fact that my parents— although banal and suburban by most measures—didn't really monitor my TV and movie consumption. My parents met in the Navy and left the service together to open a private practice. They worked a lot, were gone a lot, but always showed up and supported us when it mattered.

Nevertheless, my older siblings and old movies mostly raised me. By the age of four I was watching anything and everything. In my house that usually meant telenovelas.

However, I saw *Basic Instinct* when I was eight and have subsequently never owned an icepick.

I saw *Friday the Thirteenth* when I was twelve and have a morbid aversion to hockey goalies.

It also meant my favorite movie at thirteen was *Duck Soup* with the Marx Brothers, and my sister Rena and I could quote line for line the entire Abbot and Costello "Who's on First" bit.

But now, on a backwoods mountain road in the middle of nowhere Tennessee, I glanced around my tree-lined surroundings and I swore I heard the ominous banjo music.

Duna-ner-ner-ner-ner-ner-near-near. . .

Yeah. I was lost again.

This time it wasn't my fault. Not that it was my fault last time, but this time it really wasn't my fault. I'd been practicing for the last week. With the reluctant blessing of Dave, my security lead, Hank had taken me out three times, showing me the route to the filming location. He brought me maps. I made a mental map. I even drew my own map from memory. And I had a new cell phone, one that should have had reliable reception all over the mountain.

Driving by myself felt like a luxury after spending a week working from early morning until past midnight writing, answering emails, going into Knoxville to be seen and for interviews, and sharing a lake cabin with several burly, loud men.

Regardless, my new phone now had no reception, it was 6:47 a.m. and I was terribly and irrevocably lost. I felt like a fool. I should've just agreed to let Dave or Tim drive me. I didn't know why I was being so stubborn about driving myself.

The good news, because there was good news, was that the sun had finally decided to rise. So when I saw an official-looking sign reading COOPER ROAD TRAIL I decided to pull off. I figured, like any sane person would, that the trail must be on the map.

The trail wasn't on the map. I didn't have the energy for a breakdance map assault. Instead I exited my rental car, calmly sipped on my tepid coffee, and made a plan to walk toward the campsites I'd spotted by a creek in the distance. I figured I'd wait until someone emerged from his or her tent—assuming he wasn't carrying a rifle and wearing flannel—and then I'd accost him or her for help.

At least, this was my plan.

Not part of my plan was the very familiar-looking green pickup truck that slowly wound down the trail entrance and eventually parked next to my tiny rental car. Also not part of the plan, the perplexed smile on Ranger Jethro's handsome face as he exited his truck and scrutinized me as I sipped my tepid coffee.

Not part of my plan, but not unwelcomed.

Keeping his eyes on me, the ranger—who I could no longer call *adorable* or simply *a hot guy* now that I knew way too much about his past—tipped his hat much as he'd done before. And much as he'd done before, he said, "Miss, do you require assistance?"

Unexpected warmth spread from my belly to my fingertips at the sound of his voice in the early morning, rough and unused. Deeper. Manly. Despite the unanticipated belly flips, I was able to quip, "Aw, I bet you say that to all the lost ladies."

This earned me a wider smile. "As a matter of fact, no. I don't make a habit of coming upon lost ladies all that often. But when I do, they all have irresistible dimples and they all seem to be you."

I returned his smile, unable to help myself. Man, he was a great flirt. Like really, really great. He was able to slip in a compliment and make it sound like a fact. As well, his creepiness and cheesiness factor was a big fat zero. He made my heart beat faster, and yet he seemed entirely relaxed and unaffected.

I recognized it as confidence. And not the douche kind either. The sincere, well-deserved kind.

I let my dimples show and indulged in my desire to look at his lips, because he had nice ones. But I didn't look too long, because he also had nice eyes. "So, you're a strictly monogamous rescuer?"

He shifted on his feet, gathering a deep breath and crossing his arms over his broad chest. "More like I've been in a rescuing dry spell for several years."

"Not many damsels then? In these parts?"

He smirked but endeavored to keep his expression even. "Plenty of damsels. Just none that I'd like to rescue near as much as you."

This made me laugh, and I saw his eyes fall to my mouth. He blinked and gave into his grin. He'd complimented my smile and laugh last time I'd seen him, so I decided I ought to return the favor.

"You have a great smile, Ranger."

"Call me Jethro."

"What's wrong with Ranger?"

"Ranger isn't my name, Sarah."

That gave me a start, a twinge of something unpleasant like guilt, because Sarah wasn't my name, and yet I continued to encourage his ignorance. He didn't recognize me as a celebrity, of that I was certain, but would he recognize my name?

I hoped not.

Before I could correct him and give him my real name, he stepped forward, reaching for my mug and removing it from my hands with a gentle kind of self-assurance. He placed it on the roof of my car. I had to lift my chin to keep looking in his eyes, which held me completely captivated. They were gold and green, not brown like I'd expected.

Now he was standing close, but not too close. Just, a really good distance—non-threatening but within my reach—like an invitation.

With a truly exceptional grin, one that made my knees feel a bit weak, he dropped his voice so I'd have to lean closer to hear him. "And you've got such a beautiful voice. Seems a shame to waste it on Ranger when you could be saying Jethro instead."

I blinked, startled, because—Oh. My. Dear. Lord.—I do believe my stomach just did a somersault.

Could he be any sexier? And why, apart from the obvious, was he so sexy?

"Jethro, I hope you don't mind my saying so—"

"Say whatever you'd like, Sarah," his voice was a rumble, "just as long as you keep using my name."

Oh, gah! Another tummy cartwheel. And now I really wanted to touch him. What voodoo was this?

It took a great deal of concentration, but I continued as though he hadn't interrupted. "And please accept this as a compliment, because I mean it with all sincerity, but you are the most gifted flirt I've ever met."

His eyebrows ticked up beneath his hat, and his smile didn't waver, if anything it seemed to deepen.

"I mean it. And I've met a lot of very capable ones. I hope you've put flirting on your résumé, and if you need a reference please let me know, because as much as it's possible to love something about a near stranger, I love this about you."

He continued to study me for a silent moment, during which the urge to touch him intensified to something like an itch. He was so close, yet all I could think was that he wasn't close enough. But that was probably the point.

Well played, Ranger Jethro. Well played.

And his eyes. Don't get me started on his eyes. Just . . . don't. I can't even with this guy. So. Gorgeous. They held an invitation as well, a twinkly, heated, mesmerizing invitation. And I wanted to RSVP so hard.

Both breaking and heightening the wonderfully agonizing tension, Jethro finally said, "Coming from you, that is a compliment."

His eyes swept over my face, pausing on my mouth.

Oh, *sigh.*

Too bad I was late for work. Also too bad I'd promised Hank I would stay away from Ranger Jethro. At the time I hadn't thought I'd encounter him again, so my promise hadn't felt like a sacrifice. Hank had been overreacting, succumbing to prissy hysteria. Clearly, the ranger wasn't a delicate flower. He was self-possessed and capable.

And I was not a man-eater.

I was more of a man-sampler.

Regardless, yielding to the more responsible facets of my personality, I gathered a large inhale and glanced at my watch. Yes, I wear a watch. I hate keeping track of time on my cell phone, mostly because it distracts me. I see the texts and notifications and feel like I must respond. Whereas my watch makes no demands.

It's like, *here is the time and nothing else.* That's it. I love it. It's great.

"I hate to press the pause button on this epic awesomeness," I motioned with my hand to his entire person, "but would it be possible—do you have the time—to help me get unlost this morning? I was supposed to be someplace by five thirty and it's almost seven."

He smirked at my hand movement. Of course he did. No pretentiousness or shocked indignation from this guy, or irritation at my quick subject change. Just quiet acceptance and confidence. He was such an . . . *adult.*

Jethro rocked back on his heels, pulling his phone from his back pocket and tapping out a message. "Sure, no problem. I have time, just need to call my boss."

I recalled from my gossip fest with Hank last week that Jethro's boss was Drew, a federal game warden, engaged to Jethro's sister, and had beaten the crap out of Jethro a few years ago.

I said nothing of my knowledge, but inspected the ranger as he made his call.

Okay fine. I stared at him.

I STARED AT RANGER JETHRO. *Are you happy now?*

You would stare at him, too. He had long eyelashes for a guy. And his beard was fantastic. And it framed a really nice mouth.

Plus, I felt like I knew him. Probably because Hank had given me the man's entire life story. And yet, this guy didn't even know my real name. This was a complete role reversal. Usually people, strangers, felt they knew me. They followed my life, had seen pictures of me from my quinceañera, and had real opinions about the dress I'd worn. Opinions they wanted to discuss, and did discuss on message boards all over the glorious Internet.

I'm serious. Check out #SiennaQuinceañera. It still trends on Twitter every once in a while. You will be horrified and amused.

But back to sexy Jethro.

Now I was the stranger.

It was nice to be the stranger.

And yet, the fact Jethro had no idea I'd been acquainted with his backstory didn't sit well. It felt more deceptive than not sharing my real name. Knowledge of his history colored my thoughts and reactions to his behavior, and he had no idea he was being viewed through my gossipy lens.

"Drew? It's Jet. I'll be late. See you later," he said then ended the call. Either he didn't wait for a response or he was leaving a voicemail.

"Where are you headed?" he asked, not glancing up from his phone. He must've felt my eyes on him—because I was staring—but he didn't seem at all fazed by it.

"Um, Cades Cove."

His gaze shot to mine. "Cades Cove?"

"Yes. And I'm running terribly late."

"Are you, uh," he conducted another pass of my features, dawning realization making his eyes grow just a smidge wider, "you're an actress."

Aaaggrrrraaahh . . . boo.

He knew about the movie. It made sense, what with him being a wildlife ranger at the national park where we were filming. But I didn't like the way he'd said that, like being an actress made everything I'd said or done up to this point suspect, or less sincere.

I wasn't a fake. I was just selective about the truth. Totally different.

Not wanting the magic between us to end, I hedged, "I'm a writer." Then I turned to my car under the premise of grabbing my bag so he wouldn't see me cringe.

The irony was not lost on me; I'd just proven his instinct to be suspicious right. However, what I'd said was also true. I was a writer. I was a screenwriter.

"A writer? Really?" Jethro had already opened the passenger door for me by the time I straightened from my vehicle. He looked at me with renewed interest bordering on fascination. "Did you write this movie? The one they're filming here?"

"Uh, yes. I did. I wrote this movie." Truth.

As I climbed into his truck I realized he hadn't offered his hand like last time. I don't know why I noticed, but I did and I wondered why— both why he didn't offer and why I noticed.

"How'd you get into writing movies?" he asked as soon as he opened the driver's side door. I saw he'd also grabbed my coffee mug from the roof of my car and placed it in the cup holder closest to me, whereas I'd totally forgotten about the mug.

"In college. I won a contest." Technically true.

"What kind of contest? A screenwriting contest?" Jethro turned the key to the ignition, placing his phone on a dashboard stand, presumably so he could see any messages as they came in.

"No. I won a stand-up contest my freshman year."

"You're a comedian." His smile returned. I really liked how easily he smiled. Given his past, especially the shady criminal parts, I was amazed at how genuinely friendly and upbeat he seemed to be.

I braced myself, wanting to be honest, but hoping if I told the entire story he wouldn't put two and two together. "Well, the contest was stand-up comedy, improv, that kind of stuff. An agent—Hollywood talent agent, big deal—had been in the audience; her nephew was a contestant. After the show, she approached me. I'd always loved to write, so I showed her some of my work. She helped put me in contact with the right people to clean up my first script for submission." All true . . . except I left out the part about the bidding war between studios. I also left out that my agent wanted me to play the lead in the movie and wouldn't take no for an answer.

Though, I didn't put up much of a fight because, really? I'm going to turn down the possibility of becoming a movie star at twenty? *Yeaaaaah, no.*

Jethro was turning back onto the main road, which I noted was named Moth Run Road, and I saw another question was on the tip of his tongue.

Wanting to head off pointed questions, I hastened to volunteer, "Six years later, here I am. Getting lost in Tennessee while trying to work on my next film script."

"There are worse places you could get lost." He paired this statement with a sly grin in my direction.

"Too true. Like Russia. I don't think I'd like to be lost in Russia. Putin might think I'm a tiger and try to ride me around a mountain."

"Or North Korea. That guy might mistake you for a doughnut."

I wrinkled my nose at him. "You think I look like a doughnut?"

"No, but I do find myself wondering what you'd taste like."

I gaped at Jethro—who was giving me another sly grin—before I threw my head back and laughed. "You are THE BEST. Gah!" I smacked his arm lightly, sneakily squeezing his bicep, while he chuckled along with me.

FYI, he had a really nice bicep. Really. Nice.

But rather than give in to my instinct to feel him up while he drove me to work, I reached for my coffee mug and held it on my lap, needing to employ my hands. "That was a great clandestine flirt attack. I feel like you could teach me so much."

"About flirting?" He sounded doubtful. "I don't think so."

"Yes. Absolutely. You would make such a great character in a movie. You're smooth and witty and gorgeous. In books everyone wants the hero to be broody. But in my movies—the kind of movies I write, romantic comedy stuff—they want the guy to be clever and charming. The ladies love watching that guy on screen. Think a bearded Ryan Reynolds."

Jethro shook his head. "I don't know who Ryan Reynolds is."

I turned in the seat, again gaping, and sputtered at him. "What? How-what-who-what? How can you not know who Ryan Reynolds is?"

Rather than answering my very valid question, Jethro hit me with another sneak attack. "We can talk about this Ryan guy later. Instead, let's get back to how I'm witty and gorgeous. Tell me about that."

Laughing once more, because I couldn't help it, I rested the side of my forehead on the headrest and stared at him again. "Oh, I think you know enough about that already."

"I don't. Really." He was excellent at sounding innocent and coaxing, though he grinned like a devil.

"Do you own a mirror? Maybe start there."

Now he laughed. He had a great laugh, rumbly and carefree. Contagious.

I loved this. Loved. This.

I'd forgotten what it was like to talk to a guy who had no idea who I was. Usually, if the guy wasn't famous, he wanted to use me to get famous. I'd learned that lesson more than once.

And if the guy was already a celebrity, then everything became a competition. I had to deal with his FOMO (fear of missing out); missing out on someone more famous, more important, more relevant.

Even before my career success, I'd never hit it off so quickly with someone. I'd never met a guy and felt entirely at ease, like I didn't have to carry the conversation, fill the silence with jokes, and constantly entertain. This was easy and fun.

He was easy and fun.

So, of course, I awkwardly thought and blurted at the same time, "I just love you so much."

Not missing a beat, Jethro responded, "The feeling is mutual," before I could feel too weird about my crazy admission.

But, despite his immediate assurance, I did feel weird about it. How could I not?

I turned away and faced the windshield, holding my coffee cup with a tight grip, my heart reaching a crescendo between my ears.

This was weird and I was weird. I wasn't used to being weird. I was used to making other people feel comfortable and important. For the life of me I couldn't figure out how to unweird myself.

Turns out, I didn't need to.

"What did you decide?" Jethro asked, pulling to a stop at a flashing red light.

"What? What do you mean?" My eyes widened as I looked between him and our surroundings, worried he'd been speaking and I'd missed his original question.

He faced me, looking at me like I wasn't at all weird, like he still wanted to taste me. "You're sitting over there, having a conversation with yourself. I just wanted to know what you decided."

I studied—i.e. *stared*—at him again, thinking *this is a man who deserves to be stared at.*

"I guess . . ." I debated how to respond, then settled on the truth. "I guess I decided I'm weird. I've spent maybe a half hour in your company and just told you I love you. That's weird."

He shrugged, again not missing a beat. "It's not weird. I'm extremely loveable. Doughnut?"

I blinked. "Doughnut?"

He lifted his chin toward the road. "If we go right, we can grab a doughnut from Daisy's place. They're amazing. It's about a half mile that way. But Cades Cove is to the left, so doughnuts would be a detour. Do you have time for a detour?"

"Oh, um . . ." I frowned, surprised by his rapid subject change and seriously considered grabbing a doughnut. "I'm already late," I said, debating with myself out loud.

He flipped his blinker to the left, even though we were alone on the road, and took the turn for Cades Cove.

"Maybe another time."

I nodded, my mind caught somewhere between a doughnut and my earlier declaration of love. "Yes. Another time."

"How about tonight?" he asked, his tone conversational.

"Tonight? You want to get doughnuts tonight?"

"Yeah. I could pick you up from your film set and take you back to the lake house. Both are on my way."

"Both Cades Cove and Hank's cabin are on your way home?"

"Actually, no. Not really," he admitted, a soft smile on his lips. "But it would save both of us some time if you'd just let me drive you, both at night and in the mornings. Then you wouldn't get lost and be late. And I wouldn't have to search all the roads and trails looking for you."

I scoffed, noting self-deprecatingly, "Uh, no. I'm sure you have better things to do with your time than chauffeur me around."

"I can't think of a single thing more important than driving around a woman who loves me."

I hid my face in my hands and shook my head harder. "Oh God. You're not going to let that go, are you?"

He chuckled, clearly enjoying my embarrassment. "I'll make you a deal. You let me drive you home tonight and pick you up tomorrow. If it's troublesome for me or unpleasant for you, then we'll call it off, no big deal. But if the arrangement suits us both, then . . ." he trailed off, allowing me to fill in the blanks.

I peeked at him through my fingers. "But what are you getting out of this arrangement? I mean," I let my hands drop, "the benefit to me is obvious. But do you really want to saddle yourself with a directionally challenged, prematurely love-declaring weirdo for the next twelve weeks?"

He glanced at me, the same soft smile on his lips. But his eyes heated as they moved over my form, making my mouth dry. The earlier tummy flips now seemed like nothing in comparison to these more mature twistings and aches low in my belly.

Goodness, I adored how he looked at me.

Eventually, Jethro pulled his eyes back to the road and shrugged. When he spoke his voice was rougher than it had been the moment before. "I can't think of anything I want to do more than take you for a ride twice a day."

He glanced at me, making sure I caught his meaning.

I caught it. In fact, it hit me squarely between my legs.

And for once in my life I was too flustered and surprised and pleased to offer a retort. Because now I was thinking of going on Ranger Rides, and that thought made me hot all over.

I held his gaze, saying nothing, because there was nothing left to say, and we passed the rest of the short drive in tense silence. The good kind. The exciting kind. The *I can't wait for this day to be over so I can see you again* kind.

Well played, Ranger Jethro.

Well played.

CHAPTER SIX

"If I ever go looking for my heart's desire again, I won't look any further than my own back yard. Because if it isn't there, I never really lost it to begin with."

— L. FRANK BAUM, THE WONDERFUL WIZARD OF OZ

~Jethro~

I MAY HAVE been grinning like a fool.

I may also have watched Sarah in my rearview mirror as I drove away. She'd stood still as though a statue, staring after me, one side of her mouth kicked up in an alluring, small smile.

When we'd first met, I'd been rusty as hell. But sweet-dirty talking to a woman was like riding a bike. Mind you, it was a bike I hadn't even looked at in over five years. Of course, it helped that I'd been thinking about her all week. I'd carried on conversations in my head just in case I was lucky enough to see her again.

I wasn't going out to Hank's cabin, not after he'd been so cagey about her identity last week, so I'd been forced to bide my time. Praise the Lord for her crap sense of direction. I would see her this evening around 7:00 p.m., and tomorrow morning at 5:00 a.m. I figured that'd be plenty of time to work in an invitation to dinner.

I was still smiling as I pulled back into Cooper Road Trail and parked my truck down the slope from the ranger cabin. Gathering my things, I noticed Sarah had left her coffee mug in the cup holder. I tucked it in the mesh side pocket of my pack, so I could wash it before I picked her up this evening, then hiked up the side of the hill to the station.

Drew was already inside when I entered, sitting on the red and gold checked couch. He'd started a fire, as was his habit on chilly mornings, and didn't look up as I entered. But he did ask, "What's that you're whistling?"

I stopped—stopped moving and stopped whistling—because I hadn't realized I'd been whistling. I tried to think of the tune and came up empty on the song title. "I don't know."

Cletus appeared from someplace at my left and offered, "Sounds like that French song by that French lady. Something like Pilaf."

"No, dummy. It's Edith *Piaf*, not pilaf. Pilaf is rice." Roscoe, my youngest brother, was sitting at the square table in the corner. He'd also escaped my notice at first. Clearly my head had been in the clouds. "And the song is 'La Vie en rose.'" This last part Roscoe said like he knew how to speak French.

"Since when do you speak French?" Cletus narrowed his eyes on our youngest brother and sipped what smelled like both coffee and molasses from a blue and white enamel mug.

"What the hell are you drinking, Cletus?" He was close enough that I could lean forward and sniff the air around his cup.

"It's coffee with blackstrap molasses and apple cider vinegar. You should try it. It's good for your digestion." Cletus lifted his cup toward me.

Behind him Roscoe cringed, cradling his coffee cup close to his chest as though protecting it.

"Cletus, you're twenty-seven. I seriously doubt you're having digestion problems." I crossed to the basin sink toward the back and retrieved Sarah's mug from my pack to rinse it.

"I'm not. My plumbing works just fine, thanks for asking. But one day I will. And on that day I'll be prepared. Additionally, drinking this gives me something to discuss with senior citizens. They're always talking about their digestion."

"I have never heard any seniors talk about their digestion." I didn't roll my eyes, but I wanted to.

"That's because you don't play shuffleboard on Sundays. If you played shuffleboard on Sundays, you'd talk about your digestion and know all about everything going on in town and elsewhere."

"I have no desire to know about everything going on in town and elsewhere."

"One thing I don't know is why you're drinking coffee from a Hello Kitty thermos." Cletus sounded both interested and irked. "And why haven't you bought one for me? You know I like that Hello Kitty."

"It's not mine." His comment had me studying the pink and more pink travel mug in my hands. He was right. It was a Hello Kitty mug. And I didn't much want to explain whose it was, so I quickly changed the subject. "What're you two doing here anyway?"

"Before we get into that, don't forget our switched schedule starts this week. I'm cooking on Thursday, and you're cooking on Friday." Cletus was referring to our dinner rotation.

Each of us five men—six now Roscoe was back for summer break—cooked dinner once a week. We had an assigned night. Mine was usually Thursday, but I'd switched with Cletus because he had to get to the community center early on Fridays for the Jam Session now that it was summer.

Drew unfolded from the couch, drawing my attention to his towering form. "Regarding your question, Roscoe is with me for the next three months."

I vaguely remembered Drew telling me something about this last month. It made sense, given Roscoe had been accepted to veterinary school, for my youngest brother to shadow Drew. As the game warden for these parts, Drew was federal law enforcement. All animals—human and non-human—within the national park were within his purview.

"And Cletus is here to help you." Drew indicated to Cletus with his hat. "He volunteered."

"Volunteered? What's he helping with? Daniels and I can handle the soil science folks." I glanced over my shoulder, my attention split between Drew and my brother. Daniels was another of the wildlife rangers, and we were scheduled to meet with the MLRA soil survey leader all this week to go over topography data.

"I'm having Daniels handle that. Something else has come up." Drew frowned at me, then at his hat. "We've had, uh, a request. And I think you're best suited to the job. But you'll need Cletus, too."

Turning off the water, I set the rinsed mug to the side of the sink and wiped my hands on my pants. We were out of paper towels. "What's the job?"

Drew hemmed and hawed, saying nothing, which was unlike him. Usually he was one to talk straight.

Meanwhile, Cletus slurped his offensive brew. Loudly. His eyes darted back and forth between Drew and me.

Wanting to ease my boss's mind, I gave the room my easy grin and shrugged. "I'll do it, whatever it is. Don't worry about me."

"It's those movie people," Drew bit out, his nose wrinkling in mild disgust.

"They want a liaison, and you're it." Cletus lifted his cup toward me then took another loud slurp, wagging his eyebrows.

"A liaison? But I thought someone from the Department of Agriculture had been appointed, someone from the federal office."

At our team meeting last week, the day after my surprise birthday party, Drew had brought the rangers into the loop regarding the movie. As Sheriff James had noted at Jeanie's Bar, the movie was being filmed at Cades Cove, within the boundaries of the national park. We'd been told the Department of Agriculture was sending down some Hollywood specialist to interact with the movie folks.

We were warned that some of us might be asked to handle crowd control on days when extras were being used. But other than that, we'd been assured it wouldn't interfere with our regular schedule of duties.

"Yeah, well, the guy they sent doesn't know how to handle black bears." Drew's tone was flat and irritated.

"Why did they send someone who doesn't know how to handle black bears?" Roscoe asked the obvious question, still clutching his coffee. "Seems like a rookie mistake."

"I'm guessing the USDA was more concerned about wrangling the Hollywood animals, not the park animals," Cletus quipped.

"I got a call before sunrise about a momma bear and her two cubs. They were eating berries outside John Oliver's cabin while the production team was trying to set up. That means it's either you or me making sure these people don't ruin the ecosystem in the prairie. And it isn't going to be me." Drew was fairly notorious for being reclusive, preferring the company of no one to the company of anyone new.

"Okay." I nodded, mentally reorganizing my day and week. At the same time I realized there was a pretty good chance I'd be seeing Sarah before this evening. In fact, there was a pretty good chance I'd be catching glimpses of her all day, every day for the next few weeks.

"Why are you smiling so big?" Cletus's tone told me he was suspicious. But then Cletus was always suspicious.

Ignoring my brother, I asked Drew, "So what's Cletus going to be doing while I'm managing the bears?"

"They have a couple of old tractors, real primitive stuff, and they need help keeping the machines working. I guess their supplier didn't know they wanted the things to actually run, not just sit pretty in the background," Cletus answered for Drew.

"Fine. That's fine." I was only half listening; Cletus and his machine tinkering weren't of much interest to me. If encouraged, he would talk about it for hours. "So, when do we start?"

"Today, more or less." Drew set his hat on his head. "You're meeting with the director next Monday at noon, a week from today. Her name is Tabitha Johnson. 'Til then, you'll be scouting the perimeter, keeping bears out of the prairie. Take the traps and use The Beast to move them."

The traps were the custom-welded bear traps of Drew's design; they caged the bears without harming them. The Beast was a Ford F-350 Super Duty truck.

"Also, you might want to load up on ketamine," Drew added, motioning for Roscoe to join him.

"Sure, but I think the traps should work." I set my hands on my hips, not wanting to tranquilize the bears unless absolutely necessary.

"The ketamine isn't just for the bears." Drew gave me a sympathetic look, then promptly turned and left, Roscoe on his heels.

"I think he expects me to use the ketamine on the film folks." I chuckled, knowing Drew wasn't serious. It was pretty darn close to a joke though. I was proud of my boss, he rarely made jokes.

"Or use it on each other." Cletus gulped the rest of his coffee, smacking his lips before adding. "If these movie people are as crazy as Drew thinks they are, we can self-medicate until we pass out. It's always good sense to have an escape plan."

* * *

I WAS GLAD to have Cletus along.

I wouldn't have been able to move the traps on my own. Cletus was good company, just as long as he didn't have anything up his sleeve. The problem was, Cletus usually had something—or several somethings—up his sleeve.

Luckily, today was one of those infrequent days where we were able to share space, time, and work without me having to worry he was plotting my demise.

". . . so we're going into Nashville to play the opening set. Now I just need to convince Claire to sing the vocals, because there's no way Billy or Drew can be persuaded to come around." Cletus was referring to his bluegrass trio. My brother played the banjo every Friday night at the community center during the weekly jam session. He and two of his fellow musicians had recently formed a bluegrass band, but they were still looking for a singer.

"You've tried blackmail?"

He nodded. "With Billy, yes. But he won't budge."

"But not with Drew?"

Cletus gave me a probing stare. "Under what circumstances do you think it would ever profit to blackmail Drew Runous? He's as honorable as the Mesozoic Era is long."

"I guess no profit, if I thought on it." I grinned, ceding his point. "But what about Ashley?"

Cletus lifted an eyebrow, holding the trap base so I could crank open the door. "What about Ashley?"

"Well, she's been back in town for nearly two months, and she's got a great voice. If Claire don't work out, you could ask Ash."

"Huh." Cletus nodded slowly. "I could ask Ash. And I bet she'd agree straightway, too. Good idea, thanks."

"No problem." I grinned wider.

Arriving at this place with Cletus—where he actually spoke in a congenial tone rather than constantly plotting my demise—had taken five years and a great deal of effort. His thanking me with any sincerity was a small victory I'd happily take.

We worked in silence for a time, finishing with the first trap after forty-five minutes of setting up. The Beast could only carry four traps at a time, so we'd have to make ten trips in total over the next week. I wanted to have all the traps set and checked at least once before meeting with the film director.

"You're whistling again," Cletus remarked as we climbed back into the truck.

"Am I?"

"Yep. It's that froufrou song again, the one Roscoe can pronounce without sounding like he's from Tennessee."

"I don't even know where I heard it." I started the ignition, checking the rearview mirror.

"Momma used to listen to it when we were growing up. She'd make us dance with her whenever it was on."

"Oh yeah . . ." My recall clicked at his reminder and an image of my mother came to me, so very young to be having a brood of boys wrecking everything in her fine, old house. She and my grandmother tried their best to civilize us, with deportment lessons and mandatory reading lists, not to mention dancing around the house to French records.

"It's a love song."

69

"Is it?" I asked, pulling onto the primitive dirt road.

"Yes. So why are you whistling it so much?"

I shrugged. "Don't know." But that wasn't true. I guess I did know. I was thinking about Sarah and her chestnut eyes and full lips. It was the song that came to mind whenever I thought of her. It just seemed to fit.

"Yeah, you know." Cletus sounded irritated. "You're just not going to tell me."

I studied my brother for a beat, debating whether or not to share the truth. In the end, I decided to tell him, even though it could be used as ammunition. Drew, who had become a good friend, had counseled me on more than one occasion that I needed to show trust in my brothers in order to gain trust.

So tucking my contrary instincts away, I cleared my throat and admitted, "I met someone."

The cab was quiet for maybe a half minute before Cletus echoed, "You met someone?" I felt his shrewd eyes inspecting me before he asked, "You mean, you met a woman?"

I nodded quickly, checking my rearview mirror for no reason. We were going five miles an hour through the deserted prairie. The chances of encountering another vehicle were zero.

"So this woman has you whistling a love song?"

"I guess," I started to say, being evasive, but then corrected myself, "I mean, yes. This woman has me whistling a love song."

Glancing at Cletus, I was surprised to see a rare smile curving his lips.

"Well, that's great." He nodded, reiterating quietly, "That's really great."

This was effusive encouragement for Cletus. It left me disoriented. Hence, when he launched into his bombardment of questions, I answered plainly.

"So what's her name?"

"Sarah."

"And where'd you meet her?"

"She was lost last week coming up the mountain going to Hank Weller's place. I drove her the rest of the way."

"This is the car Duane filled with gas and moved during your surprise party?"

"Yes, that's right."

"And she's staying with Hank?"

I shook my head. "No. She's not staying with Hank at his place, she's staying at his cabin on Bandit Lake."

"Ah. Well, what does she do? Who is she?"

"She's a writer. She wrote the script for this movie."

Cletus grew still and quiet. When I glanced at him again he was staring out the windshield, his expression showing he was confused.

"What? What's wrong?" I asked.

"She said her name was Sarah?"

"Yep."

"Are you sure? *Sarah*?"

"Yes."

"Any last name?"

"No. But I haven't asked for it yet."

"And you saw her just the once?"

Something about Cletus's new line of questions had me sitting a little straighter. "No. She was lost again this morning, so I dropped her off to the movie set and made plans to pick her up after, so she doesn't have to worry about finding her way back. Why?"

"What does she look like?"

I settled my frown on him. "Why?"

His eyes widened to innocent circles. "You know I follow the film business, I was just trying to figure out if I knew of her, any of her previous works and the like, since you don't know her last name."

"Fine. She's tall, five eight or more. Curvy. Dark hair, dark eyes, dimples."

When I said dimples, Cletus huffed a peevish sigh.

Ignoring him, I continued, "She writes comedies, won a contest when she was in college."

He hesitated, then stated rather than asked, "A stand-up contest."

"Yeah. How'd you know?"

He shrugged, no longer meeting my eyes. "Just a guess. And you said she told you she wrote this film?"

"Yes," I bit out, growing irritated. "What are you not saying, Cletus? Do you know of her or not?"

He shrugged. "I think I've heard of her. She wrote a film called *Taco Tuesday* a few years back; it made a huge impression and about a billion dollars worldwide. Launched the lead actress's career. Diaz is her name. Um, Diaz just won an Oscar for best actress this year. She's probably at the top of the A-list celebrity pile right now, has been for the last two years or so. A real big deal."

This information surprised me. "Huh, how about that."

"How about what?" Cletus asked, chewing on his bottom lip. I made a note of the action because he only ever chewed on his lip when he was agitated.

"Well, Sarah didn't mention any of that when I talked to her this morning. She'd been modest about her writing." Which made me like her even more. "So it's fascinating to hear about how she's basically launched someone else's career and made no show of it."

Cletus had no response to this, just kept chewing on his bottom lip and staring out the windshield. We passed a few moments in a contemplative hush, during which I decided I should look up Sarah's film credits when I got a chance. On the other hand, maybe I wouldn't. Maybe I'd just let her tell me about herself in her own time, let things progress naturally.

"Well, anyway," I said—Cletus's prolonged silence unsettled me and I needed to say something—"you'll meet her this evening. Like I said, I'm picking her up at the end of the day. So I'd appreciate it if you made an effort to be nice."

My brother shifted in his seat. "You whistling love songs means you really like this girl, huh?"

I nodded once. "That's right."

"You've never been one to misread women," he said this mostly to himself. Then to me he put, "I'm assuming she's given you reason to believe she's interested, too?"

I grinned, nodding. "That's right."

His eyes darted to mine, then away. "It's been a long time, Jethro. Not that I've been keeping track, per se. But you haven't shown any particular interest in a woman, or women, in over five years."

"That's right," I said for a third time, finding I needed to add, "but you know why that is, why I haven't."

"I guess I do." Cletus's voice was gentle, deep in a way that communicated concern. "It's just, I know we give you a hard time, but we see you've been trying to make amends . . . with all of us. Your efforts haven't gone unnoticed."

I blinked. This wasn't the direction I'd expected the conversation to go. I pressed on the brake, bringing the truck to a stop, and held still. The moment felt fragile and I wanted to make sure he knew I was serious.

"I appreciate you saying that, Cletus," I said carefully. "But I don't plan to disappoint this girl. I'm not like that anymore. Nothing has happened yet, but I wouldn't be pursuing her if my intentions weren't honorable."

Cletus sighed, shaking his head, looking mildly frustrated. "I know that, dummy."

I eyeballed my brother, at a loss. "Then what's the problem?"

He didn't respond. Not even when I pressed on the gas again and drove us to the next trap site. He just sat in his seat looking pensive and chewing his bottom lip sore.

CHAPTER SEVEN

"Success is stumbling from failure to failure with no loss of enthusiasm."

— WINSTON S. CHURCHILL

~Sienna~

MY MAKEUP ARTIST'S name was Susie Moist.

No lie. That was her name.

Thus, I couldn't help but usually greet her as follows: "Susie . . . Moist?"

And she would always reply, "Not for you."

But not today. Today I discovered her applying Tom's makeup. Now this wouldn't be that big of a deal, except Tom was in my trailer, sitting in my chair.

So, to recap, my sorta ex-boyfriend was in my trailer, sitting in my chair, and using my makeup artist.

"Hello, Tom. Susie," I said stiffly from my place just outside the trailer. "How's it hanging?"

Susie gave me a frown that communicated she was less than pleased to be doing Tom's makeup.

Whereas Tom grinned like he was happy to see me. It was adorable. As was his nickname for me. "Sí-sí."

Hilarious, right? Because I am Latina, and "sí" is "yes" in Spanish. So his nickname for me was "Yes-yes."

. . . Don't everybody swoon all at once.

I glanced at the front door of the trailer again, making sure it had my name on it—Sienna Diaz, not Sí-sí, because Sí-sí wasn't my name—and sure enough, it was my trailer.

"Why are you in my trailer, Tom?" I made sure my tone was light, quizzical, and betrayed none of the irritation I felt. We were going to be working together for the next twelve or more weeks, and I was a professional. But I made note of the lesson: never date another actor, because one day you might have to work with him.

"I was bored. Make me a coffee. You make the best coffee." He lifted his chin and gazed into Susie's eyes, giving her his trademark smolder as she applied his lip liner. Susie was one of the toughest most pragmatic women I knew, but I could see it affected her. I wasn't surprised. His smolder up close was no joke.

He had the bluest eyes. The. Bluest.

And his hair was jet black.

And his lips were always curved in a devilish smirk.

He was physically stunning on the screen, but up close? *Forgetaboutit*. He defied description.

Dropping my bag by the door, I crossed to the coffee machine in the small kitchen and easily found the coffee beans, reminding myself that I was going to make coffee anyway.

"You look great, Sí-sí," he said to my back and I braced myself for the next comment, because I knew it was coming. "Have you lost weight?"

Yep. There it was. Right on schedule.

I was glad he couldn't see my face because I'd just mouthed, *Fuck you, Tom!* to the coffee machine.

So, let's talk about this, shall we? Since it's "a thing" for people.

I am not skinny. Or even thin.

In show business, I'm what people called fat.

In the real world, I'm what people called a woman. (Of note, a skinny or thin female was also called "a woman" in the real world.)

Sometimes I'm a size sixteen. Sometimes I'm an eighteen. Sometimes I'm a twelve. It all depends on what role I'm playing. At present I'm a size fourteen, which was my baseline unless it was the holidays. Because I loved cookies.

Did I exercise? Yes. I did yoga and strength training five days a week because it's good for me and makes me feel great.

Did I diet? No. I eat all food. Sometimes I eat salads. Sometimes I eat steak. Sometimes I eat cookies.

Did I eat to excess? Not unless it's Thanksgiving.

Did I do cardio? Hell. No. I hated cardio—as we've already established—unless it's sex or dancing. Then I'll do the fuck out of that cardio. But running? No, thank you.

Am I healthy? Yes. Like most women who are size eighteen or sixteen or twelve or six, I am healthy.

Do I give two fucks about my weight? No. I honestly don't as long as I'm healthy. And I don't know why it's such a big deal for people, why they can't accept the fact that I'm not hung up on my size. I look just like all the other women in my family, and they're gorgeous.

But, hey, if Hollywood wants to make me the poster lady for positive plus-size body image, who am I to deny them? I love the way I look, and so should everyone else.

Moving on.

Tom was one of those people who thought telling a woman "it looks like you've lost weight" was the best compliment ever. But this wasn't the reason we broke up, though it was aggravating. The reason we broke up can be summed up as follows: Tom only ever said he thought I'd lost weight because he wanted me to say it in return.

We broke up because he required constant reassurance.

"You too, Tom. Have you lost weight?" I recited the lines he wanted to hear. "Because you definitely look like you have."

He didn't look like he'd lost weight. He looked exactly the same as he always did. But if I didn't ask him, he'd start an argument.

I glanced over my shoulder and discovered him smiling at me with genuine affection. "I have. Just a little. I started the lemon water cleanse over the weekend."

I swapped a commiserating glance with Susie. She gave me a tight, sympathetic smile.

Upon my sister's advice, Susie was one of the first people I'd hired as part of my permanent staff. Marta said having a talented makeup artist who was also great at keeping secrets was like having a fairy godmother. She transformed you while pretending your dirty laundry didn't exist.

We'd become friends quickly, her crankiness and blunt manner an excellent foil for my silliness. Most importantly, I trusted her.

"Oh. Can you have coffee?" I asked Tom.

"Yes, but thanks for checking. All liquids are allowed." His startling blue eyes moved over my face, growing warm. "I've missed you."

I nodded politely but didn't respond. I hadn't missed him. He was exhausting.

Instead I changed the subject. "Did you get the changes to the script? Tabitha sent through her okay, but I didn't receive the follow-up email from production. Maybe they didn't send it to me because I originated the change?"

"Yes. I received the changes. They're good, I like what you did. I like it a lot." He nodded earnestly, making Susie mess up his under-the-chin shadow.

"Thank you. I appreciate that." I finished making the coffee then turned to lean against the counter, crossing my arms and surveying the trailer. The morning was colder than I'd expected. I made a mental note to ask production staff to bring me extra blankets just in case I needed to sleep on set.

"What? What are you thinking?" Tom picked up the mirror and looked at himself. "Is it my hair?"

I gave him a tight smile. "No, Tom. I was just thinking it's cold here in the morning. I'm going to ask production to grab me some extra blankets. Do you want me to do the same for you?"

"Oh." He immediately relaxed. "How thoughtful. Yes. It's cold, right? Could you also ask Elon to have some extra cashmeres ordered?"

He called sweaters *cashmeres* because all his sweaters were made out of cashmere. No judgment, it's just something he did. Elon was his administrative assistant, and she had three personal assistants. I didn't know any of their names because each position was filled monthly with a new person. Elon was a bit of a handful.

I pulled out the drawer next to me, searching for a notepad and pencil. Finding one, I wrote down a reminder to ask for the blankets and text Elon about his cashmeres.

"Good. You're making a list. I need more lemons, too." Tom turned his attention back to Susie and lifted his chin so she could correct the inadvertent double shadow on his neck, leaving me to my list.

Tom was going to be a handful and my patience was already running thin. Susie knew I didn't want Tom in my trailer, so he must've had help getting inside. He'd probably used an ignorant assistant director and had already been making himself at home when Susie arrived.

I'd have to speak with the production staff at some point. Stationing Dave and another of the security team outside would also help. Tom wasn't to be allowed in my trailer. Ever.

On one hand, I couldn't wait for the primary filming to be done.

On the other hand . . . *Jethro*.

* * *

JETHRO PROMISED HE'D pick me up at 7:00 p.m. in the same spot where he'd dropped me off this morning. He kept his word.

However, he was driving a different vehicle, and he had someone else with him. Both of these facts gave me pause.

First of all, the truck was huge. I mean HUGE. It resembled one of those monster trucks, except it was painted a benign blue and the wheels were normal sized. Secondly, the man with him was dressed in grease-stained blue coveralls, a black and red checked flannel, and his beard was overgrown and wild. Actually, everything about him looked a bit wild.

But then my gaze moved back to Jethro and he grinned, big and wide, which meant I had to smile. I had no choice, because his grin was happy and open, epic even.

I waved.

He waved, still smiling like he couldn't help it.

By Godzilla's tibia, I felt like a teenager. I was all aflutter with happy anticipation.

I glanced at his companion, deciding—based on the look of him—the man was even less likely to know who I was than Jethro. Thus, gathering a breath for courage, I hitched my bag higher on my shoulder and closed the remaining distance.

As I approached the gigantic truck, Jethro took a few steps forward, hitting the other man lightly on the shoulder to gain his attention. But his companion didn't look up. As I drew closer I saw the man was staring at the screen of an iPad.

"Hey you," Jethro said, his green and gold eyes warm and welcoming, though his voice was gravelly and tired, as though he'd been talking a great deal. "You left your thermos in my truck this morning. I wanted to let you know, just in case you've been missing it. It's been cleaned and it's inside The Beast." He indicated with his thumb the blue truck behind him and reached for my bag, adding, "Let me carry this for you."

"Thank you, Jethro." I let him take the bag, feeling a renewed sense of wonder at how he insisted on caring for me in small ways. Carrying my luggage instead of rolling it and ruining the wheels, remembering my thermos and cleaning it out for me, grabbing my backpack.

After spending the day with Tom Low and the other actors and egos on set, Jethro felt like a breath of fresh air. He felt real, a real person. Thoughtful. Normal. Nice.

"This here is Cletus, my brother."

My eyes moved to his companion again and I extended my hand. "Nice to meet you, Cletus."

Cletus didn't look up, but he accepted the handshake. "Pleased to make your acquaintance. Jethro said you've been having car trouble."

I lifted an eyebrow at Cletus's odd behavior, as though he were pointedly *not* looking at me for some reason. Jethro caught my eyes and rolled his, communicating with the single gesture that his brother was a special snowflake and would have to be indulged.

I gave Jethro a reassuring smile as I addressed Cletus's last statement. "Yes. Sadly, I have a terrible sense of direction. So your brother has been kind enough to help me find my way."

"I'm sure he didn't mind overly much," Cletus mumbled under his breath. "So, you're a writer?"

"That's right."

"You wrote this movie?"

"Yes." I inspected Cletus's forehead and the rest of his downturned features. His hands were big and strong, covered in either dirt or grease. I guessed both. He had thick hair, super thick, with an odd spirally curl every few tendrils. This added to the outward suggestion of his unkempt appearance. Though his hair was wild around his head and shoulders, sticking out in odd directions, it was clean and brushed. It was also two full shades lighter than Jethro's dark brown with natural blondish highlights.

His face, or what I could see of it, was too manly and square to be pretty or adorable; but there was definitely a resemblance between the two brothers. They were about the same height, with Jethro being just a smidge taller and definitely leaner. Cletus was stocky. Where Jethro looked lithe, Cletus looked strong.

"What's the movie about?" Cletus asked, still not looking at me.

"Cletus . . ." Jethro's tone held an edge of warning, like he was losing patience.

"No, it's fine. The movie is a comedy about a female FBI agent trying to infiltrate a cult and unwittingly becomes their leader. She allows the power to go to her head and starts dictating their lives."

"And of course disaster ensues," Cletus guessed with a smirk.

"Actually, no. She really helps them. She talks them out of their suicide pact, saves their lives, keeps their commune from financial ruin. But no amount of good intentions can make up for the fact that she lied."

"In the end they forgive her?"

"Nope. They try to sacrifice her to their god."

"Well, that's unexpected." Cletus chuckled, lifting his chin slightly and affording me a fuller view of his features. They shared the same nose, yet their eyes were different. Jethro's were nearly almond shaped; Cletus's were big and round and framed by ridiculously long and dark eyelashes. They brought the word *extravagant* to mind, and I was a little envious.

I continued explaining the details of the script. "But she is busted out by her partner."

"Who's been in love with her the whole time," he guessed.

"Exactly." I glanced at Jethro. He smiled at me like he was proud. I twisted my lips to the side, to keep my ridiculous answering grin at bay. I swear, at this rate of staring and grinning, Jethro and I were in serious danger of going steady and holding hands.

"What kind of car are you driving around?" Cletus asked unexpectedly.

"Uh, a Kia Ultima."

"You mean a Kia Optima."

"Yes. Sorry." I scratched my forehead, tired, the length of the day catching up to me. "You're right."

"Why'd you choose the Kia?"

"Um, I don't know. It's what they had at the rental counter."

"Do you like it? Driving it, I mean."

"Sure. If I didn't keep getting lost." I checked my watch.

I was just wondering how much longer we were going to play twenty questions when Jethro's brother lifted his eyes and looked at me. Actually, he pinned me with his gaze, making mine widen with surprise, because he did not look happy.

And in that moment I knew. I knew that he knew that I knew that he knew who I was. By all appearances, he seemed to be debating what to do next. His glare was hard, irritated, and distrustful.

I realized he'd likely known my identity the second I'd opened my mouth, maybe even before. And speaking of my mouth, it went dry.

"What'd you say your name was again?" Cletus asked, his tone flat.

"I already told you, her name is Sarah. Can we get going?" Jethro opened the cab door, motioning for Cletus to step up and sit behind the driver's seat.

Cletus narrowed sharp eyes on me, tucked his iPad under his arm, and climbed up into the truck. I tried to swallow, act naturally, as Jethro escorted me to the passenger side door.

As soon as Jethro opened it, Cletus said, "Oh, hey, Jet. Can you check the ties on the master lock in the truck bed? I think I tightened the winch, but it'd be great if you could double-check before we're leaving machine parts all over The Parkway."

"Fine." Jethro nodded, helping me up and giving my hand a squeeze before he released me and shut the door, leaving me alone in the car with his astute brother.

"I can—" I started, but he cut me off.

"I don't know why you're being dishonest with Jethro, and you owe me no explanations. I doubt I'd be interested in them anyhow. But I haven't seen my brother hopeful in a real long time. Mind, hopeful is different than happy. Don't confuse the two, because hopeful is a good deal more dangerous than happy. My only warning is as follows." Cletus paused, waiting for me to turn over my shoulder and look at him before continuing.

"He's got five brothers and a sister, all of us love him something fierce. As such, none of us are going to sit idly by and watch while he's being toyed with. So either you tell him who you are, and tell him soon, or I will."

CHAPTER EIGHT

~Sienna~

I DIDN'T GET a chance to speak with Jethro during the drive back to Hank's place, not with Cletus in the back seat glaring daggers at the back of my head. I didn't blame him for disliking me, not when it was clear I'd been dishonest with his brother about my identity.

But despite how magical, exhilarating, and honestly addictive it had been to be just some girl flirting with some guy, I was determined to explain everything to Jethro the next morning. Unfortunately, Cletus was in the truck when Jethro picked me up at 5:00 a.m.

Jethro held the door for me, giving me a wide grin and offering me his hand. "You left your thermos in the truck again last night, so I took the liberty of filling it with coffee for you. Watch your step."

After he helped me up his hand lingered in mine, entwining our fingers for the barest of seconds, sending a shock of warmth up my arm and stars in my eyes before he pulled away. I mourned the loss of his touch as soon as he shut the door and watched his easy strides as he crossed in front of the truck.

But Cletus's hard voice saying, "Sienna," by way of greeting pulled me out of my happy Ranger Jethro musings.

"Cletus," I returned, frowning.

"Have you told him?"

"When would I have told him?" My response was urgent, because Jethro was almost to the driver's side.

"You need to tell him."

"I will."

"When?"

"As soon as we're alone, somewhere quiet and private. Where we can discuss it."

"Make it happen," he whispered hastily and harshly just as his brother opened the door.

Jethro climbed into his spot and gave me a friendly smile. "How's the coffee?"

"She hasn't had any yet," Cletus answered for me, then added, "but she wants you to ask her on a date tonight, no place public. Somewhere private, for discussing things."

Jethro's eyes widened, and he glared at his brother's reflection in the rearview mirror, snapping, "Cletus."

"Don't clutch your pearls at me, big brother. Look at her, for hootenanny's sake. She's got the hots for your ugly face, Lord help her. And I know you've been thinking about her, judging by how long you took in the bathroom this morning."

I clamped a hand over my mouth just as shocked laughter burst from my lips.

"Dammit, Cletus," Jethro growled, turning the ignition and shooting his brother an incendiary look. "You are the worst. Just, don't speak. Ever. Don't speak ever again." Jethro's gaze darted to me then away as he sighed, looking remorseful. "I'm so sorry."

I placed my hand on Jethro's thigh—FYI he had a *really* nice thigh— to ease his mind and because I wanted to touch him. "No, no. Please don't apologize. He's right and he's wrong. I do have the hots for your face, but it isn't at all ugly."

At this Cletus snorted and grumbled, "Well, it ain't pretty."

Jethro pressed his lips together and I could see the hint of a smile there amidst his frustration. "Glad you have the hots for my face."

"Just ask her out already," Cletus demanded. "She ain't doing anything tonight. You two will go out tonight."

Jethro cast his brother another murderous look, but I took the opportunity to interject. "That's right. I'm not doing anything tonight."

Cletus pressed his hand to Jethro's shoulder. "Fine. It's settled then. And you're welcome. Now, if you don't mind, I'm going to sleep back here until we get to the Cove. So if you two lovebirds could keep it down, I'd much appreciate it."

$$* * *$$

I RAN INTO Tom in the staff tent during breakfast.

Actually, let me clarify that.

Tom's administrative assistant, Elon, tracked me down in the staff tent during breakfast and demanded I come with her immediately to eat with Tom in his trailer. When I politely but firmly declined, she left. And then five minutes later, Tom swept into the staff tent.

This was kind of a big deal. Tom didn't like to mingle with the production staff. I honestly didn't blame him. As soon as he entered, capable women were reduced to giggling girls. Even some of the men behaved like star-struck goofballs.

Production staff and support actors never behaved this way around me. I didn't enjoy having colleagues who lost their ability to speak whenever I walked onto the set, which was prone to happen when headliners held themselves separate from the people actually making the movie. I made a habit of making myself available from the get-go and worked on ingratiating myself to everyone, from the production assistant to the cameraman (or woman).

But I wasn't Tom Low. I didn't have fifteen years of brooding star status under my belt. Plus, Tom was a very hot guy. I'd been beyond captivated by him the first time we'd met, reduced to one of those giggling girls, blinded by his looks and importance.

"Sienna," he said, scowling at Janice Kenner who sat next to me on the bench. She was one of the lead support actresses, and we were friendly acquaintances.

"Why the constipated face, Tom?" Janice looked up from her salad. "You should try more fiber."

"I get plenty of fiber." Tom sniffed, rolling his shoulders and glancing around the tent. "I'd like a word with Sienna."

"Take a seat." She motioned to the empty chair across from hers.

Tom glared at her then at me. She was outwardly unaffected, but I knew she was enjoying his discomfort. Janice was nice to me and hugely talented, but she was also a harbinger of drama. Whereas I preferred to keep the peace.

"Hey, Janice," I nudged her with my elbow, "I'll be back; save my seat?"

She shrugged mutely and rolled her eyes. I shot to my feet before she decided to make a comment about the puffiness of his face, making the comment under the guise of concern, as she was prone to do. Capturing Tom's elbow, I steered him past the remainder of the tables to a quiet corner just outside the tent.

Feeling eyes drilling into the side of my face, I glanced at Tom, finding him tossing every ounce of his extraordinary man-handsome in my direction. It was enough to take my breath away, had I not known he was incapable of doing his own laundry.

"What's up?"

"Come to my trailer," he said, using his sexy voice. "Let's talk. I didn't get a chance to talk to you yesterday."

"Yes, we did. We talked about your lemon cleanse and your cashmeres." I tried for innocently perplexed, but the truth was I'd avoided him for the remainder of the day after finding him in my trailer. It hadn't been easy. I'd been forced to hide in the attic of one of the old houses we were using because he kept searching me out everywhere else.

His mouth hitched to the side, his glorious azure gaze moving over my features with potent tenderness. "I want to know what's going on with you. Tell me about your next script."

I tried not to outright scowl. I'd helped Tom get the role for this film. His last several movies, since the last one we'd starred in together, had been box office disappointments. Even Marta—who was his biggest fan —had admitted his career was floundering.

I shrugged, glancing at my watch. "Uh, I don't—"

Luckily I didn't have to finish my excuse because my phone rang. Marta. I held a finger out to Tom, saying "Sorry, we'll have to talk later. I have to get this," then rushed away from the tent.

"Sienna, my lovely, beautiful, wonderful sister. You haven't, I mean, has anyone mentioned anything to you?"

I smiled at the sound of Marta in such a good mood, searching for a quiet corner where I could take the call but also not be found later by Tom. "About what?"

Ignoring my question, she asked, "How are you this morning?"

"I'm great. How are you?"

She breathed a sigh of obvious relief. "I'm also great. Do you know why I'm great?"

"Do you want me to list all the ways? Because it's a very long list."

"You're cute." She chuckled, sounding pleased. "I'll tell you what happened. I'm great because I just heard from Jenny this morning. Guess who they're looking at to play Smash-Girl? Guess?"

"I have no idea. Who?"

"You."

I blinked. I frowned. "What?"

Smash-Girl? Am I asleep? Is this an awesome dream?

"They want you to play Smash-Girl! The studio is adamant. And they want you to write it."

"They want me to write it?" *If this is a dream, NEVER WAKE UP.*

"Well, co-write it."

"I'm confused. Is this going to be a superhero movie or a comedy?"

"Both. After the success of Smash-Boy, the word is Dimension Comics is scrambling to capitalize on the appetite for subversive, funny, action movies, and they thought of you first."

"So . . ." I stared off into space, my brain not quite accepting or understanding the most basic part of this conversation. "Don't I have to, you know, be buff? Isn't Smash-Girl super strong?"

"No, no, no. They plan to do a green screen with CGI capture, like they did for the Dimension movies with Bryce Boomer. It would be you when she's in normal form. The character would be a super-polite, good-natured, likable, normal woman. And then it would be CGI you when she has her freak-outs."

An avalanche of ideas rushed to the forefront of my brain, funny ways Smash-Girl could lose her cool. "Maybe, before she is able to control her powers, she goes red at the OBGYN's office when the speculum is cold, or if she's out of red wine. Or when people keep cutting in front of her at the DMV."

"Yes." Marta cheered me on, her chair making a small squeaking noise, alerting me to the fact she was bouncing in it.

"This could be great." This could be really, really great.

"Yes! This will be great. And not just for you but for all women. Think about how this could shift the industry, change people's percep-tions. For years women have been written off as not being superhero or action movie fans. Think about how this would open the door for other roles, parts for strong women. A generation of kids would look up to you. And with you writing, you can keep them from dumbing it down, pandering. Sienna, it's going to be so, so great."

I nodded, giving in to my excitement and not thinking about what this might mean for my work schedule.

Before I could venture too far down the path, Marta cut in, "Oh. Before I forget, are you going to Kate's premiere in London? I think you have to and I think you have to bring a date."

"I-uh-hadn't given it much thought recently." My mind was still going through Smash-Girl going red scenarios.

"Well, you have to go. But beware, because Tate will be there with his new girlfriend."

"So?"

"So, you two dated. It will be awkward."

"No, we didn't."

I heard my sister huff on the other end. "Yes. You did."

"We did not. I never dated Tate. We went to a juice bar after yoga once. Once."

"He still calls you the one that got away."

"That's ridiculous. He talked about his beet juice obsession the entire time. I barely said a word. I would never date someone who peed purple."

"Sienna."

"Marta."

I could tell she was trying to be serious, but I was also serious. The man drank so much beet juice it wasn't just his pee that was turning purple.

Spoiler alert: it was his face.

"Well, Kev will be there too, and the rumor is he's bringing his sister. He's telling people he's not over you yet."

"Oh my God. Are you serious?" I shook my head, disgusted. Our agents had set us up for a publicity dinner, and he'd been milking it for the last eighteen months, playing the jilted lover card. We'd never even kissed. "What a ballsack!"

"I'm just saying. Between Kev, Tate, and Tom, it's going to be a full house of your previous boyfriends. So you have to show up with a date."

I felt like screaming that none of them had been my boyfriend—except for maybe Tom, and then only for a month—but I thought better of it.

Instead I said, "Fine. Fine. I'll go, and I'll bring a date." Worst-case scenario, I'd ask my bodyguard Dave to go with me.

"Good. I'll book your travel. We'll charter a plane out of Knoxville, otherwise you'll have to make three connections."

"Okay."

"Oh, and Sienna?"

"Yes?"

"Congratulations." Her voice held a genuine smile and pride. "You are going to write an epic script and be an amazing Smash-Girl."

I was tired, but I could do this. I would do this. This was important.

Despite my lingering irritation about the London premiere, I allowed myself a small grin. "Thank you, Marta. Thank you for making this happen."

And then maybe after I did this, if Smash-Girl was successful, if I accomplished what I hoped I would, I'd be able to take that break.

* * *

THE REST OF the day passed in a blur of activity. News of the Smash-Girl movie and my potential role in it must've been leaked, although I couldn't imagine how it had managed to spread so quickly. By that afternoon everyone was smiling at me and offering their congratulations.

But I had other things on my mind, namely awesome Ranger Jethro things.

As sunset approached and my scenes wrapped for the day, I snuck back to my trailer. Dave, head of my security team, was standing outside the door. He gave me a chin lift and opened the door.

"Has Tom stopped by?" I asked, passing Dave the coffee and doughnut I'd grabbed for him on my way.

"Thanks." He accepted my offering. "I haven't seen him since lunch."

"Good."

"Sienna?"

"Yeah?"

"Are you sure you don't want us to drive you in the mornings and take you home?" Dave frowned. I could see my reflection in his dark sunglasses. "We have the day split into three shifts, and you know I'm a morning person. I don't mind taking you early. If Marta finds out about you driving yourself—"

I waved away his prepared speech, which he'd been giving me for the last week ever since I told him I wanted to drive myself. He'd said much the same again last night when I arrived home at the cabin later than he and Henry did.

"Let me deal with Marta. You work for me, not Marta. If I want to drive myself or if I want to ride with someone else, then that's my decision. Okay? You're at the cabin with me all night. You're here with me all day." I glanced over my shoulder at Henry, who'd been shadowing me. "You guys are great, and I appreciate you. But I need a little break."

He nodded somberly then took a bite of his doughnut. I stepped into the trailer and closed the door just as I heard him say, "Holy shit, this is a great doughnut."

I smirked, because everyone had been talking about the doughnuts. I hadn't eaten one yet because they were from the place Jethro had mentioned the morning before. Maybe I was odd, but I wanted to save the experience for when he and I were together.

Locking the door after me, I checked my watch, saw I had about an hour before Jethro would collect me for our date. Knowing I wouldn't have an opportunity to change at Hank's cabin before he picked me up, I'd borrowed an outfit from wardrobe.

I felt like a knockout in it.

A black knee-length dress with red fabric cutouts on either side of my waist, and a deep bosom-highlighting V-neck. It had been tailored specifically for this movie and specifically for me. I'd only worn it once before, for a promo photo shoot two months ago, but I loved it.

I took a shower, shimmied into my dress, and used Susie's makeup kit to do my face, leaving my hair to air-dry around my shoulders into messy waves. My shoe options were: red flats, black heels, or hot pink chanclas—flip-flops for non-Spanish speakers.

The spot where Jethro dropped me off in the mornings and collected me in the evenings was close to the main temporary structures, but the road was hidden. It was a secluded area with very few, if any, people passing by. But it was also unpaved, which meant I'd be walking and standing in dirt until he arrived.

I decided to slip the heels into my bag and wear the chanclas out, not wanting the black shoes to slow me down or get caught in the grass. Tapping three times on the door, I waited for Dave to return the taps, which would signal the all-clear. If Tom or Elon were present, Dave had strict instructions to explain that I'd already left.

I opened the door and he helped me down. I caught his frown when my flip-flop clad feet hit the ground.

"Sienna, what are you wearing?"

"A dress. What are you wearing?"

"You're not driving yourself, are you?" He scowled. "You have plans."

"You are correct." I hoisted my bag, which held my laptop, higher on my shoulder. I was carrying it everywhere these days.

"Please tell me it's not Mr. Low," he groaned, making a face.

"It's not Mr. Low." I laughed, hiding myself behind Dave's big form until I could ensure no one was around to catch me sneaking off.

"Is it Ken Hess?" Ken Hess being one of the other leads in the film.

Ken was a nice guy, he and I got along great, but he was very much an adorable, rising star type. Meaning, he enjoyed his new fame with a harem of on-again, off-again girlfriends. This behavior was typical for most male actors and celebrities my age, or at the beginning of their career. Ken's trajectory would follow a familiar pattern: He would string a horde of women along until his career began to flounder. Then he'd be forced by his agent and manager to pair off with another celebrity to increase his prominence and Q score.

"No, Doris. It's not Ken." Sometimes when Dave was being gossipy, I called him Doris. I also called him Doris because he had a habit of being excessively insightful. I know it's not fair to generalize about men or women, but I'd never met a guy as intuitive as Dave; he had a sixth sense about situations and people. It certainly contributed to him being a great bodyguard.

"Thank God. That guy's already slept with half of the production assistants."

"They don't seem to be complaining."

"The guy's a horndog," Dave grumbled. "Makes a bad name for the rest of us."

"The rest of you?"

"Men."

I smirked but said nothing. Dave was a good guy and a staunch romantic. Dave gave me hope that other good guy romantics existed.

Depressing truth: 99% of actors, actresses, and celebrities who date each other only do so because their managers and agents forced them into it/thought it would help their career. And that's a fact.

Which was why I was weary of male actors. However, that being said, these people would receive no flak from me. I understood the business just fine. I understood how celebrity worked. Capturing the public interest was one thing, keeping and holding it was something else entirely.

"So . . ." Dave squinted. "Do I know the guy?"

"No. Now move this way a little so I can get out of here without anyone seeing."

He didn't cooperate. "If I don't know the guy, then that's a problem. How can we provide security for you?"

"Don't worry about it."

Dave wouldn't budge. "That's ridiculous. I get paid to worry about it. Who is he?"

"He's a wildlife ranger at the park, okay?"

"Not okay."

I gritted my teeth. If we loitered in front of my trailer much longer, Tom or one of the production crew might corner me. Then I'd never get out of here.

"Fine. You can come meet him. But don't say my name and let me do all the talking."

"I'll need to run a background check."

I ignored Dave's last statement because he shifted his body, covering for me and allowing me to slip past my trailer without being seen. A minute later he was next to me, escorting me to where Jethro would pick me up.

"How did you meet this guy? Are you sure he's safe? How do you know he's not a crazy fan?"

"He's not a crazy fan," I grumbled.

"You can't know that." I frowned at Dave then at the grass under my feet. This was why I didn't want to tell Jethro who I was. This was why being with him while he was unaware of my identity was so wonderful.

"Yes, I can, Doris." I was irritated that I couldn't be trusted to make my own decisions, which was a gross simplification and exaggeration of the situation, but that's how I felt.

"We'll see . . ." Dave tilted his head from side to side, cracking his neck.

We maneuvered around the last of the tents and strolled into the open field. I saw Jethro at once, this time Cletus was nowhere in sight. Alone and standing beside the smaller green truck he'd used the first two times we'd met, Jethro smiled and waved. As usual, I couldn't resist smiling back.

He was dressed in dark blue jeans, a black sweater, and black boots. He looked . . . incredible. You know when some men dress up for an occasion, shaving and grooming and whatnot, they look like they smell marvelous? Well, Jethro looked as though he smelled like heaven. His beard was trimmed shorter, neat and tidy at his neck, lips, and cheeks. My skin prickled just thinking about the texture of it sliding against my neck, lips, and cheeks.

"Oh no," Dave muttered, drawing my attention back to him.

"What? What is it?"

"You like this guy."

I gave my bodyguard the evil eye. "Say nothing."

Dave glanced between Jethro's achingly handsome form in the distance and me. "He doesn't know who you are, does he?"

"Just let me do the talking," I whispered, even though we were still fifty feet away.

"Boy, is he in for a surprise."

"Shut up, Doris."

"Poor guy."

Jethro was looking between my guard and me; his smile curious, but just as friendly and open as usual.

Focusing on me first, he stepped forward and pressed a quick kiss to my cheek, sending ripples of lovely warmth through my body.

"Hey, gorgeous." I felt his whisper beneath my skin, and it made my chest tight and achy.

A dazed "Hi," was all I could manage, because he did smell like heaven. The texture of his beard against my cheek was everything I hoped it would be and more.

Jethro placed one hand possessively on my back and reached his other out to Dave, which Dave took for a shake.

"Hi, I'm Jethro."

My guard said nothing, but I saw he returned Jethro's smile. Though Dave's looked sympathetic . . . the turncoat.

"This is Dave." I indicated to my security team lead with a quick wave of my hand. "We work together. He wanted to meet you to make sure you're not a crazy fan."

Truth. All of it. I wasn't going to lie, but I wasn't going to make a big deal of having a security team either.

Jethro's smile widened. "Glad to see Sarah has people looking out for her."

Dave grew very still when Jethro said, "Sarah." I was relieved he still had his sunglasses on so Jethro couldn't see his eyes.

"Yes, well, that's done. So we'll be going." I directed this last statement to Dave, narrowing my eyes at him.

"Nice to meet you," Jethro said, stepping closer to me, his hand on my spine a reassuring weight. He was polite and gentlemanly and everything wonderful.

Dave nodded, shooting Jethro another tight, compassionate smile, but addressed his comment to me. "Be good."

"We will," I said between clenched teeth.

Shaking his head, Dave left us, strolling back in the direction we'd just walked. I turned in Jethro's arms, felt myself immediately melt at his quizzical amusement as he gazed down at me.

"He seems nice," Jethro said, guiding me with gentle pressure to the passenger side.

"He is. He is nice." Dave was nice. He'd been my security lead going on four years. We'd become friends. Even so, the idea of having to clear my dates—or Jethro being subjected to a background check—chafed. This was one of the reasons I'd only ever dated people in the business up to this point, they didn't require a background check or a waiting period.

Jethro opened the door, but I didn't climb into the truck. Instead, I turned to face him, and hesitated, a mounting sense of urgency filling my chest.

In a few moments, I would tell Jethro who I was. I had no control over what happened next, how he would react, if he would see me differently, treat me differently.

Maybe I was selfish . . . okay, yes. I was selfish. But I wanted one more moment of his ignorance, of being just a woman he liked. I wanted the simplicity of being any woman.

I placed a hand on his chest and gazed up at him, feeling nervous and somehow new. "I know . . . I know this is usually done at the end of the evening, but can we . . ." I licked my lips fretfully. I was being weird with him. Again.

He watched me with his perma-friendly expression, but his eyes lowered to my lips and darkened, making my heart quicken. He was thinking about kissing me; I could see it in how his mouth parted and his gaze grew heated and distracted. Rather than say anything to risk derailing his train of thought, I stepped forward, lifted my chin, rose on my tiptoes, closed my eyes, and kissed him.

And God bless Ranger Jethro, because he didn't need even a minute to recover.

His big hands gripped my arms and pulled me closer, firmly against his chest. Quickly taking control, he walked me two steps backward until my back met the truck. His mouth moved over mine. His warm, full lips softer than I'd imagined, his beard tickling my chin and nose in the best way. He swept his tongue out, tasting me. I moaned, opening my mouth as heat pooled in the center of my body. I pressed closer and his grip on my arms tightened while his skillful tongue teased and mated with mine.

BY MOTHRA'S NIPPLES, HE WAS A GREAT KISSER.

I never wanted it to end. But end it did, with him biting my lower lip, tasting it once more with a slide of his wonderful tongue, and stepping away.

As he opened his eyes, he gathered a deep, happy-sounding breath, his gaze hot and pleased and sending new shivers and longing racing through my body.

Dave was right. I liked this guy. And not just because he was thoughtful and achingly attractive—though that definitely didn't hurt—and not just because he was an incredible kisser—though that also didn't hurt. He was charming, yet artless. Straightforward, yet complex. Funny and witty, but sincere instead of sarcastic or caustic.

And he was looking at me like I was the most wonderful thing in the world.

The question was, would he still be looking at me like this when the night was over?

CHAPTER NINE

"The way to love anything is to realize that it may be lost."

— G.K. CHESTERTON

~Jethro~

To say I enjoyed kissing Sarah would be a mighty big understatement.

She was a damn good kisser, maybe the best I'd ever had the immense pleasure of kissing. It helped that her lips were like pillows and she tasted sweet. Not like strawberries or peaches. Sunshine and sweet— her own brand of it. Plus there was desperation in the kiss, an understated but raw passion I couldn't recall ever experiencing before.

Or maybe that had been me. Maybe I'd been the passionate, desperate one. No matter. Either way, she'd stolen my breath, robbed me of thought and sense. She was a master thief, and I loved her for it.

During the kiss I'd kept my hands on her arms so I wouldn't slide them up her skirt, because I wanted to. Christ Almighty, I really wanted to.

But I didn't. It was too early for all that. Way too early.

. . . but I wanted to.

The potency of my response wasn't necessarily unexpected, but it did have me questioning our next steps.

Was now the time to tell her about my self-imposed celibacy? If so, should I also tell her about how, due to my past, I'd vowed to wait until marriage? Or was a first date too early?

I was good at bluffing and flirting, but I now realized I didn't truly know how any of this worked, how dating and long-term partnerships were sustained. When was too soon to discuss this stuff? When would it be too late?

We drove to The Front Porch engaging in surprisingly easy discussion given my internal debate. Though if you'd asked me what we talked about later I sure as hell couldn't tell you, only that when she laughed at something I said, I felt twenty feet tall. And when she reached over and ran her hand down my arm, I wanted to pull the truck over and spend the rest of the night on the side of the road kissing her.

The fogginess departed as we pulled into the parking lot of the restaurant. Ultimately, I decided to bring up my past and resultant decisions when the time felt right. No need to rush.

She was talking about something that had her excited, and I forced my head out of the clouds. I didn't want to miss it.

"Comic books," she said. "So, you read them?"

I realized this was the second time she'd asked the question. I'd been too distracted to answer properly the first time.

"Yes. Used to sneak them in and read them at night when I was little. My momma was a librarian. She approved of the classics and not much else."

"Well, today I received a call from my manager because I've been asked to write the script for Smash-Girl, the movie. GAH!"

"That's great." And I meant it. "I know Smash-Girl, got into her after I finished all the Smash-Boy I could get my hands on. You know many consider her eye candy and nothing more. But they're wrong." I withdrew my keys and grabbed my cell from its holder on the dash.

"Exactly. That's how I feel. I love that her powers are similar to, but different than Smash-Boy's. That when she grows angry, she maintains her ability to reason. It's such a great allegory for how women and men actually are in life."

"I don't know about that." I scratched my neck, having not given much thought to the allegorical implications of Smash-Girl. "But I will say this: as far as superheroes go, she's way up there."

"Yes." Sarah's grin was huge. I tried to not get lost in her dimples and mostly succeeded. When I lifted my eyes back to hers, I saw she was trying not to get lost in my grin.

I reckoned we were both in danger of becoming lost in each other, and that was fine by me. It was still early, way too soon to be having thoughts of the long-term, but I imagined what it might be like to come home to her every day. Her soft curves, deep dimples, dark eyes; her blunt sensuality and seductive honesty.

It would be like winning the lottery of life.

But I was getting ahead of myself.

Here the date hadn't even really started and I was thinking on our future. She lived elsewhere and, for all I knew, wasn't keen on staying after the movie wrapped. The last five years had addled my mind.

Or maybe it's been preparing you, making you deserving of her . . .

Getting hold of myself, I disentangled our gazes and moved to exit the truck. But she stopped me with a light touch on my leg. "I have to tell you something."

"Okay," I nodded once. "Shoot."

I saw she was nervous, locked in an internal debate. It must've been heated because Sarah gathered a deep breath and fisted her hands.

Then, on a sudden rush, she said, "My name isn't Sarah."

I cocked an eyebrow at her. "It isn't?"

"No. When you asked, that first day, I had my hands in front of my face and my response was garbled. You heard Sarah, but I said . . ." She appeared to be winded. I watched her gather another large inhale and force herself to release it slowly, saying, "Sienna."

I continued looking at her, waiting for her to continue. When she didn't, I asked, "Is that it?"

"Yes. That's my name. Sienna is my name."

I grinned at her and her new name, deciding it fit her perfectly. "Nice to meet you again, Sienna."

Her eyes widened with what seemed to be wonder as they moved between mine, her mouth hitching to the side. Then she frowned again, shaking her head like she was clearing it.

"There's more."

"Oh?" I asked, unconcerned.

"Yes. You asked me before if I were an actress and I said, 'I'm a writer.' That's true. I am a writer. But I'm also an actress." The look she gave me was bracing as she added, "I just wanted to clear that up."

I nodded again. Again waiting for her to continue. And again asking, "Is that it?"

"Yes. My name is Sienna, and I am a writer and an actress. That is it."

"Okay." We watched each other. When it was clear she expected me to say something else, I added, "Sounds good."

At that, Sienna released a heavy sigh of obvious relief, "Thank you. Thank you. I was so afraid—" She cut herself off, pressing her lips together and shaking her head. "Just, thanks for not being angry."

"Angry?" I scoffed, frowning at her like she was nuts. "Why would I be angry? You should be irritated with me, calling you the wrong name for over a week."

Not waiting for her response, I exited the truck and crossed to her side. I opened the door, reaching my hand out to help her down, but she was changing her shoes. My eyes drifted to her legs, happy to have a reason to stare at the shapely calves as she pulled on black high heels.

"Nice shoes," I said, the compliment slipping out. I hoped there'd come a time when she'd wear just those shoes for me and nothing else. In fact, I filed that thought away under my *to-do* list.

"Thanks." She grinned, flashing her dimples as she finished. "I'll let you borrow them if you want."

That made me chuckle and I offered my hand again, taking hers as she climbed down from the truck. But this time I didn't let her go, instead threading our fingers together as I closed the door. As much as

Cletus had irritated the hell out of me this morning, I decided I was going to forgive him. His interference had brought me to this moment.

I took just two steps before Sienna tugged me to a stop. "So, uh, this place we're going . . ."

"The Front Porch."

"Yes. Is it very crowded?"

I shook my head. "Shouldn't be. Middle of the week isn't their busiest time. Though I think the high school PTA might meet up here on Tuesdays."

"And it's mostly locals? People you know?"

"We get a few tourists, but it should be mostly locals. Shall we?" I asked, bringing her close to my side.

Sienna gave me a big smile and nodded once. "We shall."

Hand in hand we walked into the restaurant, and that's when everything went spectacularly wrong.

We were getting looks.

Jackson James, deputy sheriff, did a double take as we strolled in the door, and Hannah Townsen, the hostess, gawped at us. Her mouth fell so far open she might've been catching flies. A hush fell over the crowd like a wave gradually retreating from the shore.

Now everybody was staring.

At first I thought this was because of me. I hadn't been seen stepping out with a woman around town in years. Most folks assumed Claire and I would be getting married eventually. Hence, I presumed these fine people were surprised to see me with someone new. I'd never corrected the assumptions because I never considered my friendship with Claire to be any of their business.

I frowned my disappointment at the two closest gaping faces: Kip Sylvester, the high school principal, and Ben Huntsford, owner of Big Ben's dulcimer shop. I'd expected better of them, better than gawking at me and being rude to Sienna by association. I bent to her ear, about to apologize for their odd behavior, when a shriek interrupted me.

"Oh my God!"

Both Sienna and I turned to find Naomi Winters approaching us, her eyes wide. But she was staring at Sienna, not at me.

"Oh my God. You're Sienna Diaz!" Naomi was now fiddling with her phone, trying to turn it on and hastening to get her words out. "I just love you. I love all your movies. You're one talented lady. Can I have a picture? Oh, this darn phone."

I frowned at Naomi, who I'd known since I could remember, and pulled Sienna slightly behind me.

"Naomi, see here—" I began, but Kip Sylvester rushed forward and cut me off, along with half of the high school's parents and teachers.

"It is such an honor to meet you." Kip pulled Sienna's hand out of mine and shook it with enthusiasm. "Can we have your autograph?" he asked, though he didn't wait for her to respond before thrusting a napkin and pen into her hands. "Can you make it out to Kip? K-I-P, like Catnip." He grinned at his joke, which sadly made no sense.

"S-sure." Sienna scrawled her name on the napkin, handed it back to Kip, and another was placed in her hands.

She'd signed five before I came to my wits, but it was sixty seconds too late. People I knew surrounded us, people I'd grown up with, people who'd been at my surprise birthday party last week. But gathered like they were, demanding and greedy for her attention, they looked like strangers.

Not helping matters, everybody was taking pictures. It was a mess of shouts for her attention. Flashes went off from every direction.

What in the ever-loving hell is going on?

I tugged the sixth napkin away from her and shoved away, giving my neighbors a stern frown and pulling her into my arms and against my chest.

I yelled over the crowd. "Now see here. Y'all need to go back to your seats and mind your manners. We're trying to go out to dinner, and I can't even put my name in."

"I wrote you down, Jethro," Hannah said from the hostess stand. "We're putting you two in the back, away from all the crazies."

A few of the said crazies protested, and I lifted my hand to keep Kip and his teachers from coming any closer. "I'm not telling you again, Kip. Take a step back. Sarah isn't here to sign napkins. She's here to eat dinner."

"Who's Sarah?"

I gritted my teeth, tightening my arm around her shoulders. "Sienna. I meant Sienna. Now y'all need to go sit down, 'cause she's signing no more napkins."

The crowd began to grumble, as though they'd been disenfranchised, but then Sienna lifted her sweet voice over their grousing. "Thank you for your kind welcome and exuberance. I'm so honored. But before I sign any more autographs or take any more pictures, I have to admit I'm famished."

"Say that line from the movie," someone called, rudely interrupting her and making my blood pressure spike.

I glanced down at her, saw she was flashing her dimples, working the crowd. I realized with no small amount of discomfort that the same smile she'd used to make me feel twenty-five feet tall earlier was being shared with these people. She was charming them, working the room, much like she'd charmed me every time we were together.

"I promise I'll stay and sign all the napkins," she said, winking at Kip and making the grown man blush. "But for now I'm going to have that steak I've been hearing so much about."

She held them captivated as she continued making promises, all the while towing me after her to the hostess stand and eventually to the kitchen where a table had been set up. I recognized our waiter as Devron Stokes. We'd gone to high school together and he was a frequent visitor to The Pink Pony. He pulled out her chair before I could, offered Sienna her napkin, and placed his hand on the back of her chair as he recited the specials.

That is, he had his hand on the back of her chair until he caught my eye, then he promptly removed his hand. Likely because I was silently communicating my desire to remove it if he came anywhere close to touching her again.

Clearing his throat nervously, Devron gave me a stiff smile. "Haven't seen you out with a woman in years, Jethro. Not since Kitty Carlisle our junior year of high school."

Ignoring his gossipy comment, I ground out, "How about you get us the wine list, Devron? And some privacy."

"Uh, sure thing. I'll be back quick."

"Take your time." My mind swam as I stared at my date.

She, too, looked like a stranger.

I watched her swallow, studying me, biting the inside of her cheek. "How are you holding up?" she asked, like I'd been the one mobbed by my neighbors.

"I'm real sorry about all that." I gestured to the main restaurant. "I wouldn't have expected them to—"

"Don't worry, I'm used to being swarmed. It happens all the time."

"It happens all the time?"

She seemed to regret her words as soon as I echoed them, because her face fell and she swallowed again. "Well, not all the time. Just when I go out in public."

"Oh," I said stupidly, horrified.

"Except by you. You've never swarmed me." Sienna gave me a sweet, hopeful smile and reached her hand across the table, palm up, an invitation for me to take it.

Before I could, Devron was back with bread, but without the wine list.

"I promised myself I would be cool and wouldn't say anything—"

"Then you should keep your promise," I grumbled.

He ignored me, continuing, "But I have to tell you how much I love your films. And you are amazing. And so much more beautiful in person."

Sienna pulled her hand away, and I watched a mask slip over her features as she dealt with Devron, giving him a warmly polite smile and thanking him for his kind words.

While she was thanking him, all I could think about was getting him alone so I could beat the shit out of his presumptuous and rude ass. I clenched my jaw, knowing the violence of my thoughts was directly related to how unexpected and disorienting the events of the last few minutes had been.

I'd been blindsided.

Here we were, wanting to have a quiet dinner, like any two normal people. Ten minutes ago I was making long-term plans, thinking about coming home to her every night.

And now . . .

Now I realized, I had no idea who she was.

CHAPTER TEN

"It's so much darker when a light is lost than it would have been if it had never shone."

— JOHN STEINBECK, THE WINTER OF OUR
DISCONTENT

~Jethro~

OUR EVENING DID not improve.

We didn't get a chance to speak again. Even though they'd put us in the kitchen—so, great ambiance—we had no peace. The cooks came over, the manager, all the waiters and waitresses. Everyone had their picture taken and their stuff signed. Three hours into dinner and she'd had only three bites.

I didn't know where I fit. Sienna seemed at ease, talking to everyone like it was her job, making them feel special. I supposed it was her job. Regardless, she was a natural.

When we finally left, I had to do some fancy driving because several people tried to follow us. I lost them on the wildlife ranger-only trails, locking the gates after me so they couldn't follow me to Hank's cabin on

Bandit Lake. I assumed she didn't want anyone knowing where she was hanging her hat.

Once we lost the last of the hangers-on, I breathed a sigh of relief.

"I'm sorry," she said, drawing my attention to her. It was the first time she'd spoken since we got in the car, having silently understood I needed to concentrate on driving in order to lose the folks following us.

She looked sorry. And worried.

"Why are you sorry? You didn't interrupt your own dinner for the last four hours. Did you get enough to eat?"

"I'm sorry our date didn't go as planned. I'm sorry I didn't tell everyone to back off. I should have. I should have—"

"No. Those are grown men and women, they know better. You were just being polite."

"I didn't know what to do. Everyone seemed to know you."

"I've known those wackadoodles most of my life, and I had no idea they were that nuts."

This made her laugh, but I was serious.

"Well, I didn't want to seem rude, not to your neighbors and friends."

I nodded, checking the rearview mirror to make sure we weren't being followed before I turned on the gravel circle for Bandit Lake. "I get that. That was kind of you, but next time you have my permission to tell them to take a flying leap."

This seemed to ease her mind. "Okay. I will."

We pulled into Hank's driveway and I cut the ignition, taking a moment to soak in the silence. It had been so loud at the restaurant. The quiet felt like a gift.

"Next time we'll go someplace with no people." She shifted in her seat, drawing my attention to her, giving me a coaxing smile. I studied the smile, couldn't decide if it looked sincere or rehearsed.

And that thought troubled me. I was good at reading people and their intentions, but only if I wasn't too invested. Once invested, I couldn't separate what I wished to be true from what was actually true.

Saying nothing, I exited the truck and walked to her side, opening her door. I offered her my hand, which she took and held on to with an iron grip. Still lost to my thoughts, I escorted her up the steps to the porch, trying to decide whether I should ask to come in.

Mostly, I wanted to talk. The evening's events had been overwhelming, so a post-game analysis felt in order. Plus, I still felt like I didn't know her at all, not anymore. And I wanted to fix that before leaving for the night.

Facing her, I gathered her arms in my hands, needing the connection, and began, "Sienna, look, I was hoping—"

I didn't get any further because the front door opened unexpectedly and a dark figure came at us. He was holding a gun.

So I did what anyone who'd just had my night would've done. I pushed her behind me to protect her, and punched the assailant in the face, kicking the gun away as he fell to the ground. The man landed hard and with an audible grunt.

"Don't get up," I ordered, feeling behind me to make sure Sienna was okay. I had a knife in my boot, and I was just reaching for it when the man spoke.

"It's me. It's Dave," he said, and it was a voice I recognized though I couldn't immediately place. He groaned, "I think you broke my nose."

"Oh no!" Sienna rushed around me and knelt next to this Dave. "Should you sit up? I'll go get ice."

"Who is Dave?" I asked stupidly, irrationally irritated that this Dave person had opened the door and gotten himself punched in the face. Admittedly, I was also irritated that a man was in the cabin at all. The fact that I'd done the punching was irrelevant.

"Dave. You met him earlier. He walked me to your car?" she rushed to explain, standing again and jogging into the house, presumably to get ice.

Two more big fellas appeared in the doorway, both holding weapons and both pointing them at me.

"What the fuck is this?" I muttered, having just reached my limit.

"Put your hands up, sir," the taller of the two ordered.

"Like hell I will."

My response did not make the man happy. He started forward as though he were going to force my hands up, when Dave—still on the ground—grabbed the guy's pant leg.

"Wait, no. This is Jethro, the park ranger. The one I mentioned earlier. He's just bringing Sienna home."

I split my glare between the three men, quickly understanding that when she'd said "co-worker" earlier, Sienna meant Dave and company were her security detail. She was a woman who had three personal body-guards. Three.

All thoughts of inviting myself inside the house extinguished.

"I'm sorry, Jethro," Dave was saying. "I heard something out here, I should have flipped the light on. That's my bad. Sorry for interrupting."

I stared at him for a long moment, where he was sprawled on the ground holding his nose. Adrenaline was leaving my system, leaving me cold and tired and feeling bad for punching him in the face.

"No, look, I'm sorry." I reached forward and offered him my hand. "Keep your head back, but you should sit up. And you," I gestured to the shorter of the two guards still standing, "go get some tissues or a napkin, something to stop the bleeding."

Sienna appeared just as the shorter man disappeared to follow my instructions.

"Are you okay, Dave?" she asked, worry plain in her voice and features.

"I'm fine."

I took the bag of ice from her and placed it gently on Dave's nose. "Okay?"

"Yes. Thanks, man."

I didn't acknowledge his thanks because I was the reason he was sitting on the floor in the first place. Instead I pulled out my phone and sent a quick message to Luke Thurstan. He was a year from retiring but still made house calls.

"I have Doc Thurstan's number, let me shoot him a text. You're going to need to get that set."

Dave chuckled. "I know. I've been punched in the nose before."

"Yeah. I figured you had." I smiled a little despite myself.

"That's Henry," Dave indicated behind him, in the direction of the man who'd left to get the napkins, then lifted his hand toward the taller fella still present. "And this guy is Tim."

I offered Tim a handshake and he accepted it, saying, "Sorry about . . . earlier."

"You were just doing your job."

A moment of silence passed, and my attention drifted back to Sienna. She stood in the entryway twisting her fingers, her eyes wide and watchful. She seemed to be biting the inside of her cheek again.

"Well . . ." Scratching the back of my neck, I tried to hide my frustration under a wry grin. I'm afraid it may have resembled a grimace.

"Do you want to come in?" She stepped over Dave's legs and came out to the porch.

"No, thank you," I answered honestly, because I couldn't wait to leave.

It wasn't because the guys were her bodyguards, or that she was so famous she made my neighbors lose their minds. The chances of us having any alone time were now zero. More than anything after the night's events, I didn't want any more audiences.

My momma always told me that men, to a much greater degree than women, have difficulty dealing with derailed plans. She was right. And I was no exception. I'd had plenty of plans for the evening. I really liked this girl. She'd felt like the beginning of something new: a reward, a gift for five years of levelheaded decisions.

But nothing since we'd entered the restaurant had gone right. Not only that, it had all gone terribly wrong in the most bewildering of ways. The evening was over. I'd planned to end it with a goodnight kiss. But for how I planned on kissing her, I wasn't keen on an audience. And I refused to end the night with a chaste peck on the cheek.

Hell. No.

She stared at me for a protracted moment, like she wanted to say something, but then she glanced at the two guys loitering in the doorway, one standing, one on the floor. Sienna closed her eyes and released a laugh devoid of humor.

"I am so sorry."

I hated that she kept saying sorry.

"Stop apologizing." I reached to take hold of her then stopped myself. We were still being watched.

"I don't know what to say," she whispered, leaning close; her lovely dark eyes turned down at the corners communicating her regret.

"Nothing to say." This time I smiled and made sure it looked sincere. "Go get some rest, and make sure this guy's nose stops bleeding."

"The bleeding stopped," Dave said, reminding us—just in case we'd forgotten—that he and Tim were still there.

I pressed my lips together and turned, slowly descending the steps. Disappointment a cold weight in the pit of my stomach.

I wished . . .

My mind was a mess of contradictions.

I wished I'd known how famous she was earlier, because then we would've never gone to The Front Porch. I would've taken her some-place truly private. Not to take advantage but to talk and just be.

But then again, if I'd known how famous she was from the begin-ning, I never would have allowed myself any interest. Her celebrity likely made anything between us a dead-end road, and I wasn't interested in dead-ends, not anymore.

Sienna stopped me with a soft, "Jethro?"

I turned and met her searching gaze; she was at the top of the steps. Behind her, Tim was helping Dave stand.

"Yeah?"

"I'll see you tomorrow, right? In the morning? You're picking me up?"

"Yes. Of course," I responded immediately. I was thrown, frustrated, and overwhelmed, but I wasn't dumb enough to miss out on a chance to spend alone time with her. She may have been named Sienna instead of Sarah, and was apparently a celebrity of huge proportions, but she was still dimples and eyelashes to me.

"Goodnight, Sienna." I mustered a soft grin.

"Goodnight, Jethro." She did not manage a grin, nor did she meet my eyes as she said the words. Her tone and expression made me think she was close to crying. That had me gritting my teeth and my heart jumping to my throat.

116

Before I could re-mount the steps and take her in my arms, curious guards be damned, she turned, walked back into the house, shut the door, and locked it. This left me ten feet away, staring at Hank Weller's closed door.

Well . . . "Fuck."

I stuffed my hands in my pockets so I wouldn't assault an oak tree or blackberry bush on my short walk back to the truck. Once in the driver's seat, ignition on, seatbelt fastened, hands on the steering wheel, I debated my options.

"What a fucking mess."

I left, careful to keep my foot light on the gas so I wouldn't inadvertently peel out of the drive. Suddenly too hot, I tugged my sweater off and made a right out of the Bandit Lake graveled circle.

I knew what I had to do next. I needed to get to The Pink Pony and get the lowdown from Hank Weller. Then I needed to do a Google search for Sienna Diaz and find out what the hell I'd gotten myself into.

* * *

"Jethro."

"Hank." I glanced over his shoulder, eyeballing the wall of whiskey behind him. The Pink Pony may have been a strip club, but Hank had the best stock of Tennessee Rye anywhere. "I'll take the George Dickel, neat."

"Sure thing." Hank eyeballed me, likely because I wasn't much of a drinker these days.

"So, what's going on, Jet?" he asked, placing the shot of amber in front of me. "Why're you here?"

His question was a fair one. I didn't typically stop in unscheduled, and never at night when the place was open.

"I need to talk to you about your house guest."

Hank grew still, but his expression became guarded and cagey. "What about her?"

If I wanted Hank to share information, I assumed I'd have to be willing to share the entire story. This approach was not in my nature, discussing my personal business with anyone aside from what was strictly necessary, need-to-know. However, I wasn't ready to let go of Sarah.

Sienna.

So I set aside my reservation and said, "I know who she is, though it took her until tonight to tell me, when we were on a date."

His eyes widened. "You? You and Sienna? Went on a date?"

"Yep."

"You? On a date? Not just fucking around. Like, getting dinner?"

I clenched my teeth. "Yes."

"Jet, you haven't—"

"Over five years. Yes, I know."

"Longer than that for taking a woman out, I was going to say. Since high school? Senior prom?"

Was everyone in this town suddenly a goddamn gossip?

"I dropped out the end of my junior year, but I guess you're right. High school was the last time I took a girl out, if you want to be technical about it." I wished, not for the first time, I didn't live in such a small place.

"Plenty of women since then," he stated.

"But none at all for a while," I corrected.

Hank gave me the side-eye. "Sorry for beating a dead horse, but are you sure it was a date? 'Cause she has a habit of going on dates with guys, but not considering them dates."

The hint of bitterness in Hank's tone gave me pause. I studied my business partner, noticed the derisive curve of his lips. He wasn't an unhappy person. He was shrewd—similar in many ways to Cletus—but generally affable.

So I guessed and asked at the same time, "You and Sienna?"

My stomach dropped when he nodded.

I decided to take a seat. "Make the next one a double."

He gave me a small smile. "If it makes you feel better, it was a long time ago, and we never made it past first base, despite all my best efforts." He added this last part under his breath.

"I don't know if that makes me feel better." I shook my head, staring at the bar. "I don't know that I want to feel better."

Hank poured my double shot and set it next to the single. "Have you googled her yet?"

I shook my head.

"Don't. Just know she's at the top of the A-list, world famous levels of celebrity. She's got a new boyfriend every week, all of them Hollywood pretty boys. But she was the same in college, before she dropped out to become Sienna Diaz. She's whip smart, funny as hell, beautiful, talented as fuck, could charm the collar off a priest. She's amazing. But she's career-focused. I've known her six years and have never seen her as serious about anyone like she is about her job. I just asked her last week whether anything had changed, whether she was inclined to settle down any time soon."

"What'd she say?" I couldn't help my perverse curiosity.

"She said settling down was the same thing as settling, and she had no plans to settle." He gave me a flat smile.

I nodded, absorbing these details, forcing myself to believe them despite how I wished they weren't so.

"Are you upset because she's had so many relationships or that one of them was with me?" he asked, dry humor permeating the words.

"Neither," I said, grabbing the double and downing it with one swallow. It burned, but the hurt felt good.

I wasn't upset she'd dated Hank. Nor was I twisted up about her having a battalion of suitors. My despondency was borne from already feeling invested in a girl who had a history of not investing.

Because I had invested. Maybe I didn't realize how much until that very moment, but I'd been making plans and calling them wishes. Not only did she not invest, apparently she was opposed to the idea.

"Don't let me have any more after this one." I pointed to the single still on the bar. "I have to be up early tomorrow."

"Fine. I won't." Hank crossed his arms, uncertainty casting a shadow over his features. "She's not a bad person, Jet. She's good people. She makes a great friend. She's just a flirt, can't help it." He was quiet for a beat, then added, "She kind of reminds me of you that way."

I lifted my eyes to him. "What do you mean?"

"Not how you are now, though you still flirt without meaning to, but you have better control over it. Whereas before you were breaking hearts without knowing, leaving a trail of frustrated hopes. You and Sienna have that in common, except you've moved beyond it—"

"And she hasn't," I finished for him.

Hank gave me a sympathetic nod. "No. She hasn't. I doubt she realizes it either. Like I said, she's a good person. She's got a big heart, but I suppose that's part of the issue. People gravitate to her big heart, her big charisma," he shrugged, adding with a grin, "and her big other things."

Now I wanted to punch him in the face.

But that wasn't my place.

And I was just as bad as he was because I'd been admiring her big other things most of the night. I'd already been imagining what it would be like to have her, what she'd taste like, and the sounds she'd make. Now it would all remain a fantasy, an unknown . . . a frustration.

I twisted the small glass on the bar, staring at the gold liquid, debating my options. But after a minute I realized I didn't have any options. I'd been building castles out of clouds because Sienna clearly saw me as a short-term diversion.

How could she not? World-famous, gorgeous, sexy, can-have-anyone-she-wants Sienna Diaz and wildlife park ranger Jethro Winston from Nowhere Tennessee?

Nope. Not going to happen.

Yep. I was a temporary distraction.

"Sorry, Jet. But the dog won't hunt."

Leaving the shot where it was, I reached for my wallet and set a twenty on the bar. "Thanks for the information."

"You don't want your drink?"

"No. You have it. I need all my wits about me tomorrow if I'm going to make it through the day without acting like an asshole."

"Your asshole days are behind you." His tone was both concerned and encouraging.

"Don't worry about me."

But I could see Hank was worried, especially when he pressed,

"Jethro, you're not special. She has this effect on everyone. You're just one of many. Don't beat yourself up; you couldn't have known."

If he was trying to cheer me up his words had the opposite effect. My mood turned from cloudy to dark. But that was okay. One could argue I had this coming, given my misspent youth.

Karma was a shithead.

Yet, it could have been worse. I hadn't traveled too far down the road with Sienna. I could still make a U-turn. And I would. And then I'd be just fine.

CHAPTER ELEVEN

"The true paradises are the paradises that we have lost."

— MARCEL PROUST

~Sienna~

EVERYTHING WAS DIFFERENT.

I felt a shift the moment I saw him the next morning, leading me to suspect the dynamic between Jethro and me had completely changed overnight. I hesitated a half second, my stomach falling, then stepped off the porch and crossed to where he waited by his truck.

He opened the door for me, as usual. And his smile was still just as easy as it had been previously, just less open and considerably less interested. He'd erected a wall. I felt like crying.

"Morning, Sienna," he said, sounding just as he always had and offering me his hand like he usually did. But instead of allowing our fingers to tangle, he withdrew immediately and shut the door once I'd climbed up.

I watched his unhurried strides as he crossed in front of the truck, admiring how he walked, how he carried himself with unaffected self-possession. I decided—meaning, *I desperately hoped*—that perhaps I was overreacting. Maybe I was allowing my worries and insecurities to color my perception.

Because I hadn't erected a wall last night. I'd collapsed on my bed and cried after the doctor left. And no, I wasn't being overly dramatic. Perhaps some of the tears were caused by mental exhaustion. Sleeping less than six hours a night and working every waking moment for the last four years would do that to a person.

But, I liked this guy. A lot. More than I'd liked anyone. He was already special to me because our brief moments together thus far left me feeling invigorated and energized. I couldn't remember the last time anyone made me feel this way. Maybe never. He was like a battery charger for my heart and brain. I wasn't ready to let go of that, of him.

"Sorry I'm a little late," he said, slipping to his seat with the grace of a man who used his body daily. "I think two of the high school teachers from last night were trailing me this morning. I had to lose them." He chuckled and it didn't sound at all forced.

And that—the real amusement, the joke about losing his neighbors on an early morning car chase, more than any other physical cue thus far —felt like a coffin being nailed shut on the possibility of *us*.

I stared at his profile as he started his truck, aware I'd said nothing thus far. I was being weird, but I didn't care.

Jethro cleared his throat, his eyes darting to mine then away. He motioned to the cup holder between us with his chin, his tone conversational. "You keep leaving your thermos in my truck. I stopped by Daisy's and filled it up. I, uh, also grabbed a doughnut for you."

I glanced at my Hello Kitty travel mug and the small box next to it.

"Thank you," I said, frustrated with myself, and him, and the situation.

"No problem," he said, frowning.

We passed several minutes and miles in silence. I sipped my coffee but left the doughnut untouched. I stared at the lid of my cup, deciding I was going to continue my pity party from last night for the rest of the day, *at least*. Maybe it would last until Halloween. Then I could dress up in a sexy Eeyore costume and make people pin the tail on me.

I was such an ass. I should have told him everything from the beginning.

He stopped at the flashing red light and glanced between the doughnut and me. "Don't you like doughnuts?"

"This is not how I envisioned eating my first Daisy doughnut."

I felt the smile in his words as he asked, "And how did you envision eating your first Daisy doughnut?"

I shrugged dejectedly, answering with a stream of consciousness. "I guess I imagined eating it with you, but you were also eating a doughnut. And maybe I get a little cream or strawberry jam on my lip. So you tell me and I try to wipe it with a napkin. But then I don't get all of it, and you cup my face, the camera cuts close—like you're going to wipe it away with your thumb—but instead you lean in and lick it away with your tongue."

The car descended into a heavy silence as I finished relaying my fantasy, the click-click-click of Jethro's turn signal the only sound. It felt thick, meaningful, unmanageable.

So I broke it.

"Sorry. I think in movie scenes sometimes."

He cleared his throat again, making his left turn. I hazarded a glance at him. He was scowling at the road like it ruined his best pair of cowboy boots.

"Sienna, I think we need to talk."

"I agree."

He sucked in an audible breath, but before he could *talk*, I said, "I'm sorry I wasn't honest about who I was from the beginning. When you didn't recognize me, it was, well . . . it was really nice. To be just Sienna —or Sarah, I guess—instead of Sienna Diaz. It's rare, meeting someone who doesn't feel like they already know me. I liked it and I like you and I know that's not an excuse for my behavior. I'm sorry."

"It's fine." He gave me a reassuring smile. "I'm not sore at you. I mean, last night was an eye-opener, that's for sure. But I understand wanting to be someone different, not wanting to be judged based on your past. I understand your perspective, it makes sense."

His empathy showed me he understood. He grinned wider, making my stomach do one of its trademarked Ranger-Jethro-induced somersaults. "I like you, too."

But . . . I held my breath, waiting for the word. Just when I thought maybe he wouldn't say it, he did.

"But you have a lot going on, and I don't want to add to any of the demands on your time."

"I see," I breathed out, feeling hollow, rejected, and keeping my eyes studiously on the lid of my mug.

Somewhere, someone was doing voodoo on my heart. It hurt so much I could barely draw a full breath.

I didn't realize until that moment just how much I liked Ranger Jethro. But now it was too late. He'd decided I wasn't worth the headache, and he was letting me down gently.

"So maybe we could be friends? Or acquaintances, whichever you prefer." His tone was so light, so undemanding and magnanimous. It made me want to slap his face. I wanted to ask him how and why he cared so little, when his previous actions led me to believe he'd cared so much.

"Friends or acquaintances," I echoed, trying both the words on and hating them.

"I don't mind driving you, seeing as how we're going to the same place every morning. But I understand if you'd like to drive yourself, or have one of your security guys do it."

Now he didn't want to drive me? But . . . that was our thing. That was how we'd met and connected.

I felt lost.

Crap.

I was going to cry again.

But not in front of him.

I turned my face to the window, rested my elbow against the door and tucked my hand under my chin. "Sure. Yeah. That makes sense. I'll have Dave take me. No worries."

He was silent for a full minute, then said, "I guess it's settled."

I nodded, though I didn't look away from the window.

And those were the last words spoken between us.

CHAPTER TWELVE

"Nothing is ever really lost to us as long as we remember it."

— L.M. MONTGOMERY, THE STORY GIRL

~Jethro~

NEWS OF MY date with Sienna spread through the valley faster than a dumb idea at an Iron Wraiths MC meeting. I couldn't go anywhere without folks eager for the scoop, questioning me. Even Reverend Seymour stopped me outside Sunday service.

"What's she like?" he asked in a hushed tone. "Is she tall? She looks so tall in her movies."

"She seems real nice," his wife added, coming out of nowhere and startling me. The woman was stealthy. "I talked to Diane Sylvester and she said Kip said she signed everybody's napkins. Did you get a signed napkin?"

Reverend Seymour gave me a kindly but prodding smile.

"She is nice," I agreed, not adding that Kip Sylvester and the rest of the people at the restaurant had not been nice. They'd acted like a herd of assholes.

"So . . .?" The Reverend nudged me.

"Sir?" I kept my tone polite, though I couldn't help but clench my teeth.

"You think I should invite her over?" Mrs. Seymour asked, her eyes impossibly large and hopeful. "With your momma gone, there's no one to invite her over. I could ask Jennifer Sylvester to make a banana cake."

Oh no. Not the banana cake.

Lord save us from Jennifer Sylvester's magical banana cake. It was award winning and inescapable. Everyone bought one for special occasions from the Sylvester's bakery, and always raved like it was the cure for cancer, impotency, and boring conversation.

Meanwhile, I hated the taste of bananas.

I shook my head stiffly. "No call for that."

Mrs. Seymour looked frustrated. "Aren't you going to see her again? Deveron Stokes said—"

"Now when were you talking to Deveron Stokes?" Reverend Seymour interrupted, frowning at his wife.

"Excuse me." I used the Reverend's rebuke as means to escape, ducking away and hurrying to catch up with my brothers across the grass parking lot.

Keeping my head down, I ignored the two or three calls for my attention and jogged to where Beau's car sat idling. Typically, most of us went to church together early on Sundays, taking a few cars, then back to the house for breakfast. Ash and Drew had already left, so had Duane and Jess. Billy, however, was at the mill, working. He was usually working on days I had off.

"Took you long enough," Beau pestered as I slipped into the passenger seat.

"What'd he want?" Roscoe asked from behind me.

"I'll give you three guesses," I grumbled, drawing a scrutinizing look from Beau.

He pulled out of the lot, and I ignored the smug smile hovering under his red beard. We drove in silence until Beau pulled into our drive, then he gave me the side-eye and said, "Don't you think it's time you told us what's going on?"

"Jess said she and Duane were stopping by the store on the way home. He needs more blueberries for the pancakes," Cletus answered as though the question had been directed to him. He was also in the back seat and sounded very concerned about our present lack of blueberries. "I hope they're not sold out."

"That's not what I meant, Cletus. I was talking to Jethro." Beau stopped in his usual spot in front of the house, and I saw Ashley's truck already parked; Ash and Drew had beat us home. I quickly exited, hoping my brother would drop the subject.

But Beau must've guessed my intentions as he swung open his door and jumped to his feet, continuing to poke at me. "Jet, we're all dying to know what's going on with you and Sienna Diaz."

"No one is dying." Roscoe unfolded from the Pontiac after I pushed my seat forward. He grinned at me as he straightened. "We're just close to apoplexy."

"Well, I'm more worried about the blueberries." Cletus climbed out on Beau's side and the frown he tossed at me was grim. "Blueberries aren't in season yet."

"Would you forget about the blueberries?" Beau hissed.

I spotted Jessica's Jag kicking up dust as it pulled up our drive. Ignoring Beau, I shut my door and made for the porch.

"I share Cletus's worry over the blueberries," I said, just to rankle Beau.

"See? Jethro's worried, and he's never worried." Cletus gestured toward me then pointed at Beau. "You should be worried, too."

Jess parked next to Beau's vintage Pontiac, and Duane held up two pints of blueberries as he stood from her fancy Jaguar.

"You can stop panicking, Cletus. I have the berries."

"Oh, thank God." Cletus held his chest and stumbled a step backward. "You should have live-tweeted your progress. I was near a fit."

Beau dogged me, on my heels as I climbed the steps. "You realize you're with a woman on my celebrity list."

"Celebrity list? What are you going on about?"

"Come on, don't you have one?" Beau appealed to my siblings and

Jess as I opened the screen door. "A list of women who you'd get a pass on from your significant other."

"What?" I snapped, not liking the concept or the fact that Sienna was on Beau's dirty list.

"I have a list." Jessica nodded toward Beau. "But mine has mostly men on it."

"Wait a minute, *mostly* men?" Duane took a shuffling step to one side so he could see his girl, his eyes wide. "*Mostly* men? Who are the women?"

"Wouldn't you like to know?" She gave him a saucy grin and a quick kiss, then to me explained, "Everyone has a list, Jethro. But it's like any fantasy. In theory, the fantasy is fine. But in reality, if I were faced with a man on my list—"

"Or a woman?" Duane put in, teasing her.

She ignored him and continued, "If I were faced with a man on my fantasy list, I wouldn't cheat on Duane. And if he were faced with a woman on his list, he wouldn't cheat. It's just one of those things people talk about. Like, if you could have a superpower, what would it be?"

"I'd like to be able to fly," Cletus responded as though her question had been asked in earnest.

"Not be invisible? Or read minds? Or be omniscient?" Roscoe suggested.

Cletus shook his head. "Certainly not. That'd be redundant because I'm already all of those things."

"Then make it rain blueberries," Roscoe teased.

"My point is," Jessica put the conversation back on track, "it's all theoretical. The list is made up of people you admire and—theoretically—would like to know, not just for their looks."

"That's true," Beau agreed. "Sienna is real pretty, and I don't think that's a controversial statement. But it's all the other stuff that pushed her to the number three spot on my list."

I felt my blood pressure spike and realized I'd curled my hand into a fist as Beau spoke, not liking that he felt free to discuss Sienna like she was public property. Of course, everyone in town had done the same. Why should Beau be any different?

Jessica must've taken note of my mood shift, because she placed her hand on my forearm. "Lots of normal people have a list, Jethro. It doesn't mean any harm. It's no big deal."

"Except I don't have a girl, so there's no one I'd be cheating on." Beau stuffed his hands in his back pockets and rocked on his feet. "So if I were faced with an unattached Sienna Diaz, I would totally—"

"Careful, Beau. I don't think that's a sentence you want to finish," Roscoe warned, then shot me a commiserating glance.

Beau frowned, but didn't finish the thought. Thank goodness. I didn't feel much like teaching him a lesson. I was tired. And, if I were being honest with myself, I missed Sienna even though she was lost to me.

But the point Beau had inadvertently raised was a good one. If Sienna and I had continued seeing each other, I would've had to deal with a lot more Beaus and a lot more dirty lists.

I opened the front door and motioned for everyone to file in, ignoring Cletus's frown of concern as he passed and Beau's searching glare. I hesitated on the porch, listening to Ashley greet my brothers and Jess as they disappeared inside.

The thought of more questions from my family, because I knew they were coming, made my stomach turn sour. And bitter. Truth was, I didn't feel much like having Duane's blueberry pancakes.

So for the first time in a long time, offering no explanation or excuse, I left my family and went for a drive.

"YOU HIDING OUT here?"

I turned, finding Claire hovering at the edge of her gazebo. I'd been meaning to fix several of the rotten deck planks for months. Leaving my family to their breakfast, I drove into Knoxville for parts, where my neighbors wouldn't question me, then to Claire's house.

"Maybe." I gave her a small smile. "Or maybe I was just hoping you'd come find me."

She rolled her eyes and crossed the deck to stand next to me against the railing. "Do you ever turn it off, Jet? Doesn't it get tiring sometimes?"

"What's that?"

"I've known you . . . hell, I guess going on twenty-five years now. I can count on one hand the number of times I've seen you not be charming."

I twisted my lips to the side, considering my friend. "You remember me when you were three?"

"Yes, I do. You were eight, and you were trying to charm me out of an ice cream cone."

"Did it work?"

"No," she answered simply, her red eyebrows arching over challenging blue eyes. "And maybe that's why we're still friends now."

"Because you're an ice cream hoarder?" I teased, liking to tease her. She was fun to tease because she didn't take any shit. Not from me, not from anyone.

"Don't be stupid." She smacked my shoulder and laughed. "You know what I meant. Maybe we're still friends 'cause I don't go around sharing my ice cream with you every time you bat those big pretty eyes. So, what I'm asking is, don't you ever get tired of charming the pants off people? Don't you ever want to just . . ." She cast her eyes around the gazebo, then lifted her face to the sky. "Don't you ever want to just be free to be yourself?"

I studied her upturned face, warmed by afternoon sunshine, and I wished—not for the first time—I wanted Claire as more than a friend. I wished I felt just a fraction of the draw with Claire that I'd felt with Sienna. Life would be so much easier if Claire and I were married. At first, after Ben died and I cleaned up my act, I think everyone expected it.

"You know," Claire sighed, her smile small, "I'm not always going to be here. One day you're going to have to find a new place to hide on Sundays."

"I met someone," I said, the words spoken before I knew I was going to say them.

She grinned, but didn't look at me, keeping her eyes on the sky. "Did you?"

I could tell by her tone she'd already heard the gossip. I frowned, frustrated all over again.

"It's over."

Now she looked at me. "Is it?"

I nodded once.

It was over, but I'd dreamed about Sienna every night since. I'd been taking up more than my fair share of time on the weekly schedule in the upstairs restroom. Maybe it made me a creeper, but Sienna had become my only muse.

Sometimes I was licking doughnut frosting off her lip like she'd described. But in one dream I was introducing her to my mother. I'd awoken with a dull, persistent pain in my chest nothing but a long trail run could help.

"Why? What happened?"

I shrugged, feeling more sullen than I had a right to, though I answered. "She was looking for a fling."

Claire eyeballed me. "And what are you looking for?"

"Forever," I answered easily, because it was the truth.

Her mouth hitched up on one side, and she looked at me as though she were proud. "Don't worry, Jet. One day you'll find your forever."

"I'm not worried." Crouching, I pulled off my gloves, set them on top of my toolbox, but then admitted, "I'm a little worried."

"Why?" She sounded close to laughter.

"Because," inspecting my left glove, I saw there was a hole in the seam by the index finger, "I'm not a good judge of character."

She didn't respond for a while, but when she did her voice held no amusement. "He was your father, Jet. It's normal to idolize your father."

I affixed a carefree smile to my features. "You didn't idolize yours."

"No. I didn't. But nothing about my daddy is charming. Your father, on the other hand, makes you and Beau look like amateur charmers. I don't think you're giving yourself enough credit. You read people like a pro."

"I'm not talking about people. I can read people just fine." I picked at the hole of the glove, stretching it. "Unless I need something from them, something meaningful, something I don't want to con or trick them into, something real. I still can't reach Billy. And I didn't see this thing with Sienna going south until it was too late. Once I'm involved, it's like I'm blind."

A bird chirped. Wind rushed through the trees, loud in the silence that had fallen between us. She knew I was right. Her reluctance to speak ended up speaking volumes. Claire was picking her words like she picked through produce at the farmers' market.

Finally, she seemed on the precipice of making a comment, but at just that moment my phone rang. Pulling it from my back pocket I studied the screen. Seeing it was Cletus, I gave Claire a small apologetic smile and answered it.

"What's up?"

"I need your help."

Cletus never asked for help, so it took me a sec to recover. "Sure thing. What can I do?"

"They called me down to the set; they can't get the Colt combine harvester to start, and they need it working for a scene they're filming tonight. I need you to come help me with it."

I hesitated, both because his request was an odd one—seeing as the twins were co-owners with Cletus in the Winston Brothers Auto Shop and much more mechanically inclined than I—and because going to the set meant I might see Sienna.

"I don't mind, Cletus. But why don't you ask Beau or Duane?"

"Duane and Jess are off smooching in the woods, and I can't take Beau to the set for obvious reasons."

I pondered that statement and decided he was right. However, being around Sienna without being free to talk to her had me debating whether or not to make an excuse. Sienna Diaz was quickly becoming more fantasy than reality, so keeping my distance, forgetting about her was the smart thing to do.

And yet . . .

"Come on, Jet. If Sienna is there, I'll hide you under a tarp."

This statement irked, because Cletus had basically read my mind. He was entirely too good at goading people into getting his way. Even so, I finally agreed, "Fine. Fine. Do you want me to pick you up?"

"No. Finish up with Claire, and meet me there later. Since I have your binding promise, you should know I'm going to need you helping me on set this whole week. I already spoke to Drew about it. He says you should have time, seeing as how the bears are mostly staying out of the cove now."

"Gee, thanks, Cletus." I wasn't surprised he knew I was at Claire's since she and I had a standing dinner scheduled every Sunday.

For whatever reason, forcing me to see Sienna all week was obviously in Cletus's plan. He liked to torture his brothers, me in particular. But as duplicitous as Cletus was, I was just as talented at being invisible. Hiding wouldn't be necessary. I'd make myself known if or when it suited my purpose.

"You're welcome. Like I said, if Sienna's about, I'll throw a tarp over you and pretend you're one of the busted-out tractors, just the man-sized, scaredy-cat variety. Oh, and ask Claire if she can pack me up some dinner before you leave."

My gaze flickered to Claire. "I'm not asking her that."

"Cletus wants some dinner?" Claire guessed, already turning back to the house. "Tell him it's fine."

"Don't encourage him," I said, only half joking.

Cletus chided from the other end, "Come now, Jethro. You should know by now, I've never required encouragement."

CHAPTER THIRTEEN

"You feel so lost, so cut off, so alone, only you're not. See, in all our searching, the only thing we've found that makes the emptiness bearable, is each other."

— CARL SAGAN, CONTACT

~Jethro~

T UESDAY WAS THE first time I saw Sienna since our date.

She didn't see me because she was on set, doing her thing.

Cletus and I were nearby. He had me holding his hand while he fixed the Colt, not that he actually needed me there. I knew my brother well enough to recognize he liked having someone present to hand him the tools in a dramatic fashion.

"Socket wrench." He held out his palm, not looking at me.

I gave him the wrench, and he passed me the wire cutters. I shifted my weight while he fiddled around for a stretch. The contraption he was working on was a real antique. Red rust dotted the yellow paint. As far as I could tell, this bucket of metal machinery was two hammer hits away from collapsing into a pile of garbage.

"Flathead." Again, not looking at me, Cletus held out his hand.

I gave him the flathead screwdriver, and he passed me the socket wrench.

"Switch out the socket, would you? I need it a quarter larger."

"Sure thing," I mumbled, thankful to have something to do other than hand off tools within his easy reach. If I thought I could get away with it, I would've been listening to one of my favorite podcasts, either *Curious Handmade* or *The Renaissance Woodworker*. But Cletus had the tendency to take offense and make trouble if he wasn't given undivided attention.

Leaving him to his hunk of junk, I walked around the harvester and some yards away to his big toolbox. Once there, I picked through the socket heads 'til I found the right size.

"Hey, Jethro. Are you here with Cletus?"

I glanced up at the question. One of Sienna's bodyguards, the one I'd punched in the face, approached from the direction of the active film set. I'd caught sight of the staffers setting things up earlier in the day. Beyond the bodyguard I saw a flurry of activity. Now it looked like they were almost ready to start filming.

"Hey, Dave? Right?" I straightened from the toolbox and held out my hand for him to shake, though my eyes kept looking beyond him to the set. Without wanting to, I was looking for her.

He gave me a quick handshake as I divided my attention between his nose, which wasn't in good shape, and the movie people behind him.

"Yes. Dave's the name."

"Hey, sorry about your . . . sorry about the . . ." I motioned to my nose.

"Occupational hazard. Like I said, I've had worse. So, um, are you here with Cletus?"

I nodded warily. "How do you know Cletus?"

"He came around last Friday and introduced himself to people."

"Did he?" That was odd. Typically, Cletus avoided people.

"Yes, sir. He said you were looking for people to help with the bears?"

"Really." I crossed my arms, wondering why Cletus would say such a thing.

Dave tilted his head back and forth as though reconsidering his words. "Actually, it was more like Cletus mentioned you're moving the bears out of the prairie so we can film, and I asked if you needed any help."

I scratched my jaw and considered this Dave. It was obvious he wanted to get up close and personal with a black bear and saw me as his front-row ticket.

"I could always use an extra set of hands, but it's my job to protect these animals."

He nodded quickly. "Of course, of course."

"Just so we're clear, it wouldn't be any help having someone along who's going to antagonize a bear. Spelling it out, you'd have to be respectful and compassionate with the creatures."

"Absolutely."

"That means no flash photography, no poking at it, throwing things at it, no—"

"I get it. I wouldn't do that kind of thing. I just . . ." Dave's eyes, still puffy and bruised, widened as he chose his words. "I'd just love to see one, while we're here."

"Fine." I nodded once, extending my hand for him to shake. He took it, a big smile on his face. My attention snagged on the activity going on behind him. Specifically, the tall, gorgeous woman walking toward the set, dressed in a garment befitting a Quaker.

My breath seized in my lungs as Sienna tossed her chestnut hair over one shoulder, giving her companion a wide, sunny smile. She made the other woman laugh. Then she laughed. The melodic sound traveled to where I stood, as I stared at her like a fool.

"Oh, yeah. She's filming today." Dave followed my line of sight, turning and standing next to me. "Have you seen her act yet? On set? She's brilliant. The camera doesn't do her justice."

I tore my gaze from Sienna, my chest and throat burning with something unpleasant, and eyed the big man next to me. He spoke of her like he was proud. I was glad. She deserved to be surrounded by good people.

I turned to leave, figuring Cletus would be near a fit if I didn't return by the time he was finished with his screwdriver, but Dave stopped me with a hand on my arm. "Here, wait. Just watch. They're about to call action."

Not intending to, I waited, I watched, entranced.

The wind tossed her hair to one side and she laughed again. Someone was called to bring it under control. And then action was called and everyone grew real still.

She spoke first. I couldn't hear her and that was frustrating. I loved her voice. Unlike actors on a stage, these folks were speaking softly. Of course, a giant microphone hung over their heads to catch all their words. Regardless, I could see well enough and what I saw was mesmerizing. She'd transformed, was an entirely different person, like she'd slipped on the skin of someone else.

I didn't know what the scene was about, but it looked like some ladies were trying to teach Sienna's character how to churn butter. Her movements were all wrong, making the usually benign up-down movement appear extremely, albeit accidentally, sexual. In fact, her movements were so ridiculously wrong—graphic in an awkward, accidental, unattractive way—they were hilarious. She was hilarious.

She looked like a damn fool. A clown. A genius.

I glanced at two production staffers and saw they'd both turned away from the set, hands over their mouths, shoulders shaking. A quick scan revealed they weren't the only ones struggling not to laugh.

Someone called cut and a chorus of laughter broke out, but Sienna didn't stop. She danced around the butter churner like it was a pole and she was the world's worst, and most oblivious, stripper. I couldn't help but laugh, unable to tear my eyes away.

"See? She's unreal," Dave said with a smile in his voice. After a tick, I felt his eyes on me, but I wasn't ready to look away. The show she was putting on held all my attention. Despite a lingering bitterness of what might have been between us, I truly did wish her well. She deserved every good thing.

Dave eventually cleared his throat, drawing my ears—if not my eyes

—to him. "It's really interesting to me, that someone who is so talented, so gifted at acting doesn't really like it all that much."

That got my attention.

I frowned at Dave and his comment. "Sienna doesn't like acting?"

"Yes. Well, no. I think she likes acting. But I'm pretty sure she doesn't like being a celebrity."

I thought on that, then asked, "Why does she do it? If she doesn't like it?"

"At first, from what I can gather, it was an accident. She thought she was selling a script. Her agent and her sister talked her into starring in the movie. It wasn't supposed to blow up like it did. And then she kept making movies. No one expected her to be as successful as she is. But there's just something about her, you know?"

"Yeah. I know." My eyes sought her out again. She'd ceased her pole dancing and was now talking to Tabitha, the film's director. Her expression was patient and interested. My attention dropped to her lips. She was biting the bottom one.

"Did you know she doesn't live in her own house? When she's in L.A., she stays with her parents."

"Why's that?" I asked distractedly, biting my lip as I recalled what kissing her was like. It had been just the once, but I remembered every detail. Sweetness and sunshine.

"Her house, the one she owns, has been broken into several times."

A shock of concern traveled down my spine and I demanded, "What? Was she at home?"

"No. She wasn't at home. Even though she hasn't said anything, I can tell she doesn't feel safe there. Even with a full security team living with her."

"Y'all always live with her? Even when she's at home?"

He nodded. "She was trying to use this time in Tennessee to get a break. I know she'd like some privacy—even from us, and I get that— but her sister talked her into having us stay at the cabin. We try to stay out of her way, but she never complains." He scratched the back of his neck. "The truth is, I feel sorry for her."

"You feel sorry for Sienna?" I eyed him warily, getting the sense he was leading me down a brick road of his own design. Obviously this guy had an agenda, why else would he be sharing details about her personal life so freely?

"I do. She's a good person, and people are always trying to use her for their own ends. She doesn't really have an advocate, anyone she can trust."

"What about her sister?" I asked before I could catch the question. It wasn't really any of my business.

She's not your business.

Dave shrugged. "Marta has Sienna's career interests in mind, so does her agent. They tag team her, push her, but they're good for her career. But at what cost, right? A person has to have more in their life than work, right?"

I nodded slowly, unable to keep myself from saying, "Maybe she doesn't see it that way. Maybe work is what she cares about right now."

"No." Dave snorted. "No, not Sienna. What Sienna wants is an advocate, a partner. She needs someone who cares about *her* health and happiness. Not just the health of her career."

I said nothing, gritting my teeth, letting his words hang in the air. I had nothing to add because it wasn't any of my business.

She's *not* your business.

Even if I wished things were different. Even if I wanted her to be my business.

She's not your business.

As my momma used to say, no use buying a saddle for a horse that doesn't want a cowboy.

* * *

BEAU AND HANK often had Mondays off. For them, that meant fishing in the morning and playing video games all day. I tried to join them the first week of every month at Sky Lake, and they'd oblige me by cutting the excursion short so I could still make it to work on time.

Though it was currently the first week of the month, I almost didn't go.

Sienna was on my mind.

Now, Sienna being on my mind wasn't unusual. But it was supposed to be unusually cold later this week and I knew—because Dave had told me yesterday—that Sienna didn't have many extra blankets in her trailer.

Since my impromptu interaction with Dave over a week ago, he'd been seeking me out, telling me all kinds of things about Sienna. She liked to read *The New Yorker*, but he couldn't get it delivered to the set, and it kept getting lost in transit to Hank's cabin. So I ordered two months of back issues, plus arranged to have new issues delivered to my house.

I gave Dave the magazine with my address cut out, reminding him there was no reason she needed to know where they came from.

Last Friday he told me she'd been craving Chinese food, but they couldn't find a decent restaurant and none outside of Knoxville. So I asked my friend and co-worker—he and his wife were from China—if they would mind preparing a meal. Dave and I put the food in takeaway containers to disguise the fact it was homemade. Again I reminded him there was no reason for her to know where the food had come from.

I also arranged for Daisy's coffee to be delivered to Sienna in the mornings. She liked it better than her own coffee beans, or so Dave had told me.

Yesterday Dave told me his security guys had scoured Hank's cabin and found only the blankets on the beds, and Sienna didn't want them to go to the trouble of bringing those back and forth to the set. He also told me the production staff had brought them blankets, but they were polyester, scratchy, and gave Tim hives. So Dave asked if he thought it would be worthwhile to send Tim to Knoxville to buy blankets or if I had any at my house.

Hence, my mind was on Sienna. I needed to get back home, round up our extra blankets, and bring them to the set sometime this week before the cold snap.

"You've been real quiet, Jet."

I glanced at Hank from my spot in the back seat, then moved my attention back to the window beside me. "I guess I don't have a lot to say."

"Seen Claire lately?" Beau asked, turning around to look at me. He was sitting in the front.

"Yep. Every Sunday. But you already knew that."

"Is she going to sing in Cletus's band?"

"I don't know." I was making a list, all the things I needed to do as soon as I got home. Cletus would be fit to be tied if I made him late.

"So . . ." Hank started, cleared his throat, then started again, "Have you seen Sienna lately?"

I met his eyes in the rearview mirror, keeping my expression blank. "No."

Beau and Hank traded a glance. I looked out the window again.

"I've been calling her, but she seems real busy," Hank pressed. Even though we'd left Sky Lake, I guessed he wasn't finished fishing.

"Maybe she is." I shrugged.

I knew she was busy. Because Dave told me she was busy, writing all the time, not sleeping much. He seemed to think I deserved a daily rundown of her activities. I didn't need or deserve a daily rundown. She still wasn't *my* business. Nevertheless, I was concerned she wasn't sleeping enough.

I added a canister of my momma's special sleep-tea blend to the list of items I needed to bring to the set.

Hank sighed like he was frustrated as he pulled into our driveway. As soon as he parked, but before he cut the engine, I bolted out my door and jogged toward the house. I had exactly twenty minutes before Cletus would be downstairs, hollering at me that it was time to go.

A quick shower and ten minutes later, I stood in the upstairs linen closet, grabbing as many spare blankets as I could hold. I kicked the closet door shut and made for the stairs. Over the bundle of quilts, I spotted Cletus standing by the entryway table, turning an envelope over in his hands and peering at the return address.

"Hey," I said.

He jumped, his hands and the envelope going behind his back. "Hey yourself," he grumped. I'd obviously startled him.

"Help me with these. And what are you hiding behind your back?" I asked upon arriving at the main floor.

"I'm not hiding anything." His tone was defensive, and yet he continued hiding the envelope.

"Yes, you are. What's that letter behind your back?"

Cletus ground his teeth, the muscle at his jaw ticking. He was thinking. Deliberating. I lifted a concerned eyebrow. No one, least of all me, wanted Cletus to be deliberating.

Abruptly, he thrust the envelope at me. "Fine. You got a letter. Give me those stupid blankets. I'll carry them out to the truck."

We swapped burdens and Cletus stomped out the front door, mumbling to himself as he went. Meanwhile, I turned the envelope over to check the return address, much like he'd been doing when I spotted him seconds ago.

My stomach suddenly hollow and hard, I wished I hadn't pressed Cletus about the letter.

It was posted three days ago, sent from the Federal Correctional Institution, Memphis, where our father was imprisoned for attempted kidnapping and aggravated assault. I briefly debated whether or not to tear it up and burn it. But morbid curiosity had me tearing it open instead.

Inside was a photo of Sienna and me, taken the night of our date. We stood by the hostess stand at The Front Porch. It was dark and a little blurry, taken with a cell phone, but we were obviously the two people in the photograph.

I flipped the photo over, knowing there would be a message but not wanting to read it. I read it anyway.

It said, *"You always were best at the big cons. I hope her bank account is as big as her tits. She can pay my legal fees."*

I heard his voice in my head as though he'd been standing next to me. A sharp, fierce surge of protectiveness and anger had me shredding the note and the photo. Grim hatred and resolve turned my insides to stone because Darrell Winston never did anything without a reason.

The picture had been a threat.

He was never going to leave me in peace.

But I could make damn sure his filthy plans never touched Sienna.

* * *

CLETUS AND I met Drew and Roscoe at the Cooper Road Trail ranger station. They hadn't yet left for the day. I brought doughnuts and coffee and bad news.

"You tore up the picture?" Drew asked, leaning back in the small wooden chair, peering at me from beneath blond eyebrows.

"It doesn't matter." Cletus shook his head. "If he hadn't torn it up, I would've torn it up."

Roscoe's attention bounced between the three of us. "What can he do? He's locked up."

I glanced at my youngest brother, both happy and troubled he didn't understand our father's true nature.

Looking at Roscoe was like looking at a younger version of myself, except one who'd been mostly spared the influence of our father. He'd been the first to give me a chance five years ago, after Ben died, when I needed one of my brothers to believe in me. I was fond of Roscoe, protective in a way I should have been for the others when we'd all been growing up.

Cletus frowned at Roscoe, looked like he was about to fill in the blanks, but instead said, "Roscoe, could you take Jethro's truck and run back over to Daisy's for more coffee?"

"You're trying to get rid of me." Roscoe shook his head.

"Yes. We're trying to get rid of you." I clapped my hand on his shoulder. "You're not the law—like Drew—and you're not sinister—like Cletus."

"Plus I want more coffee." Cletus lifted his empty cup. "I can't think without my coffee."

"I'm not leaving." Roscoe crossed his arms and leaned back in his chair, mimicking Drew's pose. "I'm not a kid. No use protecting me."

Cletus and I frowned at each other, neither of us liking the idea of exposing Roscoe to this steaming pile of horse manure, but Drew vetoed

146

us both. "He should stay. How can he defend himself against something he doesn't understand? The time will come when Darrell tries to use Roscoe for something or another."

It wasn't unusual for Drew to speak to us in this way or cast the final, deciding vote in our family. After I'd stolen his motorcycle—a fucked-up cry for attention—and he'd beaten me senseless, he'd realized who I was. He'd realized I was Bethany Winston's oldest son. Since then, he'd often given me fatherly lectures. He was a man of few words, but the words he spoke were always worth listening to.

He was the first person I truly respected to ever tell me, "I'm proud of you." It meant something, his pride, because I cared a great deal about his opinion.

Never mind the fact that he was more than a year my junior.

"Fine." Cletus acquiesced, banging the table once. "But don't make any more ignorant statements unless you bring me more coffee. I can't deal with ignorance without another cup of coffee."

Drew almost smiled, almost, but then turned a sober expression on me. "What is it you're thinking he's planning?"

I shrugged. "I have no idea. It could be anything. It could be nothing, just mind games. But if Sienna and I were really together, I'm sure he'd try to exploit it."

Cletus banged on the table again. "Now you listen here. Don't use Darrell Winston as an excuse to push that fine woman away. I already told you in the truck on the way over here, I have that man well and truly under control."

"Are you going to share your methods?" Drew asked evenly. "Or do we not want to know?"

"You don't want to know," Cletus responded, just as evenly.

"So we're just supposed to trust you?" Roscoe asked, clearly disbelieving.

"Roscoe Orwell Winston, you are making ignorant statements again." Cletus's tone was flat. "Now you have to buy me two cups of coffee."

"That wasn't a statement, it was a question."

"Ignorant questions cost two cups, so now you're up to buying my next three coffees."

"I trust Cletus," Drew said, holding my eyes. "If he said he has it under control, he has it under control."

I said nothing, because I also trusted Cletus. I trusted him with my life.

But I didn't know if I trusted him—or anyone else for that matter— with Sienna's.

CHAPTER FOURTEEN

"Stephen kissed me in the spring,
Robin in the fall,
But Colin only looked at me
And never kissed at all.

Stephen's kiss was lost in jest,
Robin's lost in play,
But the kiss in Colin's eyes
Haunts me night and day."

— SARA TEASDALE, THE COLLECTED POEMS

~Sienna~

A T LEAST ONE person was happy about the dissolution of my non-affair with capable and sexy Ranger Jethro. Marta. Well, she wasn't specifically thrilled about the terrible date or Jethro's decision to extract himself from my life because she didn't know about that.

She was happy because I'd become even more of a wretched workaholic.

"Wow, Sienna. I'm speechless." I heard Marta flipping pages, going through the first draft of my latest script. "How did you get so much work done on this?"

"I haven't been able to sleep." I'd spent the last two weeks since our disastrous first date working like a mad woman. I'd also been spending my time listening to the Breakup Songs station on XM radio and daydreaming about the children I would never have with Jethro Winston.

They would have had his eyes and my dimples.

Ugh. I didn't recognize myself. Who was this pitiful person? We'd gone on one date. One date.

One date, crazy lady. It was just one disastrous date. One epic kiss. So stop picking out names for your children.

"Can't wait to dig into Smash-Girl, huh?" She laughed lightly at what she assumed was impatience to finish my current work in progress so I could get moving on the superhero movie.

Little did she know . . .

Over the last weeks, since my disastrous dinner with Jethro, every hour I wasn't rehearsing or filming, I was writing. Or I was giving telephone interviews. Or I was getting shit done. I'd cut my sleep from six hours a night to four, because I hadn't wanted to lay down unless ready to pass out.

I was lonely, and yet I refused to do anything about it. Hank had called several times, and I'd made excuses. Both Janice and Jon had invited me along on their excursions, but I'd turned them down, preferring to work and be antisocial.

Ranger Jethro was proving difficult to forget.

"Barnaby wasn't expecting this until next month. He'll be thrilled."

"Yay," I deadpanned then shook myself. My sister didn't deserve my bad attitude. She wasn't responsible for my current funk.

I was.

I was responsible.

"So, the London premiere." Marta switched topics. She was all business this morning.

"Yes. The premiere." The *dumb* premiere.

Again, I had to shake myself. I was being negative, throwing my mood around like rice at a wedding. No one wanted my bad-mood wedding rice. No one.

I tried once more, forcing cheerfulness into my voice. "So, the London premiere. I was thinking, what if I took Dad?"

"No, no, no. We already talked about this. Kev and Tate will be there. We want people to talk. Young, sexy, carefree is what we're going for. You need to bring someone that will get people talking. We want more spotlight, not less."

"Fine." I tried not to growl the word.

"Do you want me to call Jenny? Ask which of her firm's clients are looking for buzz?"

"No. Don't do that."

She paused, clearly considering my options. To my horror, she suggested, "Even if you go as friends with Tom, people will take notice."

"No. Absolutely not."

"Fine." She sounded disappointed. "But we're running out of time."

A knock sounded on the door to the trailer, and I sat upright from my bunk. "Listen, I'm going to let you go. I just wanted to make sure you got the draft."

"Okay. No problem," my sister said, sounding distracted. "Talk to you later. And reconsider that spread in Playboy magazine."

I bit my tongue, not wanting to argue with Marta. I'd already turned down that request six times. I didn't want to have to defend my position. Again.

I moved to the door, which Dave had cracked, and signed off with a chipper, "Okay, goodbye."

Dave waited until I'd set down my phone before saying, "It's Susie, here to do your makeup."

"Okay, sounds good." I yawned, stretching as I stepped back to give Susie room to pass. I motioned to the coffee machine. "There's coffee if you need some, but that's the last of it."

She wrinkled her nose. "Sienna, babe, it's almost 4:00 p.m. If I drink that stuff I'll be up all night."

I sat in my chair and yawned again while she set to work pinning up my hair and applying the undercoat. My mind began to wander—

predictably to Jethro—and the now constant sad ache in my chest had me sighing.

"Why the heavy breathing?" Susie frowned at me, her tone and expression full of concern.

"Just tired." I gave her a smile meant to reassure.

She did not look reassured. We weren't precisely friends, but we were friendly co-workers. It's hard to truly be friends with someone when you pay that person's salary.

Lifting her impeccably manicured and triply pierced left eyebrow, she ceased applying my makeup and demanded, "What's going on with you?

"What?"

"How long have we been doing this? Four years now?"

"Almost five."

"You're depressed," she accused, her tone holding no room for argument. "You haven't asked me if I'm moist for the last ten days. For the record, I was once. But you never asked. What's going on? And don't tell me, 'Nothing.'"

I held her gaze, not wanting to explain my funk or relinquish my shoebox of sadness. If I explained my funk, then I might leave my funk. I wasn't ready to leave this funk; I wanted to wrap myself in its funkiness forever.

"Either you tell me what's up or I'll make you look like Bette Davis."

And she would, too.

"Fine, fine. I'll tell you what happened." I gathered a breath for courage. "I met—"

"A man," she finished. "It's always a man. Tell me about him."

So I did. I spent the next several minutes giving her the whole story, which ended up being a surprisingly short story. While recounting the details I realized Jethro and I hadn't spent much time together, not enough time to warrant how I felt.

"He didn't want to see you again after finding out who you were? Do you think it's because you lied at first?" Of course her questions would be blunt and to the point.

"I didn't precisely lie."

She looked unimpressed. "Honey, he thought your name was Sarah for more than a week."

"Anyway," I said, knowing she was right about my dishonesty. But there was nothing I could do about it now. "I don't think it was my lie of omission, not really. I think he saw firsthand what life would be like if he dated me, and it scared his cute beard off, and I don't really blame him. I think he came to the conclusion I wasn't worth the effort, and that was that."

Susie flattened her lips, clearly thinking this over, then shook her head. "Nah. I don't think so."

"Well then what could it be?"

"I don't know, but I don't think that's it. I doubt he considered you not worth the effort. He'd have to be an idiot to think that, and this guy doesn't sound like an idiot."

I slumped in my chair, staring forward. She was right. Jethro wasn't an idiot.

"Close your eyes." Susie tilted my chin up and applied her magic brush to my eyelids. "You should find out."

"Find out?"

"You should ask him, find out what's up."

"What's the point? He's not interested anymore." Asking Jethro why he didn't like me enough to put up with my fame didn't sound like a conversation that would go well for me.

"You don't know that for sure. You're still interested. I can tell. It's all over your face and how you talk about him. You sound like my daughter the night she met her husband, all droopy and sad and happy at the same time."

She was right. I was still interested. I was still mega interested.

"I guess I am, but thinking about him hurts." I pressed my lips together because my chin wobbled. Susie stopped applying my eye makeup. I think we were both surprised by my honesty.

"Oh, hon. You were falling for him." Her words were soft and empathetic.

I shook my head, keeping my eyes shut tight, not wanting to see her sympathy. "I'm not so ridiculous as to think I have a broken heart. We didn't know each other enough for real roots to have formed, just imaginary roots based on surface information. Topsoil roots."

"What's a topsoil root?"

"You know, roots based on wishing, not reality."

"But you're still heartsick, babe."

"But it's not real. It's because I like the idea of him, of having a safe haven, a person who is mine, who I can count on." I also knew the promise of him was made even more potent by knowing his history as told by Hank. "He was such a grown up, so capable and steady. And so handsome." I added this last part with a pathetic and pining moan, opening my eyes. Susie was watching me. Her arms were crossed and she smiled a small, commiserating smile.

Yep. His epic good looks without succumbing to the adorable label had made him a man-unicorn in my mind. Or a merman. Or a Loch Ness Monstman. He was a mystical creature.

"Capable and steady, huh?" Her smile grew. "Does he have any older brothers?"

I snorted softly. "No. He's the oldest. But he has five younger brothers."

Her eyebrows ticked up. "Think any of them would be interested in a fifty-year-old grandmother from the Bronx?"

"All of them, if they have any brains."

She grinned, then snickered, shaking her head. "Fine. So your guy is a wildlife ranger. He's handsome and steady and doesn't care about your fame."

"He does care about it, it's why he ditched me."

"Stop saying that." She pointed one of her brushes at me. "You don't know that for sure. He sounds like a dream, and he's planted himself in your topsoil. I still say you need to ask him what happened."

I studied my fingernails because I couldn't hold Susie's perceptive gaze and say what I was about to say. "I liked him, Susie. I liked him a lot. And it's an intangible like. Everything was so natural and unforced between us. I slipped into it unconsciously because liking him was so effortless. Being around him was both easy and exciting."

"You're worried you'll never have a similar connection with anyone else."

I nodded.

"But, hon. There are so many fish in the sea, and you're so talented. You're amazing."

"Maybe." I shrugged, then lifted my eyes to hers. "But how does someone like me meet a guy? I can't take out an ad on OkCupid. I can't go on Tinder—"

Now she snorted. "Trust me, nothing but bags of dicks on Tinder."

"Even so, I'll never know, because those outlets aren't open to me."

"I had no idea you wanted to be in a relationship so badly."

"I didn't either." I shrugged, feeling oddly helpless, like I had a gaping hole in my chest and no means to fill or patch it.

Her blue gaze studied me for a long moment before she said, "Or maybe it's not just any relationship you want. Maybe it's a relationship with this guy, with your Ranger Jethro."

I wanted to bury my face in my hands but I couldn't, she'd already done too much of my makeup.

The conversation had grown too solemn and I needed levity, so I scolded her. "You aren't helping my depression, Susie. You're making me feel worse. You'd be a terrible therapist."

"Please," she rolled her eyes and bent to apply shadow under my cheekbones, "I'm a great therapist. You're just a bad patient. Take my advice and you'll be happy. End of story."

* * *

IT WAS COLD the next morning. I'd spent the night on set, filming scenes well past midnight. The blankets production had sent over were given to Henry. He'd complained that they were scratchy but ultimately accepted them. Now Henry was posted outside the trailer and obviously needed the protection from the cold more than me. What I needed was hot coffee, but I was out of ground coffee beans. I needed to get moving.

I showered. The hot water helped, but as soon as I stepped out and toweled off, I was cold again. I dressed in leggings and an oversized sweater, wanting cozy comfort but unable to achieve it. Dave was still asleep on the bottom bunk. Jethro hadn't broken his nose, thank goodness. The purple bruises were now green and yellow and finally disappearing.

He'd been snoring like a fiend earlier, so I sneak-attacked him and put some Vicks VapoRub around his nose.

I know I shouldn't put medicine on people without their consent, but he wouldn't listen to me. And he was keeping me up. My mother used Vicks for everything growing up—colds, flus, allergies, coughs—even bruises and sore joints. Prescribing for her patients always included a small screw-top container of Vicks.

VapoRub applied, Dave slept much better. I didn't want to wake him now. So I decided to grab Henry and talk him into a doughnut/coffee run. I still hadn't eaten a Daisy doughnut, hung up as I was on the idea of eating my first with Jethro. Perhaps it was time to take the plunge and move on.

I would also ask him to grab some blankets from Hank's house on his way back.

Opening the door to the trailer, I peeked around it, finding Henry bundled and sitting on a folding chair. He was awake and had a hot cup of coffee in his hands.

I frowned at him because he was also eating a doughnut. It was a Daisy doughnut.

"Hey, Handsome Henry."

He turned just his head toward me and lifted his chin, a happy smile on his face. "Hey, gorgeous."

"Where'd you get the coffee?"

"Your guy brought it."

"My guy?"

"Yeah. The park ranger guy."

My heart did a sad, deflating thing in my chest. I ignored it. Stupid heart.

"You mean Jethro?" His name felt weird to say, like it was covered in sand . . . and tears.

"Yeah. That's the guy. Him and his brother."

"Cletus?"

"Yeah. That's the other guy. I like those guys."

"Oh." I stood in limbo outside my trailer. I couldn't ask Henry to go on a coffee run, not when he already had coffee and had spent most the night awake on duty. That wasn't nice.

Nor did I want to wake up Dave. It was Tim's day off, so Dave had been on duty the other half of the night.

So I crossed my arms over my chest and glanced around the temporary structures, half-hoping, half-dreading I'd catch a glimpse of Jethro.

"What, uh, what were they doing here? Jethro and Cletus?"

"They were here last night, saw how late everyone was up, so they brought coffee this morning."

I stood straighter, a shock of surprise running down my spine. "What? They were here? What?"

"Yeah. Cletus does the work on the tractors. He's here every day. You haven't noticed him?"

"No." I shook my head, feeling oddly foolish. I stepped down from the trailer and closed the door behind me. Wanting to poke at the wound further, I asked, "What about Jethro? Is he here every day?"

"Not every day. Unless he's helping Cletus or meeting with Tabitha."

"He meets with Tabitha?"

"Every Monday and Wednesday."

I thought for a second. "Today is Friday."

"He was here last night helping Cletus. Tabitha asked them to stay. But, even when he's not on the set, he's in the Cove. He takes care of the bears."

"The bears?" My voice squeaked.

"Yeah. He traps them then takes them someplace else so they don't interfere with production. Dave and I went with him earlier this week on our day off, helped him move a giant male black bear. The thing was huge, and angry." Henry stared forward as he remembered, adoration or reverence clouding his gaze. "But Jethro knew just what to do. He was so calm. He wasn't at all scared. I think even Dave was scared."

Henry chuckled at that then sipped more of his coffee, completely oblivious to my stunned gawking.

"He traps black bears?" I repeated, louder this time, my voice still squeaking.

"Yep. And other animals, too." These words, arriving from someplace behind me, made my spine stiffen and my palms sweaty.

Gulping air, I looked over my shoulder, finding Jethro and Cletus standing some feet away. Cletus had his arms wrapped around several blankets and Jethro held two containers of what I assumed was coffee in his grip. One was a Styrofoam cup, the other was my Hello Kitty travel mug.

I hadn't seen or talked to Jethro in over two weeks, thus I decided to forgive myself for devouring him with my eyes. He stood as though relaxed, all weight on his left foot, his narrow hips slightly cocked to one side. He wore his ranger uniform of cargo pants, blue button-down shirt, boots, but no tool belt or hat.

Without his tool belt and hat, he looked oddly unadorned. The simplicity suited him. But so did his belt and hat.

When I lifted my eyes, his green and gold gaze locked with mine. Though his friendly grin was in place, something about it had altered. It struck me as less friendly and more predatory. I liked it, because I imagined I was looking at him in much the same way.

"Sienna," he said, giving me a single nod.

"Hi." I breathed the word, the air between us growing electric. Perhaps the feeling was entirely one-sided, but I didn't think so. The crackling tension felt good, exciting, but also unwieldy.

"Sienna Diaz, that was mighty fine acting last night." Cletus strolled over and passed me his bundle of blankets. "These are for you. Jethro thought you might be cold."

"We thought you might be cold," Jethro clarified.

"He's been thinking on ways he might warm you up."

Jethro ignored Cletus. "We were planning on leaving these with Henry," Jethro said, like he felt the need to explain or apologize for his sudden appearance. "Didn't want to wake you up or get in your hair."

"Well now, I thought you wanted to get in her hair. Or at least you did two weeks ago." Cletus smiled widely at me, then Jethro. His comment made Henry laugh, my face burn scarlet, and Jethro frown.

GRIN AND BEARD IT

I saw Jethro slice his eyes toward his brother and administer a murderous look. "We'll just be going," he said, his voice hard. Then to me, much softer, "Where would you like your coffee?"

"Inside," I responded automatically.

His mouth hitched on one side, his wonderful gaze flickering over me again. "I'll leave it on the table next to Henry," he said, but didn't approach.

I frowned at him, at his reluctance to come any closer. A hot, uncomfortable lump formed in my chest, making it difficult to breathe. Neither of us moved.

But then Cletus placed his hands on Jethro's shoulders and gave him a push. "You heard the lady. She's got her hands full with blankets, least you can do is carry her coffee inside the trailer." Then to me, he offered, "Let me get that door for you."

Cletus jogged over, opened the trailer door, and similarly to how he'd manhandled his brother, he pushed me inside. Jethro, juggling the two cups of coffee, was pushed in next. And then the door was closed.

And then we were alone.

CHAPTER FIFTEEN

"Lost Time is never found again."

— BENJAMIN FRANKLIN, POOR RICHARD'S
ALMANAC

~Sienna~

I DON'T KNOW who was more unprepared for alone time in close quarters, Jethro or me.

We stared at each other, which was all we seemed to be capable of doing, for several long seconds. And then we both recovered at the same time, speaking over the other.

"How have you been?" I asked.

"Your scenes last night were great," he said.

We both started, paused, waited for the other to speak. And then we did it again.

"I've been just fine," he said.

"Did you see them?" I asked.

And then we both laughed. Well, I laughed. He smiled, a big generous grin, his eyes trailing over me.

"That's going in a movie." I set the blankets down on the table by the door, then took my coffee cup from him, carefully placing my hands just where Jethro's had been. "The awkward staring, the overly polite yet stunted and inane conversation, both of us speaking at once. You'll see that in a movie."

"I wasn't awkward." He dismissed the label with a teasing tilt to his lips. "You were awkward."

I sipped my coffee and gave him a very dramatic frown. "It's awkward to call someone awkward. You were just awkward."

"But before that, I was smooth."

"Oh, yes." I agreed with my words but shook my head, my eyes communicating my disagreement. "Very smooth. You were the very picture of smooth. Like an ass."

"An ass? Really?"

"You didn't let me finish. Smooth like a baby's ass."

Now he did laugh. "Very smooth, Sienna. Not at all awkward. And for the record I've never heard anyone call a baby's backside an ass."

We were bantering, teasing, so of course I didn't think about my words before I said, "Well then, obviously you need to spend more time with me."

And then, just like that, it was awkward again. Yet not like before. This awkward was less friendly and innocently disoriented. It was a frustrated awkward, a reproachful awkward, and I could see Jethro was just as irritated as I was.

And then we did it again, but this time we were joined by a third voice.

"Jethro—" I started.

"Look—" he ground out.

"Sienna, did you put that Vicks shit on my face?" Dave asked, startling us. We both turned our attention to the big, sleepy bodyguard as he stumbled out of the bunk room.

I placed a hand on my hip, annoyed by the complaint in my guard's tone and his interruption. Or maybe I was annoyed with Jethro.

Whatever.

Regardless, I regretted nothing. "Yes, Dave. You were snoring and waking me up. And you wouldn't listen to reason. My mother always—"

"Yes, yes, I know. She's a doctor, and she uses it for everything. I heard it all before."

"You're just lucky I didn't put it on your feet." I gave him a challenging eyebrow lift, daring him to tell me that the Vicks hadn't helped.

He grumbled something inaudible, then to Jethro—as though he weren't at all surprised to find him inside the trailer—he asked, "Are you around today, Jethro? I should be able to get a few hours off to help with the traps, if you need the help. We all slept here last night instead of going back to the cabin. By the way," Dave turned his thoughtful frown on me, "what time is it? I can't find my phone. And will Susie be here soon? What time does filming start? I had the schedule on my phone, but I can't find it anywhere . . ."

Dave's voice faded as he slouched through the door of the back area, leaving us alone again. Of course there was the threat of his reemergence at any moment.

I turned my attention back to Jethro. He was scowling. Again, clearly frustrated. I opened my mouth to speak but he cut me off.

"I should be going," he grumped, tearing his eyes away. "I have . . . things to do."

I stopped him with a hand on his forearm, not sure what I was going to say, but pretty certain I was about to make a fool of myself. Especially since my heart took off like racehorse as soon as I touched him.

Oh well, so be it.

Because, you know what? Making a fool of myself was my job. I was literally a professional at it.

"Wait, wait." I gripped his arm tighter even though he made no further move to withdraw. Instead, he glared at my hand. "Wait a minute. I need to talk to you."

"What about?" His voice was rough and he refused to meet my gaze. I didn't recognize this version of Jethro, and it had me feeling off-kilter, nervous.

And when I'm nervous . . .

"About the impossible anatomy of Godzilla, of course."

Then he did lift his eyes, *and* his left eyebrow. "Pardon?"

I bit back another joke, forced myself to be serious. "Sorry. I'm sorry. I don't want to talk to you about Godzilla's improbable femurs or Mothra's nipples."

"Well, that's a relief." Jethro gave me a small smile, likely in spite of himself.

"I miss you," I blurted, then shrugged. But I couldn't hold his gaze after that, so I focused on some random spot over his shoulder. "I like you. You're fun. I don't get to have much fun. And, surprisingly, not many people—in this world—are fun. But you're fun. And," doubling down, I took a deep breath and added recklessly, "I'm lonely, and I want you to drive with me in the mornings and evenings, but I'd settle for one or the other if you don't want to do both."

I didn't mention that I hadn't been lonely until I met him. Somehow that felt like walking out too far on the ledge of vulnerability. I didn't mind being a fool, but there was no reason for me to be an idiot fool.

He didn't say anything, not immediately. So I mentally pulled up my big-girl panties and loosened my grip on his arm, preparing to let him go. But then he stepped forward and surprised me by cupping my cheek with his big palm, pushing his long fingers into my hair, and drawing my eyes back to his. His hands were warm and everywhere he touched tingled with frenzied responsiveness. I wanted more.

His gaze was on my mouth and he *gazed* upon it in every sense of the word. It was a true gazing upon, not a looking upon or a staring upon. Gazing upon implies longing, and his longing was as tangible and hot as the coffee mug still in my hand.

I held my breath, gazing upon him as well.

I know, I know, I'm crazy. But my first thought was *Is he going to propose?*

Crazy.

Jethro bent his head, brushing his lips softly against mine. I instinctively chased each retreat, craning my neck and holding my breath. Once, twice he pressed a teasing kiss to my mouth. When he returned a third time, the kiss immediately turned hungry. Teeth and tongue encouraged me to open for him and I did, placing my mug on the table beside us with fumbling fingers.

Unencumbered by my coffee, I was free to touch him. So I did. I gripped his sides as he tasted me, the rhythmic slide of his hot tongue in my mouth had me pressing against him, needing to anchor our bodies together.

And then his wonderful lips left mine, his hands cupping my face and holding me still when I would've sought his mouth again. My lashes fluttered open, and I found him again gazing upon me.

Jethro smoothed his fingers into my hair then down to my neck, his eyes dazed and heated, his thumbs caressing the bare skin of my collarbone.

"I've missed you, too." His voice was low and gravelly. Paired with his touch and tremendous kisses, it sent delicious, shivery warmth racing along my nerves to my fingertips and toes.

He missed me! Yay for me. Yay for missing me. Yay for Jethro.

"It would be my pleasure to pick you up in the mornings and bring you to the set." His hands dropped, abandoning my skin, and he stepped back. Though he continued to gaze upon me, his gaze grew distant, guarded, and he clenched his hands into fists.

I nodded mutely, only able to watch him as I was not yet capable of forming words. Even so, my face split into a confused, hopeful smile.

He returned the nod with a single one of his own, saying, "We'll see you on Monday."

And then he turned and left the trailer.

I stared at the door for a good thirty seconds before his parting words untangled themselves.

We'll see you Monday.

We . . .

Who the heck is we?

CHAPTER SIXTEEN

"Your perspective on life and loss comes from the cage you were held captive in."

— SHANNON L. ALDER

~Sienna~

"I'M DISAPPOINTED IN you, Sienna."

I glanced over my shoulder and found Cletus Winston standing just behind me, holding a doughnut in each hand. We were in the dining tent, which was mostly empty. Tom had left earlier for L.A. and would be gone for the entire week. I'd been taking advantage of his and Elon's absence by spending the morning outside my trailer.

Before Cletus's interruption, I'd been attempting to work. Attempting being the operative word.

"Why is that, Cletus?"

He claimed the empty chair next to me, and I extended my hand for a doughnut, assuming one of the two was for me. I assumed wrong.

"These are mine; you can't have one." He held them away and took a bite from the one with pink icing.

Dropping my hand, I watched him chew as he eyed me defiantly.

Jethro, true to his word, had picked me up that morning. The *we* included Cletus. So it was Jethro, Cletus, and I together in Jethro's truck.

Cletus had been pointedly sullen and quiet for the entire drive. Worse, Jethro was back to being respectfully friendly, not kissing friendly. It was difficult to switch mental gears when you're expecting kissing friendly and instead you end up with one angry Winston brother and forced politeness from the other.

"Okay. Fine. Why are you disappointed in me, Cletus?"

"Because I provided means and opportunity. All you had to do was exploit the situation."

"What are you talking about?"

"On Friday? With the blankets and coffee? You think that was all by accident? That was arranged."

"Arranged?" I blinked at him while he tore off another piece of his doughnut. It smelled like it was strawberry flavored.

"Yes. Arranged."

Leaning back in my chair, I crossed my arms and examined Cletus. I decided he was odd. "You're odd."

"Yes. I am. But that doesn't negate the fact that you fumbled my pass. If we're going to make this thing happen with Jethro, I need you to bring your A-game."

"This is about Jethro?" I sat up straighter.

"Of course. What'd you think I was talking about?" Apparently I wasn't catching on quickly enough because he sighed loudly and rolled his eyes with great effect. "Do you want my help or not?"

"Yes, yes, yes," I said quickly, leaning forward at full attention. "Yes. I want your help."

"Fine then. We need to coordinate our attack." Cletus punctuated this statement by popping the remainder of the first doughnut in his mouth.

"Good. Yes. Attack synchronization." My phone rang as he chewed. I glanced at the screen, saw it was Marta, and sent it to voicemail.

Marta called back immediately, earning me a severe frown from Cletus.

"You should get that." He gestured to my phone. "You get that and I'll ruminate while eating this other doughnut."

Doing as he suggested, I answered her call. "Hey, what's up?"

"Where are you?"

"Uh, on set. Why?"

"Can you go to your trailer?"

I frowned. Whenever Marta had bad news to deliver and I was on location, she would wait until I assured her I was in my trailer.

"Is everyone okay? I just talked to Mom and Dad yesterday."

"Everyone is fine; this isn't about the family. Just go to your trailer and call me back when you get there."

"Okay. Fine."

"Good. Talk to you soon."

She hung up, leaving me perplexed and anxious.

"What's wrong?" Cletus asked around another mouthful of doughnut.

"I don't know yet." I thought about doing a Google news search for my name, but decided against it. "My sister won't tell me until I'm alone in my trailer."

"What?"

"This is how she operates." I stacked the papers I'd spread out and closed my laptop as I explained, "She's done it this way for years. She thinks I'll react like a crazy person to bad news, lose my shit in front of people and make an embarrassing scene."

"Why does she think that?"

I shrugged. "I think because I used to do that when I was five."

"You were five. That's how a five-year-old rolls."

"I know. But to her, in some ways, I guess I'll always be five."

"Hmm." Cletus studied me, and then stood abruptly. "You're going to your trailer?"

Juggling my belongings, I stepped to the side as he pushed in my chair. "She won't tell me anything until I'm there."

"Good. That's good." He nodded once, then unceremoniously jogged out of the tent, leaving me frowning after him.

He really was odd. Delightfully odd.

Shaking myself, because I didn't have time to think about Cletus

Winston's oddness, I motioned for Henry to join me on the walk back to my trailer. Once there, he unlocked the door and held it open. Inside, I deposited my belongings on the table and immediately called Marta.

"Sienna."

"Marta. I'm alone. In my trailer. What's up?"

I listened as she gathered a large breath before tearing off the proverbial Band-Aid. "Barnaby doesn't think you're right to play the role of Smash-Girl. But he still wants your script."

I let those words sink in. When they did, my stomach fell and I sunk to a chair. "Why?"

"He says you're too old."

I nodded, though I disagreed. I was twenty-five, would be twenty-six or twenty-seven when primary filming began. Assuming they were following my script, I was exactly the right age for the character. "Okay."

I was not okay. I was super angry. But I was also an adult and saw no benefit in ranting and raving on the phone with my sister.

"Also, he's worried that it would be typecasting."

"Why? Because I'm writing the script?"

"No. Because you're Latina."

Now I rolled my eyes, disgusted. "Are you saying he doesn't want to cast me in a role about a woman who is quick to lose her temper because he thinks all Latina women are quick to lose their temper?"

"No. He doesn't think that, obviously. But it's a stereotype. He's already received pushback from racial equality groups, bad publicity about typecasting a Latina in the role."

"That's the dumbest thing I've ever heard." I leaned back in the chair and swiveled it from side to side. I gritted my teeth. It was dumb. It was preposterous. "So, Barnaby is worried racial equality groups will pitch a fit about a Latina woman playing a major film role because the role happens to involve a character who turns red when angry, never mind the fact that I'm the best person for the part. However, these same racial equality groups have no problem with a person getting passed over for the role just because she is Latina. It's so dumb, it's brilliant."

"Sienna—"

"No. No. It makes perfect sense. Better we keep that glass ceiling intact rather than address the issue head-on. I mean, forget that having a Latina play the role will open up doors and encourage diversity in film. Never mind that. Much better we worry about perpetuating an outdated stereotype. In fact, they should probably just get rid of all colors but white in films. And all women. Shakespeare had it right; films should be all white men. Unless of course the character is privileged and rich. Then it should be played by a person of color, we don't want to enforce a *stereotype*."

Yeah, I was being ridiculous and petty. But I'd just lost the role of a lifetime. I was allowed to lash out and be bitter. I think anyone would be, no matter their ethnicity.

I'd grown up privileged, lived in a nice neighborhood, safe, surrounded by people who loved me. My parents were physicians, made a good living. I didn't think all white people were privileged any more than I thought all Latina women had irrational tempers.

But white actors were never denied roles that potentially perpetuated negative stereotypes about their race. So why was I being denied the role of a badass superhero?

It's so dumb, it's brilliant.

"Honey, I know you're upset. But on the bright side, they're thrilled with the last script, and the pages you already sent in for Smash-Girl. They still want you involved."

I tucked my chin to my chest, slouching in my seat and glaring unseeingly at the inside of the trailer. I didn't respond.

"Sienna? Are you there?"

"Yes."

"There will be other roles."

"I know."

She hesitated, then asked, "You'll continue to send pages? For Smash-Girl?"

I didn't respond.

"Sienna," she firmed her voice, "keep sending those pages, do you hear me?"

"I have to go."

"Sienna, you listen to me—"

I ended the call and turned off my phone, tempted to throw it. I didn't. Instead, I steeped in my frustration. But the super odd thing was, I didn't know if I was more upset about losing the part, or about the reason I lost the part. Yes, I was profoundly irritated I'd been passed over because of my ethnicity . . . but losing the part—and therefore all the associated pomp and attention attached to it—actually felt like a relief.

A knock sounded from the door. I ignored it. The knocker tried a second time, louder. I ignored that, too. The person knocked a third time, and I was just about to holler in response when I heard the door open.

"Sienna?"

I closed my eyes, blocking out the world, because the persistent knocker was Jethro.

He didn't wait for my response, just let himself in the trailer, closing the door behind him. I sensed him cross to where I sat slouched in the chair, felt his eyes move over me.

"Hey," he said, nudging my foot with his boot. "Are you okay?"

I swallowed an abundance of emotions. I was frustrated. And as I've mentioned previously, when I'm frustrated I cry.

Once I was certain I'd be able speak without crying, I said, "I'm fine."

Jethro was quiet. I felt him still watching me, so I opened my eyes and met his. His handsomeness felt overwhelming, his presence in my trailer confusing.

So I asked, "What are you doing here?"

"Cletus said you were getting some bad news."

"So?"

"So." His gaze sharpened; clearly he found my question wearisome. "I was worried about you."

I frowned at his statement, how he'd said he was worried about me as though it was obvious. It wasn't obvious, not to me. Not when one minute he was kissing me like I'm the most delicious thing since Daisy's doughnuts, and then the next minute he leaves. He picked me up this morning, and then used his brother as a third wheel so he could keep distance between us.

While I debated whether or not to ask him why he'd kissed me, and if he had plans to do it again, Jethro pulled his phone out of his pocket. He frowned at the screen. He tapped and scrolled with his thumb until he found what he was looking for. Without warning, music reverberated from his phone.

I recognized the song but didn't recall the title. It was an old recording. A woman's voice singing French words filled the space between and around us.

"What song is that?"

Jethro's warm gaze moved over me, an alluring smile just curving his lips. "La Vie en rose."

"It's beautiful." It was beautiful, but it wasn't helping my mood.

Then Jethro held out his hand. "Dance with me."

Blinking, first at his offered palm and then at his features, I asked, "Why?"

Not immediately replying, he reached for me, pulled me to my feet, and slid an arm around my waist. I allowed him to hold my body against his, fit our hands together, and sway to the lovely music. Begrudgingly, I admitted to myself he had great rhythm. Someone had taught him to dance.

Jethro dipped his mouth to my ear, his beard tickling my neck as he finally whispered an answer to my question, "Because you want me to hold you, but you don't know how to ask."

* * *

WE WERE WALKING through the prairie holding hands.

HOLDING. HANDS.

My brain shouted this fact at odd intervals, because it was both confusing and exciting.

We'd danced in my trailer, "La Vie en rose" on repeat, until I was finally ready to tell him about the bad news.

Upon retelling, I grew agitated all over again. He suggested we go for a walk under the guise of checking the bear traps. The rhythm of the walking, paired with the loveliness of the park—plus the approaching sunset streaking the sky blue and purple—made recounting my tale of woe easier.

Jethro listened attentively, with equal measures of concern and anger on my behalf. Then he expressed sympathy and support, reaching for and holding my hand.

Now here we were, and the silence stretching between us rivaled the length of our shadows.

He broke the comfortable silence with, "Something my momma used to say, something I try to remember, is *'Don't go skinny-dipping with snapping turtles.'*"

I glanced at his handsome profile, grinning at the saying because Hollywood was chock-full of snapping turtles, but was distracted by the strength of his jaw, neck, and shoulders. His hand in mine also felt solid. Jethro was coiled strength and power, and his strength felt genuine and wild. Or rather, wild in comparison to the civilized strength to which I was accustomed. My fellow actors, and I included myself in this category, cultivated strength in an air-conditioned gym with a personal trainer.

Jethro used his strength daily, as part of his job, sometimes alone, sometimes as part of a team. It felt real. He felt real. I loved that he was real.

His eyes flickered to mine, waking me from my musings.

"Uh, did she?" I huffed a laugh, shaking my head. "She sounds like a smart woman. Did she work in Hollywood?"

He grinned, but it quickly waned. "No. Her snapping turtles were more of the biker variety."

We walked a few more paces, and then I said and thought in unison, "She sounds like my mom. She likes to give me advice of a similar sort. But instead she would say something like, 'You can't make a silk purse out of a sow's ear,' where the sow's ear are shitty people."

His answering smile was wry and sympathetic.

Because I no longer wished to discuss the unfairness of Hollywood and, as I was curious, I asked, "Did you always want to be a park ranger?"

"No." Jethro shook his head, both amusement and vehemence in his denial. "Not at all. I couldn't stand the wildlife rangers growing up. They were always spoiling my fun." He was quiet for a moment, but it was the kind of quiet that promised more information was forthcoming. "I grew up wanting my own Iron Wraiths cut."

"What does that mean?"

He brought us to a stop and released my hand, folding his arms over his chest and squinting at the horizon. "That means I wanted to be a biker, a member of the gang." Then, quieter, he added, "That's all I ever wanted."

"What made you change your mind?"

Jethro's gaze flickered over my face, inspecting me before he began reluctantly, "I had a close friend growing up. Ben was his name." His eyes dropped to the reedy prairie grass reaching our knees. "We had the best time, did everything together whenever possible. He was a real good person. In fact, he was the best person. I was always getting in trouble, and he was always there to rescue me, trying to reform me." Jethro chuckled at some memory and shook his head. "I guess I counted on him for that, always thinking the best of me when everyone else saw only bad. Does that sound strange?"

"No. Not at all. I think we all need someone who sees the best in us." For my part, the concept of Jethro as a bad person felt completely discordant with reality, if not impossible. "Did you know him your whole life?"

"Yes. I can't remember my life without him in it. Until he died."

I kept my expression supportive but neutral. I knew how Ben had died because Hank had told me weeks ago, but I had the impression Jethro needed to talk about it. So I asked softly, "How did Ben die?"

"He joined the Marines, wanting to do good and make a difference before settling and starting a family. But he died in Afghanistan on his first tour. Ben was the one who wanted to be a park ranger."

"Ben wanted to be a ranger?"

His gaze grew unfocused. "That's right."

"So you became one?"

His eyes cut to mine, held them. Usually Jethro had at least a whisper of a perma-smile in his expression. It was one of the things I liked most about him, how easy-going and friendly he was. But now there was nothing happy in his looks, nothing joyful or tranquil.

"I did." He nodded once. "Because when Ben died, I couldn't stop thinking that it should have been me."

"Oh, Jethro. No." I reached for his hand but he saw my intention and placed his hands on his hips, evading my touch.

"I was a real asshole. Disrespectful to my momma, arrogant, cocky. I once tried to pimp out my sister." Jethro's lip curled and he spat the words, visibly disgusted with himself. "Rather, my father tried to and I didn't do anything to stop him. She was only fifteen at the time, but I thought he'd hung the moon. Luckily my brother Billy found out and put a stop to it. I wanted to follow in my father's footsteps, saw him as a big man. Important because the Wraiths considered him important. But the truth was, all he had was the respect of his fucked-up brothers, the gang members. He had power in a shitty little biker gang. That's all he had."

I didn't know what to say because I didn't think Jethro was finished. I remained quiet, watching him, wishing he would let me hug him or something.

"But when Ben died," Jethro's voice deepened, rough with emotion, "I took a step back and realized it wasn't the Iron Wraiths that I loved, or my father. It was the loyalty, the family, the belonging to something important, to *someone* important. That's what I'd wanted. And I'd already had that, with my real brothers. And Ben." He sounded so tortured, so remorseful, I felt tears sting my eyes, but I couldn't look away. "That's what I had with my momma and my sister, but I'd thrown it away." Jethro shook his head, his grin held unmistakable self-loathing.

"You changed," I pointed out, hating how his features were twisted with bitter anger, all directed inward. "You changed and look at you now."

"I didn't change, not the way you mean. What I did was become someone new. What I did was decide to live the life Ben never got a chance to live. I've tried to live his wishes and dreams. I want to be the person he never got a chance to be."

This statement hurt my heart. I gripped both of my hands at my chest to keep from reaching out again. "But what about the life you want to live? What about Jethro's wishes and dreams?"

Jethro shook his head again, his smile wry and tired. "Those dreams died with Ben McClure in Afghanistan. And good riddance."

I breathed out a pained exhale. "I'm not talking about the dreams and wishes of becoming a motorcycle gang member. I'm referring to new wishes, new dreams, good ones. What do *you* want to do? If you could do anything, what would it be?"

Jethro shoved his hands in his pockets and shrugged. "Not hurt people."

"Okay, so we can take axe murderer off the list."

This drew a light laugh from him. The tightness around my chest lessened as a semblance of his easy smile returned.

"I'm serious, though. What do *you* want?

Once again, I found myself being the subject of Jethro's *gaze upon*. And once again, I held my breath.

As he'd done Friday, Jethro took a step toward me, nearly closing the distance, and slid his fingers into my hair. Goosebumps raced over my skin, sensitive to his touch. I tilted my chin, wanting his mouth, because the man was truly a gifted kisser.

Also, my stomach and heart were engaged in synchronized gymnastics.

Also, I just really freaking liked him a lot.

Instead of kissing my lips, he tugged me forward and pressed his lips to my forehead. My breath came out in a confused *whoosh*.

"Jethro—"

"Hush," he said, his lips still hovering against my hairline.

Jethro dipped his chin and pressed our foreheads together, breathing me in. I gripped his wrists and gave my head a small shake, not wanting to break the contact, but I was a mess of confusion. I didn't know what we were doing. I wanted more contact, not less.

"What are we doing?" I asked, feeling restless.

"Taking comfort."

That made me smile, so I peered up at him. "You're taking comfort in me?"

PENNY REID

"Yes."

My smile grew and I closed my eyes, giving myself over to the moment.

Gradually, I heard a symphony of sounds rise around us. Wind played through the grass, rustled the small but plentiful leaves of a nearby lonely oak. Crickets and other insects chirped and hummed. I felt the beat of Jethro's heart in his fingertips and where I gripped his wrists. My heart slowed until it matched the rhythm of his.

My restlessness eased until it faded away, eclipsed by the stillness, the comfort of being close, yet barely touching. And I took comfort in him.

CHAPTER SEVENTEEN

"People take different roads seeking fulfillment and happiness. Just because they're not on your road doesn't mean they've gotten lost."

— DALAI LAMA XIV

~Sienna~

I THOUGHT JETHRO and I were moving forward, moving toward each other.

Yet after "sharing comfort on the prairie"—which I realize totally sounds like a sexy euphemism—Jethro started avoiding me again. He, Cletus, and I drove to the set every morning and that was it. He was friendly enough during the chaperoned truck ride, with Cletus in the back seat, then always painfully polite and distant when we arrived on set.

Which was why, ten days later, when I caught sight of the two of them leaving the dining tent, I moved to block Jethro's path. I was intent on strongly suggesting he come to my trailer so we could clear the air.

And by clear the air I meant find out what in Godzilla's name was going on between us.

However, before I could speak, Cletus intercepted me and announced loudly, "Ah, Ms. Diaz, I wonder if you'd be interested in coming over to the Winston homestead for dinner tomorrow. It's Jethro's turn to cook, and he makes a mean turkey pot pie."

"She doesn't want to come," Jethro said, his hands stuffed in his pockets, his mouth curved in a wry—albeit small—smile. "She's busy."

"No, I'm not," I blurted, frowning at Jethro, irritated he would assume I was busy. Or maybe he just didn't want me there. Either way, seeing him every day without touching him left me raw, but I also recognized it fed some sort of addiction. I wanted more of it, more of his time, more of seeing him.

He met my frown with one of his own, like my words surprised him. "You're not? Aren't you leaving town on Saturday?"

I clenched my jaw, standing straighter and lifting my chin. Defiance. That's what I felt. Defiance in the face of him trying to make excuses not to see me outside our structured morning truck ride.

"I have a trip Saturday, but I'm completely free tomorrow. Completely. No plans at all. I have nothing at all to do." Then to Cletus I said, "I accept. What can I bring, and when should I be there?"

Cletus gave me a crooked grin. His round eyes crinkling at the corners. "Just bring yourself. That'll be more than enough."

"Sienna."

The three of us turned toward the sound of my name and I struggled to keep a grimace from my face.

Tom was back. The last week had been so peaceful without him. He was jogging toward me, looking like an advertisement for men's casual fashion and overpriced body spray. Elon had to speed-walk to keep up.

"Sí-sí," he said as he drew closer, giving me his trademark adorable man grin. "There you are."

"Yes. I am here. Here I am." I don't know why, but I inserted myself between Cletus and Jethro. "Tom, this is Jethro and Cletus Winston. Cletus, Jethro, this is Tom Low."

"Mr. Low," Cletus said, not looking at him. "I enjoyed your film, *The Wall Street Connection.*"

"Thank you," Tom responded, shaking each of their hands in turn. He scrutinized them both. Cletus kept his eyes on the grass, whereas Jethro met Tom's gaze directly and gave him an easy smile, seemingly unaffected by the movie star's presence.

Tom clearly noticed Jethro's polite indifference to his star status. I watched with mounting trepidation as my co-star affixed his narrowed glare on Jethro.

"Do you want an autograph?" he asked with forced graciousness. "I'm afraid I don't have a pen."

"That's not necessary, sir." Jethro waved off his offer with a friendly smile, but it was still obvious Jethro had no idea who Tom was. Nor did he care.

Tom studied Jethro for a beat longer, dislike evident in his expression, then turned his attention to me.

"Sí-sí, I'm so sorry about Smash-Girl." He clicked his teeth. "Do you know why they changed their minds?"

"Uh . . ." my eyes flickered to Jethro then back to Tom, "I think they're looking for someone shorter."

Tom's gaze slid down then up my body and I sensed Jethro stiffen. The ranger took a step closer, shifting his weight to his foot behind me.

"Have you thought about asking the production staff for the low-carb option? Both Elon and I are having our meals delivered to my trailer, and they're honestly not bad. Well, not bad considering where we are."

I gathered a deep breath for patience just as Jethro's chest brushed against my back. I don't know if he meant to do it, but it felt reassuring, as though he were silently communicating *I've got your back.*

"No," I said, "I haven't asked for the low-carb meals."

Tom's attention flickered to my boobs then back to my face. "You should. Just give it a try. Maybe they'll reconsider you for Smash-Girl."

Before I could respond with a subject change or an excuse to leave, Jethro asked with a hint of irritation, "How's eating low-carb going to make Sienna shorter?"

Tom blinked once, his glare shifting to Jethro, the muscle at his jaw ticking. "I've been thinking of giving that look a try." He lifted his chin toward Jethro. "Do you have any tips?"

Jethro's chest pressed more fully against my back. "I don't know what you're talking about."

"Where I'm from," Tom tilted his head to the side, "they call your kind a hipster or a lumbersexual, with the beard and flannel and such."

Without missing a beat, Jethro responded, "Ah. See, where I'm from, they call my kind a man." Jethro gently placed his hand on my upper arm. "And this here is a woman, and so is that." He pointed at Elon.

"Ha ha, you're funny." Tom's voice lacked humor, and his grin resembled an aggressive baring of teeth. "What do they call my kind? Movie star, right?"

"No, sir."

"Well then, what?"

"I'd tell you, but you wouldn't like the word."

I felt my eyes widen before I could catch my reaction. It didn't matter, though. Because Jethro was using his hand on my arm to turn me toward him. And then he gathered me in his arms and brushed a tantalizing kiss over my mouth, with just a hint of his delicious tongue, surprising the heck out of me and making my limbs feel immediately heavy and useless.

"I'll see you tomorrow," he said in a soft, rumbly whisper. It simultaneously gave me the warm fuzzies and made my knees weak. He nuzzled my jaw, tickling me with his beard, and placed a kiss there as well.

Then he released me, tipped his hat to Elon with a, "Ma'am," and strolled off.

Tom was momentarily stunned, as was I. But I recovered first, mostly because Cletus nudged my shoulder as he walked past, leveling me with an intense but small smile. He mouthed what looked like, *How badass was that?* and stepped quickly to catch up with Jethro's departing form.

I quickly shook myself and made an excuse, citing a meeting with our director, and walked in the opposite direction. When I was several feet away, because I couldn't help myself, I glanced over my shoulder— not at Tom, but at Jethro and his unhurried stride. I noticed again that he had a really nice walk—easy, sexy, unaffected.

Yet, until that moment, I'd never truly appreciated how audaciously he carried himself, as though assured of his place as master of the universe, presiding over the kingdom of I-don't-give-a-fuck.

I mentally added his dauntless self-confidence to the list of his irresistible qualities.

CHAPTER EIGHTEEN

"I may have lost my heart, but not my self-control."

— JANE AUSTEN, EMMA

~Jethro~

I AWOKE AND glared at the clock. It was just past 2:30 a.m. I hadn't been sleeping well. I'd passed out around 9:00 p.m., but once again I'd had an irritating dream. The particulars weren't important, something about an elevator and it always stopping on the wrong floor.

The problem was, I'd been having dreams of this ilk for weeks, ever since my date with Sienna Diaz. I was frustrated, short-tempered, and it was getting worse. The only other dreams I'd been having involved us having hot sex. Sometimes it was wild; sometimes it was rough; sometimes it was slow and sweet. But it was always hot.

In summary, one way or the other, I was waking up every morning frustrated and hard.

Rubbing my eyes, I rolled out of bed, debating whether or not to pour myself a few shots of whiskey. I liked the idea in theory, but in practice I knew it was a slippery slope. No good could come from replacing one addiction with another.

That's what my present trouble reminded me of. I'd witnessed a few of my biker brothers back in the day go through withdrawals, wanting to curb their dependence on drugs or sex or booze. Some were successful, most weren't. They'd fall back into their old habits as soon as temptation presented itself.

I'd never been addicted to any vices. I didn't believe I had an addictive personality.

But that was before.

Before a few weeks ago.

Before I couldn't stop thinking about a certain gold-skinned woman with dark eyes, dimples, long lashes, and a body that inspired inconvenient—and frequently dirty—daydreams.

I stood and moved quietly, not wanting to wake Roscoe. He and I currently shared a room. The house was still undergoing renovations after years of neglect. It wasn't my momma's fault. She'd been too busy bringing up hell-raisers and trying to make us respectable to notice the encroachment of termites, the leaky roof, the wood rot, or the mold.

Walking down the hall, I surveyed the new wainscoting I'd installed last month. Most of the demolition work was done, but half the bedrooms still lacked floors. Some were missing drywall. Hence, we'd been doubling up since last November. I also planned to add two more bathrooms on the top floor. One bathroom for six men just didn't cut it.

Naturally, Duane and Beau shared a room. Duane and Jess were leaving for Italy soon, so Beau would be on his own by the end of the summer.

Billy hated my guts, so he roomed with Cletus.

I usually had my own room, but Roscoe was home for the summer.

Ashley lived in sin with Drew in his cabin on Bandit Lake, and we couldn't be happier for her. Though, I suspected he'd already proposed marriage, perhaps multiple times, and she hadn't seen fit to give an answer. Not yet anyway. She could be odd as Cletus sometimes.

I didn't bother to shut the bathroom door behind me. I was just after a glass of water. But then my attention snagged on a dirty magazine someone—probably Roscoe—had left on the counter. I say *probably Roscoe* because he hadn't quite acclimated back into the groove yet.

See, we had a schedule. The schedule was sacred. If we didn't adhere to the schedule, people were grumpy and chaos reigned. In truth, we only had three firm rules in the all-male Winston household:

One: Don't eat someone else's leftovers.

Two: Do your chores.

Three: Stick to the schedule.

Roscoe, being twenty-one and without a girl to call his own, had been messing up the schedule since his return. Duane didn't care for obvious reasons. Billy hadn't said a word, at least not to me. But Beau and Cletus were acting like Roscoe's midnight masturbating was the end of days, like we were teetering on the collapse of polite society.

"He's used all the tissues. Again," Beau had accused in a harsh whisper last night after dinner, cornering me by the outside freezer. "And there I was, all finished, like an asshole with no means to clean up. You need to do something about it, Jethro."

I'd rolled my eyes at their complaints, suggested they wash up instead of wipe up, and assured them they needed to exercise patience and restraint, but I knew I'd have to step in sooner or later and have a talk with my youngest brother. God forbid someone might have to walk downstairs to take a piss in the middle of the night. What was the world coming to?

But back to the dirty magazine on the counter.

The cover caught my attention. More precisely, the woman caught my attention. She was dark-haired, voluptuous, and something about her reminded me of Sienna at first glance.

Taking a second look, I realized any resemblance had been a trick of my imagination. This woman had big tits, but they were just big, not generous. And the proportion of her waist to her hips was all wrong. Her legs were too skinny. Her mouth wasn't the right shape, not to mention her eyes being the wrong color, holding none of Sienna's charm.

Realizing what I was doing, comparing some dirty magazine cover model to Sienna Diaz, I tucked the magazine under the counter with the others, where it belonged, and washed my hands.

Unfortunately, and not for the first time in recent weeks, I couldn't stop thinking about her. I couldn't stop comparing the two women, with Sienna coming out vastly superior in every way.

Her legs were things of beauty. And her skin glowed gold and bronze, out of the sunlight and even in the dark. And her body was hot and soft and made my mouth water. Just thinking about her had my pulse beating double.

I held the physical memory of all the times she'd pressed against me, brought the sensation out and turned it around. I'd planned to inspect the recollections as an impartial observer, but I couldn't. Soon I was pulled back in time.

Maybe it was the memory of her touch and the feel of her silky skin. Maybe it was middle-of-the-night wood. Maybe it was the way she'd looked at me, how she'd smiled, how remarkable she was. Or maybe it was merely frustrated need, but I was quite suddenly and epically hard, hot, and bothered.

Fucking hell, you'd think I was a teenager. I prided myself on self-control, five-plus years of it. I debated taking a cold shower.

Unbidden, a dream I'd had earlier in the week flashed like a dirty slide show in my mind. In the fantasy, Sienna had found me in the shower and alleviated my frustrations with her hands and mouth. But just as I was lifting her up against the tile wall and wrapping her legs around my waist, Cletus shoved a rooster in my face, waking me up and complaining, "The cock ain't crowing!"

In a way I'd been grateful. Against my will, my body was acting like I was sixteen again, waking up to damp shorts and horny fictions.

But now, standing in the bathroom, gritting my teeth at my reflection, images of fantasy Sienna taking me in her mouth . . . the ache was real and inescapable.

Cursing under my breath, I closed the door, violently flicked off the light, and leaned against the countertop. I reached into my boxers and grabbed myself, hissing, keeping my grip tight and my strokes smooth.

Given my dry spell, I was a pro at this. Usually it took less than three minutes: all business, no fuss.

But not tonight. Tonight I had an acute desire to draw out the act, to immerse myself in the fantasy, because nothing else was helping.

My chaotic mind sorted through all the ways I wanted to claim her, all the ways I'd bring her satisfaction. I wanted her naked and pleading, pressing her backside to my front, standing before a mirror so she could watch me touch and stroke and pet her body. Our eyes would meet over her shoulder and she'd arch her back, begging me to bend her over and fill her up.

In the next second I wanted her delighted and laughing, because her laugh was the closest I'd come to believing in magic. I wanted her on top, chasing her pleasure as I rolled my hips beneath, gripping her ass, watching her tits sway and bounce, watching her gorgeous face above me.

I cursed, my muscles rigid, and I came. The image of her flirty smile and seductive looks played through my mind, the only sound my heavy breathing as I tried to calm my pulse. The fantasies had been too vivid in the dark bathroom. I'd come too quickly, my mind still a tangle.

Spent, unsatisfied, and exhausted, I flicked on the light and saw to the mess. I was no closer to contentment than I'd been moments ago, and the question remained, other than the obvious, *why her*?

Our first kiss had set the tone for everything that had come after: frustration, desperation, passion.

It had been weeks since she told me I was fun. Fun to be with, fun to be around. And it was painful to hear those words from her mouth. I was spitting mad. So what did I do? Walked away like I should've? Like a sane person?

Hell, no. I kissed her, because—even though she was pissing me off —I missed her and I wanted to.

So I did.

And did I turn down her request to drive in together? No. I gave in, even though spending time in her company as a friendly acquaintance was like lying in a bed made of fiberglass.

And when Cletus told me she was dealing with bad news, I didn't think twice about dropping everything to make sure she was okay. And again when her asshole coworker showed up outside the dining tent and implied she should try a low-carb diet.

I wanted to say, *You know what else is low-carb? Shutting the fuck up.*

I wasn't thinking clearly. I kissed her again, in full view of everyone, and spent the rest of the day tortured, tasting her on my lips and cursing myself.

And now she was coming to dinner.

She'd be in my house, and yet still completely out of my reach.

CHAPTER NINETEEN

"For there is nothing lost, that may be found, if sought."

— EDMUND SPENSER, THE FAERIE QUEENE

~Sienna~

I SPENT ENTIRELY too much time trying to decide what to wear to dinner. At first I settled on dark blue jeans and a caramel-colored, off-the-shoulder shirt with a white lace camisole beneath. Dave told me it looked good.

"But do I look sexy?"

He grimaced in horror. Apparently my question panicked his delicate sensibilities.

"I need to look sexy, because I'm trying to get Ranger Jethro to kiss me and think about me naked."

If things went well tonight, then hopefully Jethro and I would be able to spend quality time together for the next sex weeks or more.

Six weeks!

I mean, *six* weeks, not sex weeks.

Six. Not sex.

Not. Sex. Weeks.

... although, I hoped some of the six weeks would be sex weeks, if you know what I mean. ;-)

Dave's frown eased and he grinned. "Oh. I see. Maybe wear a skirt?"

"Why a skirt? Why is a skirt sexier than jeans?"

"Because he can lift it easier," he explained pragmatically. "You don't say 'lifting jeans.' It's called lifting skirts for a reason."

I trusted Dave, so I changed. Instead I wore a simple blue skirt, matching V-neck top, and—at Dave's urging—nude thigh-high stockings with dark sapphire suede Mary Janes.

"The shoes are practical, flats but dressy," Dave said as he nodded his approval. "But the stockings make them sexy. Once he realizes they only go up to your thighs, he won't be able to concentrate on cooking anything that tastes good. So maybe grab a snack before you leave."

Scrutinizing my reflection, I lifted my skirt a few inches to reveal the top of the lace. I loved Dave. I was going to give him a raise.

I navigated while Dave drove. Thick mist rose around us as we descended the mountain, which struck me as strange. It hadn't rained and the sun shone brightly in the higher altitude around Bandit Lake. The sky had been blue. But here in the valley a late afternoon fog had rolled in, casting a silvery sheen over the emerald-green forests and narrow roads. The light was different. I felt as though I were looking at a fairy glen through the filter of a camera lens.

Nothing looked familiar and the whimsical lighting was distracting. Thus, I was immensely proud of myself when we arrived at the Winston homestead (as Cletus had called it) with only one U-turn between Hank's cabin and our destination.

I understood why Cletus had called it a homestead as soon as we drew close enough to the main house to see it clearly. It was a grand house. At least three stories, with possibly an attic and basement, a wrap-around porch, and Roman columns along the front. The white exterior, blue trim, and red door all appeared to have been newly painted.

And it was located on a great deal of cleared land with outbuildings in various stages of disrepair. Although one in particular, a detached garage or old carriage house, seemed to be in the middle of renovations.

I craned my neck as I exited the car, holding the two bottles of wine Henry had secured earlier from the grocery store.

"How much land do you think they have here?" Dave was also surveying the property. I didn't answer because I had no idea. He pointed to the forest behind the house, drawing my attention to it. It lay beyond an enormous, lush, green field dotted with red and purple wildflowers. "That's the national forest. This place is right on the park."

I nodded absentmindedly, distracted by the wildflower field blanketed with silvery mist.

Beautiful.

Reluctantly, I climbed the stairs to the porch. It had the natural wood luster of a recently restored antique. Seven rocking chairs lined one side. Two hanging wooden porch swings dangled at each corner, calling to mind lazy afternoons reading books outdoors, or holding hands with loved ones under a starry sky.

By all outward appearance, the house was grand, but it also felt like a home.

Dave had insisted earlier that he walk me to the door, reminding me of my dad and how he used to drop me off at a friend's house. He'd walk me to the door, meet the parents, look them in the eye, suggest a tour of the house, ask if they owned any guns, or had any vicious animals as pets.

Dave rang the bell and less than a minute later Cletus answered the door.

"Hello." He was wearing a tweed jacket and a red bowtie. He was also holding a brandy snifter.

"Hey, Cletus." Dave grinned. "How's the tractor?"

"Dead. For now. But I ordered a part from a junkyard in Galveston. It should be getting here next week. I have high hopes for its resurrection." Then to me Cletus nodded curtly, his eyes moving up and down my body in a way that felt entirely scientific. "That should do it. Y'all come in." Cletus stepped to the side, motioning for us to enter.

"Nah. I know you guys." Dave waved the suggestion away, as though the two of them were old friends.

Dave glanced over his shoulder at the long driveway, lined with old oaks, winding toward the house. "But, if you don't mind, I'd like to walk the perimeter."

Cletus nodded solemnly. "Of course."

"Nice to see you, Cletus." My smile was genuine; despite our original rocky start, he and I had become something of co-conspirators. I had no idea why he was helping me, I was just happy to have him on my side. "You're looking very dapper this evening."

"Repeat that later." He reached for my arm and tugged me into the house, calling over his shoulder, "Feel free to skulk all you'd like, Dave. Jethro will have her home before eight as we'll all be going to the jam session tonight." And with that, he quietly shut the door behind us.

"You brought wine," he whispered, releasing me and grabbing both bottles, tucking one under his arm as he juggled his snifter. "That's good. Ashley will like that. She's always complaining about the lack of wine, but Jess is a beer drinker. She don't care."

"Who is Jess?" I whispered because he was whispering.

"Duane's girl and my calculus teacher. Duane's the surly twin. Beau is the friendly one. Careful of him though, he'll try to hump your leg." He paired this statement with an exasperated eyebrow lift, like *Girl, you don't want to get me started.*

Once again, I covered my mouth with my palm to contain my laughter.

Cletus grinned at my movement, his hazel eyes dancing happily. "You are remarkably pretty when you laugh."

"Cletus?" Jethro's voice sounded from someplace behind me, sending a shock of nervous energy down my spine. "Did you get the door?"

Cletus hastily deposited the bottles on a table under an antique mirror but didn't answer Jethro. "Right," he continued whispering to me, "the kitchen is through there." He pointed down a hallway lined with framed pictures and turned me toward it. "That's where your man is, barefoot, making delicious turkey pot pie. Go."

"But, wait," I glanced at Cletus over my shoulder as he pushed me, "do I tell him I let myself in?"

"He won't ask."

"But—"

"Just go. I'll be in soon. That whole business with Tom Low today gave me an idea. I need to make an entrance."

With one last gentle shove, Cletus sent me down the hall.

I took three steps before I realized how out of control my anxiety was, and I froze.

Staring forward, eyes wide, I whispered to myself, "Don't make any jokes. No jokes. In fact, don't speak. At all."

Just as I finished my quiet pep talk, Jethro popped his head into the hallway. Judging by the initial glower on his features and then the abrupt clearing of his brow, I guessed he'd expected to see Cletus.

"Hi," I said, sounding odd, like I was out of breath. But I sorta was out for breath. And my palms were sweaty. I placed them on my thighs. I also stared at him, soaking in the sight.

Is it strange that I missed him? It's weird, right? .

"Hi," Jethro finally said, also sounding out of breath. He stepped fully into the hall, wiping his hands on a towel then tossing it to his shoulder. He was barefoot and that made me think of him naked. Don't ask me why, that's just how my mind works. I see bare feet and think full frontal.

Unable to tolerate the delicious vision of a naked Jethro while he stood before me, yet completely beyond my touch, I blurted, "I brought wine, and you have nice feet."

He blinked, the dazed quality of his gaze dissipating, and a soft smile spread over his features. "That was very kind of you."

"The wine or complimenting your feet?"

"Both. I've never thought much about feet, not when there're so many other places I could focus my energy." He held my eyes captive; his soft smile grew playful, causing a spreading heat to radiate outward from my heart to my limbs.

Ah, there it is.

I'd missed *this* smile. I missed how it made me feel. It was my favorite of his smiles. And that's when I realized I'd been spending a portion of my time cataloging his smiles.

Wanting to capture and sustain the moment, I teased, "Really? Where? And be specific. Diagrams are also enormously helpful."

"Why draw when I can demonstrate?"

"On yourself? Or do you require a volunteer?"

Jethro laughed—an uncontainable, sinister sounding snicker, low and rumbly—which made me laugh, too. Not going to lie. I was giddy with how wonderfully easy things were between us, just like they'd been before.

"Depends on the volunteer." He paired this statement with a lazy perusal of my body, from shoes to nose. When his eyes returned to mine, they were a shade darker and the amusement in his expression had an edge of something new. Something hot, but not warm.

I was just about to raise my hand and volunteer as tribute—Katniss Everdeen style—when a buzzing sounded from the kitchen, breaking our lovely flirty spell. Jethro started, blinking and frowning as though the sound confused him; and then he turned his frown on me, as though my presence also confused him, or frustrated him. One or the other.

"That'd be the crust." He tossed his thumb over his shoulder then turned, calling back at me. "Uh, come into the kitchen, and I'll get you something to drink."

I hesitated, cast adrift by his departure. Cletus's warning from weeks ago—hope being more dangerous than happiness—chose that moment to resurface. I understood now what he meant. Standing in the hallway of the Winston homestead, the danger of hope felt very real.

The buzzing from the kitchen stopped and still I loitered in the hall.

I was hopeful, and thus caught in a web of fear. The possibility of dashed hopes was scarier than I'd anticipated. As I entered the kitchen I did so cautiously, preparing myself for another rejection, but hoping it wouldn't come.

Peeking around the corner to the kitchen, I found Jethro sitting at the kitchen table pulling on boots over socks. He glanced at me, raising his eyebrows in question.

"Are you okay?"

I nodded.

He studied me, the side of his mouth hitching the longer he stared. "You can come in. I promise I won't bite."

But what if I want you to bite? The question was on the tip of my tongue when a male voice boomed from another room, interrupting me.

"No. No way. No way ever."

"Please."

"I said no and I mean no." The owner of this statement strolled into the kitchen from the far door. He wore a scowl and was tall and lean, but not skinny. Built like a runner. He had a shock of red hair standing in all directions, and a neatly trimmed red beard. His sky-blue eyes swung around the kitchen, searching for something. They landed on me for a beat, he did a double take, then dismissed my presence.

Well, that's a first. I liked him already.

He was followed closely by a cute blonde woman twisting her hands. "But, Duane, I wouldn't ask except Jackson needs—"

"Like my momma used to say, keep weasels and appointed sheriffs at a distance." Duane shook his head stubbornly.

She clicked her teeth. "Duane Faulkner Winston, don't be rude. You know Jackson would really appreciate your help."

"He can take his appreciation and shove it up his—"

"Duane Faulkner," Jethro interrupted sharply, standing from the table. "We've got company."

Duane's scowl deepened as he looked at Jethro. But he took a deep breath, inhaling patience, and turned a stoic expression on me and offered his hand.

"Hi. I'm Duane. One of the twins," he said flatly, as though meeting me was a chore. I stepped all the way into the kitchen and accepted his hand, oddly charmed by his bad attitude.

"Hi. I'm Sienna. Nice to meet you."

"This is Jessica." He placed his hand on the back of the blonde woman who'd entered with him. When he looked at her it was the first time since he'd entered that he didn't appear to be irritated. By contrast, he looked proud, or happy, or a mix of both.

"Nice to meet you, Sienna." Jessica shook my hand, giving me a lopsided grin. "I recognize you from your film roles and all that ruckus at

The Front Porch a few weeks ago. I'm so sorry those people didn't leave you and Jethro in peace. Some folks have no manners."

"You were there? At the restaurant?" She didn't look familiar. Then again, I'd been overwhelmed by faces and disappointments that evening.

"I was, but I didn't approach. I'm a teacher at the local high school, and the PTA was meeting that night," she explained.

"She teaches calculus," Cletus announced, entering from the same door Duane and Jessica had just used. With some deference, he nodded to Jessica, "Good evening, Ms. James."

"Cletus," she returned with a small grin.

"You look lovely today, Ms. James," Cletus remarked, causing the reemergence of Duane's scowl.

"Thank you, Cletus." Jessica appeared to be holding in laughter. "And may I say, you look lovely—"

"All right. That's enough," Duane cut in, stepping between them and sliding his arm around Jessica's waist. "I'm watching you, sneak. No miraculously 'finding' the mistletoe from last Christmas tonight, do you hear me?" This question was aimed at Cletus, who widened his eyes innocently.

"I am affronted by your insinuation," he said, not sounding affronted. Then, turning to me, he stepped forward, slipped his hand in mine, and tugged me toward him. He placed a soft kiss on my cheek. Now *that* I hadn't been expecting.

"You also look lovely, Ms. Diaz," he announced loudly.

"Thank you, Cletus," I responded automatically, then remembered to add, "you look very dapper this evening."

"Oh, this old thing?" he asked loud enough to be heard, kissing my other cheek, then whispered, "Is Jethro watching?"

My gaze moved to Jethro. He was watching and his scowl resembled Duane's.

"Yes."

"Good." Cletus leaned away, giving me a small smile. Further surprising me, Cletus slid his arm around my waist and pressed me to his side. "I'm so glad you're here."

I narrowed my eyes at him, wondering what he was up to. I didn't have to wait long.

Wearing an unhappy expression, Jethro walked over and gripped my arm gently, tugging me out of Cletus's hold and tucking me next to him. "None of that," he said to his brother. "Duane doesn't like it. What makes you think I would like it?"

"I don't know what you mean." Cletus sounded exasperated and put out. "I'm just trying to be friendly."

"Take your friendly somewhere else," Duane said just as another man walked into the kitchen behind him and Jessica. This new man's piercing stare moved over the five of us, landing on Jethro's hand where it gripped my waist, while Jethro and Duane ganged up on Cletus.

"I thought you didn't want to get in her hair," Cletus was saying to Jethro, his hands on his hips.

The newcomer was taller than Jethro, taller and stockier. His hair and his beard were darker, nearly black. His eyes were the most amazing shade of blue and his face was startlingly handsome. Like, I needed a minute to recover from the handsome. Beautiful, even. As I studied him I noted that his features were perfectly symmetrical. The camera would love this guy.

And yet, though he was intense levels of physically striking, he projected an air of cool disinterest. By contrast, he lacked Jethro's ever-present friendliness and warmth, warmth I'd been drawn to immediately and couldn't seem to bask in enough.

My only experience with a brooder had been Tom, and since Tom, brooders held no allure. From my quick inspection, this new guy would rival Tom in both looks and frostiness. I hypothesized he could cause a snow flurry just by sneezing.

Mr. Freeze's eyes connected with mine, and they felt like two icicles aimed at my brain. I saw intelligence there, but also something unpleasant that had me pressing closer to Jethro's side.

"You will kindly leave Sienna's hair out of this conversation. And leave off touching her as well. Keep your paws to yourself." The edge of Jethro's scowl was tinged with amusement. I loved this about him. Even when he was irritated, he had to work to keep his good mood and easy temper from taking over.

"What's going on?" Another man, this one looking like a happier version of Duane, stepped into the kitchen.

"Nothing," Duane and Jethro said in unison.

The new redhead walked around Icicle Eyes—who was still glaring at me—and stepped forward. "Holy moly, I know you. You're Sienna Diaz!"

I smiled at the newcomer, obviously the other Winston twin, and shook his hand. "Yes. You must be Beau."

His wide grin reminded me of Jethro's, as did his open manner. Although, his charm was more like an excited puppy than Jethro's brand of self-possessed manly magnetism. Regardless, he was cute and friendly. I immediately returned his smile.

"I can't believe I'm meeting you. Whoa. Look at those dimples. You should have a license for those."

This made me laugh and Jethro grumble, his hand sliding to my hip in a blatantly possessive movement. I wrapped my arm around his waist and allowed myself to enjoy his closeness.

Allow me to take a moment to express my appreciation for Cletus Winston and his entrances.

Beau's eyes moved between Jethro and me, his grin waning. "Wait a minute. Are you two . . .?" He stopped himself.

"Yes," Cletus, my new favorite person, answered the unfinished question. "Our brother Jethro has finally done right by the family and involved himself with this fine woman."

Jethro shifted uncomfortably, but made no move to release me. "We're friends," he said finally, his eyes flickering to mine, then away. "Good friends."

"Friends?" Beau's tone was edged with happy relief. "So you wouldn't mind if—"

"I would mind, and you can go make the salad while I show Sienna around." Jethro then turned us away from where his brothers were gathered, mumbling, "Sorry," as he led me out of the kitchen and out of the house.

"Don't apologize," I whispered, my lips close to his neck. I squeezed his waist and ignored the way my heart galloped in my chest. Because, honestly? I was pretty much taking this opportunity to feel him up.

Don't judge me. You would do it, too.

His stomach was rock hard and his arm felt strong and steady. He held me so close his beard brushed my temple and upper cheek, the texture sending spikes of loveliness everywhere. And he smelled good. Intoxicatingly. Good.

"That's the carriage house." He pointed at the half-restored building I'd spotted before entering the house. "I've gutted the inside. The roof is new as is most of the siding. I'll have it done in two months."

"You're remodeling it yourself?"

He didn't stop for me to take a closer look, instead keeping our pace quick as we walked through the wildflower field I'd been admiring earlier. We were in their backyard, which was immense and backed on to a forest thick with trees. I quickly inspected the wooded area, deciding it would do nicely for privacy. I wanted to talk to him, just talk. I hoped he'd give me a chance to make a pitch for Jethro + Sienna, the sequel.

"Yes. I just started last month since I'm mostly finished with the big house."

"What did you do to the big house?"

"I refinished the porch in April. Before that I stripped all the original wood moldings, the banister, and cornices, replaced all the windows. The kitchen is new, new granite and cabinets, but I'm waiting on installing the new appliances until this summer. I haven't updated the bathrooms yet or painted the inside. I want to test out my skills on the carriage house first before I rip up the tile inside the main house and piss everyone off. Plus, I'm not much of a decorator, so I need Ashley—that's my sister—to help me pick colors and finishings. She and Jess chose the exterior paint. Duane and Beau had the big house painted in one week. I ordered enough so the carriage house will match."

"Wow. That sounds like a lot of work."

He shrugged, not looking at me but continuing to hold me close to his side. "To be honest, I enjoy it. The carpentry and refinishing parts especially. It's been neglected for so long, I like making the old place new again."

We fell into a contemplative silence even though our steps were hurried. I surmised he wasn't walking fast on purpose but rather hadn't yet realized how quickly we were moving. We were almost at the edge of the field when I sensed he was about to turn us back to the house. Not wanting to return yet, I stiffened my arm, slowing our pace, and subtly steering us toward the forest.

Now was the time for my pitch. I was far too impatient to wait until after dinner. Better to know as soon as possible whether he'd definitely friend-zoned me. I was more adept at hiding disappointment than I was at hiding hope.

Clearing my throat, I announced, "I want to thank you for inviting me."

His eyes cut to mine and he lifted an eyebrow. "I didn't invite you. Cletus did."

I angled my chin and slipped on one of my more seductive smiles. "I guess I should thank Cletus, then."

His eyes narrowed. "No need to thank Cletus. I'm the one making dinner. You can thank me."

"How should I thank you?" I deepened my voice, pretty sure he would catch the general direction of my thoughts.

Jethro's pace slackened as we entered the forest, the thick under-growth hiding us from the view of the house.

"A simple thank you should suffice."

I gathered a breath for courage and made my pitch. "Is that all you want from me? Because I'm prepared to offer more."

His steps faltered and I glanced tentatively at his profile, trying to read his expression. Before I could, Jethro's hand fell from my hip. He crossed his arms and walked ten paces away to a tall pine tree, giving me his back.

I watched him for a long moment, disoriented at first. As time wore on, I began to suspect the distance he'd put between us was my answer. Heart plummeting to my feet, I was glad he'd given me his back. I was having trouble assuming a mask of friendly indifference. So much trouble I doubted I'd be able to recite the words necessary for us to transition into the friend-zone.

In fact, I doubted I'd be able to friend-zone Jethro at all. He would exist in a new zone, one entirely of his own, where I would think of him often, and with longing wretchedness. Or was it wretched longing?

His shoulders rose and fell with an audible sigh, and then he turned, again offering just his profile. His smile was pleasant but flat. Jethro uncrossed his arms, stuffing his hands in his pockets.

"This is the national park." He tilted his head, indicating to the forest surrounding us. "This house has been in the family for over one hundred years. We have fifteen acres here. Or rather, I should say, I have fifteen acres. The house and the land belong to me as the oldest. I inherited it last year, along with some other . . . stuff."

I nodded slowly, still absorbed by my disgruntlement but grateful for the subject change. "It's a beautiful home."

"It is." He faced me, the lines of his features serious, his eyes searching. "I'm hoping to raise a brood of kids in this house, on this land."

I watched him as he watched me, getting the sense he was trying to impart something important without having to come out and actually say it. I frowned when I couldn't figure out what he wasn't saying.

He continued to scrutinize me, like it was my turn to speak, so I said, "You should. This is an ideal environment for raising children. I had a lot of room to run around when I was growing up and loved it."

His frown mirrored mine, the intensity of which seemed to increase the longer we stared at each other.

At last he said, "I like you . . . a whole lot." The way he said these last words left me in no doubt of how much he liked me, but then he followed them up with, "But I'm sorry if I misled you, or made you think I was available for a fling during your time here. The fact is, I'm not. I can't see us being suited."

"You don't think we're suited?" My heart was all over the place. It had made a U-turn on its way to my feet when he said he liked me, bypassed my stomach, and now was lodged in my throat.

"As much as I wish things were different, no. No, I don't think we're suited."

"Is it because I can't read maps?" I squeaked the joke, because I was a bundle of new nerves.

His lips tugged to the side and something behind his composure wavered. "No. I think I could help you with that, truth be told."

"Then why?" I tried to swallow but my stubborn heart wouldn't budge. "Was it because I let you think my name was Sarah? Because—"

"No. Like I said before, I understand why you did that. The main problem is that you're young and you're wildly successful."

"I'm not too young for you," I contradicted, a little louder than I'd intended, taking a half step forward. "Six years isn't a big difference."

"That's not what I meant. It's not the number. It's the difference in life situation."

"So you think you're what? Old and a failure?"

He cracked a grin at the unadorned frustration in my rhetorical question, his gaze reminding me of a caress as it moved over my lips and neck.

"No. I'm not old, and I'm not a failure. But you're not just successful. You're world famous."

"And you don't want to be with someone who is world famous." The words tasted bitter as they left my mouth.

"No, Sienna. That's not it, either. Your fame doesn't frighten me. Although, if I'm honest with myself, it was overwhelming when I saw it firsthand. The real issue is that I might be good at my job, but I'll never be near as wildly successful at my job as you are with yours. And that's fine by me. My ambitions aren't career-oriented, they're family-oriented. If I have wild success, and I hope I do, it'll be as a husband and father, a brother and an uncle. It might not make a lot of sense to you, but I can't start something, invest in someone, I know from the get-go is going to be temporary."

I could only blink at him, trying my best to absorb his words.

Meanwhile, he shifted on his feet, his eyes darting over me and added, "I would want forever with you . . . or at least a shot at it."

As he finished his speech, a soft, resigned smile hovering over his handsome lips and behind his eyes, I had one thought: *Could he be any more amazing?*

Really. I wanted to know. Could he?

I would want forever with you.

Oh my dear mother of all swoony sighs—this! So. Much. This.

Instead of asking him whether or not his amazing level was at maximum, and without giving his speech the responsible consideration it likely deserved, I allowed my melodramatic nomadic heart to veto all deliberations. "Okay."

Because, honestly? Forever with Jethro, in this gorgeous house, in this secluded and beautiful part of the world sounded like perfection. It sounded like everything I never knew I wanted, but in this moment felt with absolute certainty was where I belonged.

It also might've been seasoned with a dash of escapism, but I pushed that inconvenient thought away.

"Okay." He nodded once, as though things were settled. And yet, he looked a little sad. *Why does he look sad?*

"Okay," I said again, closing the distance between us, my hands on my hips. When I reached Jethro, I pressed a kiss to his mouth, just a quick taste, because I couldn't help myself. His lips were soft and hot and perfect. But I touched him nowhere else. It's just . . . he had fantastic lips. My heart skipped back to my chest at the thought of this being the first of many kisses. "Let's do this."

His eyes were olive green today with gold flecks around the irises, and they looked confused. "Do what?"

"Let's do this thing." I pointed between the two of us. "Let's do this not-temporary thing."

He blinked. "What?"

I gestured to the house behind him. "I love your house. I'd like a tour. And if you have a sex dungeon, I'd like a chance to mentally prepare for the sex swing, but I can totally see raising our theoretical kids here. In case you haven't noticed, I have birthing hips, so that's a bonus. But you need a playground back here." I gestured to the meadow with a flick of my wrist. "Also, I must warn you, at some point my abuela will pressure you into converting to Catholicism. And all our daughters will have a quinceañera, but we'll cross those giant dresses when we come to them."

The creases in his features smoothed while I spoke, and his stare adopted an edge of wonder. "You're serious."

"Yes." I was.

And yet he appeared to be torn. "Sienna . . ."

"Jethro."

"You don't even know me."

"No. I don't, not yet. And you don't know me. But you didn't ask me to marry you. You asked that I not approach a relationship with you as something temporary. You asked for a shot at forever, and I'm asking for the same thing from you."

His hands went to his hips. His eyes moved over my features like this might be the last time we'd be this close. "You're a movie star. A celebrity with millions of fans."

"And you're a wildlife ranger who traps giant, dangerous black bears for a living and acts like it's no big deal. Tell me that doesn't sound like a heaping helping of crazy, with bizarre gravy, and a slice of mashed loco for Cocoa Puffs."

His breathing and the teetering look in his gaze told me I almost had him. Almost. Something was holding him back. He just needed one more push . . .

"These stockings are thigh highs," I abruptly announced. "Want to see?" Not waiting for his response, I took a step back and lifted my skirt, showing him where the tops of the stockings met my upper legs.

I glanced up to find Jethro's eyes locked on my legs, his gaze growing hotter.

Excellent.

"And the panties match," I volunteered, biting my bottom lip and drawing his darkened gaze back to mine.

He reached for me and stilled my hands before I could show him the underwear, too. His mouth curved in a reluctant and wicked grin. He split his attention between my lips and eyes. "You are very bad."

"Am I?" Once again, I felt abruptly winded. "I'm stunned. I thought I was very good."

"Oh, you're good." His eyebrows bounced once and his voice deepened to a rumble. "You're just also very bad."

"What are you going to do about it?" I couldn't wait to find out.

Holding my gaze and towering over me, he gained the step I'd taken, then several more until my back connected with a large tree trunk. He placed his hands on either side of my legs and lifted the skirt, his fingertips connecting with the skin just above my stockings. With an achingly light touch, he drew small circles on my legs, inching the skirt higher and higher until I was breathless with anticipation.

"You're going to be my girl," he growled, nipping at my jaw.

"No." I shook my head, evading his mouth and correcting with, "I'm going to be your woman."

He grinned again, that predatory flash I'd seen earlier returned. His eyes dropped to my breasts where they were pressed against his chest. "Does the bra match, too?"

I nodded. He groaned, capturing my mouth with a searing, urgent kiss.

His hands drifted higher on my thighs, sending sparks of heat shooting up my spine and low in my belly. Moving his fingers to the front, he encouraged me to spread my legs with his knee. His knuckles rubbed lightly back and forth over my center, still covered in white lace. Hot and needy, I tilted my hips forward as my head fell back, my hands fisting in his shirt, and I gasped for air.

"You're so beautiful." He sounded awed, out of breath. I opened my eyes, wanting to see him, and found his gaze devouring, cherishing. "You're a fantasy."

"I assure you, I'm very real." My hands stroked down the front of his chest, enjoying how his body, still sadly encased in clothing, tightened under my fingertips as my touch drifted lower. When I reached his belt he caught my wrist and bent his head to my neck.

"Don't," he growled. "I want you." The words were tortured, as much an admission as a warning.

And the ferocity of his statement sobered me, woke me from the impassioned thoughtlessness of my actions. Because as much as I'd planned to flirt and tease him into agreeing to see me again, I hadn't planned on *this*. The force of my longing, this intoxicating pull between us, the internal debate warring within me—*have sex against the tree or have sex on the ground? It's not that dirty* . . .

Yes?

Please?

Who was this woman? I didn't even recognize myself.

At most I thought maybe we'd make out, kiss a lot, grope a little. I hadn't been prepared for what it would be like to actually be touched by him. As with all things, Jethro was capable, straightforward, and in control . . . until his control had slipped, and so had mine, and desperation and passion threatened to overtake sense.

So I swallowed and closed my eyes, made myself breathe in and out, and brought my hands to his shoulders. I tried to ignore the hard length of him pressing against my stomach.

"We should take things slow." The statement meant to convince us both. As we'd just agreed, this wasn't a fling, not for either of us. We had plenty of time.

He nodded once, kissing the skin beneath my ear and making me squirm. Withdrawing his fingers from between my legs, Jethro gripped my thighs, his hands still under my skirt, as though he couldn't bring himself to stop touching me.

Eventually, he lifted his head. The friction of his beard, paired with his hot breath against the exposed skin of my neck, left me trembling.

Jethro studied me with a heavily-lidded gaze, and I almost took back my words of caution. *Almost.* Because his stare seemed dark with dirty thoughts.

I was curious. So, so, so curious. So I demanded, "Write it down."

"Pardon?" His voice was gravelly, somnolent as though I'd woken him.

"Whatever you're thinking right now, write it down. Because when the time comes, we should totally do *that.*"

His eyes moved between mine, dazed lust giving way to amusement. "Really? Even if it involves the sex swing in my dungeon?"

I wagged my eyebrows and—again because I couldn't help myself—pressed a quick kiss to his lips. "Most especially if it involves the sex swing in your dungeon."

CHAPTER TWENTY

"If you have built castles in the air, your work need not be lost; that is where they should be. Now put the foundations under them."

— HENRY DAVID THOREAU, WALDEN

~Jethro~

"YOU HAVEN'T STOPPED smiling since returning from your walk," my sister whispered, drawing my attention from where Sienna was charming Duane and Drew across the deck—having already charmed Beau, Cletus, and Roscoe—to Ashley's wide eyes. "Did something happen between you and the delightful Ms. Diaz?"

Ashley, Drew, and Roscoe had arrived during my extremely gratifying walk with Sienna. We'd all had dinner out on the deck behind the house due to the gorgeous weather. Of course, I'd also wanted to show off as many views of the house and property as possible.

Now most everybody was sitting at the two picnic tables on the raised deck. Billy and Drew were off to one side, both too big for a crowded table.

Ashley and I stood by the cooler. I was grabbing another beer, but she had tracked me down to tease and gossip.

I tried to wipe the grin from my face, but it was no use. I couldn't. "I don't know what you're talking about, Ashley."

She quietly snorted and took a step closer, her voice dropping to a soft accusing whisper. "You are a lying liar. You two can't stop looking at each other, and she blushes like a pole-dancing virgin every time your eyes meet."

"Does she?" I'd noticed the blush, but damn if I didn't like that it was obvious and others had noticed as well. And now I had images of Sienna pole dancing flashing through my brain—not the awkward butter-churning pole dancing either.

"Congratulations, Jethro. She's sweet on you. You've just taken one the world's most famous role models of feminine independence and turned her into a giddy, flustered mess of hormones."

My smile wavered, not sure about my feelings on the matter, which made Ashley smile wider. "Oh, you didn't know?"

I cleared my throat, my attention flickering to Sienna, then back to my sister. "Hank may have mentioned something."

Now her smile wavered, her eyes narrowing into suspicious slits. "Jethro, don't you hurt that girl."

I winced, her words hitting a target Ash likely didn't realize existed.

Placing a gentle hand on Ashley's shoulder, I pulled her a smidge closer. "Ash, I love you. You've been gone a long time and have only been back a few months, so I don't mind repeating myself 'cause you haven't been here to see things change first-hand." I made sure she was looking at me, really looking, before continuing. "I don't do that anymore. I haven't for a long time. I have no intentions of hurting Sienna or anyone else. Not ever again."

Ashley's gaze flashed, likely with some unpleasant memory of a younger asshole me, then dropped to the deck. She nodded stiffly. Her tone was laced with guilt as she apologized. "I'm sorry. You're right. You've changed. Sorry."

The set of my sister's jaw was a painful reminder of how, no matter how far I'd come or how many good decisions I'd made in recent years, I couldn't take back past mistakes. I couldn't undo the consequences of my selfish decisions.

"No, Ash. I'm sorry," I said, shaking her shoulder lightly so she'd look at me again. "I'm sorry, and I promise I'll do my best to make it up to you."

She gave me a brave smile that quickly turned affectionate, covering my hand with hers. "No need. You're right. That's all in the past."

I didn't deserve Ashley's forgiveness. Not yet, at any rate. I didn't know which was worse: Ashley's wanting to forgive me so quickly without my having earned it, or Billy's continued rejection despite my repeated attempts to reach out.

Regardless, Ashley had been gone during my reformation. I had a lot of making up to do with her.

"I'm serious about making it up to you. Do you need anything built? A barn maybe?" I teased.

She shook her head, her pretty face lighting up with a pretty smile. "No, but I'll keep you in mind should I require a barn."

"Come on, Billy. It's a joke." The edge in Duane's voice had me glancing over Ashley's shoulder to where the rest of our siblings were gathered.

"Was it?" Billy's response was flat. "I was under the impression jokes were supposed to be funny."

"You're the only person this side of the Mississippi who doesn't think that's funny." Beau rolled his eyes with great effect.

"That's not true," Cletus countered. "I know at least three other people who have no sense of humor besides Billy."

"It's no big deal." Sienna shrugged, apparently unfazed by Billy's bad attitude. "It's a work in progress."

"No. It is a big deal." Duane was scowling at Billy. "You've had a stick shoved so high up your ass all night, I'm surprised you can't taste it."

"Now *that* was funny." Roscoe lifted his beer toward Duane, then tossed a smile to Sienna. "But your joke was funny, too."

"No, no. Duane's was funnier." Sienna tipped her wine toward Roscoe, then nodded to Duane. "I might have to steal it."

"Thieving one of your hobbies?" Billy mumbled. More precisely, he said it loudly enough to be heard, but gave it the appearance of being mumbled in a world-class show of passive-aggressive antagonism.

Having reached my limit, I stepped away from Ashley and crossed to Billy, motioning for him to rise. "Okay, that's it. William Shakespeare Winston, get up."

"What?" he snapped, glaring at me.

"You heard me. You've got a problem with me. Not gentlemanly of you to be taking it out on Sienna. Don't take your frustration out on her. We all know you've got a problem with me, but that's no call for you to treat a guest with disrespect."

Billy stood abruptly, his eyes flashing with the fire of hatred. "What the fuck do you know about respect?"

I set my jaw. I thought I'd eventually grow accustomed to the hollow ache settling in my stomach. Although I was used to his sporadic hateful outbursts, they never got easier. If it had just been us, just the family, I wouldn't have said anything. Billy had every right to be pissed at me, for the rest of our lives if he so chose. But I wasn't going to have him make Sienna feel unwelcome or uncomfortable. Not in my house, not anywhere.

His eyes, so like my father's, pierced into me—through me—cutting and full of loathing. His lips parted, and he bared his teeth like he was fixing to volley another spiteful remark.

"Billy, please don't." At Ashley's soft reproach, his mouth snapped shut, his gaze darting to our sister, then away.

Pulling a hand through his hair, he muttered a quiet curse; it sounded like *fucking bastard*. He swallowed. Then he turned and walked off the deck without another word.

Gloom fell over the previously merry group. I hadn't seen Billy this angry in a while. He normally held back, especially in front of company, but not tonight. I wanted to apologize. But Cletus had told me after the first year he was tired of hearing me say I'm sorry. I'd taken to showing my family with my actions, knowing I needed to prove not just that I'd changed, but that I'd wanted to.

Beau was the one to break the silence. "Sorry about that, Sienna. Billy isn't usually friendly, but he's not usually an asshole, either."

"No, no. It's fine. I have a large family. We don't all get along all the time." I felt her eyes on me and I knew I would need to explain more about my past mistakes sooner rather than later.

"How large is this family?" Cletus asked.

Followed quickly by Roscoe, "And do you have any single sisters?"

Which of course made everyone laugh, because everyone wanted to laugh. They didn't want any more cumbersome drama. We'd already been through enough drama this year.

Ashley stepped next to me while Sienna answered Roscoe's question; my sister nudged me with her shoulder. "Go after him."

I grimaced. Remorse, now so familiar I considered it a friend, tightened around my lungs in a vise-like grip. "He doesn't want to talk to me."

"Maybe." She shrugged, nudging me again. "But Billy once told me, 'Apathy between family members makes the blood they share turn to water.'" She paused, allowing me a minute to think on these words, then pressed, "Billy may have several colorful feelings regarding your person, Jethro, but none of those are akin to apathy."

This made me smirk. "You sound like Momma."

"Thank you. I take that as the highest of compliments. Now stop trying to distract me and go speak to your brother."

A low chuckle had both Ash and me twisting around, searching for the origin. Drew stood just behind us, his eyes on his boots, but he wore a rare smile.

"What?" Ashley demanded, narrowing her eyes.

He shrugged, his stare lifting to my sister. "It's just, Jethro's right." My boss's eyes moved over Ashley's face with a fathomless well of affection and devotion. "You do sound like your momma, just less subtle and a good deal more autocratic."

She considered him for a long moment, then unexpectedly wrapped her arms around his neck, planting a kiss on the game warden that was not fit for polite company.

I quickly averted my gaze and descended the stairs two at a time. "Pardon me. I think I'll go talk to Billy."

I was twenty feet away when I heard Roscoe groan, "Oh, come on. Really? Go get a room. The house has like ten. Pick one."

* * *

I IGNORED THE ensuing good-natured ruckus behind me, readying myself for a confrontation with my brother. We didn't have many. He mostly pretended I didn't exist. Or, if it was a holiday, he pretended he didn't hate me for the sake of the others.

The woodshed was a popular spot for us boys when aggression was high and options for releasing it were low. Suffice to say, we had a lot of cut wood. I decided to search there first.

Billy was setting up the chopping block when I found him, wielding an axe with white knuckles. He may have loathed my person, but I had no fear for my safety. I launched into the heart of the matter, anxious to have this one point sorted.

"Listen, I know I can never make up for being a terrible brother to you growing up. But there's no call for you to be."

"You're bringing women home? Really, Jethro?" Billy brought the axe down with a furious *thunk,* splitting the log with one strike.

Yep. He was pissed.

"Yeah. So I brought a woman home. So what?"

"What about Claire?" He didn't look at me as he asked the question, but there was something about the way he said my friend's name that had me standing straighter.

"What about Claire?"

He cast his eyes to the heavens. Billy swore like he thought I was an imbecile.

Between clenched teeth he asked, "How do you think Claire is going to feel?"

I stared at him, not understanding his question. "About what?"

"About you stepping out with someone else, jackass."

The question surprised me so much I laughed. "Claire couldn't give

214

two shits who I see."

"Really?"

"Yeah. Really." I eyeballed my brother's back, deciding he'd lost his mind. This was the longest conversation he and I had shared in over ten years. He never spoke to me, not if he could help it, and now he couldn't shut up about Claire McClure.

"You go over there every Sunday, Jethro. You can't tell me nothing's been going on. You two, you're always together." He brought the axe down again with another furious strike.

"That's because we're friends, Billy. You should try it, having friends. It's nice."

"You two are not friends." His statement sounded like an accusation, one that troubled him deeply.

"Yes, we are. We've been friends since Claire married Ben. Just because he died doesn't mean we stopped being friends."

"Right." Another angry strike of the axe, another split piece of wood.

"Right, what? What are you so aggravated about? That I have friends, even though I'm not deserving? Or that Claire is one of them?"

My brother said nothing, just glared at me over his shoulder.

"What the hell, Billy?"

I was so tired of this. Both he and Ashley were right, apathy makes blood turn to water, but in that moment I prayed for apathy. His grudge, how he wore it like a badge, was wearing me down, pushing me to not care what he thought or what he did.

"You know what?" I shook my head, aggravated and exhausted and over his perpetual rotten attitude. "I don't have time for this right now. I don't have time to say I'm sorry for the millionth time for being a miserable excuse for a human being when we were growing up. I have a guest over—yes, a woman—and I'm so fucking tired of you hating me. If you're going to be mean, go someplace else."

He caught my arm as I moved past, his fingers grasping, but not punishing. I met his glare, expecting to see more of the same, but instead, the searching, hopeful quality there nearly knocked me on my ass.

What the hell?

"You and Claire, you never . . .?" His voice was strangled, as though the thought had been suffocating him, maybe for years.

The man looked tormented by the thought.

I turned and faced my brother. "No. Claire and I have never so much as kissed. We did a lot of hugging when Ben died. I used to stay the night at her house. On the couch. We slept together once, just slept, while I held her and she cried. That was the night we got the news."

Billy's eyes moved over my shoulder as I spoke, focusing on nothing. I saw his thoughts were turned inward, like he was sorting through a burden too big and heavy for his shoulders alone.

"But you haven't . . . I mean, there's been nobody. You had no girls over, and I haven't seen you with anyone else since Ben died."

I nodded, but I couldn't keep the hard edge out of my voice. "That's right. Because I had bad habits, Billy. Habits that had me treating women like shit. Treating you and Momma and Ashley and everyone else like they didn't matter. Habits that made me hate myself. So I decided to change."

Billy's hand dropped and so did the reinforced walls in his gaze. He blinked, his gaze penetrating, like he was seeing me for the first time in a long time.

So I took advantage of the moment, because I didn't know if I'd ever have it again.

"I'm sorry."

He flinched and looked away, at the wood pile, at the shed, anywhere but at me.

I wasn't finished. "I'm sorry you had to be the responsible one. I'm sorry our father beat you senseless instead of me. I was the oldest, I should have protected you. I should have protected all of you. I'm sorry I was a crap brother. And I want to make it up to you, however I can. Tell me how to make it up to you, Billy."

I watched him swallow, saw his eyes were rimmed with emotion and knew he hated I was there to witness it.

I took a step back, giving us both space, and held my hands out, palms up, beseeching. "Tell me what to do."

CHAPTER TWENTY-ONE

"Don't grieve. Anything you lose comes round in another form."

— RUMI

~Jethro~

"I PROMISED **DAVE** you'd have Sienna home before eight, so no driving to Hawk's Field and making out in the car."

"Cletus," I warned, wrapping my arms around Sienna from behind and pulling her back against my chest. I couldn't be too irritated with Cletus. He was the reason Sienna had come over at all—him, and his meddling.

The evening had gone from fine to good, good to fantastic, fantastic to unpleasant, and unpleasant to miraculous.

Billy and I had returned to the deck together. We weren't holding hands or singing Kumbaya, but we weren't tossing insults at each other either.

No one remarked on Billy's storming off. Dessert was served, during which Billy made a point to sit next to Sienna and apologize like a gentleman. He also laughed at all her jokes. Although he avoided my gaze for the remainder of the evening, I knew things between us must've shifted because he'd told a story about us two as kids.

We'd broken into Mr. Tanner's junkyard to steal toilet seat lids. We'd covered them with Saran Wrap and placed them in public restrooms. Everybody was laughing, me most of all. I'd forgotten about the incident. We were close as kids, before all the bad that comes with being a teenager and wanting mischief of a more destructive kind.

It was good to remember, and it was good he hadn't forgotten.

Now we were gathered on the front porch. Cletus, Billy, Beau, Roscoe, Drew, and Ashley were off to the jam session at the community center. Duane and Jess were off someplace else. I was fixing to drive Sienna back to her place. I didn't think Green Valley was ready for Sienna Diaz to show up at a jam session. Not yet. But it was an occasion to work toward.

"Now, let me finish, Jethro," Cletus protested my interruption. "It's not polite to cut people off when they're in the middle of a thought. As I was saying, don't go to Hawk's Field, that's too long a drive. Go to Duane and Jessica's love nest down the road, over by Wright's Ridge. No one knows about that place and I bet Duane keeps the sheets clean."

Jess winked at me and said, "We both do and you're welcome."

While Duane grumbled, "Thanks, Cletus. Now everyone knows about it."

"Not everyone," Cletus said with an air of obliviousness. "I haven't told Jessica's brother Jackson about it." Turning to Sienna, Cletus took her hand and placed a kiss on the back of it. "Thank you for coming, Ms. Diaz. I hope you plan on returning soon."

"Thank you, Cletus. I'll be happy to return anytime I'm invited."

"You're always invited," I murmured in her ear, causing her to tilt her head reflexively as I tickled her neck with my beard. Her body shivered, just a subtle tremble, but it was enough to remind me of how very close I'd come to taking her against a tree.

For the record, I'd been very close.

Finally releasing her hand, Cletus noted conversationally, "If you come next Wednesday, I'll let you try my sausage."

I gathered a breath for patience and squeezed Sienna's waist.

"Here we go," Drew said as he swapped a knowing look with my sister.

Meanwhile, Beau rolled his eyes and released a disgusted snort. "Not this again."

"Cletus's famous sausage is famous," Jess added helpfully, her eyebrows bouncing. She was already giggling.

Not missing a beat, Sienna asked, "How do you make it? Do you bake it?"

"No way. The heat isn't right. In order for the sausage to mature, it needs the right type and application of heat. It needs heat on all sides, and wet heat is best."

"You are the worst," Billy said, though his mouth hitched on one side.

"This joke never gets old." Jess was now laughing so hard she'd gripped her stomach, tears leaking from her eyes.

"It does when you have to hear it every month for ten years," Duane complained, but couldn't quite manage a scowl.

"My sausage is no joke." Cletus frowned, wagging his finger through the air like *we* were all juveniles.

"So you grill it," Sienna supplied, moving the conversation back on track.

"That's right."

"Good." She nodded once, sounding thoughtful. "In that case, I insist you taste my thighs and breasts."

These words, so calmly and earnestly spoken, rendered us all speechless.

Even Cletus.

I do believe we stared at Sienna in a collective state of paralyzed suspension, no one quite knowing how to react to her offer.

I felt her shoulders shake, so I shifted to the side, wanting to catch her expression. Her irresistible dimples flashed in full force and she giggled as she explained, "I have a great mojo chicken recipe. We can grill the chicken and sausage together." Then to Cletus she said, "It'll help with the wet heat."

I looked to the heavens, hidden by the porch ceiling. "God, thank you for sending me this woman."

Meanwhile, Cletus blinked once as though startled, but then a slow grin spread over his typically solemn features.

Beau, holding his hand over his heart, took the bait. "Sienna, I would be honored to taste your thighs and breasts."

I shot him a warning glare. "Don't you say that to her." But I couldn't keep my face straight either.

"What? What did I say?" Beau tried to sound and look affronted. "I was talking about her chicken. Obviously."

Cletus's grin had grown into an immense smile as his gaze moved over my woman with plain appreciation. "Well played, Ms. Diaz. Well played."

In fact, everyone was either smiling or laughing. I glanced at each of my younger brothers and my sister, trying to remember the last time we'd all been together *and* laughing. Last Christmas came pretty close. Before that, it had been a few days before our momma died. She'd requested we tell her jokes, so we did our best to be funny for her.

This was different.

Different because no one was on their best behavior. No one was pretending for the sake of the others. Every one of us were just ourselves. We were enjoying each other and our growing family—Drew, Jess, and now hopefully Sienna.

I couldn't help but think it was a perfect moment.

And then, as usual, when things were better than good, I couldn't help but think I didn't deserve to be a part of it.

* * *

"I have to admit, I was hoping you'd take me to Hawk's Field or Jess and Duane's love nest," Sienna said on a sigh as soon as we pulled onto the gravel circle around Bandit Lake.

Her words put a smile on my face. "I could turn around."

Sienna sighed again. "No. I have an early flight tomorrow. I have to be up and at the airport by 4:00 a.m."

"Where are you going?" I knew she had a trip as I'd overheard people on set talking about her leaving for the weekend.

"I have a meeting in L.A. about a script I finished a few weeks ago. They're already moving forward with the casting. It's a quick trip, I'll be back on Sunday night." She frowned at Hank's place as we pulled into the drive. "Will you call me? While I'm gone?"

The edge of vulnerability I heard made me want to hold her close and reassure her with slow, deliberate kisses. Problem was, if I held her close I'd be telling myself a few kisses weren't enough. I'd want a taste of her breasts and thighs, and I wasn't referring to her mojo chicken recipe.

"Of course." I slid her an easy smile, then handed her my unlocked phone. "Type in your number."

I walked around the truck to her door as she programmed her contact info. When I opened her door, she took my hand and allowed me to help her down, entwining our fingers and keeping hold of my phone.

"We need someplace with good light," she said distractedly, frowning at the darkness of early evening. "Come up here on the porch."

I let her tug me behind her and lead me up the stairs. She was on a mission and from my place behind her I was graced with a great view of her ass and legs. With each swish of her skirt I was reminded that her stockings ended halfway up her thighs. And that reminded me of touching her skin.

By the time we made it to the porch and she flipped on the overhead lights, I'd forgotten she had my phone. Sienna turned, opened her mouth to tell me something, but I stopped her by capturing her bottom lip with my teeth.

Her breath hitched.

Her eyes widened.

Her body tensed.

I liked that I'd surprised her, could taste it in the air between us.

I licked her lip and slipped my arm around her waist, gripping a handful of her ass. I needed the flavor of her on my tongue and the softness of her body beneath my grip. I wasn't going to lift her skirt on the porch, but I could show her how much I wanted to.

Sienna moaned, long lashes drifting shut, relaxing against me while she swept her tongue out to invite me in. She arched, her body stretching along mine, pressing her tits to my chest and her rounded ass into my palm. Everywhere our bodies met, heat spread like wildfire. Spikes of cold and hot traveled up my spine and down my legs, causing my hips to roll in an instinctive rhythm.

Pulling her mouth from mine, Sienna said on a gasp, "Jethro, this is such a bad idea."

I was about to ask her if she wanted me to stop when she dug her fingers into my scalp and brought my mouth to her neck. "Don't stop."

Her contradicting messages had me smiling against her skin. It may have been a bad idea, making out on the front porch of Hank Weller's cabin for anyone to see. Well, anyone passing by—which no one ever did —or her guards to stumble upon—which was more likely. But I didn't want to let her go.

"I want to touch your heat." I nipped the underside of her jaw, telling her what I wanted to do but couldn't presently make a reality. Not yet. "Slide my fingers inside."

"Holy shit I love your accent," she breathed out in a rush, more like *holyshitIloveyouraccent*. "Say something else."

"What do you want me to say?"

"Anything! Anything that makes you hot."

"What about making you hot?"

"I'm guessing anything that makes you hot will also make me hot."

"Fine then, I want to leave love bites here." I palmed her breast and massaged, rubbing my thumb in a slow circle around her nipple. I wanted to suck her skin between my teeth, and soothe the sting with my tongue. "I want to feel you beneath me, panting, moaning . . ."

My face was still buried in her neck, my fingers pulling aside the edge of her shirt to expose the skin of her shoulder, when I heard a soft click.

I stiffened, a new kind of adrenaline—the kind laced with frustration and dread—pumped through my veins. I immediately lifted my head, searching for the source of the sound. Preparing to smash both the cameras and the heads of any voyeurs lurking nearby, my initial sweep revealed no one but us.

Sienna was watching me with a dazed, but sublimely happy expression. And her arm was raised to one side, the screen of the phone facing us. Set to camera mode.

It took me near a full minute before I comprehended that Sienna had used my cell to snap a picture.

"What did you—"

"Look. I'm going to make this my avatar on your phone." She caught her bottom lip between her teeth and gave me a naughty grin, then showed me the screen. It was a picture of us making out, her head thrown back, her neck and shoulder exposed, and it was very, very hot. Sienna continued on a seductive whisper, "So every time I call . . ."

I shook my head, both loving and hating her idea. "You are so bad."

"If I'm so bad, then why are you smiling, Ranger?"

I stole another kiss, rolling my hips against hers because I now knew she liked it, waited until I felt her body tense with urgency, then pulled away and snatched my phone from her fingers.

Walking backward, I enjoyed watching her chest rise and fall with heavy breaths, liked how her eyes were clouded and hungry. Grinning, I left her on the porch and tossed my answer over my shoulder as I strolled away. "Because you're also very, very good."

* * *

I WAS IN trouble.

My cell phone company alerted me late Sunday afternoon that I'd nearly used up all my text messages for the entire month. I suspected the seventy-five or so texts I'd exchanged with Sienna since Friday night were the cause.

So I called and upgraded to the unlimited plan.

But that's not why I was in trouble.

I was in trouble because I've never been the text-messaging sort. I figure, you got something to say and you expect me to pay attention, it better be important. If it's important, you call or stop by.

It took just three minutes and one quick exchange with Sienna on Saturday morning for me to change my tune.

Sienna: *What are you doing?*
Jethro: *Cutting buttresses for the carriage house. You?*
Sienna: *Thinking about you.*

Yep. That's all it took. I read and reread the words for at least a full minute, probably longer. Three words on my phone staring back at me, evidence that what we had between us wasn't one-sided.

Two hundred twelve messages and thirty-six hours later, I was in deep, drinking the text-messaging moonshine and waiting for my next fix. Of course it helped that every time she sent a text I got an eyeful of the avatar she'd set next to her name. Plus, she was just as irresistible via phone as she was in person.

Sienna: *If you re-arrange the letters of Jethro, you can spell 'Hot Jer'*
Sienna: *Also 'OJ Reth', 'Thor Je', and 'JT Hero' All of which would make an excellent name for a DJ.*
Jethro: *Whereas yours spells 'A sin' with 'ne' left over.*
Sienna: *FYI mine also spells 'insane'*
Sienna: *So watch out!*
Sienna: ;-)

I chuckled, covering my mouth with my hand. Throughout the day she'd sent various pictures of herself doing funny things. In one she'd posed with a guy on Hollywood Boulevard who was dressed like Smash-Boy, both of them making angry faces, with the caption: *"You make Smash angry when you don't send shirtless pictures."*

We'd been doing this since she left, sending dumb stuff back and forth or just conversing about our day.

Jethro: *Insane and Sienna... That's quite a coincidence.*
Sienna: *I often wonder if my parents did it on purpose.*
Jethro: *What time do you get in tonight?*
Sienna: *Past midnight.*
Jethro: *Do you want me to pick you up?*
Sienna: *No. Get your sleep.*
Sienna: *And dream of me.*
Sienna: *Naked.*
Sienna: *I mean: you should sleep naked. And dream of me.*
Jethro: *But not you naked?*
Sienna: *If we're both naked then I want details!*

We also texted about our families. She had a large one too, three sisters and two brothers, and they sounded like fun. Getting ahead of myself—again—I liked the idea of our kids having cousins on both sides, lots of aunts and uncles nearby and lots to visit. Sienna was the youngest and I learned her manager was her oldest sister, Marta.

Sienna: *Send a picture of yourself so I can show Marta.*
Jethro: *No.*
Sienna: *What? WHY??*
Sienna: *I want to tell her about us. I can't tell her if you don't send a picture. She'll want photographic evidence.*
Jethro: *I don't do selfies*
Sienna: *That's not what your brothers said...*
Sienna: *GET IT?*

"What is so funny?"

I glanced up, finding Claire peeping out of the kitchen, an expectant smile on her lips.

It was Sunday afternoon and, as was my habit, I was over at Claire's, checking in to make sure she had everything she needed. As usual, she'd invited me to stay for dinner. As usual, I'd accepted.

"Nothing." I shook my head, slipping my phone in my pocket and resuming my work on her kitchen drawer. I was fixing the roller track.

"You're still smiling," she teased, stepping into the doorway and placing her hands on her hips. "This wouldn't have anything to do with a certain movie star, would it?"

I tossed her my best impression of irritation, but it wasn't very effective seeing as how I was still smiling. "None of your business."

She returned my glare, the effect also lost since she was still smiling. "Come on, Jet. I'm dying here. Cletus said you had her over for dinner?"

"You two girls gossip about anyone else? Or just me?"

"Stop being coy. I'm excited for you." Claire sounded exasperated. "Cletus seems to approve, and if Cletus approves then she's got to be great."

"She is great," I said without thinking, the words slipping out easy as breathing.

"Then tell me about her. How did you meet? How serious is it? What'll you do when the movie wraps up?"

I was with her until the last question, and then I felt my smile slip. "We haven't talked about what happens when the movie wraps, but we'll figure it out, I guess."

"You guess? Meaning you'll still be seeing each other after?"

"I hope so."

Now that was an understatement.

"I'm so happy for you." The quiet sincerity in her tone had me looking up from the drawer and into her big sapphire-blue eyes. "I'm so happy to see you finally putting yourself out there. I was starting to worry you'd never fill that house with kids."

"Now hold on." I stood, picking up the fixed drawer and scooting past her into the kitchen. "This thing just started. Ain't nothing serious yet."

"Come on, give me some credit."

I didn't have to be looking at Claire to know she'd just rolled her eyes.

"We're taking things slow."

She snorted. "Well, now I *know* it's serious. You have to promise me you'll bring her over for dinner. I promise not to embarrass you too much," Claire said, and then added under her breath, "though I might embarrass myself."

I smiled, but kept my back to her so she wouldn't see. "What about you?"

"Don't start with me. Maybe I've got plans you don't know about yet."

I fit the drawer in its slot, rolling it back and forth a few times to make sure the movement was smooth before turning to tease my friend. "No, no, no. If I'm taking chances with my heart, maybe it's time for you to do the same."

She folded her hands under her chin and blinked several times. "Oh my apple pie. Jethro Winston, taking chances with his heart. I never thought I'd see the day."

"Very funny. Now why don't you tell me what's going on with you and Billy?"

Claire stiffened. Her hands dropped and her smile dimmed. "What did you say?"

"You heard me. Why would you tell Billy that you and I were involved?"

Her smile vanished entirely. A flash of remorse and guilt passed over her features, almost too quick for me to see before she succeeded in masking her emotions. Claire was real good at this, hiding her feelings. It had been a survival technique, learned over the course of a bitter childhood.

"I never told him that." Her tone was flat and defensive.

"Did you ever strongly imply that we were together?" I meant to tease her about this. However, based on her reaction, I was careful to keep my tone light but devoid of playfulness.

She said nothing, just glared at me with blue eyes that held so much wisdom it physically hurt to look at her. I knew she'd been ill-treated as a child. She was the only daughter of Razor, the president of the Iron Wraiths motorcycle club. Saying he'd been a bad father would be like calling Cletus mildly unconventional. She'd escaped the club when she was a teenager and had married Ben at eighteen.

Ben had treated her right, but I knew his gentleness could never make up for the years of abuse that came before.

I tried a different approach; I could usually charm her if the need arose. "If you didn't imply it, did you infer it?"

She cracked a regretful smile, just a small one, and turned away. "I'm sorry."

"You're sorry for what?"

"I'm sorry if I've caused any problems between you and your brother."

I stared at her back for a long time, watched her shoulders rise and fall as I waited. She said nothing. I swear, this woman was as stubborn as a boulder.

"Claire, I don't know what's going on, or what happened between you and Billy, but—"

"Nothing happened between me and . . ." she paused, rubbed her eyes with the base of her palms and took a deep breath, "between me and him, not for a long time. Not since before Ben. Not since we were teenagers."

Not since we were teenagers . . . This was news to me.

I crossed my arms, seeing my good friend in a new light. "Well now, you got me feeling like I deserve some answers. I didn't know anything had ever happened between you and Billy."

Her shoulders fell and she shook her head. "It was so long ago, Jethro. I'm sorry if my silence on the matter caused you trouble, I truly am. I didn't infer or imply. I promise. I just . . ." She lifted a hand to her chest and rubbed her ribs just beneath her heart, turning her head to give me her profile, like she couldn't bring herself to look at me. "I just didn't deny anything when he asked."

"And what gives him the right to ask?"

"Exactly." Now she did look at me, her eyes hard and her whisper fierce. "He doesn't have a right."

CHAPTER TWENTY-TWO

"The greatest hazard of all, losing one's self, can occur very quietly in the world, as if it were nothing at all."

— SØREN KIERKEGAARD, THE SICKNESS UNTO
DEATH

~Sienna~

JETHRO DIDN'T SEND me a selfie.

Instead he sent a picture of him and a gigantic black bear in the background. The bear was in a cage and was asleep or had been tranquilized. Jethro was crouching down next to the cage, but at a safe distance, not looking at the camera. My heart gave a happy leap, tingly pinpricks of warmth dancing beneath my skin. I smiled wistfully, at least it felt wistful on my lips.

He was so handsome to me. He was the handsomest.

Jethro: *This is the only picture of myself I have on my phone. It'll have to do.*
Sienna: *You have no selfies on your phone? Seriously? None at all?*

Jethro: *Nope.*

Sienna: *You are the only human in the world with a smart phone and no selfies.*

Jethro: *I'm pretty sure Drew has none on his phone either.*

Sienna: *Drew doesn't count. Ashley said he reads poetry to her. He gets a free pass.*

Jethro: *Is this your way of telling me to read poetry to you?*

Sienna: *No! Not at all!*

Sienna: *I want you to read poetry to me. this is my way of telling you to read poetry to me.*

"Who are you texting?" Marta asked from behind the couch, startling me.

I glanced over the back of the sofa where I was sitting. She was at my shoulder reading my screen. I immediately pressed the phone to my chest.

"Marta. Don't read my text messages."

"Why can't I see? Who is it?"

"You can't see because it's an invasion of privacy, you weirdo."

She gave me a patronizing look. "You know you have no privacy."

Marta was referring to my Cloud backup account being hacked three years ago and how hundreds of my pictures had been made public. Unfortunately for the gossip pages, the most risqué image they found was me in a two-piece bathing suit one of my college friends had taken and texted to me. The media—we're talking CNN, Fox News, MSNBC, et. al.—had spent months debating whether or not my waistline was healthy or attractive.

Meanwhile, I was turning down dicks—both figurative and literal dicks—left and right. I should note that some of the literal dicks weren't attached to figurative dicks, which was nice. I went on a number of promising dates, but work always got in the way, and then my movies were hitting records. Finding dates with non-figurative dicks became increasingly difficult after that.

I don't know what the media ultimately decided about my chances of dying alone and sexually starved because my tummy lacked a six-pack. I was too busy being happy with my body and making blockbusters.

You know, crying myself to sleep on my big pile of money.

"Just because it's happened in the past," I continued to clutch the phone to my chest, "invasion of privacy is never okay. Would you want me looking at your personal messages?"

"No. But I'm not a household name. You can't expect the same level of privacy as everyone else. People are interested in you. If you want to maintain this level of success, you have to expect some invasion of privacy. You know this."

We'd had this conversation one hundred times, but it had never started with her being the one spying.

"Yes. I understand that. But you're not just my manager. You're my sister, and I expect more from you."

Marta had the decency to look mildly ashamed. "You're right. I'm sorry. I shouldn't have looked. Now, are you going to tell me who you've been texting?"

I smiled, unable to stop myself, because I'd been texting Jethro.

Too happy to think about how Marta might react, I announced, "I met someone."

Marta's eyebrows bounced high on her forehead. "In Tennessee?"

"Yes!"

She looked at me for a long moment, her eyes losing focus like she was going through a file drawer inside her brain. "Is it Tom? Are you two back together?"

"No. No, no, no."

"Ken? Because that could work, especially with the promotional tour for the film coming up."

"No, Marta. My guy isn't an actor."

"Is it Joe?"

"Who?"

"The junior executive producer. You met him at the casting event."

"No." I had no idea who she was talking about. I knew the producing team, because they'd stopped by the set last week, and none of them were named Joe. "I don't even. No. It's nothing like that. He's a park ranger."

"Who is?"

"My guy. He's a wildlife ranger. He works at the national park." I scrolled through my text messages until I found the picture of him next to the cage and showed it to my sister.

She stared at the image like it confused her, and then suddenly she laughed.

I watched her loss of composure for a full minute, because now I was confused. I even checked the picture to make sure I hadn't zoomed in on the bear. Nope. The screen displayed Jethro's handsomest face.

"Oh, Sienna. You're hilarious." She was holding her stomach, shaking her head.

"What? Why is this funny?" For once I didn't like the sound of someone laughing.

Marta wiped her eyes, her laughter becoming short bursts of chuckles. "What?"

"I said, why is this funny?"

My sister blinked at me, waited, like she expected me to deliver a punchline. When I didn't, all humor fled from her features. "Oh my God, you're serious." She grabbed the phone and looked at the screen again, her face grimacing in horror. "You've got to be kidding me with this. Oh . . . Oh my God. What is this picture?"

She turned the phone toward me and pointed at Jethro's avatar, the photo I'd taken with his phone of us making out on the porch. He'd sent it to me so I could make it his avatar as well.

"It's us. Kissing. You see, Marta, when a boy likes a girl, it's this thing they do with their lips—"

"He is all over you. Who took this picture?"

"I did."

"You did?"

"Yes. I took it with his phone and then he texted it to me."

She stared at me blankly, in a way that reminded me of a bomb about to detonate. But when she spoke she did so in an eerily calm tone.

"You're telling me that the park ranger has this picture of the two of you on his phone? And you took it?"

"That's right."

Marta stared at me like I'd lost my mind. "Are you trying to ruin your career? What is going on here? Do you need a vacation so badly that you're sabotaging yourself?"

"You need to calm down." I swallowed past a thick knot of something uncomfortable in my throat. Marta's assessment was mostly wrong, but part of it rang with uncomfortable truth. Maybe part of me—a very small part of me—saw Jethro and a life with him as an escape from everything I hated about being a celebrity. Maybe.

But so what? If being with a man I adored gave me the impetus to change my life for the better, gave me the strength to plot a new course, then where was the harm in that?

"Calm down? When he sells it to TMZ along with all the sordid—fake—details of your love affair, don't expect me to clean this up."

I snatched the phone away, a weird mixture of embarrassed and angry heat slithering up my neck. "What is wrong with you?"

"What is wrong with me? You think you're dating a park ranger. In Tennessee! How do you think people are going to feel about that?"

"Who cares?"

"You should care."

"No. I shouldn't. I absolutely shouldn't care." And I believed this. My mantra since the success of my first film had been: Never care about media opinion. Work hard. Do what's right.

But Marta cared. And more frequently than I wanted to admit, her caring had the habit of affecting my career choices. Her caring was why I hadn't yet taken a vacation. Ultimately it was my decision, but the thought of letting her down had been unbearable.

Until now. Until I had something other than myself to fight for.

I wasn't sure whether I was more concerned about disappointing my eldest sister or my manager. Sometimes I forgot who she was most to me. Perhaps she forgot, too.

"How can you say that?" She looked like she wanted to strangle me.

"Because if I allowed myself to care about what the talking heads were saying, I would be horribly unhappy and nowhere near as successful as I am now."

"That's ridiculous," she ground out angrily, marching away from me toward her desk.

"It's not ridiculous. It's true." I followed her across the room. "They call me the fat funny lady, Marta. I'm plus-sized at a size fourteen, which —whatever, I don't care about the label, plus-sized is fun-sized—but this business hates that I'm average-sized and successful. They hate that I'm a woman and write funny movies."

"We are not average-sized for film, Sienna. We are big. We are fat. Pretending we're not fat doesn't make it so."

I ignored her spiteful comment. My sister had always struggled against her natural shape and I knew her size—our size—was a sore spot for her. I'd always hoped to show her through embracing my gifts that she didn't need to measure herself against society's silly mandates.

"But we are average for the US. Size fourteen is the average. You can't read an article about me without the writer bringing up my audacity for not caring, criticizing me for not starving myself. So you think I should listen to that crap?"

Marta lifted her voice over mine before I finished speaking. "You think you're successful because you don't care? Well guess what, you're successful because *I care*. Because *I* push you. *I* am the only reason you are taken seriously. You would be nothing if it weren't for me."

I flinched, my ears ringing in the sudden silence. I couldn't be more surprised if she'd slapped my face.

Seeing my expression, or maybe realizing what she'd just said, Marta covered her hands with her face and released a loud exhale. "I'm sorry. That came out wrong."

I ignored her apology and presented the facts as I saw them. "You're wrong. I am successful because I don't care about media opinion. If I cared then I wouldn't be writing comedy film scripts, because women aren't as funny as men."

"Sienna—"

"I wouldn't be acting in film, because actresses are a size zero and five foot two."

"I'm sorry—"

"I wouldn't have won an Academy Award for best actress, because only white women—usually named Meryl Streep—win that award. And never for a comedy role."

"You've made your point."

"Every step of the way I'd been scolded for being happy with myself. How *dare* I be happy with who I am, my size, the color of my skin, that I can make both men and women laugh. So you think I'm going to let you or anyone else make me feel ashamed about Jethro?"

"His name is Jethro?" Her tone held a worried edge. "Really? Couldn't you at least have messed around with a park ranger named Chris or Carter? It has to be a Jethro?"

I slow blinked because I was angry. I waited a full five seconds, simmering in my temper until I had control over it, before responding with forced calmness. "Yes. It has to be Jethro. And I love his name. And we're not messing around. We're falling for each other. I'm halfway in love with him already."

Marta looked at me, just looked at me, her expression one of frustrated helplessness and begrudging acceptance. So I looked at her in return, daring her to push me on this. I understood she believed she had my best interest at heart. But she didn't. My best interests, my career, my success? Of course, yes.

My heart? Obviously not.

"Fine. We will . . . I guess we'll talk about this later." My sister glanced at her watch, then leveled me with a dispassionate glare. "You'll be late for your flight if you don't leave soon."

I met her stare straight on. We engaged in an old-fashioned stare down. I half expected a tumbleweed to blow across her office.

She broke the silence and eye contact first. "Sienna, it's time for you to go. You can glare at me later."

"Okay. I'll go." I nodded but needed to clarify one point. "However, you should know, the only way we're talking about Jethro later is if you're ready to apologize and be excited for me. Otherwise we're not talking about him at all."

CHAPTER TWENTY-THREE

"I cannot conceive of a greater loss than the loss of one's self-respect."

— MAHATMA GANDHI, FOOLS, MARTYRS,
TRAITORS: THE STORY OF MARTYRDOM IN THE
WESTERN WORLD

~Sienna~

ON MONDAY MORNING, when Jethro picked me up, he was distracted.

And not a good, happy distracted. He was troubled. I sensed it in the way he smiled as he approached the porch, swiftly kissed me good morning when I met him halfway, held my hand tightly as we walked to his truck.

He opened the door for me as usual. I climbed up, worried something new had happened since we'd last texted, something that had him rethinking the progress we'd made on Friday. Unlike all last week, Cletus wasn't present. It was just the two of us. I spotted my Hello Kitty mug in the cup holder, but when I reached for the mug I found it empty.

And so I worried my lip, feeling gun-shy because the last time we'd been alone in the car on the way to the set he'd broken things off.

As soon as Jethro pulled onto the main road I blurted, "If you're going to break up with me again I wish you would just say so, but I wish you wouldn't because—as I've already established—I really like you and think you're making a mistake."

Jethro turned wide, confused eyes on me. "What? What are you talking about?"

"Are you going to call things off again?"

"No . . . why? What happened?"

I hesitated. The argument with my sister happened, but it didn't affect my relationship with Jethro and wasn't really pertinent to this conversation.

Being happy with oneself and pandering to no one was the quickest way to scare the hell out of people. And right now, Marta was scared of me. I endeavored to shrug off the persistent weight of unpleasantness that had been plaguing me since leaving my sister yesterday. She would come around, mostly because I would give her no choice.

I answered honestly. "Nothing happened. Did anything happen with you?"

"Not that I know of."

"So we're still in agreement? We're still a dating couple who are not temporary?"

"That's correct." He grinned like he enjoyed hearing the words out loud.

I released a sigh of relief. "Thank goodness. Because I was about to get Mexican mad."

"What's Mexican mad?"

"Same as regular mad, just with me speaking in Spanish so I could call you an asshole without you knowing. You would suspect, but you wouldn't *know*."

"Oh." He nodded as though digesting this information. "Then why don't you just call it Spanish mad then?"

"Because Mexican Spanish is different than Castilian Spanish— Spanish from Spain. Just like Dominican Spanish is different than Cuban

Spanish, or Venezuelan Spanish, or Costa Rican Spanish. The Spanish I would use to curse you, should the need arise, would be of the Mexican variety."

"Ah, I get it. In Tennessee we have our own way of speaking, idioms that don't make any sense to the rest of the English-speaking world."

"Like what?" I was all ears. I loved this kind of stuff.

"Well, let's see . . ." He shifted in his seat as we stopped at the light, his eyes moving over me. "My momma used to get mad and say, 'Well that just dills my pickle!'"

This made me grin. "Did she really?"

"Yep." Jethro nodded once, a rumbly chuckle making his shoulders shake. "Cletus also says it sometimes."

Now I laughed. "That fits him somehow. My new goal in life is to get your brother to say those words."

"He plays banjo in a band and is real judgmental of people who can't sing. This one time he said, about a fella who was trying to jam with them, 'He couldn't carry a tune in a bucket.'"

I snort laughed. "See that one would translate well in any language. Speaking as someone who can't sing, that's mean, but it's also funny."

"It is mean." Jethro turned his attention back to the road and made a right. "But then, Cletus is kind of mean."

I studied Jethro's profile, thinking about his assessment of his brother. Cletus didn't strike me as mean. Clever, perceptive, odd—yes. Mean? No.

"I don't think he's mean."

Jethro gave me a sideways look. "Yeah, well, you didn't grow up with him. When he was a kid, he was really mean. Used to make other students cry." He paused, obviously lost in a memory, and then added, "He use to make his teachers cry, too."

"But that was when he was younger."

"So?"

"So, don't you think it's a little unfair to judge your siblings now for labels assigned to them when they were kids?"

Jethro's easy smile morphed into a thoughtful one, and he raised an eyebrow at me, like he found this concept intriguing but didn't quite understand enough to agree or disagree with my point.

So I explained. "Growing up, I was the funny one."

"What?"

"I was the clown. That's all I was. My oldest brother was the artist. My other brother was the disappointment. My sister Maya was the beautiful one, and Rena was the smart one. Marta was the serious one. I was the clown."

Now he looked vaguely dismayed. "What does that even mean?"

"It means people expected me to be funny, because I was funny when I was a kid. But they never expected me to be anything else—smart, serious, beautiful, creative, or disappointing—I was just funny. And if I wasn't funny, well then they assumed I wasn't feeling well." I glanced around our surroundings, realized he'd taken us on a detour. "Where are we going?"

He must've been absorbed in our conversation or his resultant thoughts on the matter, because he blinked a few times and glanced at the road like he was surprised by where we were.

"Oh, I wanted to pick up coffee before we went in. We have plenty of time."

"Good plan." Now I understood why my mug had been empty. "Anyplace in particular?"

"Daisy's." He paired the single word with a sly grin.

Immediate and thrilling anticipation had me smiling like an idiot and leaning forward in my seat. "Really?"

"Have you had a doughnut yet?"

I shook my head vehemently. "No. No, I haven't. I've had none of Daisy's doughnuts."

"Then this'll be a treat."

I stopped myself from bouncing in my seat. Since relating my Daisy doughnut fantasy to Jethro some weeks ago, where I imagined he would lick the smudge of frosting from the corner of my mouth, the fantasy had grown more delectably scandalous. Frosting on nipples—both his and mine—may have been involved. It wasn't even about the doughnut or the frosting.

It was the licking, the tasting, the savoring. The idea of him devouring me, him being insatiable for me.

"What about my family?" he asked suddenly.

"What?" I panted, lost in my lusty thoughts.

He shifted in his seat again, his hands opening and closing on the steering wheel. "You've met my siblings. What labels do you think we grew up with?"

A moment was necessary for my brain to switch tracks, but when I did I saw that Jethro was frowning. His usual good-natured temperament had been eclipsed by something dark.

My first instinct was to avoid the question and respond, *I don't know*. Based on what I knew about Jethro—both from him and from others—his label likely hadn't been a good one. It had been unkind, though perhaps well earned.

I took too long to answer. His brow clouded with murky melancholy as his eyes darted to mine. "You can say it."

"I didn't know you growing up."

"But you can guess." Jethro gripped the steering wheel tighter and swallowed; his tone was hollow and quietly demanding as he insisted, "Guess. Please."

I pressed my lips together in a flat line, not wanting to add any more fuel to his fire of perpetual self-recrimination.

So instead I said, "Jethro, labeling kids isn't fair—it doesn't matter if the label is good or bad. It puts them in a box and makes them feel like they have to live inside it."

We were quiet after that, my words hanging between us. He was considering them. As he pulled into the parking lot in front of Daisy's, I was relieved to see his brow clear and a soft smile whisper over his features.

But then he said, "Billy was the responsible one. Cletus was . . . well, he's the odd one. Ashley was the beautiful one. Beau was the charmer. Duane was the quiet one. Roscoe was considered the overachiever, or something like that. And I was the disappointment."

My heart twisted. His words physically hurt me. He may have made bad decisions as a kid, as a teenager, but shaking off a label affixed during childhood was almost impossible.

"You're not a disappointment." I grabbed his hand as soon as he parked, brought it to my lap and cradled it there. "Your family is so proud of you. Most people live up or down to the expectations set by their label. Very few people are able to transcend it."

"I know." He gave me a charming shrug. Both his expression and words were laced with a healthy dose of self-confidence. "I turned it around."

Then he grinned a charming grin.

My mouth parted with surprise and I marveled at this man. "How do you do that?"

"Do what?"

"In one breath you're so negative about yourself, and in the next you're singing your own praises." An astonished laugh tumbled from my lips.

"I'm negative about who I used to be, Sienna. But not who I am now. I admit though, sometimes I don't feel deserving of my own happiness." He turned his hand in mine and threaded our fingers together, bringing my knuckles to his lips. He brushed soft kisses over the backs of my fingers, and when he spoke his words were introspective. "It's frustrating, as you say, having the history of the label. I see it in people, the way they look at me, what they expect. They expect dishonesty. They expect me to be a joke."

I felt compelled to say, "People expect me to be a joke, too."

Jethro gave me a soft, sympathetic smile. "You are more than the jokes you told when you were five, or eight, or thirteen."

"And you are more than the mistakes of your youth. You are more than the label you've been assigned by people who might love you, but don't really know who you are anymore."

His gaze captured mine, heated, and then dropped to my lips. "I suppose it's part of why we seek out a partner. Why we're driven to build a new family, pursue new friendships. There's freedom in being a blank canvas to another person and having some control over what is painted on that canvas."

I studied him in the weighty silence, feeling a kinship that went beyond liking, or even extreme liking. It was a shared understanding that only comes from living through similar experiences.

Jethro had been the disappointment.

I'd been the clown.

Individually we had become more.

But together and with each other, we didn't need to be our labels.

We were free to just be ourselves.

* * *

COFFEE? CHECK.

Doughnuts? Check.

Alone with Jethro in my trailer with the door locked? DOUBLE CHECK!

My call time wasn't until 10:00 a.m., but Jethro had to check the traps before then. If any bears had been caught over the weekend, he needed to haul them out of the cove before midday, before the sun heated the prairie.

Even so, we had at least an hour until he had to leave.

I pushed the chairs out of the way, leaving just a small circular side table in the middle of the space and an expanse of unencumbered carpet. I placed two plates on the table and stood back to survey my work. Jethro lifted his eyebrows at me while I arranged the furniture. He stood off to one side, holding the doughnuts and his own coffee.

"What are you doing?"

"Setting the stage."

"For what?"

"Be quiet. Let me think." I studied the setup and decided it would have to do.

I grabbed the box of doughnuts—he'd procured four, all with icing—and placed one on each plate. I set the remaining two still in the box on the kitchenette table.

"Okay," I grabbed his hand and pulled him over to the small table, motioning for him to sit on the carpet, "let's have doughnuts."

He sat.

Actually, he semi-lounged.

Jethro placed his coffee on the small table and leaned back at an angle on one arm, his long legs stretched out in front of him, crossed at the ankles. My tummy fluttered with excitement as I sat on the floor next to him and picked up the frosted confection. I was going to smudge the corner of my mouth with frosting.

And then he was going to lick it off.

And then we were going to kiss.

And then . . . good things after that. Hopefully including, but not limited to, rolling around and making out on the carpet like teenagers.

Holding Jethro's eyes with mine, which were heavily lidded and hot with interest, I took a small bite, careful to dab the side of my mouth with the frosting.

But then something unexpected happened, and it startled me out of my sexy thoughts.

The doughnut was insanely delicious.

Insanely. Delicious.

It was still warm from the oven, and yet it melted on my tongue. It was sweet, but tempered by a center filled with rich, smooth, bitter high-quality chocolate crème.

Unable to help myself, I moaned, "Oh my God."

Jethro's lips quirked to the side, his eyes on my mouth, and—right on cue—he leaned forward. "You have something just there."

I ignored him, swatting his hand away, and took another bite, speaking around a mouthful of heaven on earth. "Holy shit, this is the best thing I've ever tasted."

Jethro rolled his lips between his teeth, his eyes bright with laughter, and watched me devour the doughnut.

I continued to moan with each bite, licking and sucking my fingers until it was gone. Completely preoccupied, I didn't notice the shift in his mood at first. I was just about to lick off the last of the crème when he caught my wrist, forcing my attention to him. My protest died on my lips as the weight and intensity of his gaze hit me all at once. He looked hungry.

To be more precise, he looked ravenous.

Jethro brought my finger to his lips and sucked it into his mouth, his tongue darting out to lick the junction between my index and middle finger. The light, slick touch sent unexpected trembles to my lower belly and pulled a soft whimper from the back of my throat.

"As I was saying," his darkened gaze drifted hotly from my eyes to my lips, and he used my hand as leverage to tug me forward, "you have something . . ."

He didn't finish the sentence. Instead he licked the corner of my mouth and then delved his tongue ardently between my lips, caressing mine hungrily. Jethro's grip on me shifted. His arm came around my waist, supporting me, while my hands cupped his jaw.

In a controlled and graceful movement, he rolled me onto my back, held himself above my body, and claimed my mouth. I felt his fingers on my thigh, sliding the hem of my skirt higher, skimming fingertips between my legs. Instinctively, I arched and strained, wanting to be touched, needing him to touch me.

"Undo your shirt," he ordered, pulling his mouth from mine and fastening it to my neck.

"Why don't you—?"

"Because I'll rip it off."

Well okay then.

With eager fingers, I undid the buttons while he pressed his thigh between my legs, sliding against me. The rhythm was both intoxicating and frustrating. I felt empty, greedy for his skin.

When I finished with my top I set to work on his buttons, but he batted my hands away, his mouth moving to the center of my breast, groaning as he sucked me through the black mesh of my bra and into his mouth. Mindlessly, my hips rocked, searching for friction, for his touch.

I don't know if it was the doughnut—*food of the gods*—or the sexy, sexy man above me, but I was already hovering on the edge of my orgasm.

"Please," I panted, grabbing his hand from where he drew light circles on my thigh, and pressing it to the front of my panties.

His eyes blazed a trail from my breasts, over my exposed throat to my lips. He slipped his fingers into the lace waistband with achingly slow and measured movements, stroking a tight circle around my center while bending his head and licking my lips.

"Please," I said again, chasing his mouth as he withdrew, his teeth and tongue skillfully lavishing my jaw, neck, and shoulder with biting kisses.

"You are so lovely," he said, his voice a deep growl. "And these sounds you're making . . ." He paused as though he were listening.

I hadn't realized, but I was making sounds: soft, impassioned hitches in my breathing.

Our eyes clashed, his were darker than usual. "These desperate little moans, I'll never get enough of them, never get enough of you."

I began to spiral, holding his wrist as I curved my body toward his expert touch, unable to control or stifle my cries of ecstasy.

That's right. *Ecstasy.*

Pure, one million percent solid-gold ecstasy.

He felt so good, I forgot how percentages worked.

And he must've known what he was doing, because as soon as the first wave of ecstasy receded, he stroked me again, hitting all the right spots, faster and harder than before.

I lost my mind a little after that, lost even more control of my response, lost my ability to temper the volume of my enthusiasm.

In retrospect, I remembered grabbing fistfuls of his shirt, the sound of his name tumbling over and over from my lips, how his pants-clad leg slid against my bare thighs, how he captured my mouth at my peak and gave me a hot, crushing, devouring kiss.

And then I was falling slowly, drifting on a cloud back to earth, being wrapped in his strong arms, gathered to his chest. He pressed his lips to my forehead in a cherishing kiss as I clung to him, feeling every inch claimed, though he was still fully clothed.

Jethro holding me was ecstasy.

That's right. *Ecstasy.*

That's what it was.

CHAPTER TWENTY-FOUR

"As long as I could hear his voice, I was quite lost, quite blind, quite outside my own self."

— ANAÏS NIN

~Jethro~

HOLDING SIENNA WAS hard.

No.

Scratch that.

I was hard while holding Sienna. Holding Sienna was heavenly.

That's better.

I smoothed my hand up and down her back, down the silky skin of her lush thighs, and over her magnificently rounded backside, sadly still covered in lace panties. Her satin-soft curves beneath my fingers did very little to help the rigid situation south of my belt. But that's all right. It fed a different addiction.

Now that I'd touched her, watched and felt her come, I was mentally rearranging my schedule for the rest of my life. I was going to do this every day. Touching her now, after her gratifyingly loud and spectacularly animated release, calmed me even as it stoked a frenzied fire of need. I wanted to touch her everywhere. And for always.

"What are you thinking about?" she asked, snuggling closer and fitting her leg between mine. The action gave me more access to her thigh, specifically the innermost expanse of soft skin.

"I'm probably going to be a very tactile boyfriend," I said against her forehead, taking advantage of her new position by trailing the back of my knuckles between her legs.

Her breath hitched.

"How do you feel about public displays of affection?" I asked.

Sienna responded on a whisper. "Are you talking about holding hands or something that could get us arrested?"

"Someplace in between."

"Jethro, if you keep doing what you're doing, I don't care if it's doggy style on the red carpet, just as long as it's with you."

Well now, that conjured all kinds of pleasant images.

I know it's not polite to remark on the status of a lady's panties, but my woman was wet and supple, swollen and aroused. My thoughts naturally shifted to how very satisfying the feel of her would be, right this minute, just as she was.

Especially given the state of my head, right this minute.

"Fuck," I groaned.

"Okay," she said.

I laughed.

Removing my fingers, reluctantly, from between her legs, I grabbed a handful of her backside. "I'm going to kiss this."

She giggled and nipped at my neck. "You should. We should start every day with you kissing my ass—both figuratively and literally."

I laughed again, kissing her forehead and tightening my arm around her shoulders.

But then she said, "I'm serious. This is me officially petitioning that you and I start sleeping together. How do we make that happen?"

I tensed, because to say I liked the idea—a lot—would be an understatement. But I was trying to be careful with this thing between us.

Clearing my throat, I proceeded with caution. "So, I build things. I work with wood."

"I'd like to work with your wood," she mumbled, and I knew she was trying to make a joke. I heard vulnerability in the joke, the way she couldn't quite meet my eyes. She was clearly nervous; perhaps feeling like she'd revealed too much with her official petition, been too forward.

I leaned back so she could see me smile, but also so I could see her and gauge her reaction as I spoke. "As a carpenter I know for a fact, if you want something to last, you have to build it to last. If we wanted to establish something lasting, we can't build our foundation on just the physical."

"You mean lust."

I smirked at the disappointment in her tone. "Yeah, I guess I do. Even if we have enough lust between us to build a city."

This earned me a quick smile, but she continued to press, "We don't have to do anything, we could just sleep. Cuddle."

"What do you think the chances of us *just sleeping* would be? Because I don't think they're very good."

"I'm up for the challenge."

"I'm not."

Another quick, surprised grin claimed her features, revealing dimples and brightening her eyes. "So you find me irresistible?"

I answered immediately, with blunt honesty, "Yes."

She grinned wider, then tried to wipe the excited happiness from her face and replace it with solemnity. "I believe in you, Jethro. I think you can resist. Don't sell yourself short." Now she was teasing.

"You're wrong." I wasn't teasing, and pressure was building at the base of my skull, because I was about to admit to something that might send her running.

She continued to tease. "I sleep in footie pajamas. I own three pairs. No one is sexy in footie pajamas."

"Sienna—"

"And I have a variety of green beauty masks I can wear to bed; I think one is even called *repellant*. Is smells like wet dog."

"I haven't been with a woman in five years."

"And I-I," she stuttered, stopped, and stared at me. Blinking and edging an inch away, Sienna's lips parted and her eyes went wide. "What? What did you say?"

"I haven't been with anyone in five years."

"You mean you haven't been in a relationship for five years?"

I searched her expression as I spoke, looking for some sign as to how much of a big deal this would be for her. "Well, that's true, too. I haven't had a girl since high school, to be honest. But what I meant is I haven't, uh, slept with anyone in over five years."

"Whoa! Whoa . . ." Her first *whoa* was an inhale, a gasp. And the second *whoa* was an exhale, a sigh.

I watched her, keeping my gaze steady. Though her dark eyes were expressive, I was having a hard time getting a read on her thoughts.

Abruptly, she removed her leg from between mine, pulled down her skirt to cover herself, and demanded, "But why? Why would you do that? Not only to yourself but to all the single ladies?"

"Because I didn't want to hurt anybody." Propping myself up on my elbow, I cupped her cheek, pushing my fingers into her hair and caressing the smooth, gold skin of her neck. "I had a problem, treating women like they were disposable."

"Were you a sex addict?"

I frowned at her question, having not considered that possibility before, but then dismissed it. "No. I don't think so. I was addicted to the lifestyle, not one thing in particular. Though addicted might not be the right word. More like, it was all I knew. Using women had been part of the lifestyle of the club. When I left, I had to break all those patterns and habits. I stopped drinking, messing around, stealing cars, lying, cheating, conning. I went to school, to work, and kept my ass at home every night until new habits formed. Better habits. Until I trusted myself."

"Do you drink now?"

"Yes. But not to excess like before."

"When did you start going out again? At night?"

"A few years back. But not every night, and not to places where trouble would find me."

She studied me from where she lay on the carpet, her brow pensive. "You drink in moderation, you go out in moderation, so why not date in moderation?"

"Because drinking and going out only have ramifications for me. Dating in moderation, as you put it, comes with the possibility of hurting someone else."

Something clicked behind her gaze. "You didn't want to lead someone on."

I nodded, because that was exactly right.

"You mean to tell me you haven't met a woman you liked in the last five years?"

"I've met plenty of women I liked, but I'd always decide to wait a little longer. When push came to shove, I found it plenty easy to walk away."

Her pretty eyes widened until they were almost round. "But not with me?"

"Not with you."

"Why?"

I searched her gaze, found myself lost in her eyes.

Getting the sense I was taking too long to answer her question, I finally just admitted, "I honestly don't know. It's everything about you, I guess. Everything together that makes you impossible to leave, impossible to forget."

And that was the truth.

Her cheeks warmed with a pleased blush at my words. "Jethro." She said my name tenderly, lifted her chin as though to kiss me, but I evaded her mouth.

"There's more."

"More?" Sienna's mahogany gaze widened again, her lush lips forming circle and a pout. I had to bite my lip to keep from biting hers.

"Yes." I nodded firmly, gritting my teeth and steeling my resolve. "I decided a long time ago that I wouldn't . . . that the next woman I made love to would be my wife."

She stared at me, her eyes growing impossibly wider. Seeing I was serious, she jerked backward and sputtered, "But . . . but . . . what about . . ." Apparently having trouble forming the words, Sienna motioned to her body with stilted movements then blurted, "What do you call what we just did?"

I tried to keep a smile from my face because she was just too fucking cute. "Third base."

She growled, lifted up on her elbow, and jabbed a finger at my chest. "Well I call that making sweet, sweet love, buster."

"You're right, that was sweet. But I'm talking about a home run and you know it."

I kept my tone reasonable and gentle. She was teetering on the edge of real anger, her eyes flashing fire. I reached for her. She began to draw away but I held on.

Bringing her palm to my heart I laid it all out. "I'm falling for you, Sienna. I have been since I helped you down from my truck that first day when you were lost. You touched my hand and that was it, whatever you want to call it. I was hooked. I am hooked. It might be an arbitrary line in the sand, but I needed the line to keep me walking the straight and narrow. Wanting to wait doesn't mean I don't want you."

"I know," she admitted reluctantly and I saw she was melting, her expression a mixture of helpless and hopeful. "You are pure evil, telling me this now, now that I'm addicted to you."

A twinge of regret—of concern that I'd inadvertently hurt her—had me frowning, and I scooched an inch away. "I see—"

She grabbed fistfuls of my shirt and tugged me closer. "No, no, no. You're not going anywhere. Don't even think about it."

"I wasn't going anywhere," I said, my voice rough. I brushed a sheet of soft, thick hair from her shoulders, trying to ignore my desire to wrap my fingers in it and pull, expose her neck, bite, and mark her perpetually sun-kissed skin. "I'm just sorry if you feel I misled you."

"I don't." She shook her head. "I don't, I mean—when would you have brought it up before now?"

"I appreciate you being so understanding."

Her mouth opened then closed as she stared at me, finally saying, "I understand, but I don't. I mean, if you're in a committed relationship—and since we've discussed the possibility of forever, I would call this a committed relationship—I don't see the need to wait until marriage. I don't understand that. But given what you've told me about your past, I understand that you might not trust yourself. And so you, as you say, drew an arbitrary line in the sand."

I slid my hand down her body, feeding and torturing my need to touch her, until my fingers met the bare skin of her thigh. "I made the decision in order to keep from hurting someone again."

"Sure, okay. Maybe. I'll buy that. If you know sex is off the table, you won't be motivated by it." She squinted at me. "But maybe it's also a way to keep yourself from getting hurt. Maybe it keeps you from losing control, from fully investing in someone who might leave you."

I glared at her. Her words struck a chord, and it was an uncomfortable one. My first instinct was to reject her assessment. Of course I wasn't trying to protect myself. That was just silliness. That would make my sacrifice a selfish one.

But the longer she stared at me with her serene expression, patience in her eyes, the better I could see past my initial impulse. I liked to think I could've settled down a hundred times over in the five years. But that wasn't true. I have a healthy dose of ego and self-confidence, quite possibly bordering on arrogance. But when it got down to brass tacks, what woman worth having would want me for something other than a fling?

"What are you thinking?"

My gaze cut to hers—to this gorgeous, clever, strong woman—and I made two decisions: first, I might not ever truly deserve her, but I would work every day to be a man who did. I would work to merit her trust, loyalty, and love. I would earn it no matter how freely she might be willing to give it.

Second, I was going to break my rule. I was going to make love to her when that's what it was. It wouldn't be just sex, and it certainly wouldn't be fucking around. When the time was right, regardless of whether or not we were married, I was going to take that gamble.

"Jethro?" Her eyes were wide, her features bracing. My silence and the look in my eye must've been making her nervous.

"I was just thinking," I tempered my expression, gave her a warm smile, and kissed her shoulder, "we should get Daisy's doughnuts every morning."

CHAPTER TWENTY-FIVE

"*Aging is not 'lost youth' but a new stage of opportunity and strength.*"

— BETTY FRIEDAN

~Sienna~

USIE ARRIVED JUST as Jethro was leaving. He tipped his hat with a rumbly, "Ma'am," needing to bend at an angle to clear the trailer door because he was so tall.

She didn't say anything, just turned her head as he walked past, her eyebrows suspended over a stunned blue gaze. We both watched him saunter away through the south-facing window.

Then she said, "Whoa."

I nodded, my eyes still on him and his audacious stride. "Yeah. Whoa."

He turned the corner, slipped out of view, and we both sighed.

"Nicely done." Susie patted me on the back.

I grinned, biting my lip, feeling oddly shy. "I know, right? And he's more beautiful on the inside than he is outside."

"How is that possible?" Susie looked back to where he'd disappeared, frowning out the window.

I shook my head slowly. "I don't know."

"He looks like he's good with his hands."

Immediately, I flushed scarlet, because I now had intimate knowledge of how *very* good he was with his hands. But then my heart twisted, because I might never know how good he was with other parts.

Namely, his penis.

And I really, really wanted to know what he could do with his penis. Based on the way he rolled his hips when we made out, I was pretty sure he was a master dill pickler, if you catch my meaning.

Susie's gaze slid to mine and she gave me an impish smile. "Aha."

I laughed, hiding my face behind my fingers. "Ahhh. I like him so much."

She pushed my shoulder. "Good. You're a gorgeous girl, but your real beauty lies within, doll. You deserve someone in your life who makes you happy."

"Thank you, Susie." She may have been my employee, and we might always have that barrier between us, but I didn't realize until that moment how much I'd needed someone to be happy for me. On that note, I needed to call my mom, because I suspected she'd be happy for me.

But then Susie *had* to add, "And makes you moist."

"Thank— Ugh!" I gagged, laughing again.

She laughed too, wagging her eyebrows. "I'm serious. I was worried about you last year. Tom is pretty, but I knew he wasn't the one for you."

"Well, what can I say? His looks and star-power made me stupid for five minutes."

We turned to the interior of the trailer, and she began setting up to do my makeup.

"But what's interesting," I continued, reaching for my coffee as I sat, "now I don't find him attractive at all. I mean, I can see he's good-looking, but he does nothing for me. It's like, I see him, and my vagina— afraid of his impotency—plays dead."

She grinned at that. "So, not moist?"

"No. Not moist." I chuckled. "More like a damp, wet blanket."

"Yes. I agree." She snickered, applying the undercoat to my face and neck.

We were quiet for a while, and I found myself smiling at intervals, remembering events from the morning, some small thing Jethro had done or some detail about his face. And then I would frown, because of the giant celibate elephant in the room. And then I'd smile again, because he'd kissed me senseless before leaving.

I was lost in these reflections when Susie, who apparently had been lost in her own reflections, broke our comfortable silence and offered philosophically, "Think of how much better the world would be if people craved compliments about the beauty of their heart rather than the beauty of their face."

The unexpected wisdom of her words startled me. She smiled softly at my surprised expression, and I found myself looking at her, entranced.

I noticed, maybe for the first time in our acquaintance, she had wrinkles around her eyes and her mouth, deep crinkling creases made deeper by her grin.

They were laugh lines.

And they were breathtaking.

And so was she.

* * *

"WHY DO I feel so weird about this?"

Jethro slid his eyes to mine, then back to the road. "I don't know. She doesn't bite."

I stared at the artichoke dip I held on my lap. "You have dinner with her every Sunday."

He nodded. "That's right."

"I'm meeting the woman you've had dinner with every Sunday for over five years. She's not a relative. She's a friend. A good friend." I reiterated the facts.

"Yep."

"I'm meeting the other woman. Or am I the other woman?"

Jethro lifted an eyebrow at me. "Neither of you are the other woman. There's no reason to be uncomfortable."

"I'm not uncomfortable. I'm just feeling weird, and I don't know how to un-weird myself."

"Well, don't un-weird yourself on my account. I like you weird. And Claire will, too."

We drove in silence, me with my thoughts, Jethro with his, until I blurted, "I just don't understand how you have dinner with a woman once a week, every week, who isn't a relative, and not try to make a move." I didn't add *especially this woman.*

Last Tuesday Jess, Duane's girlfriend, had shown me a picture of Claire. I'd mentioned to Jess that Jethro and I were going over to Claire's house for dinner and Jess pulled out her phone to show me a picture. Apparently they were really good friends and taught together at the local high school.

I momentarily forgot how to blink because this Claire woman was gorgeous.

No. That's not right.

She was *fuckingly gorgeous.* She was so gorgeous, her beauty deserved the f-bomb used as an adverb.

How could Jethro spend time with her every week, week after week, and not succumb to her? Cletus told me she was tough and smart. Duane told me she was sweet and kind. Beau told me she was a great cook and had "real pretty eyes." Roscoe told me she was his favorite teacher in high school, and he'd paired that statement with an eyebrow wag.

Side note: Roscoe was too freaking adorable for his own good. End side note.

Billy, however, had remained stonily silent on the matter of Claire. I was growing accustomed to Billy's stony silence.

So why hadn't Jethro made a move?

I was already a little in love with her, and I hadn't even met her yet.

"Not every week. Sometimes I have to travel for work. On those Sundays, my momma would invite Claire over for dinner. But, as far as I know, she never . . ." Jethro's easy expression morphed into a thoughtful frown, his eyes growing unfocused, like he'd just realized something of importance.

"She never what?"

He shook himself. "Sorry. She never accepted the invitation. She hasn't been to our house since she was a teenager."

"You didn't answer my question. Why haven't you made a move on Claire? According to your family and Jess, she's an ethereal goddess of perfection."

Jethro rolled his eyes. "Yeah, well, I know Claire better than they do. She's human enough, got scars and flaws like everybody else. Plus, I don't think about her that way. We've known each other since we were kids. She's like a sister to me. Objectively, I can see that Ashley is beautiful on the outside, but when I look at her, I see her heart and her warts in equal measure. It's the same with Claire."

"Okay, that makes sense. But just so you know, I have no warts. I *am* an ethereal goddess of perfection."

Jethro grinned, pulling onto a long dirt driveway leading to a small white farmhouse with a red door and navy trim. "I never doubted it."

His eyes conducted a quick, appreciative sweep of my body before he closed them briefly and exhaled, like he was trying to control himself.

Meanwhile, my stomach was a bundle of nerves.

Despite what he said, with his sister just recently returned after an eight-year absence and the passing of his mother, Claire was *the* woman in his life. She was important to him. They may never have been romantically involved, but what she thought mattered. Also, she was single. Jethro told me she was an only child and had no family to speak of. She had no other person in her life to make dinner for on Sundays.

I felt like a usurper.

I also felt a little irritated with her for making me feel like a usurper even though she'd done nothing but exist.

How's that for mental health?

Claire's house had flowers in boxes under the windows and along the porch. Gorgeous, neatly trimmed topiaries sat on either side of the porch steps and the door. The house looked like something out of a magazine.

"Wow," I said, scanning the front yard. "This is a really pretty house."

Jethro grinned like he was proud. "It is, right? I added the porch two years ago. The boxes were Claire's idea last spring. I painted them to match the trim."

I gaped at Jethro. "You built her porch?"

He nodded, completely clueless as to how that news sounded to me. "I did. And the gazebo and deck out back. I've done a little work around the house, from time to time."

A little work. You know, like building porches, decks, and gazebos.

Maybe this news wouldn't have struck me so acutely if Jethro and I had been together longer, or if we'd been physically intimate since the Daisy Doughnut incident last Monday. But we hadn't. This thing between us was new and tentative and just a week old.

Dating a guy who wasn't trying to get in my pants every ten minutes was a new experience for me. It was . . . unnerving.

Good. But unnerving nonetheless.

Thus, I couldn't think of a single thing to say that wasn't a joke, so I just stared at his dashboard.

Jethro parked and grabbed the pie he'd made from the back seat. I took the opportunity of him walking around the truck to take a deep breath, giving myself a mental pep talk: *You've got this. You go in there and be charming. You charm the freckles off her face! Do it!*

He opened my door and helped me down, tangling our fingers together as we walked to her front door.

"Don't be nervous," he whispered, squeezing my hand.

"I'm not nervous. I'm Sienna. How many times do I have to tell you my name?" The terrible joke slipped from my mouth before I could catch it.

He cocked an eyebrow at me, his lips twisting then flattening, but said nothing.

I was nervous.

Maybe Jethro, Claire, and I can live together in harmony. Maybe she can be my sister wife. Yes. That was the answer. She could have her pretty farmhouse and custody of Jethro on Sundays. I could have him the rest of the week. And if she touched him, I would claw her eyes out.

Perfect. Solution.

Jethro knocked on the door, then slid his eyes to mine. "You look like you're anticipating eating a bug."

I didn't get a chance to respond because Claire immediately opened the door, almost like she'd been lying in wait.

And fuckingly hell, Claire was even more gorgeous in person.

"Hi!" she shouted at me, her very pretty eyes big and excited.

"Uh . . ." I glanced at Jethro—he was no help as his features were carefully expressionless, and he was looking above her head at the door jamb—and managed to say, "Hi—"

She stepped forward and pulled me into a hug. "I am so excited to meet you!" She was still shouting.

Jethro saved the dip, taking it from my hands so Claire could squeeze me tight. Our eyes met over her shoulder. He was trying not to laugh. Trying and failing.

She pulled away, holding me by the shoulders. "I'm sorry. I'm being weird. I'm just—I love you so much."

My eyes widened at her confession, and she covered her mouth with her hands.

"Oh my God. I'm sorry. I'm just nervous. Look at me, I'm a terrible hostess. Please, come inside." She stepped back, stumbling over her own feet. She was clearly flustered, her cheeks burning red. "I promised myself I wasn't going to be a creeper. And here I am, being a creeper." This last part she seemed to say to herself.

And it was the best thing she could have said because now I was completely at ease.

She was a fan.

Claire McClure is a fan of Sienna Diaz.

It never occurred to me that she would be a fan. Honestly, it didn't. Maybe I'd been spoiled by my time with Jethro and his family. They'd all been so cool about it, almost disinterested. Whereas Claire was not disinterested.

"I promised myself I wasn't going to be weird, either." I smiled at her, and she blinked at me like I was dazzling.

"You could never be weird," she said, her voice full of adoration, her eyes dazed and dreamy.

"All right, all right." Jethro grabbed my hand and pulled me inside, through a living room to the dining room. "Stop being a wackadoodle, Claire. Pull yourself together. And shut the door. We have dip. What's for dinner?"

* * *

CLAIRE WASN'T QUITE an ethereal goddess of perfection, but she was pretty darn close. And she was an excellent cook. Everything was comfort food but with a twist. Homemade crusty Italian bread, with red pepper-cherry preserves and goat cheese as a delicious variation on bruschetta. Oh yeah, she made the goat cheese herself. From goats. Her neighbor's Nigerian pygmy goats.

She also made the preserves. She canned her own jams and jellies.

For the main course, she'd made macaroni and cheese, but with spinach ziti and an asiago Alfredo lobster sauce. She made her own pasta. The salad was made with romaine lettuce, peppers, chives, and tomatoes from her summer garden. It tasted like fresh heaven.

Bickering with Jethro, talking about cooking, and my compliments about her food seemed to pull her out of the star-struck trance. Jethro knew just what buttons to push, and I followed his lead, when she stared at me or vocalized (ad nauseam) how much she loved my movies, and how she admired me, and that I smelled really, really good. But by the end of dinner, thanks in large part to Jethro, she'd relaxed.

We'd both relaxed.

And I discovered I had a little bit of a crush on Claire McClure.

"Yes, yes! Buster Keaton was brilliant." I pointed at Claire, nodding enthusiastically. We were discussing silent film movie greats and, as it turns out, we had the same opinions about everything.

"Don't get me wrong. Charlie Chaplin was wonderful in *The Gold Rush*, I love a good chicken suit gag, but I just don't think you can compare it to *The General*. I mean, that train was moving. The whole time. And he's jumping on and off like it's a trampoline."

"So much yes! He was a physical comedian, but not in the same way as Chaplin. His physical comedy was smarter, wittier. And his timing, there has never been anything like it. And the end, when he tries to kiss Annabelle but has to keep saluting the soldiers . . ."

We both giggled, remembering the same point in the movie. Claire mimed the salute scene, perfectly mimicking Buster Keaton's exasperation, launching us into renewed laughter.

Jethro snagged my attention, slipping his fingers into mine and bringing my knuckles to his lips for a soft kiss. His smiling eyes ensnared mine, heated and cherishing, making me feel warm and cherished. He looked happy.

He gave my hand another squeeze then stood, quietly picking up our plates and strolling out of the dining room.

"I've always said, a man's place is in the kitchen." Claire lifted her voice so he could hear, winking at me.

He must've heard her because he called back, "Shut your mouth, woman, or you're not getting any pie."

"You brought pie?" she hollered, suddenly serious.

He didn't respond. She turned her attention to me.

"He brought pie? I didn't see pie when y'all walked in."

I shrugged, hiding my smile behind a sip of wine. She didn't see the pie because it had taken her thirty minutes to stop staring at me when we arrived.

"Thank you so much for having me over."

She smiled a brilliant smile, her cheeks blushing pink with pleasure. "The next time we meet I promise I won't go gaga again. And I am so sorry about that. I see now that you're a normal person. Just like everyone else." She nodded, then added with stellar comedic timing, "Except funnier, cleverer, and smelling like gardenias."

"Claire—"

"And with mile-long eyelashes."

"Stop—"

"I can't stop. Sorry."

I grinned at her silliness. "Please don't apologize."

"No. I will. I promised myself I wouldn't act like a fool. But faced with the reality of you on my front porch, I lost my mind, and I'm sorry. It might take me a while, but I'll eventually stop putting my foot in my mouth." She lifted her glass of red wine toward me. "Wine helps. So call me when you're a half hour away next time, and I'll drink a glass."

We both laughed at this suggestion. She was the picture of charming self-deprecation.

"You two go for a walk." Jethro reappeared and began stacking the leftovers.

"I should help with the dishes." I stood to gather the glasses, but Jethro snatched the nearest one from my grip.

"Go on now. I want you to see the gazebo. I thought I might put something similar behind the old house and I want your opinion."

I knew what he was doing. Now that Claire wasn't tongue-tied, he wanted us to spend more time together. He wanted us to be friends. Things had been going swimmingly, but now a stirring of self-consciousness reignited in my stomach. Being Sienna Diaz, movie star, was easy. Tiring, but easy. It was a role, a mask I could slip on at will.

Being myself wasn't usually as easy. Jethro had made it easy for me, which was one of the reasons I loved being around him. I glanced from him to Claire. She was watching me with hopeful eyes.

"I'll bring the wine," she offered, grinning at me. "I promise I won't smell you again, unless you want me to."

And again, just like that, my nerves dissipated. "I'll only go if you promise *to* smell me."

"Deal." She hit the table as she stood, and then plucked her wine glass and the bottle from the table. "But seriously, you do smell good. What perfume do you wear?"

I followed her out the French doors that led off the dining room, catching Jethro's small pleased smile as he turned back to the kitchen.

"Honestly, I don't even know. My sister sends it to me. She also buys all of my other products—makeup, moisturizer, shampoo, everything—and I use what she sends."

"Do you mind asking her for me? I can't find anything I like."

"Sure. Absolutely." I made a mental note to have a bottle of whatever it was sent over, because the goat cheese alone deserved a hundred gallons of fancy perfume.

Claire and I crossed her deck, down the steps to a flagstone path. The gazebo was in the distance, illuminated by floodlights, and covered in blooming fuchsia bougainvillea and white jasmine. The night air smelled heavenly.

"This is beautiful." I skimmed my fingertips over the white flowers.

"Jethro built it a few years ago, and I trained the vines to climb the lattice. This is my favorite time of year to be outside. There's nothing quite like the smell of jasmine and a starry summer sky. Plus, in a little bit, the lightning bugs will come out and give us a good show."

I inspected the craftsmanship of the gazebo, noting the small details along the rail: vines and long petaled flowers etched into the cedar. "Did Jethro do the carving, too?"

She nodded proudly. "Yes he did. That boy can do just about anything with wood."

I lifted an eyebrow at that, how it sounded, but knew she'd meant it innocently. The carvings were beautiful.

"This must've taken forever," I mumbled to myself. How long had he spent working on this gazebo? Claire's house was finished and perfect, meanwhile his own home wasn't even half restored.

The silence stretched. I felt Claire's eyes on me, so I lifted mine to hers. She wore a small smile, her blue eyes clever and assessing. I had the distinct impression she could read my thoughts.

She gathered a deep breath and sat on the swinging bench, her eyes never leaving mine. "I'm really glad I had the opportunity to meet you."

Her voice sounded different. Deeper. Wiser. Her giddy silliness now subdued.

I strolled to the swinging bench and sat next to her. "We should get together again before I leave. I can cook next Sunday if you want. If you don't mind my tagging along—not all the time, I don't want to impose— but I'll still be here for a month or more and—"

"But I won't be."

"You won't be?" I frowned at her, not understanding.

"That's right. I won't be here. I was called last month by a friend of mine who works for a community college in Nashville. They're looking for an adjunct, to teach music theory and drama. She thought I might be a good fit. I interviewed two weeks ago and . . ." she shrugged, her eyes drifting over my shoulder, "I got the position, and I'm going to take it."

"Oh." I blinked at her. My heart sunk. "Jethro didn't say anything."

Claire studied me, the side of her mouth hitching with a soft smile. "Jethro doesn't know yet."

I felt my eyebrows jump. "Jethro doesn't know?"

"No." She shook her head, her soft smile dropping from her lips, but lingering behind her eyes. "I'm so happy for Jet. I'm so happy he found you. His heart was lost. Lonely. And now it's not. And that's because of you."

Perhaps my time in Hollywood, spent amongst image-obsessed double-talkers, had changed my expectations of conversation, but the emotion, sentiment, and sincerity behind Claire's words caught me completely off guard. I opened my mouth to respond but found myself at a loss.

She reached forward and covered my hand with hers. "I hope I'm not putting too much pressure on you or making too many assumptions."

"No! No, not at all. Where Jethro is concerned, please put all the pressure on me. Pile it on."

She chuckled. "Good. I'm glad to hear it. He deserves to be happy, and so do you."

We shared a smile then swung in silence, turning our attention to the stars in the sky. I used the time to organize my thoughts regarding Claire while endeavoring to stealthily scrutinize her. This woman in Jethro's life was on the precipice of leaving it. I suspected that as much as she'd been a constant for him, he'd been a constant for her.

So why was she leaving town? Why now?

Before I realized I was speaking, I thought and asked at the same time, "Claire, when did you decide to take this new job?"

Her bright eyes cut to mine, seeming to glow like sapphires with their own internal brilliance. "I guess I made up my mind on Tuesday."

"When will you tell him?"

"I don't know. Not yet. Probably not 'til my bags are packed, and I'm on the other side of the state. I don't really like goodbyes, so he'll understand. I'm not leaving the country, just the county. I'll come back to visit."

I inspected her open features, deciding that if she could be assertively candid, then I could, too. "I hope this is a silly question, but you're not leaving because of me, are you?"

"No," she responded too quickly, sighed, then amended, "not really. Not in the way you think. There's no reason for me to stay here. There hasn't been a reason for a long time." Her gaze moved to her fingers and she fiddled with the Band-Aid wrapped around her thumb. "Has Jethro told you about my, uh, husband? About Ben?"

"Yes. He told me what a wonderful man he was."

"He was wonderful." Her smile was sad, and she lifted her eyes to the sky. "When we first got the news about Ben, I told myself I was staying to help his parents and to help Jethro. I wanted to be there—here —in case they needed me. But it's been five years. Five years of hiding away, in this pretty house, with its pretty garden, watching the world go by." Her gaze dropped to mine and she added in a cheerful tone, "Even the McClures are trying to get me moving. In fact, Carter McClure— Ben's daddy—was the one to put my name on the short list for this position."

We shared a smile. Silence stretched. Seconds turned to minutes. Claire's eyes turned unfocused and introspective, and she frowned.

"I ran into somebody on Tuesday. Someone I used to know."

I wanted to ask her who it was, but her voice was distracted, as though she spoke without consciously meaning to do so. I waited for her to continue.

"We had ugly words." She shook her head, clearly trying to dispel the memory. "I left him and I felt . . . lost and upset. And then Jethro called, sounding so happy, asking if he could bring you to dinner. Both things happening on the same day felt like a sign. I always told myself I would leave when Jethro was settled, when the McClures were in a good place."

"How do you think Jethro will take the news?" I honestly wanted to know, because I worried for my guy.

"Jet? Oh, he'll be fine. No doubt. He just wants me to be happy." She wrinkled her nose at my concern, like I was silly. "I think you two should move into the house after I leave, if I may be so bold. You'll have no privacy at the Winston place with those boys, and Jethro has done so many upgrades here, this place feels more like his than mine."

I glanced over my shoulder at the pretty house and spotted Jethro, just stepping out of the French doors.

"When an opportunity presents itself, and you have a choice of either living life—risky as it might be—or continuing to do what's expected . . ." Claire paused, waiting for me to meet her gaze, a knowing smile curving her lips.

She was quoting me, one of my favorite lines from my first film, *Taco Tuesday*.

I returned her grin and finished the quote, "You have to grab that regal centaur by the mane and ride it over the rainbow of opportunity."

We finished together, "Or else it might mistake you for a unicorn and try to impregnate you."

"I love that movie." She grinned, shaking her head. "I always thought, like a wackadoodle, that you and I would be best friends one day."

"Ah, I see. You've set this whole thing in motion—between Jethro and me—just so we could meet and be best friends."

She shrugged, then giggled. "You make me sound like Cletus."

That made us both laugh again. I watched her, feeling humbled and oddly light, because this woman loved my films and wanted to be my friend. And Claire McClure was clearly one of those rare souls who was more concerned with the beauty of her heart than she was with the beauty of her face. I decided I loved her. It was friend-love-at-first-sight. I would be sad to see her move away.

I also decided, if things didn't work out with Jethro, I would ask her to marry me and request she make goat cheese bruschetta every Sunday.

CHAPTER TWENTY-SIX

"In the middle of the journey of our life I found myself within a dark woods where the straight way was lost."

— DANTE ALIGHIERI, INFERNO

~Sienna~

TEN DAYS AFTER the doughnut dalliance, and four days after dinner with Claire, I called my mother.

I called her after a date with Jethro.

Technically it had been our fourth date, if you counted the disaster at The Front Porch over a month ago as our first date, and my introduction to Daisy's doughnuts as our second date. Our third date had been a middle-of-the-night movie date in Knoxville.

Tonight, our fourth date, had consisted of a dinner picnic and dancing on the prairie. Afterward, he'd dropped me off at the cabin, giving me a toe-curling, spine-tingling kiss. He left me, alone to my bed and wishful thoughts for the remainder of the night.

I didn't count dinner with his family or Claire as a date. I'd given the matter a lot of thought, defining what was a date and what wasn't.

Because, by now, I figured we should be ending the night *at the very least* necking and making out in his truck.

But that wasn't happening.

So I called my mother.

"Sienna, mija, you're calling. What happened? Are you okay?" She sounded concerned. We had a scheduled call every Sunday night when I was filming because my work schedule and her work schedule were so crazy. In between films, I would fly home and spend a few days with her and Dad. We frequently texted during the week, sharing funny thoughts or *I love yous* or *I'm going to strangle your father*, but Sunday was our day to talk. We'd missed our last two Sunday calls, which happened from time to time, so I hadn't told her about Jethro yet.

Today was Thursday, and it was past midnight for me. So I understood her concern.

"Nothing has happened, nothing bad anyway. I just—I just wanted to talk to you."

"Oh." I heard her release a relieved breath. "I'll never turn down a call from my lovely daughter. How are you?"

"I'm good, I'm good," I said, nodding even though she couldn't see me. "Actually, Mamita, I'm good, but I need your advice."

"Vicks."

"What?"

"Whatever it is, use Vicks."

"Ha ha." I rolled my eyes. Usually when I called unexpectedly it was because I had a cold or some other mysterious ailment and needed my mother's soothing presence and her medical expertise. "I don't think Vicks is going to work this time."

"Oh, well then sex."

I coughed, choking on nothing. "What?"

"Sex, mija. You sound on edge. You need a release."

This was a new approach, much blunter than usual. Typically she'd say, "You need a man, let me set you up. I know a nice boy."

When I was younger, I didn't understand her meaning and I would grow indignant, angry she thought I needed a man. But as I grew older and heard her say the same thing to my older sisters, I realized *You need a man* meant *You need to get laid.*

But this was the first time she'd just come right out and said it.

My neck heated with an involuntary blush, but I pressed on. "So, that's sort of what I want to talk to you about."

"Oh." She sounded surprised. "Do you need some resource materials? Toys?"

"No!" I blurted, huffing a laugh. "No. I-I met someone."

"Ooohhhh . . ." she sing-songed. I could almost see her wiggling in her seat, the giant grin on her face. "Tell me about him. Does he need resource materials?"

Now I was really laughing, but chided, "Mamita, let me speak."

"Sorry, sorry. Go ahead."

I gathered a breath for courage, because Marta's reaction—for better or for worse—had me feeling gun-shy about sharing Jethro with my family.

"His name is Jethro. He's a wildlife park ranger here in Tennessee." I paused, bracing myself for her reaction.

She didn't say anything at first, and my heart rate doubled.

I was just about to make a joke when she said, "In the Old Testament Jethro was the name of Moses's father-in-law. That will make Abuela very happy. It's a good name. And he treats you well? With kindness?"

I collapsed onto my bed, my heart swelling with gratitude. Clearly, I'd been silly to think my mother would share any of Marta's concerns. *Thank God for my mother!*

"Yes. He treats me so well. He is amazing."

"Tell me about your young man. Leave nothing out."

I smiled at the ceiling of stars above me and spent the next half hour telling her everything. Well, almost everything. I didn't tell her about how we almost had sex against a tree behind his house. Or how we'd attacked each other in my trailer after I ate the world's best doughnut. I shared details about his past—a little about Ben, nothing about his criminal pursuits or the Iron Wraiths—enough to make it clear he'd made poor decisions as a youth, but had changed his ways.

I finished telling her about our first two dates and moved on to date three. "So I mentioned to him last week, while we were driving to the set—"

"He still drives you every morning?"

"Yes. We drive in together in the mornings, and then usually after work we have dinner with his family."

"His brothers?"

"And his sister and her fiancé."

"And his family, they are good people?"

"Yes. They are the best. The. Best. They kind of remind me of the Marx Brothers, the shenanigans and hijinks. I love them."

"That's good. Your children will resemble—in looks and temperament—your husband's siblings and your siblings."

I tried to feel irritated she would jump to this conclusion, that we might be getting married and having children, but all I felt was excitement. Even so, I reprimanded her. "Mamita, we've just started dating." I couldn't have her getting carried away. One of us needed to be sensible.

"Yes, but you are telling me about him. You've never told me about anyone before. He is the one, I feel it in my bones, and my bones never lie. And you spend so much time with him—in the mornings before work, in the evenings. Do you still enjoy his company?"

"Yes. So much. Spending time with him is comforting and thrilling and energizing. He is so easy to be around and to talk to. He makes everything calmer but more exciting. I don't know how to describe it. It's like, when we're together, we're in a bubble."

"Hmm . . ." I could tell she was smiling, but she refrained from voicing her thoughts, instead putting the conversation back on track. "You were saying about your third date."

"Oh, yes. I mentioned to him that I missed going to the movies as a spectator. You know I haven't seen a movie, just gone to the theater to enjoy a film, not a big splashy premiere for work, in years. So it turns out Jethro knows the owner of an old theater in Knoxville and he arranged for a midnight showing of *Duck Soup*."

"Ah, that's one of your favorites."

"Yes. I don't know how he knew that, he wouldn't reveal his sources, but he knew."

"I like this guy."

"I like him, too."

My mother waited for me to continue. When I didn't, she prompted me. "But?"

Closing my eyes, I released a long exhale. "But, after the movie he drove me home, carried me upstairs—because I was asleep—kissed me goodnight, and left."

"Okay . . .?"

"We kiss. A lot. But we've done nothing else for ten days."

Again she was quiet, but I could tell she was thinking, not waiting for me. Then she asked, "What did you do tonight? Was it dinner with his family again?"

"No. Tonight was a date. He made a picnic, and we had dinner on the prairie. And we danced."

"You danced?"

"Yes. He made a playlist and we danced. Then he brought me home, kissed me goodnight as usual, and now here I am."

"What kind of music?"

I frowned, not understanding her question. "What do you mean?"

"What kind of music did he play? The playlist?"

"Um, slow music. Ballads, some Frank Sinatra, that kind of thing."

"He held you close? The whole time?"

I thought about her question and realized she was right. "Yes. He held me close the whole time."

"So you are doing more than just kissing. You think it's a mistake all those songs were slow? No. He wanted to touch you. He is sneaky and clever. I like him even more."

Her conclusion made me feel better. Much better. And yet, I was still alone, tangled in want and frustration, wishing he were here.

"He is a gentleman. He sounds very complex. He has layers, like an onion."

"Exactly. He lives his life simply, but he's not simple."

"Well put. He's a man, mija. Men live simply, but are not simple. Boys are simple, but do not live simply. They don't understand what is important. Jethro isn't one of your boys. Your father and I, when we met, we were still very young. We became adults together, we grew together and challenged each other. Jethro is already a man; he will expect you to behave like a woman. He will challenge you. Are you ready to be so serious with someone?"

"Yes," I answered without hesitation. "I am. But I don't know what to do about the kissing."

"What do you mean?"

"He wants to wait, to have sex, until he is married. I'm not sure how to initiate something other than a kiss."

Again, my mother was quiet for a time, obviously thinking about this new information.

"Is he a virgin?" Thankfully, the question sounded coldly clinical. Speaking to my mother about sex was always easier when she wore her doctor's hat. We'd always talked freely, but she was still my mother.

"No. Like I said, he didn't make good decisions when he was younger." I went on to rehash how he had been trying to redeem himself through his actions and had felt enforced celibacy for the last five years was necessary to avoid hurting anyone. I further explained that we'd been intimate in some ways, just the once, but he'd drawn a line in the sand regarding that one thing.

"I see." Again, she paused and deliberated.

Before she could launch into a new set of questions, I added, "I respect his decision, and I'm not pushing for him to cross that line. But it would be nice to do something other than kiss and dance. We spend very little time alone other than the time in the truck, driving to work. I feel so much for him, and I love the time we spend together, and yet—when he leaves me at the end of the day—I have all this pent-up affection and no outlet."

I heard her teeth click and her tone change from clinical to momma bear. "Well, you need to tell him that. You need to say exactly that. We are not living in Victorian times. I applaud you for supporting him and his boundaries, but you are feeling neglected. He doesn't have to break his vow in order to satisfy his woman. You need to tell him and give him a chance to make things right."

I nodded, her words bolstering my confidence. "Yes. You're right."

"I have resource materials if he needs them."

I grinned, shaking my head. "No. No he doesn't need them. I just—you're right about everything. I know he wants me—"

She snorted. "Yes. He wants you. Never doubt that, mi hermosa. He would be a sexless idiot if he did not."

"Thank you."

"It's the truth. You are very hot. Just like your mother."

I shook my head and giggled. "I will speak to him."

"If he is as you describe, if he is thoughtful and kind, then he will do something about your feelings. He will want to make things right for you, even if it makes things difficult for him."

I frowned at this. "What do you mean?"

"Put the pieces together, mija. He feels for you. He is a gentleman. He doesn't want to break his vow, but he wants you fiercely. It sounds like he avoids situations that place him in temptation—dinner with his family, late night movies so you'll be tired after, or leaving you at home early after a picnic. You are a very big temptation."

"So . . . should I not tempt him?"

"Of course you should tempt him," she contradicted, then added in a sly tone, "it's good for a man's soul to be tortured in this way."

I frowned, not understanding how torturing Jethro was good for him.

As though reading my mind, she huffed impatiently. "Trust me. I am your mother. I know what's best."

* * *

ARMED WITH MY mother's advice, I waited.

I didn't confront him.

I just waited.

Like a coward.

I'd never been a coward before. It was an odd and unpleasant state of being. But it was also safe.

Jethro didn't make me a coward. I made me a coward, more precisely, my feelings for him did. Every day, every moment we spent together, they grew bigger, and I grew quieter. I felt myself retreating, but didn't know what to do about it. Saying nothing felt so much safer than admitting the truth and risk pushing him away.

And so, there we were, after our third midnight movie, sitting silently in his truck. We had time because Jethro only arranged for midnight movies on evenings when I didn't need to be up early the next day and he had the day off.

I wasn't nearly as tired as the last two middle-of-the-night showings. Upon Dave and Susie's urging, I'd taken a nap in the afternoon. Jethro didn't appear to be tired either. He seemed wired, on edge. He'd kept shifting in his seat during the movie, especially when Humphrey Bogart grabbed Ingrid Bergman and kissed the hell out of her.

Now the movie was over. We were both wide awake, staring out of the windshield of his truck.

Completely alone and nowhere to go.

And I was hot. Thick, twisting tension coiled in my belly. I wanted him to touch me. But the celibacy elephant and three weeks of just kissing had me wondering how to ask.

Or should I just touch him?

Or what the hell was I supposed to do?

It was the same debate I'd been having since the Daisy Doughnut Dalliance.

"Hey," Jethro said, making me jump. He laughed lightly at my reaction, grinning at his steering wheel. "Sorry. I'm sorry. I didn't mean to startle you."

I smiled at him, trying to swallow past these random nerves. Being awake and alone with him and not having someplace to be felt significant, foreboding. I wanted to make a joke, but I also didn't want to make a joke.

"So, hey," he started again, his voice quieter. "Are you tired?"

"No. Nope. Not tired." I shook my head more vehemently than necessary, as though I were denying an accusation of murder rather than sleepiness.

His grin grew. "You want to do something else?"

I nodded resolutely. "Yes." But again said nothing else, because I didn't want to start bartering for physical affection.

This something else, will we be alone?

Can we make out?

What will it take for you to put your hand up my skirt?

I'll make you a cake if you touch my boob.

I bit my lip to keep from offering baked goods in exchange for intimacy.

Jethro studied me, his eyes narrowing, his knuckles growing white where he gripped the steering wheel too tight.

"Shall we?" he asked, his voice like gravel.

I nodded, my heart fluttering. "Yes," I whispered.

He frowned, his eyes dropping to my mouth and growing unmistakably heated. I held my breath and watched him. The air heavy between us, saturated with things unsaid.

Breaking the moment, Jethro breathed out forcefully and suddenly, tearing his gaze away. He gritted his teeth and started the truck.

We drove in silence. We drove in complete silence for a very long time. Complete silence, being an unnatural state for us, only perpetuated the tension. Despite not wanting to make a joke, my desire to break the tension with levity grew and grew until I could contain it no longer.

So I said, "Knock knock."

His eyes flickered to mine then back to the dark road. "Who's there?"

"Owl."

"Owl who?"

"Owl give you a kiss if you tell me where we're going."

Jethro's eyebrows furrowed for a split second, then his brow cleared. The truck's headlights made his grin visible.

"The great thing about 'Owl' knock, knock jokes is that they work for everything, all situations," I said, using an instructional tone. "Owl give you a high five if you help me with this thing, or Owl make you a cake if you stop being an asshole."

He nodded his agreement, but his smile waned. Jethro pressed on the brake, slowing the truck and flipping on his right turn blinker.

I inspected the darkness beyond the windshield, seeing nothing but mountain road and forest. Then, quite suddenly, I spotted a turn off, large bushes concealed the view of a dirt path. I held on to the door and the armrest, the truck rocking back and forth as we traversed the uneven and unpaved road.

We drove another three minutes, never exceeding ten miles per hour, nothing but inky darkness and the shadows of tall trees, before Jethro said, "This is Hawk's Field. Or, we're almost there. Just another half mile."

"Hawk's Field," I echoed, the name sounding familiar, but I was unable to place it.

"That's right. I thought we could check out the stars. There are no lights up here, and it's a clear night." His voice was tight, but he sounded perfectly reasonable, his plan innocent.

Nevertheless, his statement caused riots.

My body was rioting.

Is that really what he wants to do? Park in the middle of a field in the middle of the night and look at stars?

That had to be code for something, right?

Right?

Before I knew it, he'd parked and had stepped down from the truck, opening the door behind the driver's seat. The sound of him rummaging in the back of the cab woke me from my stupor. Shaking myself, I exited the vehicle.

I'd dressed casually for our date: Converse sneakers, black leggings, and a long-sleeved pink cotton tunic. I wasn't cold, but the air held a slight chill. If we stayed outside for too long, I'd likely become cold. I didn't want to stand around lamely, so I walked around to his side just as he tossed a bundle of something into the bed of the truck.

"Can I help?"

Jethro glanced over his shoulder. The interior lights of the truck illuminated his outline. "Sure. Hold this flashlight."

I accepted the big flashlight and quickly found the on/off switch. Jethro tossed two more bundles onto the bed of the truck then shut the cab doors, waving me forward to follow him to the back. He lowered the tailgate, and with one impressive jump, hopped up to the bed, Dukes of Hazzard style.

"Can you shine that in here? Just for a minute."

"Sure." I lifted the flashlight and peeked over the side so I could watch him work.

The bundles he'd tossed in earlier were sleeping bags, blankets, and pillows. I stared at them and him as he worked, the earlier body riots continuing and increasing in severity. He was making a place for us to lie down. Next to each other. So we could look at stars.

Right.

"Are you okay?"

I blinked up at him. He was frowning at me. The line of his brow told me he was concerned. I nodded quickly. "I'm good."

Jethro glanced at the makeshift bed then back to me, the line of his brow now determined rather than concerned. "Let me help you up."

"Uh, no problem. I can do it." I placed the flashlight on the open tailgate and jumped up easily, using the strength in my arms to lift my body the rest of the way. I might not have been a sexy park ranger who hauled live black bears around and made it look easy, but I was a sexy Hollywood actress who did yoga daily.

Despite my ability to climb into the truck bed without assistance, Jethro was right there before I could straighten. He slipped his arm around my waist and steadied me unnecessarily, holding my hand. His thumb swiped the inside of my wrist, and he brought me flush against him.

As soon as I stood, he kissed me, a quick touch of his lips to mine. Then he kissed me again, and it felt unplanned, like he couldn't help himself. He lingered, punctuating each pass of his mouth with hungry nips of his teeth and licks of his tongue. His hands drifted lower, caressing and squeezing as they went.

"I've missed you." His voice was low, surprisingly desperate, and gravelly; my head was swimming. He lifted my tunic, his large, hot hands splaying on my sides, his thumbs drawing circles on the skin just beneath my bra. His lips lowered to my neck where he dotted the sensitive underside of my jaw with the same biting kisses.

I inhaled sharply as he slid his fingers lower and into my leggings, grabbing handfuls of my backside. And then, with his pelvis pressed against my lower belly, I *felt* how much he'd missed me. Instinctively, I brought my fingers around to the front of his jeans between us and cupped him. He hissed, his body growing tense and still as I rubbed with the base of my palm.

My head swimming became brain drowning and I moaned, shifting an inch away and reaching for the buckle of his belt. His breathing quickened and so did mine, and when I finally, *finally* circled my hand around his length, we both shuddered.

I loved the feel of him, the dichotomy of hard and smooth, the involuntary, primitive, and yet controlled nature of his arousal. Taking action was always a choice. But the physical evidence of how Jethro saw me, how he desired me—*wanted me*—was raw and honest and impossible to deny.

I needed to feel him, taste him, consume him. In much the same way I'd hoped Jethro would be insatiable for me, I was—in that moment—insatiable for him. And something happened that had never happened to me before.

I actually wanted to give a man a blow job.

Not only did I want to do it, I felt like I might go batshit crazy if he didn't let me do it. I felt the frantic need in my chest and the tips of my fingers, on my tongue and low in my belly. Armed with this need and intent on my goal, I began lowering myself to my knees, tugging his boxers and jeans down as I went.

But Jethro—who had been standing so still as I'd touched him, as though he'd been afraid the moment would disappear or prove to be a figment of his imagination—stopped me. His eyes flew open, just visible under the starlight. His searched mine and gripped my arms to halt my movements.

"Wait, wait. What are you doing?" His words were breathless and held an unmistakable air of panic.

"I'm heading downtown," I answered, equally breathless.

He blinked at me, didn't move, and said nothing.

So I pushed his jeans down his hips and moved to kneel.

He stopped me again.

"Don't—"

I reached for him again, gripping the smooth, thick length of him and stroking, effectively cutting off his words. His eyes closed again and his forehead met mine, but he didn't loosen his grip on my arms.

"Jethro, I want to."

He groaned. It sounded tortured.

And perhaps thinking about my mother in that moment was a little weird, but I did. Specifically, I thought about her words, *It's good for a man's soul to be tortured in this way.*

Without thinking, I asked, "Are you afraid of temptation?"

He shook his head. "God, no. Just being with you, just seeing you. Fuck." He mostly swallowed the expletive, his hips rolling in a way that made me think the movement was instinctual, then added on a rush, "You breathing tempts me."

That made my heart do happy backflips and I smiled, feeling bolder.

Lowering my voice to the octave reserved for seduction, I pressed, "Then what are you afraid of?"

"I'm not afraid."

"Then what—"

"I don't want you to have any regrets."

Oh, Jethro . . .

I removed his fingers from my arm and placed them on my shoulder. Then I lifted my chin and gave him a tender kiss, a gentle kiss. Paired with my tight, rough strokes I hoped it conveyed the weight of my affection, the complexity of my feelings.

"I will never regret you," I whispered solemnly.

He released a shuddering sigh and I felt some of his tension drain away.

Those seemed to be the magic words, or maybe what I was doing inside his shorts was magical. Whatever it was, he didn't try to stop me this time as I knelt on the cushion provided by the sleeping bags, bringing his shorts all the way down as I lowered myself, enjoying the feel of his legs as I skimmed my fingers over his thighs and behind his knees.

Darkness pressed in on us, cloaking my movements. Though I was greedy for the sight of him, the moonless night obscured his bare skin.

But I could feel him, still heavy and hard and smooth. With no further prelude, I took him in my mouth and moaned.

I moaned because a bone-deep satisfaction warmed my blood as he filled me. With each pass of my lips and each of his ragged breaths, a growing fulfillment blossomed, ballooned, eliminating the void carved out by weeks of frustrated longing. Now I was able to indulge myself, I felt the full weight of my desire. My pent-up frustration dissolved.

I'd wanted to give without expectation of receiving.

I'd wanted to suffocate him with affection and touch.

I'd wanted to love him.

And so I did.

CHAPTER TWENTY-SEVEN

"No effort that we make to attain something beautiful is ever lost."

— HELEN KELLER

~Jethro~

"Sienna—" I reached for her.

"Jethro." She stepped away.

"You're killing me here."

"You look healthy to me," she said, moving the flashlight up and down my person as I tried to buckle my belt.

I tried to grab her again but she moved away again, flicking off the flashlight, sitting and settling on top of the sleeping bags, out of my reach. So I chased her, kneeling in front of her drawn-up legs and wrapping my hands around her thighs.

"You can't just do what you just did—"

"You mean give my boyfriend a spectacular blow job?"

I frowned because it was more than that. Calling what she'd done just a blow job was like calling Beethoven's *Moonlight Sonata* just a song. It hadn't been part of my plan for the evening. I'd wanted a repeat of what happened after her first Daisy doughnut, at the very least, but I'd hoped for more—more of her sweet sounds, more of her bare skin. I'd also planned to take my time with her body, learn every soft curve.

But she'd surprised me; in that moment I'd never wanted anything more than her mouth on me. Although, *want* might have been an under-statement.

"You can't expect me not to want to return the favor." Again, *want* might have been an understatement. I tugged on her legs, already antici-pating the taste of her.

"It wasn't a favor."

"Then a gift."

"It wasn't that either." Her tone was more serious than I'd expected, so I stopped tugging and endeavored to make out her features.

It was dark, but we Winston boys could see better than most with very little light. With no moon in the sky, the stars alone illuminated her gorgeous face. I wanted to see her naked body under the starlight, her tits rise and fall with excited breaths as I slid my tongue inside her . . .

Jesus fucking Christ.

I couldn't breathe with how much I wanted her.

Sienna turned her face away, giving me her profile. She looked to be studying the surrounding blackness.

"Sienna." I tugged on her legs once more, wanting her to lift her hips so I could ease down her tights and expose her exquisite skin.

She covered my hands with hers, halting my movements, and she had emotion in her eyes as she brought them back to me. "Why haven't you been coming inside my trailer? In the mornings?"

Her question sounded like an accusation. It took me a moment to respond, but then she cut me off with another question before I could.

"And why haven't you spent any alone time with me other than when we're rushing to the set, or to your house for dinner, or to the cabin? You just drop me off and leave."

She sounded hurt and her eyes were wide with it. And her hurt burned me.

"Sienna . . ." I struggled for the right words. Her anger blindsided and perplexed me. I needed to make things right.

I needed to hold her, and I saw she needed me to hold her, so I did.

I gathered her in my arms and laid us both down on the sleeping bags. She didn't fight me, she snuggled closer, burying her face in my neck and gripping my shirt.

Now that we were touching, I started again. "We haven't been spending time alone because there's no place for us to be alone."

"What about my trailer and my room at the cabin and—"

"Sunshine, those places aren't private."

"They are private."

"Not private enough. 'Cause, Sienna, you're not quiet when you come—not that I'm complaining. I'm not. Not at all. I love everything about making you feel good."

She huffed. "Are you telling me you haven't been—haven't been . . . se avienta el mañanero because you require complete privacy?"

"What does that mean?"

"Literally translated, it's *throwing the morning one*, you know— getting it on in the morning."

That made me grin, because we were definitely going to be *throwing the morning one* with frequency; hopefully sooner rather than later. I'd have to learn the Spanish words and whisper it in her ear to wake her up.

Tucking that thought away, I quickly responded, "I don't require complete privacy." But then I thought more about her question and had to amend my answer. "I don't require it. But I want it."

She chuckled. It sounded frustrated. "You're going to have to explain yourself."

I tightened my arms around her and tangled our legs together. "For right now, especially for right now, I want what happens between us to be between us. I know that pretty soon things are going to change. I know I'm going to have to share you with all the dirty list makers. But for now, I have you to myself. What we're building is between just us, and that's important. I'm not ready to share, not yet."

She was quiet, like she was thinking on my words. I didn't push. Instead I rubbed her back, slipped my fingers under her shirt. I was after her skin.

Abruptly, she caught my hands on their way to her breast. "This whole time, you've been stalling? Because you wanted complete privacy?"

"Just for now." I tried moving my hand again, but she had a firm hold on me. I could easily break it. I didn't. Instead, I waited.

"I thought . . ."

When she didn't continue, I shifted away so I could see her face. Her eyes were searching for mine and she brought her fingers to my cheek like she was touching me in lieu of seeing me.

Now she'd released my hand, I continued my upward progress until I cupped her through her bra, loving the generous weight and yielding suppleness of her breast. I began pulling down the cup, planning to take her nipple between my teeth. I moved my knee to the junction of her thighs and my mouth watered in anticipation.

"What did you think?" I whispered.

"I thought, since you're trying to wait until marriage, you didn't want to do anything with me."

"What?" My single word arrived sharper than I'd intended. I saw we had some things that needed discussing. "No, no, no. God, no. All I think about is you, doing things to you. And trying to figure out how to do those things away from prying eyes and ears."

Her lips flattened. She didn't look convinced.

I pressed a quick kiss to her sweet lips. "Sienna, this afternoon, did Susie tell you to take a nap?"

She hesitated for a minute before admitting, "Yes."

"And Dave?"

"Yes."

"I asked them to do that. I have hot chocolate and champagne in the truck. And tequila. I put the sleeping bags, blankets, and pillows in the cab on Monday. I've been counting down the days, putting all the pieces in motion. Getting you alone, out here and awake, this has been in the works since early last week. I'm desperate for you." I kissed her again, pulling down the cup of her bra and sliding my palm over her perfectly shaped breast.

Fuck. She felt so fucking good. Heaven in my hands.

I wanted her. Right now.

I wanted her little, panting, hitching breaths and her loud, abandoned moans. And now I knew she was a happy screamer, I wanted her screams, too.

"Wait." She twisted her mouth from mine and caught my hand again. "Wait, stop."

I stopped, but groaned my dissatisfaction. "What? What is it?"

"I don't want you to go down on me." Her words were breathless but I heard conviction in her tone.

"Why?" I asked through gritted teeth, because I *did* want it. As much as I'd needed her mouth on me before, I needed my mouth on her sweet body. Needed the taste of her. N*eeded* it.

"Because I didn't give you a blow job because I wanted reciprocation. I did it because I need you to-to-to accept my affection. I have feelings for you—deep, important, overwhelming feelings—and I have to be able to show you how I feel."

"Fine. Done. You can show me while I taste you." I moved to kiss her again, shifting my thigh between her legs.

"Jethro, stop. You're not listening to me." Her grip on my roaming hands tightened and I growled my frustration.

My patience was at an end.

I couldn't be this close without taking some part of her for myself, so I pulled my hands and body away. I rolled onto my back, shoving my palms into my eye sockets. My heart galloped. Blood pounded between my ears and rushed with needful intent to my dick.

"Let me know when you're calm enough to talk," she said, her tone even. Completely fucking reasonable.

She didn't apologize and I was glad. She had nothing to be sorry for.

But, Christ almighty, I was shaking with how badly I needed to touch her. I was sweating with it. And that wasn't her fault.

Time. I needed time.

And space.

I pushed myself upright and edged to the tailgate, jumping down. In my peripheral vision I saw she'd also sat up and was trying to figure out what I was up to. Likely, to her eyes, I was a black mass against the dark field and sky.

"Jethro?" She sounded uncertain. I didn't like that.

I cleared my throat and tried to mimic her earlier reasonable tone. "I need a drink. You want something? I have hot chocolate."

She hesitated before asking, "Do you think it's still hot?"

"Should be. It's in my camping thermos."

"Then yes, please."

I walked to the driver's side and opened the door while I considered taking off my shirt. I was still hot. I knew of a pond not far from here I could jump in. It wouldn't be precisely cold at seventy or so degrees, but it might do the trick.

I fished out the thermos and tequila, shut the doors, walked back to the tailgate, and poured her cup first. She'd crawled on her hands and knees to where I stood and I had to look away. Seeing her in that position inspired all kinds of frustrating thoughts. I set the mug just in front of her, pulled the cork from the bottle of Patron, and took a short drink.

I needed to clear my head, not get drunk. The burn helped, sobered and slowed my frenzied pulse.

"You're drinking tequila?"

I nodded, then remembered she couldn't see me. "Yes. I'm drinking tequila."

She was quiet, like she was picking her words, then said, "You're upset."

I tried the words on and they didn't quite fit. "I'm not upset. I'm frustrated."

"Why are you frustrated?"

A humorless laugh burst from my lips. "Because I've been planning this evening for weeks, and instead of me making you feel good, I get a *Moonlight Sonata* of a blow job and then I'm not allowed to touch you."

"And why do you want to touch me so badly?"

I glared at her, seeing she was trying to subtly tell me something, or bring me to a specific conclusion. "You're trying to lead me someplace, to some conclusion? Instead, why don't you just come out and say it?"

"Fine. I'll just say it. You're frustrated because you want to show me how much I mean to you, and I won't allow it, correct?"

"That's one way of putting it." Another way might be, *I'm obsessed*

*with your body, with touching you and tasting you and bringing you
pleasure, and yet you seem indifferent.*

"I know how you feel, because that's how I've been feeling for
weeks."

I stared at her, growing irritated all over again. But this was a new
kind of irritated, like she was punishing me for not being a mind reader.

"You've been frustrated for weeks?"

"Yes."

"You never said anything."

"I know. I should have. I'm sorry."

"Yes, you should have said something. If you've been feeling frustrated, you should have told me."

"How could you not know?" she demanded, her words loud and irri-
table. "Did you really think I'd be happy with no physical intimacy?"

"So you're punishing me? Because I'm not all-knowing? You think I
haven't been frustrated too?" I lifted my voice to match her volume.

"I'm not punishing you." She reached for my hand and held it
between both of hers, sending the now familiar spike of magic, of
belonging and longing, racing up my arm. But now confusion and resentment muddied it.

"Then what are you doing?" I ground out between clenched teeth,
because I didn't want to holler at her.

"I want to talk about this before I lose my nerve, because I've been
wanting to talk to you for weeks and I've been too afraid."

I blinked at her new confession, most of my furious resentment
morphing into concern. My mouth went dry with it. She'd again
surprised me.

I choked out, "You're afraid of me?"

"No, no. I'm saying this wrong." She huffed like she was frustrated
with herself and quickly added, "I promise, if you still want to savor my
papaya after we finish talking, then I will gladly strip naked and sit on
your face. But first, we have to talk."

"Then talk. Tell me. And don't be afraid of me." I'm sure my request
sounded like a plea because the thought of Sienna being scared of me
settled like shards of glass in my stomach.

"Okay." She nodded once, gathered a deep breath, then said on a rush, "I want to be able to show you how I want you without worrying who is going to overhear or see us. I'm not talking about being an exhibitionist, but I can't go another two weeks until you arrange for complete privacy. I don't like being afraid that I'm pushing you further than you're willing to go. So before additional touching commences, I need you to know that I want you, all the time, but I don't want to lose you. I guess I'm afraid of losing you."

"You—" I took a moment to sort through her words, picking out the actionable items. "You want more, and you want it more often, and you don't care about privacy."

"I care about privacy, but not to the point where we do nothing because someone might overhear. And I don't want to lose you."

I shook my head at this last bit. But then remembered again she couldn't see me.

"I wish we weren't having this conversation in the dark," I mumbled as I climbed back into the bed of the truck. I pulled my fingers from her grip, found her hot chocolate, and tossed it into the grass.

"I know I can be pushy," she said, still explaining herself. "I have these big feelings for you and they make me clumsy. When I couldn't do anything with them, it made me sad. Everything about what I feel for you is new to me. I don't know what I'm doing. I know the celebrity thing is a headache, already a lot to deal with, I didn't and I don't want to push you—"

"You're not going to push me away," I whispered firmly, easing her back on the sleeping bags. I gripped her wrists, holding them trapped on either side of her as I planked above. I fit my knee between her legs, but applied no pressure. "And you being a celebrity isn't going to scare me off. I know I'll have to share you, I know. And I'm coming to terms with it. I want to be someone who builds you up, not someone you have to worry over. Don't worry about me."

"I can't help it."

"You have to trust me. I trusted you, when you said this thing between us wasn't temporary. No amount of celebrity headaches or you telling me how you feel is going to send me running."

How could she think that?

Sienna gathered a deep breath, her breasts pressing against my chest for the barest of moments. "I won't ask you to cross your line."

"I appreciate that, but you should know—"

"But I will do things that make keeping your vow difficult. And I might or might not do them on purpose."

I smiled. Despite the anxiety and worry in her tone, her last statement sounded like a threat.

A sexy and enticing threat.

I lowered to sweep a quick kiss over her lips. "I look forward to these things you might or might not do on purpose. Thank you for warning me. Now you got to promise me that you won't be afraid, that you'll tell me what you're thinking, no matter what."

"I promise." She made the promise on a sigh, and I felt the tension ease where I held her wrists.

I kissed her once more, sucking her bottom lip between mine. I loved how she tasted, sweetness and sunshine.

"Good," I said, then sat up on my knees and grabbed the pillows lining the left side of the bed. "Now, let's get going."

"Uh . . . we're going?"

"Yes. No need to fold up the sleeping bags." I stood and jumped down to the ground, crossing back to the driver's side door. "We can just stuff them in the back."

She grabbed the side rail and shimmied over, as close as she could get to me while still kneeling in the truck bed. "So, now you don't want my papaya?" She sounded confused and aggrieved.

I chuckled. "Oh, no. I very much want your papaya. And I want you sitting on my face while I take my time with your papaya, like you promised."

"Then why are we leaving?"

"Because your bed back at the cabin will be more comfortable than these sleeping bags. And if I need to get used to people being around to hear your screams of ecstasy," I shrugged, unable to contain my grin, "then we might as well get started right now."

* * *

WE MADE IT back to the cabin in record time and I had papaya before going to bed.

Then I stayed the night and held her.

And then I had papaya again before breakfast.

Best. Papaya. Ever.

But it was more. She was more. So much more. Was it because of five years of celibacy or because of the woman herself? *Has to be the woman.* How had she doubted my feelings for her? Pleasing her—my woman—cherishing her, loving her had no comparison. Satisfaction, desire, fulfillment were woefully inadequate words. So responsive. So incredible. So . . . *mine.*

I drifted downstairs with a big smile on my face after 10:00 a.m., leaving Sienna in her room. She was asleep again. Naked. Leaving her had been difficult, but I knew she'd wake up hungry. My plan was to drive over to Daisy's Nut House, pick up doughnuts and caffeine before she woke up, then keep her in bed all day. Naked.

But the smell and sounds of freshly brewing coffee had me stopping in my tracks as I passed the kitchen.

I glanced inside. Dave and Tim were sitting at the kitchen table reading the paper. I spotted an open box of doughnuts on the counter. Chances were, both Dave and Tim had heard Sienna last night. Likely, they'd also heard her this morning.

So I walked into the kitchen.

"Hey, these doughnuts spoken for? Or can I steal a few?"

Dave looked up from his paper and didn't appear even a little bit surprised to see me. "No, no. Take as many as you want."

"Yeah. We picked up extra on purpose. From the sound of things, you two are probably hungry," Tim added, giving me a knowing smile.

It wasn't lascivious.

It was just *knowing.*

I didn't mind. In fact, I liked that he knew. I decided everyone should know.

Meanwhile, Dave hit Tim in the back of the head. "What's wrong with you?"

"What?"

"That was rude."

"What? What did I say?"

"He doesn't want you talking about her that way and neither do I."

Tim dropped the paper he was reading and tossed his hands in the air. "I didn't say anything."

I grinned at their bickering; it reminded me of my brothers. "No, no. It's fine. Tim didn't say anything untoward."

Dave narrowed his eyes on me. "He needs to learn respect."

"But she's loud with Jethro. A woman isn't that loud unless she's having the time of her life. She's got to be starving. That's all I'm saying," Tim tried to explain again, which only served to piss Dave off more and make me laugh harder.

"Jesus Christ, Tim. Shut your fucking mouth." Dave hit him again.

"Watch your language, New Jersey." Tim swatted Dave's hand away.

Dave moved to smack him again but stopped when the sound of the front door opening pulled our collective attention away from the hole Tim had been digging. I looked at Dave. He looked at me. All three of us moved for the foyer.

But the tension left me when I heard Hank Weller's voice call, "Hey. Anyone home?"

"We're back here," Tim hollered back, releasing a relieved breath, taking his seat again.

Dave also stopped and his shoulders relaxed, though he whispered to me, "I know it's his cabin and all, but I don't like how he lets himself in. How can I keep her safe if people drop in unannounced?"

"He comes by?"

He nodded. "He used to call and she'd beg off, say she was too busy. So he started coming by unannounced, at least once a week for the last month."

"Why?"

"He's just like the rest of them." Dave gave me a single eyebrow lift, his tone telling me everything I needed to know.

I crossed my arms as Hank appeared in the doorway, watched as the expectant smile on his face wavered when he caught sight of me.

"Jethro."

"Hank."

He straightened, his eyes narrowing as they took in my bare feet, jeans with no belt, and white T-shirt. "What are you doing here?" Hank asked.

"Making Sienna scream," Tim mumbled too low for anyone but me to hear.

"What was that?" Hank looked between the two of us.

"Nothing." Dave glared at Tim, apparently he'd also heard the big man's mumble, then pointed to the kitchen counter. "Do you want some coffee? We just made some."

"Uh, sure." Hank made a show of looking around the kitchen and then sidestepping and glancing over his shoulder to the living room. "Where's Sienna?"

Tim started, "She's—"

"She's still asleep."

Hank's eyes widened, his eyebrows jumping high on his forehead. "Still asleep? It's past ten."

"So it is." I nodded once.

My business partner inspected me again. "She never sleeps past seven, let alone ten."

I didn't like that he knew when Sienna slept, so I allowed an edge of irritation in my voice as I put the question to him, "Why're you keeping tabs on Sienna's sleep habits, Hank?"

My business partner stepped fully into the kitchen and mimicked my stance. "Why're you here, Jethro?"

Dave cleared his throat and tapped Tim on the shoulder. "I think we'll finish our breakfast in the, uh, other room."

Tim grabbed his coffee cup, newspaper, and half-eaten doughnut and followed Dave out of the kitchen, leaving Hank and me swapping glares.

Neither of us spoke for a full minute or more, likely because we both already knew the answer to each other's question.

Finally, Hank asked, "You decided to ignore my advice?"

The fact Hank was the first to break the silence was unsurprising. He'd always been impatient, too curious for his own good.

"Did you give me advice?" I leaned my hip against the kitchen counter.

"You know what I'm talking about." He crossed to the coffee maker and poured a cup, giving me his profile. "When she leaves you in the dust, you can't say I didn't warn you."

I studied the unhappy curve of his mouth, saw he believed his own words. "Why are you really here, Hank?"

"Same as you, I suspect. I like her. She's beautiful. She makes me laugh. She tells great stories. She makes me feel good." He turned to look at me, blowing steam from the coffee cup and taking a sip before adding, "Except, Sienna and I are friends. When she leaves, I'll still know her. Whereas, you . . ." He shrugged, his eyes full of sympathy.

"Hey. Is there any coffee left?"

Both Hank and I turned toward the entrance to the kitchen. Sienna stood just inside the doorway, rubbing sleep from her eyes. She wore a black silk bathrobe that covered just as much as it showed, and based on what it showed I was pretty sure she was naked beneath it.

Without waiting for us to respond, she walked into the kitchen and headed directly to where I stood. When she reached me, she wrapped her arms around my neck, pressed her body to mine, and placed a sweet kiss on my mouth, nibbling my top lip as she pulled away. I grabbed her waist before she could retreat too far and confirmed my earlier suspicion. She was naked under the robe.

I fought a groan. I also fought the urge to sweep her in my arms and carry her back upstairs. Her tits were built for my hands. The idea of unwrapping her from the black silk had my blood pumping thick and urgent. She might not mind the caveman display, but I wanted Hank and everyone else to see I was nothing but confident where Sienna Diaz was concerned.

"I love that mouth," she said with a sleepy grin, her eyes on my lips as she pressed her thumb to my chin. "And I love this beard." She kissed my chin. "And I love this nose." She kissed my nose. "And I love this neck." She kissed my neck, her body inadvertently sliding against mine.

I kept my eyes studiously forward, but didn't hide my satisfied grin. In my side vision I could see Hank gawking at us.

"There's still coffee." I pushed her rich, chestnut hair from her face and angled her chin so I could steal another kiss. "Or we could take these doughnuts and head back to bed."

"Look at you, smartest man alive." She pushed on my shoulder playfully. "When we're in L.A., every Saturday will be spent in this way. I demand it."

Hank cleared his throat. Actually, he choked on a sip of coffee.

Sienna's head whipped toward the sound, her eyes wide, her mouth parted in surprise, and she gasped. "Hank. Crap. Geeze. I didn't see you. Sorry." She pressed closer to me, turning me slightly so my body hid hers.

"No, no. I'm sorry. I should have, uh, I should have called first." He waved away her apology, his gaze flickering to mine. His held speculation and maybe a hint of awe. "In fact, I would have called, but I was cleaning out the shower drain at the strip club, and you'll never guess what disgusting thing I found."

Sienna sighed tiredly but gave him a patient smile, tugging me by the fabric of my shirt toward the stairs. "I'm tired of games, Hank. Even that one. Is there anything else? Did this month's payment go through? For the rent?"

Hank nodded, looking sufficiently dumbfounded and maybe even a little contrite. "Uh, yeah. It cleared last week. There's nothing else."

"Good," she said, then to me, "Grab the doughnuts, I'll meet you upstairs."

Sienna gave me a quick kiss and a sly grin, lowering her lashes, heat and promise in her eyes. Then she turned and skipped lightly on her feet out of the kitchen. My last glimpse of her retreating form was her full, round backside draped in black silk.

I exhaled. It wasn't a loud exhale, but it was necessary. Because that woman took my breath away.

The kitchen descended into weighty silence. I counted to ten before sliding my eyes to Hank's.

"Well, I'll be." He shook his head, looking at me with unveiled wonder. "Jethro Whitman Winston, I'm impressed."

"I don't know what you're talking about, Hank Herman Weller." I'm pretty sure my smile was as arrogant as it was pleased.

"No. Really. I'm impressed. I never thought I'd see Sienna . . ."

"What?"

"I don't know. I just thought she'd always be single, never get serious with anyone."

"Even with you?" I asked, because it was a question that needed asking. Hank seemed stunned, but if he was jealous he was hiding it well.

His gaze when hazy as he considered my question. "Honestly? No. Not even with me. We don't suit, we didn't in college and we don't suit now." His eyes refocused on me. "Don't get me wrong, I'd switch places with you in a second. I'd be a fool not to." He grinned, and quickly added, "But if she was going to tie herself down, settle, I'm happy it's with you. You two, you're good people. You deserve each other."

"I appreciate that, Hank." I was surprised but pleased I didn't have to deal with jealousy where he was concerned.

He was my business partner and friend; I'd hate to lose him as either.

I openly inspected him and I needed to add, "But I have to contradict you on one point. Sienna hasn't tied herself down, nor has she settled, and neither have I. It doesn't work that way, not when it's the right person."

"So she's like Redbull? She gives you wings?" He lifted a teasing eyebrow.

I shook my head. "More like she's the sun, and she makes every minute better than the last."

His grin waned, an expression of skepticism and confusion on his face.

I chuckled. "Don't worry, one of these days you'll understand." I reached for the box on the counter and moved to follow my woman. "Now if you'll excuse me, I can't forget the doughnuts."

CHAPTER TWENTY-EIGHT

"Things are sweeter when they're lost."

— F. SCOTT FITZGERALD, THE BEAUTIFUL AND
DAMNED

~Sienna~

J ETHRO TOOK ME to Daisy's Nut House for our eighth date.

We arrived to a sign that read, Closed for a Private Party. He'd bought out the entire restaurant. It was just Jethro, Daisy, and me, and a candlelit dinner for two of hamburgers, steak fries, hot sauce, and milkshakes.

He'd suggested a booth in the back, but I requested the diner counter. I couldn't remember the last time I'd been able to sit in a restaurant at the diner counter. It felt so brazen to be out in the open, like I was on display with no consequences. The words *magnificently liberating* came to mind.

Sitting beside me on a stool, Jethro watched me with a wry expression as I added a generous amount of sriracha to my Swiss and mushroom burger.

"What?" I squeezed the sriracha out in a smiley face shape on top of the burger patty.

"Nothing." He shook his head, still grinning, still watching me in a way that had my stomach and heart doing gymnastics.

"No. Tell me. What is it?"

He hesitated for just a second before saying, "It's just, I like that you eat hot sauce because it means you can handle surprises in your mouth."

I squinted at him. He probably thought the statement was funny, or shocking, or cute, or all three. Admittedly, he was right. It was funny, shocking, and cute—but only coming from him. Jethro's flirting was typically light and teasing, respectful. He was so rarely lewd. Well, apart from when we were in bed. Thus, I kinda liked his lewd flirting. It felt special, like he reserved it just for me.

Jethro and his layers, one of which was apparently thinking about giving me surprises. In my mouth.

I waited until he took a bite of his hamburger before I asked, "How do you feel about pop rocks, then?"

Jethro coughed, his eyes bulging, and he covered his mouth with his napkin. He might have been choking to death on ketchup and laughter. I took this as a sign to continue.

"Because, if you think hot sauce is a surprise, you should try pop rocks and Coke. I mean, that's like setting off a bomb of *what the fuck did I sign up for* inside your mouth."

"Stop," he rasped, reaching for and gulping his water, still laughing and choking.

I continued to squint at him, but was now grinning widely.

Tears had formed in his eyes, and he wiped them away, still chuckling. "I promise, I will never surprise your mouth if you promise never to tell a joke when I've got food in mine."

"Agreed."

We shook on it. Instead of letting my hand go, he kept it in his on his thigh, curling his fingers around mine. I couldn't remember ever holding someone's hand during a date. It was such a simple, affectionate gesture, as though he couldn't stand having me close and not touching me.

I loved him for it.

I love him.

I blinked. The unbidden thought caught me off guard and was made even scarier because it *wasn't* too soon. Since Hawk's Field and the fun that came after, we'd been considerably more open about our relationship. He stayed with me most nights. We drove to the set together then made out or just shared each other's company in my trailer. People on the set were talking, but we couldn't be bothered to care.

We'd done everything but cross his line, and I believed he enjoyed my tempting him just as much as I did.

I was mad for him.

Everything was grand.

We were perfect together.

If my life were a movie script, the timing would have been just right. Two months, eight dates, a few ups and downs—actually, a lot of ups and very few downs—and no insurmountable issues.

I loved him. I trusted him. I wanted to be with him all the time. He treated me like I was precious to him, like I was the most important thing in his life, like I took priority. And I hoped he knew I felt the same way for him. I couldn't imagine my life without him.

"You know, I still don't know much about what you actually do."

"What I do?" I squeaked, jumping, trying to keep up with the conversation even as I was endeavoring to not freak out about the fact I loved him.

I'd never been in love.

But I loved Jethro.

I love him.

"Yeah, your job. We've talked about your writing, but you don't talk much about acting."

What a funny comment. Had we really never talked about my job? I was sure I'd rambled incessantly about acting at some point.

"My job?"

"Yes."

An unbidden smile claimed my mouth and my heart skipped a few beats. "So you haven't looked me up?"

"Nope." He smiled, clearly pleased I was pleased.

Yep. I love him.

"Not at all? No googling, or yahooing, or binging?"

"I don't know what binging is, but it sounds like something we should try later."

"No. We shouldn't. It's the shameful receptacle of thwarted hopes, where dreams and searches go to die," I joked, because I now knew I loved him and thus was nervous.

"We should definitely steer clear of shameful receptacles of thwarted hopes." He smiled at me even as he studied me, his voice a rich, velvety baritone. I even loved his voice. Actually, I especially loved his voice.

Then he asked, "Does talking about your job make you nervous?"

"No. No, not at all. I guess I can't believe we haven't talked about it yet. I mean, it's usually the only thing people want to talk to me about."

He clearly didn't like my offhanded confession because his resultant frown was severe. It was the truth—people usually only wanted to talk to me about my job, my movies, or what it was like to be an actress—but I hadn't ever admitted the truth out loud, nor had I ever explicitly realized it as a thought.

And yet, with Jethro, we'd known each other for months and this was the first time he'd asked me about it. Actually, there had been one other time, when he'd thought my name was Sarah and I told him I was a writer. Other than that one incident, he'd asked me all manner of questions—what I thought, what I wished for—but never about being an actress or a celebrity.

I rushed to answer his question, not wanting to dwell on the depressing truth of my impromptu confession. "Okay, let's see. My first film, *Taco Tuesday*, didn't have much to do with tacos. It was about a girl who grew tired of the words used to describe women, but hardly ever used to describe men."

"Like what? Give me some examples."

"Okay, like feisty. Or buxom. Or dainty, perky, prissy, slutty, bitchy, and prude."

He nodded thoughtfully. "Yeah, okay. I can see that. I've never called a man feisty, or slutty for that matter."

"And you wouldn't. It just isn't done. A woman is a slut, but a man is a man-slut. Why is the default gender of a slut a woman? Why can't sluts just be sluts instead of having to differentiate the gender?"

"Yeah. Let them all be sluts."

"That's what I always say. I'm very careful to refer to my sex-worker friends as escorts, not man-tramps or men-wenches."

Jethro laughed, his smile lingering for a long time after his chuckle tapered. I loved the sound of his laugh, and I loved that he laughed so freely, without reservation. I loved how vulnerable he was to happiness, truly open to the possibility of it. His willingness made being around him relaxing, easy. So easy, everyone else's company felt difficult and challenging in comparison.

When I realized I was staring at him and his charming face, I shook myself, returned my attention to my food, and gathered my wits. "Anyway, this girl, Kate was her name, she grew irritated with how words were used so she started insulting women with words reserved for men—like dickface—and men with words reserved for women—like prude. But then her rant was picked up by the national news, went viral, and she became a reluctant spokesperson for feminism. It was a satire-comedy, like a buddy movie that made fun of both men and women and our first world struggles, feminists and meninists."

"Meninists?"

"Oh yes. Men's rights activists."

The way Jethro both lifted and furrowed his eyebrows told me this concept perplexed him. "You made that word up."

"No. I didn't. I swear. They exist and they have twitter accounts and all hate me."

"What the hell is a men's rights activist?"

"Well, if you asked Kate, the main character from *Taco Tuesday*, it's a coven of dainty, sassy, wee men, who are quite perky, headstrong, and prudish, and who fret about how society is eroding their privilege. But if you ask me, it's a bunch of guys who don't have enough to do, suffer from micro-IQ scores, and can't get laid, so they hate on women."

"Huh." I could see his expression still held confusion and disbelief. In the end he shrugged. "So, why did you write it? Why'd you write the script?"

"I love to write. I've always loved writing much more than performing, giving voice to the imaginary people in my head. And movies. I love film. But I wrote this particular script because so much about our culture is inadvertently hilarious. I enjoy poking fun at sensitive topics, because you can achieve a lot more with humor and entertainment, reach more hearts and minds, than with the most thoughtful and well-researched letter to the editor. And because most of the words used to describe only women—not all, just most—are really rather negative or condescending. Like the term 'working-mom.' No one says 'working-dad.' Why do we do that? Don't mothers have it hard enough?"

"Buxom isn't negative." Referring to my earlier word list, Jethro's eyes darted to my chest then back up. He didn't apologize, but he did smile.

So of course I had to tease him. "Did you just look at my chest when you said 'buxom?'"

"Yes." He nodded once, his eyes warm and playful.

"And why did you do that?"

"Because the word describes what you have going on in that area. Just like, the word clever describes what you have going on here," he motioned to my brain, "and the word beautiful describes what you have going on everywhere."

Warmth bloomed in my chest and I couldn't help my grin. "Oh, you're good."

"Yes. But sometimes . . ." his eyes dropped again, this time conducting a slow perusal from the heels of my shoes to the locket around my neck, heating every inch of my body with his gaze until it collided with mine, "sometimes I'm very, very bad."

* * *

WE WERE IN his truck driving to his house after dinner, enjoying each other's company, when Marta called.

Her name flashing on the screen hit me like a bucket of ice water being thrown on the evening. I stared at my phone and debated what to do.

"What's wrong?"

I glanced at Jethro. He was obviously concerned about my sudden mood shift.

"Uh, it's just my sister." I rejected the call. "I'll call her later."

"Which one?"

"Marta."

"Your manager."

"Yes. That's the one." I swallowed stiffly, wondering if the time had come for me to tell him about the argument she and I'd had when I was in L.A. We'd been texting each other and emailing since the fight last month, our discussions limited to business topics only. This was the first time she'd called. Before I could decide what to do, she called again.

"You should get it." Jethro lifted his chin toward the phone. "It might be important."

"It's never important," I grumbled, but I answered the call anyway. "Hello?"

"Sienna," Marta said by way of greeting, which would have been fine except she'd said my name like she was trying to talk reason into me, like *Now, now, Sienna. Calm down.*

So I mimicked her tone. "Marta." *Now, now, Marta. Calm down.*

Clearly, she hadn't been expecting that, because it took her several seconds to speak again. Before she did, she cleared her throat, and I heard her chair squeak. She was at work. Even with the time difference it was still late for her to still be at the office.

"I'm calling about the Smash-Girl script and the London premiere."

I grimaced, having forgotten all about the London premiere. Again. *When was that again? August?*

"Where are you with the script? Barnaby called again this morning asking for a status."

My grimace intensified, because I hadn't thought much about the script since they'd un-casted me from the role.

"Sienna?"

"Yes. I'm here."

"Anything more I can share with Barnaby?"

"Not yet."

She sighed, sounding disappointed and irritated, but she said, "Fine."

"I'm still thinking things through," I hedged.

That wasn't like me and Marta knew it. I'd allowed it to lapse, which wasn't professional behavior at all. I needed to work on it or officially step aside. I could blame it on writer's block, but Marta knew me better than that.

"And London? Do you want me to reach out to Tom's people?"

"Tom's people?"

Jethro shifted in his seat, drawing my eyes to him. He wasn't looking at me, as his attention was on the dark road, but I could see he didn't like the mention of my co-star.

"You have to go with someone, he was your most recent—"

"No," I interrupted her. "Tom isn't my most recent anything." Then, on a whim, I said, "I'll bring Jethro."

His eyes cut to mine, his eyebrows suspended in question. I mouthed, *Just a minute.*

Again, silence followed by a chair squeak. I made a mental note to order her some WD-40 for that chair.

"Do you think that's a good idea?"

"Yes."

She huffed. "Okay, forget our conversation when you were in L.A., forget that I think you're making a terrible mistake hooking up with this guy. Forget all of that for a minute and just think about this. I can't believe I have to spell this out, but consider this: if you take the park ranger to this event—"

"Jethro. His name is Jethro."

She ignored me. "Then everyone will know about the two of you. His life will never be the same. People will dig into his past. Celebrity bloggers and websites will pick him apart. He'll find himself on the cover of magazines, newspapers, photographed at work, wherever he goes. He'll be the object of much fascination. Is that what you want? Is that what he wants?"

I held my breath.

. . . crap.

She had me there.

Biting my lip, I attempted to think of a rejoinder. I came up blank.

"I don't know," I finally admitted, my heart sinking. I'd been so busy being with Jethro, living in this perfect bubble we'd created, I hadn't thought about the ramifications of what being with me publicly would mean for him.

"The event is in one week."

"Okay." *Crap.* My pulse doubled.

"I'm chartering a plane."

"Fine. Okay. Fine."

"Do you want me to reach out to Tom's people? He could fly over with you. You could both say you're going as friends. It would delay having to make a decision about . . . about Jethro, give you some time."

"No." My response was immediate. I'd rather go alone than with Tom. "Let me talk to Jethro."

"I need an answer by tomorrow."

"Fine."

"Good night, Sienna." Her voice held hesitation, as though she wanted to say more, then with a surprisingly soft and affectionate tone, she said, "Sweet dreams."

I smiled at her tone, some of the anger I'd been carrying around since our argument dissipated. Unfortunately, it was quickly being replaced with panic.

"Good night, Marta."

Ending the call, I continued to stare at the screen, unable to meet Jethro's gaze.

The heaviness of what I'd been stubbornly ignoring for the last months saddled itself on my shoulders. I felt foolish. I felt idiotic, stranded by my own willful blindness. Marta had just pointed out major, serious issues that should have been obvious to me. Issues Jethro and I should have discussed prior to now.

Prior to our first date.

Prior to agreeing to more than temporary.

And prior to my falling in love with him.

Now I felt the weight of it, like a slap in the face or a punch in the stomach.

I felt it all.

"What's wrong?" he asked, placing his hand on my legs and squeezing. "More bad news? Do we need to go dancing?"

I managed to crack a smile at that but couldn't sustain it. My thoughts were turning pragmatic. And with pragmatism came some depressing truths.

I'd been selfish because I liked him so much. He wanted more than temporary with me, but he couldn't possibly know what that meant in real-world terms. He may have had an inkling based on our first date and from the looks we'd been getting around the set, but he really had no idea.

By his own admission during dinner, he hadn't looked me up yet.

Resting my elbow on the window sill, I placed my forehead in my hand and closed my eyes, exhaling in an effort to diffuse the foreboding swelling in my chest.

"So, when I was in L.A., Marta and I had a disagreement. She saw the picture of us on my phone and . . ." I sighed, all my words were irritating, so I rushed to finish. "She didn't like it. She's worried about the photo getting out."

"I'm not sharing it, if that's what she's worried about."

I sighed again, trying to ease the tightness in my chest. "It's not just that. I have to go to a film premiere next week in London." My voice was strained.

"Okay. That doesn't sound so bad."

I swallowed, finding my mouth dry and my tongue coated with dread. "It's complicated. I need to go with someone."

"A date."

"Yes. I need to go with a date. Someone who will help my image and create the right kind of buzz," I said flatly, echoing Marta's words from so many meetings and phone calls and lectures about the capricious nature of success, how it could vanish in the blink of an eye.

"I'm going to be real honest, Sienna. I'm not going to be happy if you go with someone other than me on a date." His tone was firm, like he meant business, but also measured and coaxing, like he was trying his hardest not to turn the statement into a mandate.

"I don't want to go with anyone other than you, that wouldn't make me happy either."

He paused for a second before asking, "Then what's the problem?"

I covered his hand with mine, and he immediately turned his palm upward, tangling our fingers together.

"If you decide to come with me, to the premiere, then everyone will know about us."

"So?"

"So are you ready to lose your privacy? Are you ready for people to dig through your trash, hack into your phone, and take pictures of you at work? While you grocery shop?" I tried to keep the bitterness out of my voice and mostly failed.

He shifted in his seat. I assumed his hesitation meant he was coming to the same realization as me.

Suddenly, I had a heartbreaking thought: Jethro and I had been doomed from the start. Or at least an open relationship was doomed.

My mind scrambled to find a solution. *Maybe he would consider a relationship in secret*, where his privacy could be protected. Maybe if we kept everything between us discreet . . . But we hadn't been discreet. People on set knew. Strangely enough, it hadn't hit the gossip mags. *Could we contain things? Keep them here?*

"Yes."

I frowned, not knowing what question he was answering. "Yes, what?"

"Yes, I'm ready to lose my privacy and have people dig through my trash. I'll have to warn Cletus, though. He disposes of odd things from time to time. Maybe I should move out of the homestead, get a place in Merryville."

I gawked at him. "What? How can you even consider this?"

He looked at me, his eyebrows arched over hooded eyes; his gaze slid meaningfully up and down my body, like I was the crazy one. "I think I'll suffer through."

I grinned despite myself and despite the situation, but reality soon won out over his charm. "You don't understand. We're not just talking about now, Jethro. We're talking about your past. Everything you've ever done would be turned into media fodder. Every embarrassing arrest photo, every painful story. You would be giving up your privacy—both past, present, and future—to be with me."

His fingers tightened on mine. Now he was frowning. I tore my eyes from his profile because looking at him was starting to hurt. We drove in silence, and I could almost hear his mind working, going back over my words.

I wanted to suggest we go the secret relationship route to protect his privacy for as long as possible, and it was on the tip of my tongue, when he said, "You're afraid my past will hurt your image."

I flinched because his tone was heartbreaking, and I immediately contradicted him. "No! God, no. Nothing embarrasses me."

He pulled his hand from mine. "But it would, right? I've been arrested plenty of times, there's plenty of photos for them to use. Plenty of sordid stories from my past. I would hurt your image and your career."

I gaped at him, baffled by the unexpected direction of the conversation. "Don't worry about that. Don't worry about my image."

He said nothing, but was gritting his teeth, his knuckles white on the steering wheel.

I was just about to reiterate that my image wasn't at issue when he asked, "How bad?"

"What?"

"How bad would it be? Could you lose more film roles?"

I opened my mouth to respond but no sound came out. I didn't want to lie and say no. The truth was I didn't know because I hadn't given the matter much thought.

But he took my silence as confirmation and cursed.

"Jethro—" I reached for him and he flinched away, startling me. I wanted to reach for him again, but it seemed my touch was now unwelcome.

A sharp, stabbing pierced my chest, my lungs rigid, inflexible. I couldn't draw a full breath. I'd never seen him like this. He'd been angry during our first date, a bewildered, frustrated anger.

But this was different.

He was angry but also something else, unwieldy and dark. And he felt faraway, removed from me. He'd opened a chasm between us.

I tried again using a carefully calm tone, though panic made every beat of my heart painful and sluggish. "Jethro, it's not about my image. I've never cared about my image, what people say."

"Do you care about your career?"

I ignored his question. "This is about your privacy."

His jaw ticked. "I'm taking you to the cabin."

"Will you stay with me? Tonight?"

He shook his head but said nothing.

I pressed my lips together to keep my chin from wobbling, but couldn't quite manage to keep my voice steady as I reminded him, "You promised me. You promised me that my celebrity wouldn't send you running. You said I could trust you."

"Sienna, this isn't about your celebrity. This is about my past hurting your future."

"Don't do this." I wanted to reach for him again, frustrated tears burning my eyes. "Stay with me. Stay the night, and we'll talk it through."

"Not tonight." Jethro didn't look at me when he spoke, but his voice was unrecognizable, hard and cold as granite. "I need time."

CHAPTER TWENTY-NINE

"*Ever has it been that love knows not its own depth until the hour of separation.*"

— KAHLIL GIBRAN

~Jethro~

"TIME," SHE ECHOED.

I made no move other than to turn left toward Hank's cabin. I said nothing because I couldn't speak, not yet. I was too angry, too frustrated. I couldn't think past the string of curses and profanities hurling through my brain.

It didn't matter how much I'd changed, how hard I'd worked to become something different, better than the garbage I'd been. My past was still hurting people, or had the potential to hurt, and this time it would be Sienna.

"You need time," she said.

I didn't like her tone.

She sounded hollow and anxious, close to tears. But I couldn't do anything about her tone just now. I couldn't find the wherewithal within myself to pacify and soothe, tell her everything was going to be just fine. I wasn't a liar, not anymore.

I didn't know whether or not everything would be *just fine*.

We pulled into Hank's gravel driveway and I eased on the brake. I tried to ignore the sense of hopelessness as we pulled to a complete stop. Neither of us spoke. I was too busy trying to think of ways to obscure my past.

Maybe . . . maybe I could ask Cletus for help. Maybe he could figure out a way to remove all my arrest records from the law enforcement databases.

But that still left all the people who knew me growing up. That still left plenty of stories and willing storytellers, eager to share tales of my misdeeds. I didn't blame them. I'd been the one to mess up my life. I'd earned every mortifyingly scandalous element of those stories. I was responsible.

And, of course, there was my father. If the picture he'd sent weeks ago was any indication, he'd be the first person in line to exploit our relationship. I heard his words again, the message on the photo, as though he were sitting in the truck with us.

You always were best at the big cons. I hope her bank account is as big as her tits. She can pay my legal fees.

I cursed under my breath, wanting to smash something.

What the hell had I done?

He was a loose cannon.

Shit.

Sienna deserved better. She didn't deserve to be tarnished by association. She didn't deserve to be linked to my father.

My job, as her man, was to take care of her, see to her needs and well-being. Not cause embarrassment, not be a stain on her reputation. Not make her job harder. I'd already darkened the lives of my own family. I couldn't live with myself if I hurt her chances for success.

I couldn't.

And I wouldn't.

She cleared her throat, her hands balled into fists on her lap. "How much time do you need?"

I shook my head but didn't answer. Instead, I exited the cab and walked around to her side, opening her door and offering her my hand.

She didn't take it and made no move to leave the truck.

"Jethro," she exhaled a broken sigh, "talk to me."

I dropped my hand and met her pleading dark eyes, hating myself for putting sadness there.

"Just give me time," I said, removed from the moment.

"What are you thinking?"

I tried to breathe in, but the tightness around my lungs didn't permit it. "You know what I'm thinking."

"You're overreacting." She jumped down from the cab, shut the door, and placed her hands on my shoulders, narrowing her eyes at me. "Nothing has to be decided right now. We can . . ." She paused, swallowing with effort, and when she spoke next her voice cracked. "I know it's not ideal, but we can date in secret for a while, just until—"

"Hell. No," I growled.

A visceral, vehement rejection of the idea pounded through my veins, setting my brain on fire.

I hated it. I hated lying. I hated denying and pretending.

Her hands dropped from my shoulders, her eyes widening by what she saw on my face. Sienna tried to take a step back, but the truck behind her halted her progress.

And it wasn't just the thought of lying to everyone. Over the last weeks I'd given Sienna's fame serious thought, but obviously not enough, not about things that mattered. *She mattered. More than anything.*

See, I'd been preoccupied with her status on countless dirty lists, like Beau's for example. I'd come to a measure of peace with this reality. She was famous and beautiful, smart, funny, and sexy. Of course she was going to be on these lists. Of course men and some women would think about her in that way.

If being with Sienna meant thousands, if not millions, of people lusted after my woman, I could deal with that. Fine. Okay. So be it.

Just as long as the world knew she was mine.

Sure, my fixation on that aspect of her fame likely made me a blind caveman, a reactionary Neanderthal, but it was what it was. Among others, I suffered from the human conditions of jealousy and pride. I've never claimed to be perfect.

Nor have I claimed to be smart.

If I'd been smart, I would've considered how my past—how being with me—might affect *her* future.

"I'm so fucking stupid," I grumbled. My forehead falling to my fingers. I stepped away from her, turned, giving her my back.

"I don't care what anyone thinks." Her voice was small, and I hated the sound of that, too. Hated that I was responsible for that as well.

"You should," I said. "You've worked hard for what you have. You can't throw it away just because you fancy a hick from backwoods Appalachia."

"Jethro."

I walked back to the driver's side, each step feeling wrong though I knew they were right.

"Where does this leave us?" she called after me.

"I don't know," I said honestly, because I wasn't ready to give up, but I couldn't see a way forward. All routes were blocked by decisions I'd made a decade ago.

That was my fault. It was all my fault. And now I was finally paying the price.

* * *

"YOU'VE CHOPPED ALL the wood."

I didn't look over my shoulder. I recognized the speaker. Billy. He was right. I'd chopped all the wood at the woodshed. And now I was swinging a double-bit felling axe at a pine some yards into the forest behind our house. I wasn't even fifty percent into the trunk, though I'd been at it for over an hour. Nor was I ready to stop. Not by a long shot.

When I didn't answer he said, "We don't need more wood, Jet."

I wrenched the blade from where it bit into the trunk and swung again.

"Jet?"

316

"Fuck off, Billy."

Last night, after dropping off Sienna, I'd driven myself to the Dragon Biker Bar, the club headquarters for the Iron Wraiths.

I'd wanted a fight.

I'd wanted to beat the shit out of someone and have the guts beaten out of me.

Raising hell, getting drunk, getting high wouldn't have felt good, but I had thought it had to feel better than the cavernous abyss of misery.

I didn't go in. I couldn't. My past may have lost me a chance with Sienna, but I still had five brothers and a sister. I hadn't lost them. They'd given me a chance. I couldn't let them down.

But I could destroy a tree.

Billy didn't leave. "What did you do to the carriage house?"

I didn't respond.

"It looks like someone took a sledgehammer to your new framework."

"Fuck. Off."

He sighed. I sensed his presence behind me, standing silently, while I took satisfaction in the jarring pain running up my arms every time I buried the axe into the trunk.

Then a second voice spoke. "Jethro, did you chop all the wood?"

Cletus.

I sighed, shaking my head.

Cletus continued, "We don't need all that wood. What are we going to do with a split pile of wood that big? It's like you're inviting termites over for tea."

"I asked the same thing," I heard Billy whisper, "and he destroyed the upstairs framework in the carriage house."

"I can hear you, dummy." I pulled the blade from the tree and glared over my shoulder, finding my brothers frowning at me. "Can you hear me? I said—"

"Fuck off. Yes. I heard you." Billy's tone was flat, aggravated, but he didn't budge.

Cletus glanced between us, a thoughtful eyebrow raised. "I take it something happened with Ms. Diaz?"

I slid my eyes to Cletus, grinding my teeth, but said nothing. If I spoke, a string of curses would erupt like a volcano. I still hadn't beaten the shit out of anyone, but the day was young. And Cletus was a good fighter.

As though reading my mind, Cletus stiffened. "You will do no such thing. I haven't had breakfast yet, and this is my best smoking jacket."

"Then leave."

Cletus grunted, his mouth a flat line, then threatened, "If you don't tell me what happened, then I'll pay a call to Ms. Diaz and—"

"You won't," I ordered sharply, taking a step toward my brothers.

Cletus raised his hands between us as though warding me off. "Then tell me what happened."

"What'd you do to her?" Billy lifted an eyebrow, his gaze cold and assessing and irritating as hell.

"I did nothing," I seethed between clenched teeth, tossing the axe to a nearby stump so I wouldn't throw it at Billy's head.

Billy's frown intensified. He clearly didn't believe me. Judgment was written all over his face, and in that moment I hated him.

Without thinking I asked, "What'd you do to Claire?"

Billy flinched, the stone steadiness of his expression cracking with surprise. "What?"

"You heard me." I wiped the back of my hand across my brow. "What'd you do to her? Why does she hate you so much?"

Billy blanched as though I'd sucker-punched him, and I was immediately remorseful for asking the question.

This, what I was doing, the mind games, the lashing out, wasn't who I was. Even at my worst, I'd never done this shit. This was my father; this was how he operated.

And now I hated myself, too.

Before I could apologize, Cletus stepped between us. "This ain't about Billy, this is about you deforesting the Great Smoky Mountains National Park for superfluous firewood, firewood that's about as useful as a screen door on a submarine. Now, I'll ask you again, what happened with you and Sienna?"

The fight drained from me, leaving my body tired and my head pounding and my chest hurting. "We're over."

The words felt final and wrong, rang empty and desolate, hung heavy in the stagnant summer air.

I'd been repeating them to myself, trying them on, because I couldn't figure a way around the mountain of my past. But I also couldn't let her go.

And because I was growing desperate, I was also trying on her idea of dating in secret. Unfortunately, that suggestion, thinking on the ramifications of it, led me to destroying the upstairs framework in the carriage house. So I'd moved to the woodshed.

Maybe by the time I cut down this tree, I'd be more at peace with her proposal of a concealed relationship.

"Fuck." I shook my head. "Maybe we're not over. I don't know."

Cletus placed his hands on his hips. "Why are you over? Did something happen at Daisy's?"

I shook my head. "No. She got a call from her sister on the drive back. Sienna has a . . . a thing. A movie premiere in London she's got to go to this week, and she needs to bring a date."

Cletus scrutinized me, as though he expected me to continue. When I didn't, he prompted, "So? What's the problem?"

"So . . ." My gaze flickered to Billy. He was back to stonewalling me, his arms crossed, his mouth a rigid line. "So, it can't be me."

Cletus *tsked* impatiently. "Why can't it be you? You got plans or something? A cake to bake?"

"Because, Cletus, then everybody would know about us. Because, if we go public, then news people will dig into my past. And how do you think America's sweetheart is going to look saddled with me? An ex-con named Jethro, from backwoods Appalachia, with a GED and an album full of arrest photos."

Cletus's frown was severe, fuming. "You're not an ex-con. You were never convicted."

"Same difference. I didn't get caught, but I did it. We all know I did it."

Cletus's eyes moved over me. "So she broke it off."

"No." I shook my head, a humorless laugh tumbling from my lips. "I'm breaking it off. I'm going to have to break it off."

"You?" Billy asked abruptly, another fracture of surprise in his granite-like expression.

"Yes. Me."

"Why?" Billy pressed, clearly captivated by my words.

"Because I can't do that to her," I ground out between clenched teeth, yelling at him, feeling wretched all over again, angry all over again, hurting all over again. "I can't wreck her career, her image. I can't do that. You don't do that to someone you lo—"

I was about to say love. I turned, gave them my back.

You don't do that to someone you love.

Damn it all to hell, but I was in love with Sienna Diaz.

Falling for her had been like breathing. Natural, easy, necessary. Inescapable. And the thought of spending the rest of my days without her had me drowning in panic.

Cursing, I moved to pick up the axe but was intercepted by Cletus. "Whoa. Wait. Wait a minute." His hands were again held out between us, his eyebrows suspended over concerned eyes. "Now hold on. What did she have to say?"

I shrugged. "It doesn't matter."

"What she wants doesn't matter?" he baited.

"I didn't say that. Of course what she wants matters."

"Then what does she want?"

I shook my head, closing my eyes. "She doesn't want to invade my privacy. And she wants us to date in secret."

"What? What does that mean?"

"She's focused on what this means for my privacy. She's worried I'll have no privacy; that I'll be giving up too much. So she wants us to hide our relationship."

"And you're not worried about that? About your privacy?"

"God, no." I opened my eyes, my words forceful. "I don't care about that. I'd gladly give up my privacy if I could be with her, but not when my past is going to—"

"Tarnish her image, yes. I know," Cletus finished for me, waving my words away, a frown etched into his features.

"And it's not just hurting her career. You saw that photo Darrell sent. You read his note. Do you think our father is just going to leave us in peace?"

"No," Billy answered honestly for both him and Cletus. "He'll try to exploit the hell out of you. He'll try blackmail; he'll try everything."

"Don't you worry about Darrell Winston." Again Cletus waved this concern away. "I can deal with Darrell Winston. Forget about him. I got him under control."

"How can I be sure?" I pressed my brother. "This is Sienna. I can't take any chances."

"Jethro Whitman Winston," Cletus's eyes were flinty and stern, "you're going to have to trust me. Let it go."

We glared at each other. I didn't know if I could let it go.

But then he ground out, "Have I ever let you down? Have I ever failed to keep a promise? I'm telling you. Let. Me. Deal. With. It."

I gritted my teeth. Cletus was right. He was sneaky and sinister, mean even, but his word was sacred. In the end, his meanness was why I ultimately trusted him to deal with Darrell.

"You need to focus your attention back to your woman, how you're going to make this right."

"Maybe we should just date in secret," I said, but the same visceral rejection as before drummed outward from my chest to my fingertips, making my skin and lungs burn.

"Don't do that," Billy said, shaking his head emphatically. "Do it in public, or don't do it at all. Don't hide what you have. The lies will destroy you and her. It'll turn what's beautiful between you ugly."

I glared at Billy, surprised by his words, and hating how wise and true they were. But I was desperate and grasping at straws. We stood in the relative silence of the forest. I heard nothing, saw nothing, because I felt nothing but hopelessness.

Billy was the first to move, to break the stillness of the moment. He removed his dress shirt, tossing it over the branch of a nearby tree. His eyes skated over my dirty, sweaty clothes. Then he removed his undershirt.

Crossing to the axe, he picked it up and offered it to me.

"Here," he said. "Take it."

I glanced at the axe handle then at my brother. "What are you doing?"

He shrugged, but I saw a glimmer of something like sympathy buried deep in his eyes. "We'll take turns. And when the tree comes down, I'll help you drag it to the pit, cut it into sections."

I swallowed. My eyes stung and my lungs labored as though I were surrounded on all sides by smoke. I was suffocating.

My voice was rough, gravelly as I asked, "Why?"

"Because you're my brother," he said, as though it were obvious. "And you need my help."

CHAPTER THIRTY

"I am free, and that is why I am lost."

— FRANZ KAFKA

~Sienna~

M Y HEART WASN'T working correctly.

First of all, it hurt. Especially when I breathed. Or sat. Or stood. Or walked.

And also, it was thumping oddly, skipping beats, pumping blood either too fast or too slow.

It was broken.

"Sienna?" Dave called, knocking on my bedroom door.

My room, the master suite, was on the third floor and the guys were staying on the main level. The entire second floor was taken up with a viewing room/entertainment area/bar combination that looked over the lake. Most of the ceiling in my room was comprised of a massive skylight. The night sky and stars were my nightly view and the windows tinted automatically during the day to shield the space from the sun.

I ignored Dave and continued to stare at the sky. I'd been doing this since Jethro dropped me off.

That's not true. At first, just after he left, I'd spent several minutes calling him all kinds of names, in both English and Mexican Spanish. I'd slammed some doors. I'd brushed my teeth with vigor. And I'd started on the Smash-Girl script, deciding she would initially grow red and angry because all men were fools.

I was frustrated. My laptop screen eventually blurred because of my tears. So I had lain on my bed and stared at the sky. My heart wasn't working properly. It was broken.

"Sienna?" Dave called again.

I shook my head, but that hurt my heart, so I stopped. A moment passed, and then I heard Dave's retreating footsteps. Some more time passed. I honestly didn't know how long. The sun was hidden by clouds and the skylight had tinted automatically.

I blamed my broken heart. Had it been working I might have been more capable of keeping track of time.

And then my door opened.

I turned my head—which hurt my heart. Cletus. He stood just inside my room, his expression inscrutable as he watched me.

"Cletus," I said, not recognizing my own voice.

"Ms. Diaz." He nodded once.

"My heart is broken," I said.

He nodded again like he already knew, but now his eyes shone with sympathy. He crossed to the bed and sat next to me, grabbing for and holding my hand. "Yes. That's why I'm here."

"Please tell me you're going to fix it." My vision blurred because I was crying again.

The side of his mouth hitched though he looked troubled. "I'm going to try."

* * *

CLETUS MADE ME take a shower. I cried a lot in the shower.

And then he made me a cup of tea and gave me a Tylenol. He ushered me to the back porch so we could look over the lake.

"A nice view always helps," he said, adding sugar to my tea.

"I don't take it with sugar."

He pressed the cup into my hands. "Sweet tea always helps."

I huffed a laugh and drank the sweet tea. It kind of helped.

"Now tell me what happened," he instructed, using a grandfatherly voice. I lifted an eyebrow at him because I was fairly certain we were approximately the same age. And yet something about his somber expression and the brightness of his eyes made him appear so much older.

"Have you talked to . . . to him?" I asked, sipping my tea, the syrupy concoction coating my tongue with sweetness.

"Yes."

I gathered a bracing breath. "What did he say?"

"I'll tell you in a minute. First, I want to hear what happened from your perspective."

So I told him. I told Cletus everything.

I started at the beginning, recounting how we'd met, how I liked Jethro so much from the start, and ended with how angry I'd been last night.

"Why won't he even consider dating me in secret? It's not uncommon in Hollywood. People do it all the time."

"Sienna, pause a minute. You've just used a double negative; obviously you're distressed. Think about what you're proposing. You're asking Jethro to deny the two of you are together. You're asking him to lie about it, like it's wrong and needs to be hidden."

"But it wouldn't be like that."

"'Course it would. And you'd never be able to visit him here, not in Green Valley. This is a small town. There are no secrets here. People have already seen you two out and about. Right now they might be pacified thinking you're just friendly. But he's already been cornered more than once. Saying nothing adds fuel to the fire. It's not a matter of keeping a secret, it's a matter of lying all the time. To everyone."

I couldn't hold his earnest gaze, so I glanced at my tea. It looked like perfectly normal tea. But it wasn't normal. It was sweet tea because Cletus had made it sweet.

"Jethro told me some of what he's done, about his past."

I heard Cletus shift in his chair, the sturdy weight of him causing the wood to creak. "Yeah. What about it?"

"Maybe if I knew more, I could mitigate some of the fallout."

"Ask him."

"I did." I met Cletus's gaze directly. "He hasn't told me a lot about his penchant for stealing, his time in the Iron Wraiths, or much about your father. But enough that I can piece a few things together. I understand his shame. He also said he used to string girls along. He also said he used to use women, the women at the motorcycle club, treat them like they were disposable."

Cletus scratched his jaw, his eyes losing focus as his thoughts turned introspective. "See now, that's where things get messy. He might have guilt about that because our momma raised us better. But those women hang around that club for one reason only, and that's to get laid by a member of the Iron Wraiths. He used them, and they used him. As long as both parties participated as consenting adults, rationally I can't find any fault with his actions. Irrationally, though, I think both participating parties are gross."

"You think men who have sex with lots of women are 'gross'?" I'd never heard a full-grown man describe promiscuity as gross.

"Yes, I do." He nodded firmly. "All that swapping of bodily fluids? Disgusting. Indiscriminate sex is like indiscriminate pie eating. I might enjoy the pie, but then I find out it was baked in a dirty kitchen, drooled and sneezed on by nut jobs, baked by a nut job who wants me to eat her dirty pie every day. Next thing you know I have a stalker, dysentery, and herpes just from one ignorant bite of pie. I keep my kitchen clean and discriminate and so should my partner. Plus, I don't want someone telling me Pop-Tarts are pie. Pop-Tarts aren't pie. I can tell the difference. I don't want a half-assed baker."

Despite the situation, I couldn't help my small smile. "So you're looking for a virgin kitchen, Cletus?"

"No, no, no. I didn't say that. Ideally, I'd like a chef who keeps a clean kitchen but knows a thing or two about baking, or at least makes a solid effort. If she doesn't know how to bake or isn't good at cooking, I guess I could teach her. But . . ." he shrugged, "I like the idea of being with someone where we can both teach each other to cook new—*quality* —recipes."

"In non-analogy terms, please."

"Fine. I'm after a woman who likes sex but doesn't put the lust part above the intelligence part. She could have a hundred partners for all I care, just as long as they've been vetted for psychopathic tendencies. I have four rules. Number one: don't invite a person into your body if you wouldn't invite her into your kitchen. Number two: the act needs to take place in a clean environment. Number three: precautions need to be taken to protect from disease and pregnancy. And Number four: don't ration the passion, i.e. put your best fuck forward."

I had to press my lips together. Even in my current state of despair, *put your best fuck forward* was hilarious. "I might have to steal that, Cletus."

"Go right ahead. I ain't using it for anything profitable."

Wanting to get back to Jethro's guilt, I asked, "So these women at the motorcycle club? They didn't take precautions?"

"It's not just the women, that's what I'm saying. Neither party thinks about any of the above. Not the women or the men, no one has a clean kitchen, everyone is serving Pop-Tarts and calling it pie, and the kitchen is full of sociopaths going around being violent fools. It's gonorrhea city up at that place. And that's why I think it's gross."

"And Jethro?"

"Well, he didn't think about it until he did think about it. And when he thought about it, he stopped. And then he called the health inspector. And now he's kept his kitchen spotless by not baking anything for anyone, just for himself."

"This is the basis for all his guilt? That he made thoughtless, horny decisions as a youth?"

"He told you about stealing cars?"

"Yes. But he was never convicted, right?"

"That's right, but he did it regardless. Never paid for it either. I think that bothers him, the stealing and not being punished for it. He was going to turn himself in, but my momma asked him not to. She asked him to go to school instead, be a man we would all look up to. She said, and I agreed, he could make up for his thieving by doing right by his family. He wouldn't have done a lick of good locked up."

"He still feels undeserving though. He still feels like he should be punished."

"I think so. Never mind all the shit he put up with when he was thieving, from our father and the club. If you ask me, he's already paid his debt. But, uh," Cletus hesitated, scratching his jaw, "there was this one time our father tried to do something untoward concerning Ashley."

I nodded, noting softly, "Jethro told me about that."

"Then I assume he told you about Roxy and Kim?"

I tensed. "No. Who are they? Are they club women?"

"Yes and no. Yes, they became club women, but Jethro introduced them to the lifestyle. And now they're both hooked on drugs and live at the club, getting passed around by those sociopaths. He blames himself."

"Ah . . . I see." And I did see. And that was a big deal.

"Kim thought Jethro was her old man, and he likely lied to lead her on. And Roxy, who he also led on, was half in love with him when he took her to the club the first time."

"What has he done about it? I mean, has he tried to help?"

"Yes. But neither of those ladies are interested in his help."

I was almost too afraid to ask. "What happened to them?"

"Well now, Roxy is still there. But we haven't seen Kim in ages. Jethro was going to offer marriage to one of them a few years back, Roxy I think, just to get her out of the club. But Drew counseled him against it, meaning he talked sense into Jet. And these women aren't the only ones he brought into the Iron Wraiths, but they're the only ones that stayed. Suzie Samuels for instance. Once she figured out Jethro was stringing her along, she set fire to his motorcycle. She hates his guts and spews obscenities at him every time their paths cross. That's the way most of them went—the Tanner twins, Suzie Samuels, Gretchen LaRoe to name a few. He's got a pack of females in these parts who hate his guts and would happily speak to your news people about how terrible a person he is."

"Oh my goodness. Why doesn't he leave?"

"I suppose he feels he deserves it, after how he mistreated them and all he's done."

Hearing names paired with Jethro's misdeeds made his past feel more real. The names gave weight to his guilt as well as his concern about hurting my image.

Even so, he wasn't the same person. He'd proved that. Five years of living a different life, making good decisions, and being honorable was proof enough for me.

"I don't know what to do," I admitted. "Tell me what to do, Cletus."

"It's simple. Tell the world you're together and deal with the consequences. End of story."

I frowned at my tea. "And take away Jethro's privacy? Throw him to the wolves? Give these women a stage for their scorn?"

"Yes. If that's the price of being with you, I know he'll gladly pay it. You're acting like Jethro is some delicate flower. That man feels remorse for his wrongs, but he's not hiding from his sins. He's more concerned about what this'll do to your image."

"I don't care about that. I honestly don't. If I had to choose between being an actress and Jethro, I'd chose him each time."

"You don't care about being an actress? A celebrity?"

"No. I mean, I like that the work I've done, the work I'm doing, might pave the way for others like me. Women in film who don't all look one particular way. If I've given hope to one little girl who thinks she has weight issues or brown skin or an odd sense of humor that—yes, you can be successful and no, there is nothing wrong with being different. Being different should be an asset. I like that I might have contributed to changing the perception that women aren't funny. I like acting, performing. Worst-case scenario—and keeping it real here—having Jethro in my life might knock me off this ridiculous pedestal, but it's not going to get me blacklisted. I can still perform. It might not be in A-list, big-budget movies. I might not be America's sweetheart, but screw that. Please believe me when I tell you being with him, sharing my life with him, means more to me than being any level of celebrity."

Cletus set his tea on the table between us with a *thunk*. "He doesn't care about his privacy. You don't care about your image. So why not just trust each other and move on?"

"It's not that simple."

"It's as simple as dry toast."

"You're encouraging me to knowingly hurt him."

Cletus grunted impatiently and threw his hands up. "We're talking in circles. Here's reality: People get hurt and they move on or they don't. You can't have it both ways. You either get to be famous, and deal with the hassle that comes with it, or you leave it all behind. Own your shit, Sienna. And let Jethro own his. And then get married and own that shit together."

Cletus stood, clearly frustrated, and stomped away from me to the back door. He disappeared into the house only to appear three seconds later to add, "And while you're at it, beget me some nieces and nephews."

* * *

OWN YOUR SHIT. And let Jethro own his.

2:25 a.m.

I was exhausted.

I couldn't sleep.

Cletus's words from earlier in the day were bouncing around, commandeering my thoughts. He was right. He was very, very right. My job meant that privacy was a luxury, but so what? Either I was going to live my life alone, avoid relationships, give in to the fear of hurting the people I cared about, or I was going to own my shit.

So . . . where did that leave Jethro and me? I wasn't going to jump unless he was with me. I couldn't make this decision for both of us.

I glanced at the photo of us on my phone, the one I'd taken of us kissing. Just then, I received a text and my heart jumped to my throat.

Jethro: *Are you up?*

I quickly messaged back,

Sienna: *Yes.*
Jethro: *I have something to ask you, a new proposal.*
Sienna: *Ask me.*
Jethro: *I'm coming over.*
Sienna: *Okay.*
Sienna: *I miss you.*
Jethro: *I miss you so much. Sorry I left. I'll be right there.*
Sienna: *I don't care about my image. I wish you would believe me. If I lose film roles, so what? I love my work but I'll love it just as much working on smaller films.*

I checked my phone obsessively for five minutes. When he didn't respond, I sent him another message.

Sienna: *What would you do if I sent this picture of us kissing to every celebrity blogger and reporter I know?*
Jethro: *Don't.*

I quickly typed a new message.

Sienna: *I'm going to do it.*
Sienna: *And I'm going to send them your full name and social security number.*
Sienna: *And a picture of me giving the double middle finger salute.*
Sienna: *Naked.*
Jethro: *Hold your horses, woman, I'm on my way.*

I leapt from my bed and darted out my bedroom door. Running down the steps, I had to temper my footfalls when I reached the second landing. I didn't want to wake Dave and Tim.

Henry was on duty, and I spotted him as soon as I cleared the last stair. He was sitting in front of the TV, watching a baseball game and looked over his shoulder as I appeared.

"Can't sleep?" He looked nervous, like he expected me to burst into tears at any moment.

Shaking my head, I darted to the foyer. "No, no. Jethro is coming over. I'll let him in. Watch your game."

I paced in front of the door, peeking out the window every five seconds. After an eternity—sixteen minutes—the headlights of his truck appeared, filling the windows and momentarily blinding me. I grabbed the door handle, thinking maybe he wanted me to meet him outside, but then stopped myself.

I didn't want to meet him outside. I didn't want to have this conversation in his truck. I didn't want to make it easy for him to say goodbye, if that's what he was planning.

Stepping away from the door, I walked back to the living room and loud-whispered to Henry, "Get the door when he knocks and send him upstairs—got it?"

Wide-eyed, Henry nodded and stood from the couch. I jogged up the stairs back to my room and paced the length of it, straining my ears for the sound of Jethro's approach. Not a minute later I heard footfalls on the stairs. I tried to swallow but I couldn't. My hands were shaking so I placed my phone on the dresser and turned to face the open door.

And then he was there, hovering just outside my room, his eyes moving over me. He was still gorgeous, dressed in a white T-shirt and dark jeans, boots and no belt. His hair was in disarray, and he looked tired. He'd obviously dressed in a hurry.

But the sight of him filled my heart with impatience and anxious joy.

So, in other words, hope.

"Come in."

His eyes lifted to mine, and I felt a pang when I saw how guarded they were, how bracing.

"You should probably put a robe on," he said gruffly.

I glanced down at myself, saw I was in my normal pajamas—pink cotton sleep shorts and a matching camisole. Of course, when Jethro had slept over I'd been naked.

I stuck my hip out and placed my hand on it. "Don't be ridiculous. I'm not putting a robe on."

"Sienna."

"Jethro."

I admit, I used my sexy voice.

His eyes heated.

"I'm not putting a robe on."

And I wouldn't. I wasn't going to put a robe on because if he was here to break up for good, I wasn't going to make it easy.

No. Way.

"If you can't control yourself, then don't control yourself. You have my full permission to ogle and/or touch me however you like." My breath caught on the last word because as I spoke his eyes narrowed, sharp and predatory, and he took a step into my room.

Holding my gaze captive, he closed the door behind him. With his signature unaffected confidence, he crossed the space and stopped just in front of me, inches separating us. I lifted my chin, balled my hands into fists. I had to force myself not to take a step back. The weight and intensity of his stare was almost too much to endure. But I did.

His eyes dropped to my mouth then to my neck, slid along my collarbone, raising goosebumps wherever his gaze focused. He lifted a large hand and placed it on my arm, the heat and strength of him had me sucking in a breath. His fingers pulled the strap of my top to one side, baring my shoulder to his eyes. Tingles raced down my spine, blossomed in my chest, made my heart thunder between my ears.

His eyes on the skin he'd uncovered, Jethro said, "I'm in love with you."

I blinked at him, at his admission.

"You . . ." My lips parted and I blinked some more. "I-you . . ."

I was well and truly stunned, because those weren't the words I'd been bracing for.

Meanwhile, Jethro continued staring at my skin, his thumb rubbing a slow circle on the front of my shoulder, as though spellbound. He pulled the strap farther down, his other hand doing the same to the second strap until my chest was bare to his eyes. Bending at the waist, his strong fingers sliding to my back and pressing me forward, he licked a wet trail around the center of my breast, sucking me into his mouth with an abandoned groan.

We were moving.

He was moving us, walking me backward to the bed. My fingers were in his hair, my nails anchored to his scalp, holding him to me. Tingly sparks ignited beneath my skin, racing over my body. Large, strong hands held me in place as he devoured my skin, biting and sucking, soothing the marks with his hot tongue.

And I was moving.

I slid my hands to his jeans, enjoying how the muscles beneath his plain white tee tensed and hardened under my fingertips. Unfastening the button, then the zipper, I reached for him, my fingers greedy. He hissed as I cupped and stroked him through his boxers. The feel of him, so hard and ready, awakened some primitive part of my mind.

"I'm in love with you," he repeated, but this time I got the impression he was speaking to himself. His fingers dug into my hips, his thumbs dipping into the band of my shorts, hooking in the elastic. "I want to make love to you."

"Jethro," I panted, his words sobering me only slightly, the anticipation both sweet and tortuous.

His mouth met mine, and he kissed me tenderly, yet I could feel how he held himself back. Every muscle strained, tight, rigid.

"Silly Sienna, smart Sienna," he continued on a low growl against my lips, one hand threading through my hair, the other dipping into my shorts and panties, inching them down my hips. "Sexy Sienna."

I rushed to say, "I don't want you to do something you'll regret."

He hesitated, but just for a split second, and then he was wrapping the bulk of my hair around his hand and tugging, exposing my neck. The action made me arch, my breasts lifting. He lavished the exposed skin with hot, hungry kisses, my shorts and panties now past my hips to my thighs.

I wanted him, badly. Yet even though his touch burned like fire, my blood simmering—my body hot and aching—I didn't want him for just one night. I couldn't remove this thought, this worry from my mind.

He loved me.

He loved me and wanted to make love to me. Right now.

Meanwhile, I wanted the forever he'd promised and didn't want to do anything to jeopardize it.

"Wait." I withdrew my fingers from his pants and gripped his shoulders. The wet trail he left exposed to the cool air made me shiver as he traveled lower, easing me onto the bed.

"Do you want me to stop?" he asked gruffly, using his knee to spread my legs as soon as my back hit the mattress.

"No. I don't *want* you to stop. But I—"

"Shhh." His hot breath fanned over my stomach, his hands tugging at the camisole around my waist, lifting it so he could tongue my belly button.

I groaned then swallowed, removing my hands from his shoulders, squeezing my eyes shut, and forcing myself to concentrate. And when I did, I said the first words that popped into my head.

"I love you, too."

By Mothra's nipples, I LOVE THIS MAN!

It was everything about him, from how he was a truly talented flirt to his epic levels of capability. No matter what it was, he had it handled. Nothing in the world was more alluring than a capable man.

Jethro's hands stilled on my thighs. In fact, he stopped moving, period. But I heard him breathe, felt his heart beat against my thigh.

"And this isn't temporary," I continued abruptly, pressing my fists into my closed lids. "And you made a promise to yourself, that the next person you would make love to would be your wife. I don't want you to break your promise, but—Godzilla's modzilla, Jethro—if you don't stop right now, I will cheerfully contribute to your downfall and then you'll never be rid of me."

Saying nothing, he skimmed his fingertips around to the backs of my legs and lifted my knees, placing them over his shoulders.

"Oh. God." I swallowed the words, gripping the sheets on either side of me reflexively, because in the next second his hot, wet, skillful mouth was on me and my body strained, entirely tuned to that one blissful spot.

He wasn't quiet either, lapping with his tongue, sliding his fingers and groaning as my breath hitched. It felt so good, sinful and right. And I kind of hated that he was a master at this. I especially hated that he had me so turned on I couldn't savor the feel of him. I was coming apart too soon, my body in various states of anarchy.

Unlike the other times he'd brought me to climax, this time he didn't draw it out, didn't chase the second release. Instead he let my legs drop, and stood. I opened my eyes, watched as he pulled several condoms from his back pocket and tossed all but one to the nightstand.

Ensnaring my gaze, he dropped his pants, ripped open the square packet with his teeth, and smoothly rolled a condom down his length.

"Do you want me to stop?" he asked gruffly, reaching for my knees again and spreading my legs.

I shook my head, too stunned by what was happening to give voice to my consent. Also, I was impressed at his condom-rolling skills. I mean, he was super fast.

He paused. "Sienna?"

"Don't stop," I breathed, choking on desire and amazement.

With sure movements, he placed a knee on the bed and shifted his hands to my hips, lifting me, sliding his length against my sensitive center. I shuddered and writhed, reaching for him, feeling empty. Then, with a graceful roll of his hips, he entered me.

Slowly at first and not all the way. He took his time, torturing me as he stretched my swollen flesh, though his eyes were blazing. Once again, the intensity there burned. And this time I felt branded.

"Jethro," I moaned, still reaching for him, near panic with my need to touch him.

Finally, *finally* he bent forward, smoothly lowering my hips to the bed and planking over me. I greedily touched him everywhere, wanting his skin, his warm chest against mine. But he continued to hold himself at a distance, rolling his hips like a gifted dancer. He didn't thrust. He rocked. His movements were fluid, stroking me with the most intimate part of himself. It was maddening and so unlike anything I'd ever experienced.

It was perfection.

The view of his arms and chest and stomach bracing his weight while he expertly rocked into my body had me gasping and closing my eyes. I felt him everywhere, though our bodies met only where I lay my hands and where he made love to me.

Fuck.

Fuck, fuck, fuck.

He made love like he walked. Like he spoke. Like he lived. With complete confidence and artless self-assurance. It was straightforward, passionate, and beautiful.

It broke something in me, something I didn't consciously know existed. A wall I'd built with jokes, flippant comebacks, and careless shrugs. He broke my shield against all those who'd ever criticized my inability to fit in or conform.

Because what he thought mattered.

How he touched me, how he saw me, what he said, and how he spoke to me mattered.

I wanted to please him.

I wanted to drive him crazy, open myself to him, trust him completely.

I wanted to be truly vulnerable.

I wanted him to dominate and cherish and use my body.

I wanted him to want me, need me.

I wanted him satisfied but insatiable, always craving more. Always thinking of me.

With those thoughts spiraling through my mind, tears in my eyes, and frantic longing in my heart, I came apart again, his name tumbling from my lips over and over like a plea.

"I love you," he growled, kissing my face, my neck, my chest. As my body intuitively tightened around his, his movements quickened but were no less graceful and hypnotic.

"I love you," I echoed, and then repeated, "I love you."

And then he captured my mouth with his, and he came. Jethro Winston was my forever person. I would never be strong enough to let him go.

CHAPTER THIRTY-ONE

"We have faith that there is purpose. We hope for things we can't see. We believe there are lessons in loss, power in love, and that we have within us the potential for a beauty so magnificent, our bodies can't contain it."

— AMY HARMON, MAKING FACES

~Jethro~

EVERYTHING WAS GOING according to plan, just in the wrong order. But that was fine. I'd arrived with an agenda. I could now cross off the second item on my list.

We were lying on her bed above the sheets, facing each other, kissing, petting, and getting worked up all over again. I was naked, but she still had her camisole around her waist. I wanted to remove it so I could see and touch her entire gorgeous body.

I started lifting the top and she stilled my movements, the look in her eyes snagging my attention. She looked worried.

"You can tell a joke if you want," I offered, my voice rough because speaking sense wasn't coming easy, not after what we'd just done. Not with what we were still doing.

Her eyebrows bounced upward. "Why would I do that?"

"Because that's what you do when you're anxious about something." I palmed her breast, loving how it overflowed in my hand, and I had big hands. Really big hands.

Even though her skin held a flush from our earlier lovemaking, the pink intensified, and she ducked her head.

"Does it bother you?"

I lifted her chin, forcing her to meet my eyes. "No. I love it." I brushed a kiss over her luscious lips and whispered, "I love everything about you."

She sighed, and it sounded wounded, sad.

I shifted back so I could see her, noticed she had tears in her eyes. I pushed my fingers into her hair and held her face so she couldn't hide again.

"Sienna, honey, what's wrong?"

"I care what you think."

I lifted an eyebrow at this. "And that's making you cry?"

She nodded and wrapped her leg around mine, like she was securing our bodies together.

I grinned at her and her beautiful face, and said, "I care what you think."

She sniffed. "Please don't regret a single thing that just happened. It was so beautiful. I think I'd have to murder you if you regretted the hottest lovemaking of all time."

Shaking my head, my eyelids lowered as all parts of my body recalled each exquisite moment. Each hitch of her breath, each reflexive movement. The moment she admitted her love might never be surpassed, but the feel of her supple body, her heat, her submissive, greedy arousal came in a close second.

A very close second.

I'd likely have to take her again soon, just to make sure.

I attempted to soothe her. "I'll never regret a second of being with you. Being with you is where I belong."

Her breaths were coming faster than usual; obviously she was still fretting.

"What can I say to calm your fears?" I whispered, kissing her nose.

"I don't know," she said, and she looked serious, her eyes darting between mine.

I studied her, wondering if now was the right time to ask her to marry me. But everything was happening backward. She was supposed to be dressed when I arrived. We were supposed to talk, sort through our troubles. I was supposed to make my case.

Then, after she was wearing the ring, we were supposed to make love.

"I've been thinking about your proposal," I started carefully. She was skittish, and I didn't want to frighten her off.

"Which? Which proposal?"

"That we see each other in secret for a time."

She swallowed, and her leg tightened over mine. "Oh?"

"You should marry me," I said suddenly, ripping off the proverbial Band-Aid and nodding at the wisdom of my words. "We should get married."

Her lips parted, and I was pleased to see most of the anxiety plaguing her expression had disappeared. However, in all fairness, the anxiety was replaced by surprise. She blinked, her mouth moving but no sound coming out.

"Hear me out." I smoothed my hand from her neck to her hip, tugging her body an inch closer, my grip tightening. "You think we ought to date in secret—"

"I don't think—"

"Just listen. I hate that idea. I do. I hate it. Now, part of my hate is because I don't want to lie to folks. But the other part is selfish. I'm in love with you, and the idea of us being a secret makes me want to break something." *Or cut down all the trees on the mountain.*

Her gaze turned warm and soft, and her lush body relaxed into mine, making it difficult for me to think.

"I never—"

341

"Let me finish," I growled, the words coming out much gruffer than I'd intended because my heart was now beating at a breakneck pace.

And I wanted her again. I wanted her crying my name and losing her mind. I wanted her begging me to do dirty things, hearing her soft moans and watching her body bounce and ripple and yield beneath mine.

So, yeah.

I was gruff.

"So what I propose is that we do this in secret, at first. We do this slowly, and I work with someone to help lessen the fallout."

Her face scrunched. "Like an image consultant?"

"Sure. Fine. Just someone who'll help soften the edges of my past for general consumption, so you aren't paying the price for my past misdeeds. And I'd pay for it all." I had plenty of money. My momma came from money; in addition to the house and land, I'd inherited two million dollars last month when I'd turned thirty-one. I'd done nothing with it. It was in a bank in Knoxville collecting dust.

"Jethro—"

"And I'll sign a prenup, or whatever. I don't care about your money."

"I know you don't."

"But we'd get married now, before the movie wraps."

"Wait—"

"I know it might not make sense to you. And I know this is fast, but I'm certain."

"Listen for a—"

"I could deal with keeping things secret in the short term, if we were engaged," I finished, frowning so she'd know I was dead serious and had given the matter serious thought.

I couldn't see her, not really, because my heart was beating in my throat, and I was nervous as hell. So it took me a full minute before she came back into focus, before I stepped out of my own way long enough to see her soft, wondrous smile.

"Yes," she whispered, her smile beaming back at me. Sienna shifted on the bed, arching her back and straining so she could kiss me.

It took me another few seconds to comprehend that she'd accepted. And when I did, I finally exhaled.

"Yes?" I couldn't believe it.

I held her smiling gaze as she nodded, grinning wildly.

"Holy shit," I cursed, beyond happy, beyond joy and elation. I was equal parts euphoric and stunned.

Wrapping her in my arms, bringing her body flush with mine, I kissed her. And then I made love to her again, taking special care of my woman.

Because I'd just won the lottery of life. Sienna Diaz was going to be my wife. The least I could do was show my betrothed how much she was loved.

* * *

I FISHED THE ring out of my pants pocket while she slept—after we'd made love for a second time and as the sun rose. I slipped it on her finger where it belonged. She stirred just as I fixed it into place.

Her lashes fluttered. She saw me and reached for me. I grabbed her hand, pressed our palms together, and brought her wrist to my lips. She gave me a sleepy smile. But then she blinked, her eyes snagging on her third finger, her gaze sharpening, and her mouth opening.

I grinned. She looked like a cartoon character—exaggerated wide eyes, gaping mouth, disbelieving wrinkle between her eyebrows—I loved how expressive she was.

"Holy shit." Her gaze moved back to mine and she repeated breathlessly, "Holy shit."

I grinned wider. "It's platinum, a two-carat, old mine cut diamond, passed down on the Oliver side of the family for three generations, from father to oldest son. Each giving it to their betrothed. After my grandmother passed, my momma—who was an only child—kept it in a safety deposit box my daddy didn't know about."

Before meeting Sienna, I'd tried to give the ring to Drew for Ashley. He'd turned me down, saying, *"Your momma wanted you to have it, for your woman. She liked to talk about you as a father, raising your own babies. She thought you'd make a great dad someday."*

Even I appreciated the epic nature of this ring. An heirloom, impressive, irreplaceable, important beyond its monetary value. Priceless. It caught and captivated the light. Glittering like a thousand stars. The ring looked important. And that was good, because it communicated to her and to the world how I saw her. She was important, impressive, and irreplaceable to me.

"This is my ring?" Her words caught, her voice cracking.

I nodded, happy she was happy. Her happiness was all that mattered to me. "This is your ring."

Her eyes filled with tears, and she moved them to mine. "This is my ring. And you're going to be my husband."

I laughed, though my throat was also tight with some emotion I couldn't quite pin down. It was more than contentment. More than relief. More than joy. It was all of those things and more.

I decided it was love, because nothing else had ever come close to feeling this good.

CHAPTER THIRTY-TWO

"When the debate is lost, slander becomes the tool of the loser."

— SOCRATES

~Jethro~

W E DIDN'T ANNOUNCE our engagement to my family. I hated lying, yet I would in order to protect Sienna. But I wasn't about to ask my family to tell falsehoods. So we said nothing during the few days that followed our engagement, neither confirmed nor denied the truth. Luckily, no one asked. They just eyeballed the ring and arrived at their own conclusions.

Though Cletus was huffing more than usual since he caught sight of it.

She wore the ring on her right hand most of the time when she was on set or when we were at my house. But when we were together, just the two of us, she'd slip it onto her left and stare as though she expected it to disappear.

Like now.

We were in her trailer, five days after my proposal, the sun just rising in the sky. Though we hadn't planned to, we'd spent the night. I'd stopped by with takeout from The Front Porch, expecting to take her home after. One kiss turned into several kisses, then kisses all over, then urgent lovemaking on the kitchen table.

Neither of us wanted to leave after that. She was off to London in the morning and this was our last stretch of time together before she left.

So Sienna had made coffee and we'd talked until late, sharing one bunk. The twin bed should have been uncomfortable, but it wasn't. The small space meant I held her tight all through the night and that suited me just fine.

"You're staring at it again," I teased, drawing her attention to me.

She started, her gaze flickering to mine. "I'm sorry. I didn't know you were awake."

I slid my hand from her back to her thigh, savoring the feel of her. Christ, I wanted to touch her everywhere at once.

"Why are you apologizing?"

"I don't know." She laughed lightly, then sounding like she was speaking to herself, she added, "I'm just not used to caring so much about what someone else thinks."

I inched my head back and stared at her profile, thinking on her words.

She must've felt my attention, because she closed her eyes, cleared her throat self-consciously and joked, "I think I'm going to be a very clingy fiancée. You'll be tactile, and I'll be clingy, and we'll be very happy just as long as we sleep in a twin bed and call each other seventeen hundred times a day."

I chuckled. She was joking, but her words held a kernel of truth. It didn't take a mind reader to see she was afraid.

"It's good to care, Sienna. It's good to care about what others think, but only when those other people matter."

She lifted her chin and gazed at me, her long lashes brushing against her cheeks as she blinked. "But how do you balance it? I mean, I care what my parents think because I love them and know they love me, and I trust their judgment. But, in the end, I always just do what I think is best."

"Then that's what you keep doing. I trust your heart and so should you."

She hesitated, searching my eyes, then blurted, "But I don't want to let you down."

I caught my bottom lip before I grinned. "You won't."

"My parents have to love me, so does my family. They have no choice. We're stuck with each other. I do stupid things and I know *they'll* forgive me. But you, you could just leave me and—"

I cut her off with a kiss, because she was talking nonsense.

Once I had her restless and out of breath, I broke the kiss and smoothed her hair from her face. "I don't do things by halves, Sienna. I tell you I love you, I mean it. I ask you to marry me—"

"Technically you never asked."

I ignored her, though the truth she spoke made me smile. "I'm not going to change my mind. After your sister called, after she pointed out some hard truths, I needed time. And I took it. And I couldn't let you go, though part of me thought it would be for the best."

"It wouldn't. It wouldn't be for the best. You should never think that."

"I won't. I've made my decision—selfish as it is—and so have you. We're in this together. We have a good deal to learn about each other. You can't ever be certain of another person, and that's where faith comes in. I've asked a lot of people to have faith in me when I didn't deserve it, and I'm asking the same of you now."

Her fingers gripped my bicep, squeezing. "You do deserve it."

I nodded. "Fine then. I deserve it. You should give it to me, and move on from your worry."

"But don't you see? It's not you, Jethro. It's me. Do I deserve your faith?"

"Do you want my faith?"

"Yes." She shook me a little for emphasis, her single-word answer loud in the small trailer. "Yes, I want it. But I'm not used to considering someone else in my decisions. I'll need your patience."

"Then you have it."

"Thank you." She sighed.

347

But I wasn't finished. "I'll give you my patience, but don't expect me to be a statue or a doormat. If you make me angry, I'm going to let you know."

Her eyes widened and lost focus, clearly thinking back on a memory. "You're a little scary when you're angry."

I lifted an eyebrow at this and frowned, concerned. "I would never, ever hurt you, or touch you in anger."

"Oh, I know." She lowered her eyes to my neck. "It's still scary, though."

I studied her, the way she was biting her lip. "Sienna, I might leave to cool off, but I'll always come back. That's part of the promise I made when I gave you this ring."

She nodded, still not looking at me, but then she said, "I guess I just have to trust you."

"Yeah. Just like I have to trust you."

Her mouth tugged to the side. "Trust me to not drive you crazy?"

"Oh no," I laughed, "you'll definitely drive me crazy. I have no illusions about that. Your name is *Insane* after all."

She scrunched her face and pinched my shoulder. I flinched away, still laughing, and grabbed her hand to halt her assault.

"What I meant was," I waited for her to meet my eyes again before continuing, "I trust you. I have faith in you that no matter where you go or what you're doing, in the end you'll always come back to me."

* * *

I LEFT SIENNA'S trailer wearing yesterday's clothes and a big smile. Who knew tight quarters could be so much fun? We couldn't get far enough away from each other to allow any measure of space. So of course accidental touching became on-purpose touching. I blamed my size and hers.

In other words, we were perfect for each other.

"It's the lumbersexual."

I looked up, finding Mr. Low strolling toward me, an unpleasant expression on his face. Now here was a guy who was an asshole. I hated these guys because they reminded me of who I used to be.

I nodded my head once in greeting but had no intent to actually stop and converse. Unfortunately, his plans didn't align with mine.

Blocking the path so I'd have to stop or walk into him, he held his hands up between us and said, "Aren't you going to say hello? Or is that business about southern manners an exaggeration?"

I stepped back, thinking it would be a bad idea for him to be within easy punching distance, and shoved my hands in my pockets. "Morning, Mr. Low."

"You can call me Tom. After all," he shrugged, "we've both fucked the same woman."

Yep. Good. Thing. He. Wasn't. Within. Punching. Distance.

Good decision.

I blinked at him once then turned on my heel and walked away. I would take the long way around to my truck. No biggie.

He jogged after me.

"Hey. Where are you going? Busy planting trees or whatever you Boy Scouts do?"

I made a list of what needed to be picked up from the grocery store for dinner. Making lists helped. Cletus had taught me to do that. Not many people knew, but Cletus had a terrible temper. As a kid his tantrums were legendary, and as a teenager his rage made him blind.

He kept it all locked up now by making mental lists whenever he felt the urge to pummel someone.

Of course, he also hatched maniacal plans of revenge against anyone who crossed him. Beau and I often considered giving Cletus a hairless cat as a present, so his James Bond supervillain image would be complete.

But then Tom pushed my back, making me stumble forward a few steps.

I didn't like to be pushed.

Righting myself, I turned slowly. Mr. Low was obviously after a confrontation.

"What do you want?" My voice was gruff, but that's to be expected. I kept my hands in my pockets, another trick I'd learned from Cletus.

"Man," he shook his head, sneering, "she did a number on you. You actually think you're special, don't you? People are laughing at you."

I stared at him, giving him nothing. Running late for work wasn't a worry. I figured he'd wear himself out eventually.

"I know you're a simple people, but do you honestly think *Sienna Diaz* is interested? In you? Her sister would never allow it. You have heard of Marta, haven't you? Sienna listens to her sister about everything. See, Marta and I are good friends, and I know she hates the idea of you. You're already as good as gone." He chuckled, and it was forced.

I tried to ignore his words, but some of them hit a target. Just as we hadn't told my family, we hadn't told Sienna's. We knew Marta was definitely not Team Jethro. Yet.

And yet, Mr. Low wanted me to doubt. He wanted chaos. I refused to give it to him.

So, I needed kale from the store, and tomatoes, and feta. We already had garlic and onions.

"You're nothing," he spat. "When filming wraps, you're gone. And then she's off to her next fuckbuddy."

Man, I really wanted to shut his mouth. Breaking his jaw would do the trick. Instead I started making a new list of how many ways I could wreck his pretty face.

"Hey!" He stepped directly in front of me and snapped his fingers in front of my eyes. "Can you hear me, hillbilly? Or are you too stupid—?"

On instinct, I grabbed his wrist and wrenched it behind his back, shoving him away. He stumbled then fell to one knee.

"You're drunk, old-timer. Go home." I readied myself for a right hook, because how he was crouched lent itself well to a surprise punch in the face. That was assuming Mr. Low even knew how to fight.

Mr. Low straightened and turned, rage in his eyes. I guess he didn't like being called "old-timer." Honestly, I suspected as much. That's why I'd said it.

"Fuck you." He seethed. "I'm not old."

I shrugged, unable to contain my smirk. *That was childish. Shame on me.*

"Are you finished?" I asked, pulling my phone from my pocket and glancing at the screen. I still had time, but that didn't mean I wanted to spend any more of it in Mr. Low's company.

His eyes flickered to my phone. "Let me guess, she took a picture of the two of you, right? While you were kissing?"

I stiffened, my glare lifting to his.

He grinned. "She put it on your phone, right? Made it her avatar?"

I frowned, unable to conceal my stunned confusion.

He laughed. "I know because she did the same thing to me. She does the same thing to everyone. It's all part of her little game."

My heart did an odd sinking thing, and my mouth fell open, my mind a mess of contradictions. I'm ashamed to say, he almost had me doubting her. Almost. He was a good actor, plus he was motivated.

But then he said, "She wants you to go with her to London, to the premiere. Marta will talk some sense into her."

And that was his mistake.

His words came into focus, the key fit into the lock, and the door opened wide.

I laughed, saying, "Of course," mostly to myself.

Mr. Low's eyes narrowed into slits. "What's the joke, hick?"

I surveyed him, this successful man, this icon of film, of our society. Here was a person who cared too much about his image, but spent no time on what actually mattered. I felt sorry for him. His life was sad.

"What?" he snapped, obviously not liking how I was looking at him.

"Let's see it." I kept my tone gentle, showing him he had my pity, not my anger.

He stiffened. "Let's see what?"

"Let's see the picture. The one Sienna put on your phone."

He took a half step back. "I don't have my phone on me."

"Bullshit."

He held himself rigid. Though he was a really good actor, I recognized he hadn't expected me to call his bluff.

I shook my head, pressing my lips together in a sympathetic smile.

"Sienna didn't put a picture on your phone. But her sister obviously told you about the one she put on mine."

My words did not settle well with him. His bitterness and helplessness was just as plain as the nose on his face. Mr. Low's eyes flashed with hatred. He wanted to hit me. Wanted to beat the tar out of me, make me bleed. Again, I felt sorry for him. It must've sucked to be so incapable.

I glanced at my phone again. It was past time for me to leave. "We don't believe in false pleasantries around these parts, nor do we kick a fella when he's down. So I'll just say, bless your heart, and leave it at that."

CHAPTER THIRTY-THREE

"Until you've lost your reputation, you never realize what a burden it was or what freedom really is."

— MARGARET MITCHELL, GONE WITH THE WIND

~Sienna~

I CALLED MY mom on my way to the airport. Dave was driving. Henry was next to me in the back, and Tim was in the front passenger seat, leaving me with both hands and all my attention free. I hadn't spoken to her since she'd given me advice about Jethro. She and my dad had been on a cruise and were due back today. I'd missed our phone calls.

Selecting her number, I tapped the call button and waited. It went to voicemail.

"Hi, Mom. It's me. I'm on my way to the airport for London and miss your voice. I know you get back today. Call me when you get this. I might be on the flight, but I'll call you back when I land. Love you and Dad."

Peering at my screen, my heart sunk. I wanted to tell her about Jethro.

No. That's not right.

I needed to tell her about Jethro. I wanted her to know her advice had been correct, and that she had been right. He was my one. And I was his.

I needed to share the news about our engagement. I needed to hear her scream and get excited and ask me when we would start having babies. I was the first of her daughters to get married, though Maya and Rena were in committed relationships, they were both career focused and had no immediate plans to have children; that was me just months ago. Whereas my brothers and their wives brought up children as a *maybe someday* concept.

My mother had lamented, loudly and frequently, to all of us on several occasions about how she wanted grandchildren.

"I love you all, so smart, so capable and accomplished. I'm so proud of you. But where are my grandchildren?" she would ask, her hand on her hip, her eyebrows raised. *"Who am I going to give my china to? Hmm? Who is going to inherit my jewelry?"*

These were the things she fussed over, but we all knew she just loved babies and wanted one to spoil and squeeze.

Dave dropped Henry, Tim, and me off at the side terminal reserved for chartered flights and parked the car. After checking in and meeting back up with Dave, we were ushered to the tarmac where the jet was already waiting.

I held my phone the whole time, hoping my mom would call me back before we departed. Thus, I received Jethro's text message as soon as I started climbing the steps to the plane.

Jethro: *I got hold of your publicity person and have a phone appointment on Monday.*
Sienna: *I already miss you. I wish you were with me.*

I sent the text, irrational anger rising in my chest, making it hard to swallow. I hated that he wasn't with me. I hated we were keeping our relationship a secret, our engagement a secret. I hated we hadn't *officially* told his family, but I understood why we hadn't. But I still hated it. I hated that my mother and father had decided to go on a cruise and weren't answering their phone.

But most of all, I hated that I hated everything.

Jethro: *I'll come next time, when we're sorted.*
Sienna: *I should have hidden you in my suitcase.*
Jethro: *It's not big enough.*
Sienna: *That's what she said.*
Jethro: *You are the funniest.*

"Mr. Low. Didn't expect to see you." Dave's surprised statement pulled my attention away from my messages to the interior of the aircraft.

Sure enough, Tom was lounging on one of the benches, holding a glass of water with lime.

"What are you doing here?" I didn't make any attempt to hide my dismay.

"I offered him a spot."

I turned my head, saw Marta standing by the cockpit, an unconcerned expression on her features.

Her smile growing warm as she glanced at Tom, she continued, "I thought it would be nice. I'm sure the filming schedule has been crazy, and with all your writing, you haven't had any downtime."

I gaped at my sister, certain my horrified expression said it all. *Now she acknowledges I need downtime? Now?*

She blinked at me, looking bewildered. "Is there anything wrong?"

I leaned close and whispered, "Yes. I'd rather fly in a dog crate, in the luggage compartment, than spend ten hours trapped in a plane with that insufferable asshat."

Her mouth flattened. "Sienna."

"Get him off the plane, or I'm not going."

She gritted her teeth. "You're being rude."

"No. You're being rude and presumptuous."

She huffed. "You can be such a diva sometimes."

Lifting my voice, I said, "No. I'm not. I'm never a diva. I'm paying for this plane, so that makes it my plane." Turning to Tom, I motioned to the door. "Marta shouldn't have offered you a seat. I want you to leave."

Tom's surprised gaze moved from me to my sister. When his eyes moved back to mine, they were hard and his expression made me take a step back.

"Is this because of what happened with your bearded friend? The one you've been fucking on the set?"

Marta gasped.

I didn't gasp. I heaved a sigh because I was bored. "Oh, for the sake of Rodan's ceiling fan, would you just leave without making a big scene? Is that possible? There are no Academy members here to see your drama. You can't use this for your reel. Just leave."

His brow darkened and he stood, smoothed a hand down his shirt front, and then grabbed the Louis Vuitton overnight bag at his feet. "You're washed-up. This guy is going to make a laughing stock of you."

"Well, I hope so. In case you didn't get the memo, I'm a comedian."

He paused as he moved past me, then turned, his blue eyes prideful and beseeching. "I could have helped you, Sienna. I still can. That's why I'm here. To help you and your sister clean up this mess."

My anger fizzled, leaving me tired. "It's not a mess, Tom. Jethro is not a mess. He's what I want. I'm in love with him."

"Even if that means throwing everything away?" He sounded truly perplexed.

I shook my head and sighed. "If you don't fight for what you love, then you have nothing worth losing."

* * *

WE WERE OVER the Atlantic when Marta finally spoke to me.

"I can't believe you made him leave." She shook her head for the hundredth time. Though she'd been giving me the silent treatment, she'd shaken her head every three minutes since takeoff.

"I can't believe you asked him to come."

She gave me a disbelieving look. "Sienna, we're all going to the same place. It's ridiculous he should fly separately."

"No. It's not. We dated, Marta. I dated Tom. We only dated for one or two weeks, but I broke up with him for very valid reasons, all having to do with how irritating he is."

"I've never seen him be anything but nice to you."

I snorted. "Really? Well, a few weeks ago he suggested I try a low-carb diet if I wanted to win back the Smash-Girl role."

She stared at me, biting the inside of her lip, then shook her head. "Okay, yeah. That's an asshole thing to say."

I threw my hands up. "Finally."

"Finally what?"

"Finally you admit that Tom Low doesn't walk on Jell-O and smell like gardenias."

Her lips pulled to the side. "Gardenias are my favorite."

"Exactly. Sometimes I wonder if you like him more than you like me."

Marta gave me a rare smile. "Well, he is prettier than you are."

That made me laugh, even as I narrowed my eyes on her. "And he knows it, too."

Her grin waned as we traded stares. "I'm worried about you."

"Why?" I asked softly, happy we were getting to the heart of the matter without yelling at each other.

"I'm worried about this guy."

"Jethro."

"Yes. Jethro. What do you know about him?"

Now I was grinning. "Everything. He used to steal cars."

"Oh my God." She covered her face with her hands.

I couldn't help but enjoy her horror, because—when she actually met him—I was sure she was going to love him.

"Don't worry, he was never convicted."

She made a little hysterical sound but said nothing.

"And he gave me this ring." I held my hand out.

Marta peeked from between her fingers. Then her hands dropped to her lap. Then she turned wide eyes and a gaping mouth on me.

"Holy shit." She grabbed my hand and yanked it toward her. "Is this real?"

I nodded, knowing she meant the ring, but answering the unasked question. "Yes. This is very real. He's talking to Annie on Monday. You know, the image guru we used when my phone was hacked. He's agreed to see me in secret until she can help us develop a plan. We're getting married."

Marta's gaze lifted to mine, a mixture of worry and frustration. "I don't know what to say."

"Say you're happy for me."

"I can't. I can't lie to you. I love you and don't want to see you hurt."

"Neither does he."

"But you will be hurt, Sienna. Being with him is going to hurt your image, you have to know that."

"Which is why we're not going public yet."

"It doesn't matter when you go public, your actions have repercussions. You're behaving like a child."

"I know my actions have repercussions. I'm not a child, and you have to stop treating me like I'm a child. I've decided even worst-case repercussions are worth a lifetime of happiness and freedom."

"You're giving up your career."

I shrugged. "Honestly, I doubt that. I'll always have a career, but it might not be as an A-list actress."

She shook her head at me. "How can you give that up? You could do so much good."

"But at what price personally? If I'm miserable and lose the only person I've ever loved, I lose the chance to have happiness, meaningful fulfillment, kids, a new family—an awesome, weird, wonderful family— will I look back on my life and think, *I'm so glad I worked as hard as I did and filled my life with money, parties, and empty relationships?* No. The answer is no. I might be giving it up, but I'm doing it on my own terms."

She frowned, pressing her lips together, then nodded tightly. "Fine. I'll fly back with you to Tennessee. I'll meet him."

My smile was immediate and, without thinking, I grabbed my sister and pulled her into a tight hug, yelling, "Gah! You're going to love him."

She hesitated, but then her arms wrapped around me, and she

returned my embrace. "I hope I do. Because, despite what you think, I do want you to be happy."

"I know." I nodded, pulling away so I could see her face, and she could see mine. "I know. But, Marta, he doesn't just make me happy. He takes care of me, such excellent care of me. And I take care of him."

* * *

ARRIVING SOLO TO a movie premiere was a lot like going to any average theater and seeing a movie by yourself. You get *the looks*. Everyone wondering what you're doing by yourself, asking you if you're lost, asking you where your date or person was.

People treated a single female alone at the movies like a cancer patient.

Of course, people treated a single man alone at the movies like a pedophile, so—between the two—I'd rather garner sympathy than suspicion.

Luckily, and to my surprise, I wasn't receiving any pitiable looks or concerned smiles as I walked the red carpet and posed for the cameras. The image I'd accidentally cultivated meant no one seemed to be taking my single status as something to be pitied.

"Sienna!"

"Are you making a feminist statement?"

"Over here!"

"You go, girl!"

"Five questions! We have just five questions!"

"Where's Tom?"

"Have you lost weight?"

"We love your dress!"

"You look hot! Can I be your date?" one photographer hollered, trying to turn my head toward his camera.

Another pap called back, "She's Sienna Diaz, she doesn't need a date. And your ugly arse isn't good enough."

This exchange made me laugh and the resultant flashes were blinding.

359

The hours were blurring together. We'd arrived in London just ten hours ago. Since that time, I'd met with the producers for my next film, given seven magazine interviews, was fitted for the dress I was currently wearing, had my makeup and hair done twice—once for a photo shoot and then again for this evening—and still managed to trade several texts with Jethro.

But I'd missed the call from my parents. I would call them back from the bathroom inside the theater, if I ever made it inside.

Stepping away from the cameras, I walked to the media section and to more calls for my attention. I recognized a reporter acquaintance who I actually really liked and respected. He stood to one side among the throng, against the barricade, and wasn't yelling at me. A small smile quirked his lips and when our eyes connected his eyebrows raised in question, *Do you have a minute?*

I gave him a warm smile as I walked to him, cameras following me, the crowd growing quieter so we could speak. I liked Arval because he never asked me about my diet. He never asked about my beauty regimen or my workout routine or questions about whether Latinas make good lovers—yes, I was actually asked that question during an interview earlier in the day.

I'd responded, "I think the real question is, when did they start allowing perverts into press junkets?"

"Sienna." Arval gave me a nod. "You look lovely."

I glanced down at myself. "Oh, this old thing? I made it."

He chuckled; like everyone else, he knew the dress was some ridiculous designer concoction.

"Shall we get down to business?"

"Please do." I motioned to his microphone.

"What are you working on right now?"

"Too many things." I laughed, turning on the charm for the camera. "We're just wrapping up filming for *The Cultavist* in Tennessee, and I start filming *Strange Birdfellows* in September."

"Are you writing anything now?"

"Uh . . ." I hesitated, not sure how to respond. "Yes. I'm working on a script for a superhero project."

"There were rumors you were supposed to star in that, is that true?"

"We were discussing the possibility, yes. But I can't speak of the outcome, as nothing is set in stone. I'm really trying to focus on the script first and foremost, so I've been embracing anger and calling it research."

Out of the corner of my eye I noticed Tom had arrived. He was currently smoldering at the cameras. He was also alone, his date nowhere in sight.

"Embracing anger?"

"Yes. Someone cut me off in traffic, so I applied a red face mask, chased the person down, and threatened to smash their Prius. Unfortunately, the police were not amused."

"That didn't really happen, did it?"

"No. It didn't. But it might. So here's a message to all your viewers at home." I faced the camera and spoke earnestly, "Don't cut me off in traffic."

Arval grinned, nodded, writing himself a note on a small notepad, then asked, "And what do you think about filming in Tennessee? Are the locals friendly?"

His question gave me pause and I did a double take, studying him. But his expression was innocent, so I decided the question must be as well.

"Tennessee is gorgeous, but it's one of those treasures you don't want other people to find out about. It's perfection just how it is, and the locals are among my favorite people in the universe."

"I heard gorgeous, you must be talking about me." Tom slid next to me, slipping his arm around my waist and placing a kiss on my cheek. I tensed and, by some miracle, kept the grimace from my face.

"Of course we were," I quipped. "We were just talking about you and your gorgeous Pomeranians. You know, the dogs you just adopted from that animal shelter?"

Tom's lids lowered, giving me a vitriolic stare, but his smile didn't waver. Tom hated dogs.

"You adopted a Pomeranian?" Arval asked, clearly disbelieving.

Before Tom could speak, I cut in, "Oh yes. And not just one. A whole litter."

Arval glanced between us, an eyebrow lifted. Everyone knew Tom hated dogs; he'd famously refused to work with a German Shepherd some years ago on a police movie, insisting his body double be used for all scenes involving the K9.

Trapping my gaze, Tom smiled and said, "Have you seen Sienna's ring?"

I gritted my teeth and shot daggers at him, my heart jumping to my throat.

Don't you dare.

His smile widened. *Watch me.*

"Isn't it lovely?" Tom lifted my right ring finger and showed it to Arval. "But it's on the wrong hand, don't you think?"

A stunned hush fell over those who were watching and listening, followed by an eruption of questions from all sides.

"Sienna, are you and Tom engaged?"

"Why did you arrive separately?"

"When is the wedding?

Arval blinked at us, clearly surprised, but then quickly recovered, addressing his question to me. "Are you two making an announcement?"

As I held Tom's smirking gaze, frantic questions being haphazardly thrown in my direction, something in me shifted.

I was mad, and I'd been mad since Jethro had left my trailer yesterday.

I was mad at Tom, obviously. He was a douchenozzle.

But I was also angry with myself. If I'd brought Jethro, if I'd followed Cletus's wise words of owning our shit and facing the music, then everything about this moment would have been different. I wouldn't be standing here feeling like a fraud.

Yes, there would be fallout. Yes, I might lose a few film roles. Some doors might shut, but did I really want to walk through those doors?

If Jethro had been standing next to me, the road would've been rocky, but at least we would be facing it together. And I would have been true to myself.

For the first time in my career, I felt like a coward. I felt like a sell-out. And I hated it.

In that moment, Jethro's words, spoken with such love, came back to me: *"Now, part of my hate is because I don't want to lie to folks. But the other part is selfish. I'm in love with you, and the idea of us being a secret makes me want to break something."*

I wanted to break something.

First, Tom's nose.

Second, each and every preconceived notion about who I was. I was ready to be free.

Decision made, I held Tom's gaze and gave him a brilliant smile. "It is on the wrong hand. Thank you for pointing that out."

His eyes widened with surprise and interest, clearly he was curious what I was up to.

Very carefully, I slipped Jethro's grandmother's ring—my engagement ring—off my right hand and placed the ring where it belonged. Then I turned it to the crowd of cameras in front of me, holding it up as though I were flipping them off with my ring finger instead of the middle one.

"I'm engaged to be married. My fiancé couldn't make it today. He's too busy humanely trapping gigantic black bears and setting them free in the wild. I can't wait for you all to meet him. His name is Jethro Winston, and he's a wildlife park ranger in Tennessee. We're completely in love, and we'll be getting married in the fall, when the leaves change."

I grinned, my heart swelling with the rightness of the moment. I turned to Arval to see if he had any more questions, but he just stared at me, his mouth hanging open. I didn't see Tom's expression because I wasn't looking at him. I didn't care whether he was angry or putting on a show. It didn't matter. What Tom thought didn't matter.

Because, as Jethro had said, it's good to care about what others think, but only when those other people matter.

CHAPTER THIRTY-FOUR

"Death is not the greatest loss in life. The greatest loss is what dies inside us while we live."

— NORMAN COUSINS

~Jethro~

"A RE YOU DRINKING that stinky coffee again?" I wrinkled my nose at Cletus, inspecting the paper bag and coffee mug he'd brought inside my truck because I smelled something rank.

"No. I only have one cup of my special brew a day."

"Then what smells bad?"

"Garbage."

I squinted at my brother. "Garbage?"

"Yes. Garbage smells bad. So does sulfur. And poop."

I sighed, rolling my eyes. "I meant, why does it smell bad in here? What is in that bag?"

"You didn't ask why it smelled bad in here, you asked *what smells bad*. How was I supposed to know you didn't just want a list of things that smelled bad?"

Glaring out the windshield, I had to bite my tongue before I snapped at my brother. He was being surly on purpose.

We were driving home for the day, but first we had to stop by the Piggly Wiggly and grab a few things. I'd trapped five bears, more than usual, and was exhausted. After driving them up The Parkway to the release grounds, I'd turned back around and picked up Cletus from the set.

He'd been rude from the get-go. But really, he'd been in a bad mood since seeing grandma's ring on Sienna's finger. The only thing for it was to ignore him.

I rolled down my window, needing air. Whatever Cletus was transporting in his paper bag smelled like three-day-old fish and burnt popcorn.

We drove in silence the rest of the way. Well, mostly silence. He kept sighing.

I pulled into the lot and jumped out of the car, heard him shut his door too, and made for the grocery store. I tried to make quick work of picking up the items on my list, but in the produce aisle my attention snagged on the bouquets of roses by the bananas.

There were several different arrangements. Sienna would be back by tomorrow afternoon and the thought of greeting her with flowers, just to see the smile on her face, appealed to me.

"Get the white ones, with the pink tips."

I glanced over my shoulder and found Jennifer Sylvester next to me. As usual, she was in an expensive-looking dress and super-high heels, her long blonde hair pulled up in a loose but fancy bun. She had on pearls. She was also holding a big, dirty crate of bananas. I frowned at her, at this little slip of a woman, looking like she was ready for church, holding a giant crate of bananas

I stepped forward to take her burden. But before I could, she set the crate on the floor and reached for the roses.

"These are the ones she'll like. They're called moonstone roses." Jennifer smiled up at me with her violet eyes, placing the bunch in my hands. "Moonstone roses smell the best, and they smell even prettier when they open."

Jennifer's eyes weren't just violet, they were full-on purple. I'd never seen anyone with eyes like hers. Her real hair color was raven black, I remember the color from when she was a little girl, but her momma had started dying it blonde when Jennifer was a teenager.

Kip Sylvester, Jennifer's daddy and the principal of the high school, didn't like the attention his daughter's dark hair, pale skin, and purple eyes garnered, so she'd grown up more sheltered than most. She was nice enough, but she was usually making everything more awkward than needed.

Bless her heart.

I gave her a small smile. "Thanks."

"You're welcome." She returned my smile with one of her own, then bent to retrieve her bananas.

I set Sienna's roses down in my cart and moved to pick up the crate. "Jennifer Anne Sylvester, this crate is too big for you."

She grumbled as I took the crate away from her. "It's fine. I have to carry it once a week, I'm more than used to it by now."

"You'll break your neck in those shoes, and then what will I tell your daddy? Where are we going? To your car?"

"I said I'm perfectly capable of carrying my own bananas." She reached for it but I shifted to the side, lifting my eyebrows expectantly. She huffed, rolled her eyes like a kid, and said begrudgingly, "Fine. Follow me."

Leaving my shopping cart by the roses, I followed Jennifer past the registers and out to her BMW. She'd popped the trunk and opened it all the way so I could drop the crate inside.

"That wasn't really necessary. I know you don't like bananas."

I stepped back so she could shut the trunk and turned a surprised expression on her. "And how do you know that?"

"Because you've never ordered my cake."

Well, she had me there.

She quickly added, as though she was afraid she'd offended me, "To tell you the truth, I don't really like cake all that much. And I don't like baking them."

This was surprising, because Green Valley was famous for three things: the jam session every Friday night at the community center, the trout fishing at Sky Lake, and Jennifer Sylvester's banana cake.

I crossed my arms, studying her upturned face. "Is that so?"

"Yes." She paired this with a single nod. "It's like, how many times am I going to have to make the same goddamn cake? Sorry for my profanity, but I get worked up when I talk about cake."

"Understood."

She didn't seem to hear me. "Just 'cause I'm good at making cake doesn't mean I want to make it for the rest of my life, you know? Just 'cause you're good at something doesn't mean that's what makes your heart happy. I sometimes feel like I've become the banana cake lady, and I'm only twenty-two. But that's it. That's who I am. My life is set, and there's no escape. I'll be ninety-nine years old, still making banana cakes at my momma's bakery."

"So why don't you do something else?"

Jennifer lifted her eyes to mine, frowning, a wrinkle of consternation appearing between her eyebrows. "You know what I'd love to do?"

"What's that?"

"I'd love to have my own kids, my own house. I'd love to be a stay-at-home mom and spend all day with my kids, taking care of the house, taking care of my husband. And if I can't do that, then I'd love to work in a preschool. I'd love to work with kids, doing crafts all day, reading to them, playing. I love babies."

"Then you should do that."

Gradually, her face fell and she nodded politely, looking away. I got the sense I'd said something untoward, but didn't have a clue what.

"Well . . ." She took a step back. "Thanks for carrying my crate. I have to get to the bakery and work on that particle accelerator."

"What?"

"Just kidding. I'm not an astrophysicist. I bake cakes." Her smile was small and forced. She turned away and crossed to the driver's side door, opened it, then slipped inside.

I stared after her, watching as she started her car.

Jennifer Sylvester was famous for three things: her banana cake, her purple eyes, and being odd.

Giving my head a shake, I turned from her black BMW and made my way back toward the store. I was just at the crosswalk when Jennifer pulled her car up next to me and tapped on her horn.

She rolled down the window and waved me over.

"What's up?"

"I forgot to tell you. Some news guys were at the store when I first arrived to pick up my bananas, a big swarm of them. They were asking for directions to your house."

I straightened, thinking her words over. "My house? What did they want?"

She shrugged. "I don't know for certain. But if I had to guess, I'd say it probably has something to do with you and Sienna Diaz being engaged."

My mouth fell open and I gaped at Jennifer Sylvester. "How did you know we're engaged?"

"She told everybody at that fancy movie premiere earlier today. It's all over the Internet."

* * *

"*I'M ENGAGED TO be married. My fiancé couldn't make it today. He's too busy humanely trapping gigantic black bears and setting them free in the wild—*"

Cletus pressed pause on the YouTube video and frowned at me. "She makes you sound like some sort of backwoods hippie."

"Shut up, dummy. Play the rest of the video." I motioned to his phone where he'd pulled up the video of Sienna from earlier in the day. It was amateur quality, the sound garbled in places by all the background noise.

Given the five- or six-hour time change, it was late night in London right now. This footage had been shot sometime around 3:00 p.m.

Cletus grumbled something. Eventually he pressed play while I listened and scrolled through my text messages. She hadn't messaged me. I tried calling her phone. It went to voicemail.

"*I can't wait for you all to meet him. His name is Jethro Winston, and he's a wildlife park ranger in Tennessee. We're completely in love, and we'll be getting married in the fall, when the leaves change."*

I glanced at Cletus's screen, saw she was smiling as though she'd just done something brilliant. Meanwhile, Tom Low looked like he'd just swallowed a live rat.

Questions were shouted at her from all directions, but that's basically where the video ended. Cletus tapped his screen and slipped his phone back in his pocket.

"Well, hell. Was that so hard?" He was grinning.

I dropped my phone to the cup holder and gripped my truck's steering wheel, staring out the windshield. "I can't believe she did that."

"From the looks of it, Tom Low put her in a bad spot. He was insinuating that she and him—"

"I saw the video, Cletus. You don't need to break it down for me."

Surprisingly, he snapped his mouth shut, his eyebrows lifting high on his forehead, his eyes going wide. I could almost read his mind, hear his internal thoughts as though he were speaking. No doubt it was something like, *Settle your feathers, crusty britches.*

We sat mostly in silence for a long time. He was drumming his fingers on the passenger side door. The beat reminded me of a ticking clock.

"What am I going to do?" I asked the car. "Should I talk to those reporters? What if I end up hurting her career even more? It seems like I shouldn't be talking to anyone until I discuss the matter with Sienna first. Which is what she should have done."

"Why don't you want to talk to them?"

"What if they ask about my past?"

He shrugged. "Tell the truth. Well, tell the truth about everything except the criminal stuff. No one really expects you to answer those questions."

Not looking at my brother, because I wasn't really speaking to him, I said, "I'm disappointed. Actually, I'm pissed off. We'd agreed on a plan and she went and did what she wanted. And now the very thing I was trying to avoid is going to happen."

"You'll have to punish her for sure."

I blinked, my gaze cutting to him. "I'm not going to punish her, what are you talking about?"

"Well if she did something to disappoint you, then obviously you'll have to teach her a lesson."

"She's not a child, Cletus. She gets to make her own decisions, do what she thinks is right. If she told those reporters the truth, then obviously . . ."

As I spoke it became clear that Cletus was trying to hide his smile. I studied him and realized he'd been pulling my leg, leading me to the water so I could decide to drink it.

Laughing, I shook my head at him. "You're an asshole."

"Yeah." He shrugged, laughing too. "I am."

We sat together for a stretch, each lost to our own considerations. I was debating how to go about approaching these news folks. How to engage them and be an asset to my woman. I decided being friendly yet firm was in order. I'd invite them for a chat—not inside the house, the porch would do just fine—I'd introduce myself, ingratiate myself.

I'd make them love me.

"If he tries to hurt you or Sienna, I'll kill him."

Cletus's casual threat pulled me out of my thoughts. I turned to look at my brother. The set of his mouth was grim and his eyes were sharp, almost painfully bright.

"Excuse me?"

"Darrell. He won't be bothering you or Sienna. Don't you worry about him. He knows, as long as he's in prison, I can get to him."

I gaped at my brother for a full minute, an inferno of hatred behind his eyes and cool determination casting his features in harsh lines. Not a look I'd seen on his face in a very long time.

"Cletus, you're not a murderer. You wouldn't do that."

He gave me a wry smile and turned the ignition, looking like someone I didn't recognize. "It wouldn't be murder, big brother. It would be self-defense. Or at least I'd make sure it appeared that way."

What the . . .?

I could only stare at my younger brother as he pulled out of the parking lot, the earlier icy determination and heated resolve replaced with his usual air of detached peculiarity.

"Should I take the valley road? Or do you think Moth Run would be quicker?" he asked unnecessarily, his tone now easy and affable.

The truth was, I didn't have time to think about Cletus's statement right now, or whether he actually had the ability to reach our father in jail and put an end to him, to all his threats. I had a bunch of news people waiting for me at the house and had to put on a good show. I needed to put my energy toward that.

But when this media mess with Sienna resolved, I would have to confront him about it. My family had already lost enough to our father. The man was a plague. A disease. A stain on the memories of our childhood. I knew Cletus had suffered, just like we all had. Although not in the same way, Cletus had lost just as much as me because of Darrell Winston.

But now I wondered what, specifically, Cletus had lost. It must've been something substantial to fuel such hatred.

Regardless, it didn't matter whether my brother thought his actions—or potential future actions—were justified, I couldn't allow Cletus to lose his soul, too.

* * *

I TRIED SIENNA'S phone one more time as we pulled into our driveway. She didn't pick up.

Even from a distance I could see the front yard littered with strange cars. Media people milling about, holding cameras, smoking cigarettes. I counted five vehicles total: four were local news vans, one looked to be a rental car from the airport. They were on us like fleas on a dog as soon as Cletus parked, calling my name and knocking on the windows of both doors.

"These people are nuts." My brother locked the doors, gaping at me in horror. "Why are they knocking? What do they think? We're confused about whether or not they think we should stay in the car? Parasites."

I smiled at my brother, like I didn't have a care in the world. "Don't say anything. Let me do the talking."

"I won't say anything. I'll let you do the talking," he echoed and removed the key from the ignition. Cletus turned to the faces nearly pressed against the door. He flicked his wrist motioning for them to step back. "Okay, okay, I know you want to speak to my brother. But I can't get out of the car if you're blocking my path, genius."

Meanwhile, I rolled down my window and two microphones were shoved in my face.

"What do you have to say about Sienna Diaz's announcement earlier today?"

"Does she know about your criminal past?"

"What does your family think?"

"Are you using Sienna to become famous?"

I let them shout their questions at me for a few minutes, careful to keep my expression calm and my smile easy. Each flash of the camera was searching for an unpleasant picture of my face. I figured I'd be the man who conned Sienna Diaz, ruined America's sweetheart if I didn't play my cards right, or donned one sinister expression.

When it was clear they were growing tired, I spoke over them. "Now, just hold on. I'll be happy to answer everyone's questions. But I'd like to do so on my porch, in the shade and out of the heat, if you don't mind. There are plenty of chairs for everyone, and I have lemonade in the fridge. It's hot out here, and I could do with a cool drink."

Their general steam and fervor, or fear that I'd rush into my house and call the cops on them for trespassing, seemed to wane at my offer and they exchanged furtive glances. Quietly, and en masse, they shifted away from the truck so Cletus and I could exit.

I stepped out, giving each of their distrusting faces a small welcoming smile, then turned to Cletus as he walked around the truck toward the porch. "Could you bring out some lemonade for these fine folks? And a bucket of ice. We'll be on the porch."

Cletus scowled, but he nodded, casting disapproving glares around the crowd like he was cataloging each of them for one of his sinister plans. I breathed a sigh of relief when he disappeared inside without saying a word.

"Forgive my brother. It was a bit of a shock coming home to such a ruckus." Before anyone could speak I turned to the reporter closest to me and extended my hand. "I'm Jethro Winston. What's your name?"

CHAPTER THIRTY-FIVE

"Love is the longing for the half of ourselves we have lost."

— MILAN KUNDERA, THE UNBEARABLE
LIGHTNESS OF BEING

~Sienna~

"I CAN'T BELIEVE we're lost," Dave grumbled, shaking his head at the mountain road. "I mean, I only had to drive up here from the airport that one time, but I seriously thought I knew the way. Everything looks the same."

"Why don't any of you have your new phones?" Marta complained, shaking her head at all of us. "I ordered you those phones so you would have reception on the mountain."

I shared a sheepish glance with Henry. He and Tim were sitting with me in the back seat. We'd all left our Tennessee phones on the kitchen table at Hank's cabin, not wanting to carry two phones with us to London.

"Guys, I think we need to pull over," Tim said. Actually, he moaned it.

"What's wrong?" Dave glanced at us through the rearview mirror.

"Tim's carsick." Henry shifted away from Tim. "Or he's about to be."

"It's because of the switchbacks." Dave nodded at his own assertion.

"Thanks, Captain Obvious," Tim groaned, covering his mouth with a big hand.

"Pull off there." Marta pointed to an overlook, a frantic note in her tone.

Dave eased us off the side of the road. As soon as the car pulled to a stop, both Henry and I bolted out of our respective doors. Tim was a little slower to exit, crawling more than walking.

The sun was low in the sky as it was still early morning. We'd left directly from the film premiere in the wee hours of pre-dawn London time. I was reasonably well rested, having slept the entire flight back to the States. But now I was anxious to get home so I could call Jethro and tell him in person about the premiere. I wanted him to have some time to prepare before Arval ran his footage this week.

Gravel crunched beneath my feet as I walked to Marta and slipped an arm around her shoulders. She exhaled a tired laugh and rested her head on my shoulder.

"No wonder you were lost up here. At least we know which direction is east, but you were driving in the middle of the day."

I glanced around the overlook, smiling to myself. "You know, I think this is the same overlook where I pulled off that first day. Just think of this as us giving you the authentic mountain experience."

She lifted her head and gave me a hopeful look. "Do you think you can find your way back from here?"

"Maybe. I think we use this road to get to Jethro's . . ." I trailed off because the sound of an approaching vehicle had us turning our attention to the road.

A green truck appeared. It was Jethro's truck. I immediately laughed. Of course.

Of course he'd be driving past. Right place, right time.

Marta glanced between the road and me. I released my sister and walked to the edge of the overlook. He'd passed us but was now putting on his brake and making a U-turn.

"Hey, that's Jethro's truck," I heard Dave say from behind me.

"What do you think of this Jethro?" The speculation in Marta's tone made me smile.

Henry chimed in. "Jethro? Oh, he's the man. Did you know he traps bears?"

I glanced over my shoulder just in time to see Dave give Henry a wan look, then affix an air of earnest concern to his features. "Jethro is a good guy. He takes really good care of your sister. Did Sienna tell you he didn't know who she was at first?"

Marta split her attention between Dave, the approaching truck, and me. "No. She didn't mention that."

"You're going to love him." Henry was the definition of effusive enthusiasm. I was pretty sure Henry had a crush on my fiancé.

Hearing the engine cut off, I turned my attention back to the truck and saw Roscoe was with him. I waved, grinning wide and excited, and quickly walked over to them.

Jethro was also grinning and my heart fluttered impatiently at the warm welcome in his gaze. He was really just too handsome. Pretty soon I was running like a goof and threw myself at him. His strong arms immediately came around me, squeezing me tight.

I sighed, happy and content.

Hopeful and unafraid.

"I missed you," I said, holding him tighter so I wouldn't tackle him and make love to him on the gravel.

His hand pulled through my hair. I let the sound of his deliciously gravelly voice and sweet southern accent wash over me as he said, "I missed you, too."

* * *

I WAS PLEASED when Marta was warmly polite—which was more than what most people received—when she and Jethro were introduced.

Of course it helped that Roscoe, who apparently knew how to turn on and off his charm, had already buttered her up by saying with a hint of suggestiveness, "You must be Sienna's younger sister. I'm Jethro's younger brother."

I tried not to laugh at how that comment made her blush and smile, though she did roll her eyes at him good-naturedly.

We loaded up in the car, Tim riding with Jethro in his truck this time while Roscoe squeezed in the car with us, and we were escorted back to Hank's cabin. Jethro and Roscoe helped carry in our bags, carrying and not rolling so as not to ruin the wheels, then made to leave. They'd been on their way to work, but invited us to dinner.

I followed Jethro out and pulled him to the side, letting Roscoe continue on to the truck.

"I have to tell you something." I kept my hand on his bicep so I could hold him in place. But also so I could feel him up. I loved his arms. They were so muscular and strong. Thinking about them turned me on, so touching them gave me delicious twisty feelings low in my belly.

Smiling at me like he knew what I was doing, his eyelids lowered. "What do you have to tell me?"

I sighed, because how he dropped his voice made me think about us alone and naked. I wished we were alone and naked right now.

"Sienna, if you expect me to pay attention, you're going to have to stop looking at me like that."

"Sorry, sorry. It's just, I really missed you."

"And I *really* missed you, too."

"No. I mean, I really, really missed you. I know we're coming over for dinner tonight, but do you think there's any chance you could meet me this afternoon for lust?"

His lips quirked to the side. "You mean for lunch?"

"Yes. That's what I said, right?"

He laughed, his eyes bright and he gained another step closer, bending slightly to capture my lips in an achingly soft kiss.

"What did you want to tell me?" he whispered, his eyes moving over my face, making me feel cherished. But his question brought me back to reality.

"Oh!" I gripped his other arm. "Don't get mad."

His smile was soft and patient, and rather than saying anything, he waited for me to continue.

I gathered a deep breath for courage and then said on a rush, "I may have told everyone that we are engaged when I was at the premiere yesterday, but don't worry, we have a few days to come up with a plan before Arval runs his—"

"I know. Someone already put a video of it up on YouTube."

I started at that. "What? When?"

"Yesterday afternoon, Tennessee time. I saw what happened."

I grimaced. "And you're not mad?"

"I was mad," he said matter-of-factly, though he didn't look mad now. "We'd come to a decision together, came up with a plan."

"Yes, but Tom was trying to—" I stopped myself. "No. That's not really the reason I did it. He gave me a push, but—honestly?—I wanted to do it. I hated that you weren't with me, and I hated that I'd asked you to lie."

Jethro hesitated, frowning, considering my words. I didn't like that he was mad, and even if he seemed perfectly calm, he was frowning. He rarely frowned, not with me. The pressure in my chest grew and I became aware that my grip was likely painful. I told myself to let him go, but I couldn't. I held on tighter.

He seemed to sense my growing unease because he placed his hand over mine and pried it off his arm, bringing it to his lips for a kiss. "I'll come by this afternoon. We'll discuss everything then. Okay?"

I nodded, pressing my lips together so I wouldn't demand he stay and sort things out right this second, in the front yard of Hank's cabin, with my sister, his brother, and my bodyguards as onlookers.

"Okay. Fine," I finally managed to say.

His mouth hitched to the side as he studied me. "Do you want me to bring lunch?"

I nodded, distracted, but deciding I had faith in him. I had faith in us. We were solid, no matter what.

Then he said, "And you'll bring the lust?"

My eyes cut to his and I saw the warm teasing there, the easy flirtation, the interest and adoration in his gaze.

"Okay. You bring lunch, I'll bring lust, and we'll both . . . eat."

His eyebrows bounced at the suggestiveness in my tone, then he flashed me my favorite smile. Despite the way it made my knees weak, I lifted on my tiptoes and brushed a kiss to his lips. My anxiety melted away, leaving only trust in this remarkable man and excitement for our afternoon rendezvous.

* * *

I ASKED DAVE to drive me to the set after spending the morning with Marta. I didn't have any scenes to film, but the trailer would provide a (mostly) private space for Jethro and me to talk.

I also brought along my black silk bathrobe. I'd been placed in charge of the lust, and I took that charge seriously.

Dave waited dutifully outside the trailer; I'd given him strict instructions to allow no one but Jethro to enter. Meanwhile, I changed into my birthday suit plus the robe. While I was waiting, an idea came to me for the Smash-Girl movie, so I flipped open my spare laptop and set to work.

I lost track of time. When I finally glanced down at the computer's clock, two hours had passed. I rubbed my eyes and stretched, glancing around the trailer, surprised to find Jethro sitting at the kitchen table. He was sipping on a drink through a straw, flipping through a notebook and scrolling through his phone.

"Hello," I said.

"Hey, gorgeous." He wrote down a few lines in the notebook, copying them from his phone, then flipped the book closed, and brought his eyes to mine. "All done?"

"For now. How long have you been sitting there?"

He checked his phone again. "About an hour and a half."

"Jethro, you should have interrupted me."

He shrugged. "You were working, and I had a nice view. A nice view always helps."

I felt my mouth tug to the side. "Is that something your mother used to say?"

He nodded, his smile growing. "But I doubt she had this view in mind when she said it." He indicated to me with a lift of his chin as he stood, shoving his hands in his pockets. "I brought lunch."

I stood as well and lifted my palms away from body. "I brought lust."

His eyes heated as they swept over me. "Yes, you did."

We indulged for a moment in mutual ogling. He was wearing his ranger uniform, but his tool belt rested on the table next to his hat, and his shirt was unbuttoned, and his hair was in disarray. He was my strong, capable, sweet man and I wanted to be close to him. But before we ate lunch or succumbed to lust, we had a few things to discuss.

Thus, I blurted, "I'm so sorry."

His eyes cut to mine. "Why are you sorry?" I didn't miss the hint of amused exasperation in his tone.

"Because we agreed to one thing and I did the opposite. I behaved selfishly, not thinking about the consequences of my actions, and I'm sorry."

Jethro shrugged, his eyes sliding over my shoulder to the swell of my breasts, saying distractedly, "Live and learn."

I stared at him, stunned and irritated at his laissez-faire words. "Live and learn?"

He nodded, a smile threatening to break free. "That's right. Now you know. Hindsight is twenty-twenty. Live and learn."

"I know what it means, Jethro," I snapped, growing both more and less aggravated—which didn't make any sense—by his teasing.

"Good. I guess we're on the same page, then." He continued to devour me with his gaze, touching me nowhere, like he was memorizing the sight of me.

"Really? Are we?"

"Yes." He nodded once, slowly.

"Enlighten me."

"I will."

"I can't wait."

"Here we go."

"Let's hear it."

"Hold on to your hat."

"I'm not wearing a hat."

"Well, hold on to your underwear then."

"I'm not wearing those either."

Jethro opened his mouth to respond but then snapped it shut, his gaze lifting to mine again, giving me another amused yet exasperated look.

"We . . ." he started, his voice full of authority, pausing just long enough to treat himself to an evocative, lingering sweep of my body. Then he started again, his voice deeper. "We make plans together; we both stick to the plan."

"Okay. Yes."

"Or if you want to change the plan, we discuss it."

"Makes sense."

"Good," he said firmly, like everything was decided, then added unexpectedly, "So I guess I have something to tell you."

"What's that?"

"Yesterday, after your video, I tried calling you because there were reporters camped out at my house."

I immediately grimaced. "Oh, no."

"Oh, yes."

"What happened? What did you do?"

"I invited them for lemonade on the front porch and answered a few of their questions."

"Was it terrible?"

He shrugged. "It wasn't so bad. But they already knew all about my past, showed me my arrest record, asked how I thought audiences were going to react to America's sweetheart hooking up with an ex-con. I pointed out that I wasn't an ex-con, as I'd never been convicted, and if they printed as much I'd have to sue them for slander. But other than that awkwardness, our chat was mostly pleasant."

I nodded, absorbing all of this. "Okay . . . okay. We'll be fine."

"Sienna," his eyes searched mine, and he closed the distance between us, gathering my hands between his, "it's just starting. This week might be tough. You have to let me help you; you have to tell me what's going on so we can work together. Things might come out, stuff I haven't told you—not because I'm keeping secrets, but because there's so much, I haven't gotten to it yet, or I just simply forgot. Ask me questions. Don't be afraid of making me angry."

"I will, and I won't. I mean, I will ask, and I won't be afraid," I promised solemnly. I was actually really impressed with how well he took the news of what had happened at the premiere. I'd expected him to be more upset.

"We're in this together," he said, and that made me smile.

"We are, aren't we?" I asked, feeling an odd sense of wonder. "It's you and me, partner."

We swapped stares, smiling at each other. I think we both appreciated the finality of the moment. I felt the truth settle around us, in our little bubble of awesome. Our bubble might be pierced, but I trusted we'd always be able to patch it.

Our past would always be part of us, but it would never wholly define us, either together or as individuals. Each moment was a decision. We could either live up or down to people's expectations, or blow them completely away. We had no control over what other people decided to think, but we did have control over our own actions, who we wanted to be, and how we lived our life.

From now on, it was Jethro Winston and Sienna Diaz against the world, defying our history, ignoring the labels others might assign. If I became lost, I knew I could count on him to find me, and vice versa. We had faith in each other, and that's all that mattered.

Well . . . maybe not quite.

What my family thought mattered, and I would always take their advice seriously, even though I might not follow it.

What Jethro's family thought also mattered, but I was certain they'd be pleased with whatever made Jethro happy. No worries there.

What Jethro thought mattered and what I thought mattered.

And everyone else could go dill a pickle.

"I love you, Jethro Whitman Winston." I slipped my hands from his and pulled the tie holding my black silk bathrobe closed. "I can't wait to make you crazy, fill your house with children, and furnish our sex dungeon."

He grinned down at me, a mixture of amusement and wickedness. He slid his large, wildly strong hands into my robe, opening it and exposing my body to his eyes and touch. I shivered, because I loved how he touched me, how he cherished me.

"I love you, Sienna Diaz." His voice was a low rumble, and he captured my mouth with a soft, savoring kiss. "You are sunshine and sweetness, but you're so much more than that. You are strong and beautiful, brave and wise. And you are funny."

"I am. I'm the funniest," I quickly agreed.

"You are." He nodded, looking at me like I'd hung the moon and stars, and then added on a whisper, "But it's not my house, love. It's our house. And I can't wait for you to tell our kids all the jokes."

I laughed, but then gasped, because Jethro Winston—my soon to be husband—was being very, very bad.

And, as usual, it felt very, very good.

EXTRA SCENE – SOMETIME LATER...

"WHAT'S THAT?" I gestured to the notebook in Jethro's hands while I dished myself a piece of pie.

We were on a picnic. The leaves were changing and the wedding was just one week away. Thus, we were also sort of hiding from our families.

Cletus and I had been doing yoga every morning since Jethro and I'd returned from wrapping *Strange Birdfellows* in Washington state. The yoga helped, and Cletus was great. But time alone with Jethro someplace outside, away from the constant swarm of reporters that had followed us everywhere since outing our relationship, was what I'd been craving.

"Poetry," he said, opening his arms and patting his lap. "Put your head here."

I lifted an eyebrow at his instruction. "You always want me to put my head there."

"Ha ha." He rolled his eyes, but he smiled. He always smiled. "Come on, gorgeous. You need a break from the wedding stuff, and I've been working on this notebook for months."

I eyed Jethro speculatively. "Is that really poetry?"

"Yes. You said you wanted me to read you poetry. So I copied some down in this book."

"Really?"

"Yes."

"Is it your poetry?"

"No. I transcribed them. I asked Ashley for some suggestions, she's a poetry nut, and a few are favorites of mine."

"You have favorite poetry?"

"Yes," he said on an exasperated exhale, patting his lap again.

"Are you telling me the truth?"

"My momma loved poetry. It's how she met Drew. She ran a poetry meeting at the library and he, being new to town, showed up. He writes it, though. I do not. But I have one of his in here. Ashley emailed it to me yesterday when I told her I was taking you out today. I haven't read it yet, just printed out the attachment about an hour ago."

"Holy cow. Drew writes poetry?"

Drew, or what little I knew about him, seemed to be a man of few words. He looked like a Viking but struck me as a gentle giant. The fact he wrote poetry left me stunned.

"Drew writes poetry. You want me to read that one first?" Jethro flipped through the pages of his notebook and withdrew a folded piece of paper, poised to start reading.

"Wait! Before you start." I set my plate to one side then crossed to him on my hands and knees. Once I was next to him I lay down, resting my head on his lap and folding my hands over my stomach. "Okay, now start."

He grinned at me like I was a goof. "You finally agree? This is the poetry-reading pose."

"Yes. I agree."

"Then I'm reading you poetry every day."

I reached above my head and pinched his thigh. "Stop being a dirty mister and read the damn poetry."

His grin widened, but he acquiesced. Attention back on the journal, he cleared his throat, and then he began.

"I see you.
A weapon to wield.
Tightrope above, No net below,
Start.
Need water, Need air, Need forgiveness,
Acceptance a mantle, hopelessness a shield,
Apart.
I see you.
Rejection causes blindness,
Reset, renew,
Restart.
Forgiveness on your mind, Love in your heart.
I see you.
Son to one.
Brother to many.
Friend to me.
Now husband.
Soon father.
I see you."

As Jethro read, the steadiness of his voice diminished as it slowed. He swallowed thickly between the lines beginning with *Brother* and *Friend* and finished the last *I see you* in a hauntingly roughened tone.

When he finished he continued to stare at the words, his throat working, his eyes darting over the page. I frowned my concern, reaching a hand above my head once more. But this time I squeezed his thigh, wanting to offer reassurance.

"Hey," I said, drawing his eyes to mine. "Are you okay?"

He nodded though he looked lost.

I sat up, twisting at the waist. I'd planned to hold his hand, but Jethro set aside his notebook and reached for me, turning my body and bringing me to his lap. I straddled him and wrapped my arms around his neck, giving him a soft kiss.

"Thank you." His words escaped on an exhale.

"For what?"

"For giving me a chance. For wanting to know me."

I gave him a disbelieving smile, tilting my head back so I could see him. Without thinking, I said, "Of course I gave you a chance. Do you know how hot you are? You are seriously hot."

Jethro smiled in return, yet it didn't quite reach his eyes, and that had me frowning again. I could've kicked myself. My instinct was to be silly in all serious situations. Sometimes that silliness made me thoughtless.

I shook my head, shoving instinct out of the way and inviting true depth to visit. I gave myself permission to feel the moment.

"That's . . . that's not what I meant. Let me try that again."

I gathered a deep breath and steadied myself by counting the colors in his iris. Green, gold, brown, and blue.

I started again. "Of course I gave you a chance. You are deserving of every good thing, Jethro. I know you struggle with feeling you deserve good things, and I admire you for your struggle, because I think a lot of people would move on or make excuses for their bad choices and behavior. You could blame your father—and I think you absolutely should to a certain extent—or you could blame a hundred different other influences and factors. But you don't."

His answering smile was smaller, but I was happy to see it reflected in his eyes. His gaze traveled over my features, warm and cherishing.

I slipped a palm to his chest and pressed it there. "You have a good heart. Thank you for letting me know it. And thank you, Jethro, for wanting to know me."

We swapped small smiles and good feelings until Jethro pushed his fingers into my hair, lifting it as though measuring its weight.

"You are so beautiful," he said, his attention skimming from my hair to my neck to my chin. "I don't think I knew what beauty was, until I met you."

"Uhh." The involuntary sound tumbled from my lips, both a grunt and a sigh. I felt his words and the sincerity behind them like an arrow to my heart.

His eyes sharpened and he studied my face with interest. "What? What's wrong?"

"You and your saying of sweet things, it does something to me. You do something to me."

Jethro's mouth hitched to the side with a pleased smile. "Happy to hear it. Because when I'm with you, I feel like I'm both flying and falling."

"Uhh!" I sigh-grunted again and quickly pressed my lips to his. "I thought you said you don't write poetry?"

"I don't."

"Stop lying to yourself and the world. You are a poet, and you don't even know it."

He pressed his lips together, clearly trying not to laugh. Again, I was being silly. Funny was my default, but my default felt right this time, so I went with it.

"You should get a permit, but don't attempt to outwit, and here's a tidbit." I pointed to my shoulder, "This is my armpit."

Jethro laughed, scrunching his face at me like I was funny and weird —which I was—and gifted me with a smiling kiss. "You're going to be my wife."

I nodded. "And you're going to be my husband."

He rested his forehead against mine and we sat together for a long moment, breathing each other in, until I asked, "Are you giving me comfort?"

"Yes, Mrs. Winston-Diaz."

"Good, Mr. Winston-Diaz."

Jethro closed his eyes, a small grin curving his mouth, and whispered like it was a secret, "Thank you for being lost."

I smiled and whispered in return, "Thank you for finding me."

-The End-

ACKNOWLEDGMENTS

I receive emails from all over the world (India, Nigeria, Pakistan, France, Greece, Australia, etc.) in which readers tell me how much they identify with my nerdy, smart, ambitious, and capable women characters. When asked which of my characters they identify with the most, over 60% of my readers say Janie from *Neanderthal Seeks Human* and *Neanderthal Marries Human*.

I think that's pretty freaking awesome. Awkward doesn't care who your parents are. Smart doesn't consult your skin color. Because being smart, awkward, having an affinity for nerd culture, and falling in love are—in fact—universal concepts.

Last year, a reader pointed out to me that all my main characters thus far have been of Northern European ancestry. She asked me, "Why are all your characters white?"

And I responded, "Because that's what I know. How can I write and do justice to a person of color? I've never been a person of color."

She smiled and said, "But you write men, and you are a woman. You write about male auto mechanics in the Tennessee foothills and you're a female scientist from California."

She had me there.

So I penned a blog post asking my readers of color to email me. I asked that they share their experiences growing up in the United States. I made a request: "Tell me what I don't know."

I received over 500 responses. And it turns out I don't (didn't) know much.

In addition to basic data gathering and information (e.g. several women of African descent pointed out that some African Americans / blacks don't like getting their hair wet and therefore don't like to go swimming; I did not know that) readers also shared a range of stories and experiences that ignited my imagination. New, exciting ways of seeing the world, perspectives I never would have discovered if left to my own paltry well of experiences.

One woman (a 3rd generation American) wrote, "I have more in common with you—culturally— than my cousins in India."

This is true. She is right. If I can write a man, or an ex-CIA agent, or a medical doctor, then why can't I write a person who happens to not be of my same/similar ancestry?

Sienna Diaz was originally slated to be Sienna Foster. But as all the events (above) unfolded, I decided there was absolutely no reason Sienna couldn't be a woman of color. In fact, making her a Latina (in my opinion) actually added additional/surprising layers to the character. And all of these new layers were wonderful.

I have to thank people. This book, more than any other I've written, was definitely a group effort.

First and foremost, I have to thank Angela Houle. She is the reader (she's also a stellar editor) who originally asked me why none of my characters were of color. Thank you for asking the question.

Second, I have to thank the 500+ readers who responded to my initial request for information. I plan to continue pilfering their experiences for the benefit of my future books (Sienna is the first of many to come!)

Third, my BETA readers who specifically helped me with the character of Sienna: Felicia Valadez, Michelle Linnborn. Elizabeth Lopez, and Melissa Breit. When I sent these ladies an early version of the book, I asked, "Please help me make her authentic. Not a stereotype and not white-washed. Help me make her real." Each of these ladies responded with suggestions, comments, and notes regarding experiences/perspectives growing up in the United States as a 1st or 2nd generation Mexican (or part Mexican).

In fact, one of Sienna's lines in the book was taken verbatim from Felicia Valadez's BETA notes, as follows: "We all grew up knowing who she was and being told we *must listen or La Llorona will find you.* I'm still not sure if the lesson is listen to your parents or La Llorona will find you and kill you, or listen to your Mexican mother because she might go crazy and kill you. Oh sure, she'll spend eternity crying and searching for you, but she *will* kill you." (chapter 4)

It made me laugh out loud, so I used it (with her permission).

I also want to thank my BETA reading team (Shannon, Tracy, April, Heather, Amber, Angie, and Becky), as well as my editors: Marion, Karen, and Iveta. I lost all of my content changes (18k words) the day this book was due back to my editor for a second read. Marion and Karen pulled me through to the other side. Without their support and encouragement, I think I would have shelved the book indefinitely. Instead, I wrote 23k words in 56 hours.

Last, but not least, I want to thank my family. I wrote this book under extreme circumstances (teething baby, closing on a new house, selling our house, packing for a move across the country, etc.) and would not have been able to finish it without the support and understanding of my family.

Wishing you the best, Penny Reid

ABOUT THE AUTHOR

Penny Reid is the *New York Times*, *Wall Street Journal*, and *USA Today* Bestselling Author of the Winston Brothers, Knitting in the City, Rugby, Dear Professor, and Hypothesis series. She used to spend her days writing federal grant proposals as a biomedical researcher, but now she just writes books. She's also a full time mom to three diminutive adults, wife, daughter, knitter, crocheter, sewer, general crafter, and thought ninja.

Come find me -
Mailing List: http://pennyreid.ninja/newsletter/
Goodreads: http://www.goodreads.com/ReidRomance
Email: pennreid@gmail.com ...hey, you! Email me ;-)

OTHER BOOKS BY PENNY REID

Hypothesis Series

(New Adult Romantic Comedy)

Elements of Chemistry: <u>ATTRACTION</u>, <u>HEAT</u>, and <u>CAPTURE</u> (#1)

Laws of Physics: <u>MOTION</u>, <u>SPACE</u>, and <u>TIME</u> (#2)

Irish Players (Rugby) Series – by L.H. Cosway and Penny Reid

(Contemporary Sports Romance)

The Hooker and the Hermit (#1)

The Pixie and the Player (#2)

The Cad and the Co-ed (#3)

The Varlet and the Voyeur (#4)

Dear Professor Series

(New Adult Romantic Comedy)

Kissing Tolstoy (#1)

Kissing Galileo (#2, read for FREE in Penny's newsletter 2018-2019)

Ideal Man Series

(Contemporary Romance Series of Jane Austen Re-Tellings)

Pride and Dad Jokes (#1, coming 2020)

Man Buns and Sensibility (#2, TBD)

Sense and Manscaping (#3, TBD)

Persuasion and Man Hands (#4, TBD)

Mantuary Abbey (#5, TBD)

Mancave Park (#6, TBD)

Emmanuel (#7, TBD)